Cold dread trickled down Morhion's throat. In the minutes since he had last looked, the shadowking had grown. Its midnight wings had spread wider, and it had raised itself slightly off the platform, leaning on a long, muscular arm that looked as if it had been carved from polished onyx. He could not see the shadowking's visage, but curving obsidian horns sprang from its brow. In time with the creature's throbbing wings, the Shadowstar pulsated against the creature's torso, glowing brightly one moment, fading to dark the next. Soon the shadowking would be whole.

High above, the shadowsteeds cried out as they caught sight of their enemy again. They folded their wings and dove once more. Morhion had no more offensive spells left.

Slowly, the shadowking rose to its feet. It was horrifying in its darkness, yet majestic as well, a vast creature of sculpted onyx muscle, with horns and talons like black ice. The outlines of the creature's face flowed, taking shape. It was nearly complete.

"Behold the King of Shadows," Morhion whispered in awe.

THE HARPERS

A semi-secret organization for Good, the Harpers fight for freedom and justice in a world populated by tyrants, evil mages, and dread concerns beyond imagination.

Each novel in the Harpers Series is a complete story in itself, detailing some of the most unusual and compelling tales in the magical world known as the Forgotten Realms.

THE HARPERS

THE PARCHED SEA
Troy Denning

ELFSHADOW
Elaine Cunningham

RED MAGIC
Jean Rabe

THE NIGHT PARADE
Scott Ciencin

THE RING OF WINTER
James Lowder

CRYPT OF THE SHADOWKING
Mark Anthony

SOLDIERS OF ICE
David Cook

ELFSONG
Elaine Cunningham

CROWN OF FIRE
Ed Greenwood

MASQUERADES
Kate Novak & Jeff Grubb

FANTASY ADVENTURE

Curse of the Shadowmage

Mark Anthony

CURSE OF THE SHADOWMAGE

First Printing: November 1995
Printed in the United States of America.
Library of Congress Catalog Card Number: 94-68155

9 8 7 6 5 4 3 2 1

ISBN: 0-7869-0191-8

TSR, Inc.
201 Sheridan Springs Road
Lake Geneva, WI 53147
U.S.A.

TSR Ltd.
120 Church End, Cherry Hinton
Cambridge CB1 3LB
United Kingdom

As always, there are many people whose help and inspiration made this book possible. There are some of them I even want to mention. Allow me to thank:

Carla Montgomery, friend and fellow wordsmith, for once again reading a work in progress; and for letting me know when things needed changing and, perhaps more importantly, when things were just fine.

Brian Thomsen, Executive Editor of TSR Books, for giving me the chance to continue a tale unfinished.

Pat McGilligan, my inexhaustible editor of four novels, for reading yet another one.

And Loreena McKennitt, recording artist, for the haunting and evocative music of *The Mask and Mirror*.

For my mother—
Esther Elizabeth Anthony
—with love.

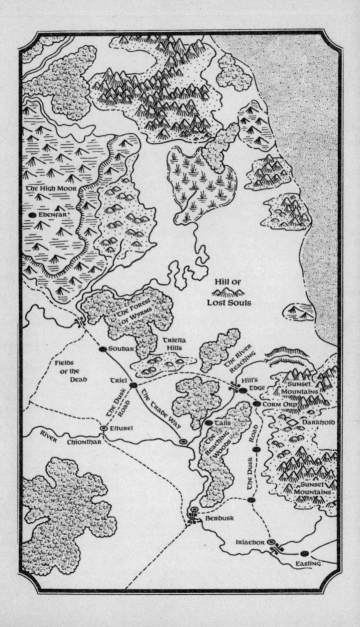

Prologue

Night.

 It mantled the city of Iriaebor, veiling all with the soft stuff of darkness. A thousand spires loomed silent and mysterious as sentinels above the shadowed labyrinth of the Old City. Selune had long since fled beneath the western horizon with the luminous orb she bore nightly in her silver chariot, and false light—the first pale omen of dawn—had not yet touched the eastern sky. It was the darkest hour of the night, the hour caught in the rift between one day and the next, when the world is the most still and magic the most strong. The Darkling Hour, some called it. The hour for thieves and wizards.

Kadian was no wizard. Not that he lacked brains enough to study the arcane arts, or was deficient in the nimbleness required for the intricate rituals that shaped magical energies into spells; he possessed both characteristics in no small quantity. Once, when Kadian was a boy, a white-haired mage on the Street of Runes had noticed

these qualities and, gazing at the barefoot street urchin
in pity, had taken Kadian into his tower as an apprentice. An hour later, the kindly mage had gaped in round-
mouthed surprise as Kadian deftly pinned the old fellow's
moon-and-star robe to the wall with a knife and made off
with three enchanted rings, a sack of gold dust, and the
mage's best magic wand. These days, the only sort of
magic Kadian worked involved moving without sound,
scaling impossibly smooth walls, and opening unopen-
able locks. If these required no mystical incantations to
perform, they were no less remarkable for that fact.

Guttering torches cast wavering shadows across the
intersection of the Street of Jewels and the Street of
Lanterns. Kadian used these pools of darkness to good
advantage as he moved to an alcove in a stone wall. He
was a big man. His broad shoulders and pale hair came
from his father, but he had his mother's grace. More than
once, he had heard it whispered that there had been an
elvish tinge to her blood, so she had been graceful indeed.

Kadian hunkered down to wait. The alcove provided
good vantage of the squat building across the street. Its
windows were heavily curtained, but from time to time a
corner of the fabric stirred, as if someone were peering
outward, and a thin ray of crimson light spilled into the
street along with the dissonant music of wicked laughter.
For a while the only comings and goings were those of
the rats searching for food in the filth-strewn gutters.
Finally the building's door opened, a thin figure stumbled
out, and the door quickly closed again.

The figure paused, wobbled precariously, found some
small reserve of balance, and lurched across the cobbled
square. Passing through the flickering circle of light
beneath a smoking torch, the figure was revealed for a
moment. He was thin, so emaciated that the possibility
of some wasting disease could not be discounted. Gaudy

finery draped his bony frame: ruffled shirt, ridiculously puffy breeches, and a doublet of yellow silk that clashed hideously with his sallow complexion. A thick coating of powder failed to disguise the deep pockmarks that savaged his pinched face. The ugly, foppish man continued to weave his way down the Street of Lanterns.

Kadian's bared teeth glowed in the dimness. "Slumming tonight, milord?" he murmured wryly. A dagger glinted sharply in his hand as he slipped soundlessly from the alcove. The waiting was over.

The drunken petty lord was so easy to follow that it was almost unfair—almost, for Kadian had never been of the opinion that life was meant to be in any way fair. Justice weaves as Justice sees, or so his mother had told him. Kadian pursued his quarry through the tortuous streets of the Old City. Overhead, countless spires wove themselves together in a tangle of spindly bridges and midair causeways that blotted out the starlit sky. Beneath the towers, the narrow streets were no less tangled, forming a maze in which the unfamiliar or the unwary could all too easily find himself lost.

A short distance ahead, the nobleman hesitated at a crossroads. He looked first right, then left, then—and now a bit dizzily—right again. At last, apparently at random, the foppish lord plunged through the left-hand archway.

Kadian's smile broadened. "Wrong choice," he whispered with a feral smile. That way was a dead end. Gripping his knife, he hastened through the archway.

Kadian came upon the petty lord moments later, in a small cul-de-sac lit by a single greasy torch. Realizing he could go no farther, the nobleman turned around and found himself facing Kadian. His expression of astonishment sent fine cracks through the thick layer of powder that coated his face. Swiftly, surprise gave way to dread.

The man licked his rouged lips. "What . . . what do you want of me?"

Kadian spun the dagger casually on a fingertip before returning it firmly to his grip. "Come now, milord," he said chidingly. "There's no use in stating the obvious, is there? You know exactly what I want."

The petty lord's reply was limited to a small, strangled squeak as he sidled clumsily backward. Kadian moved smoothly toward him. As he did, he felt a peculiar prickling on the back of his neck. It was a sensation all good thieves experienced when being watched. But Kadian could see no one who might be doing the watching, nor even any windows through which watching eyes might peer unseen. There were only the shadows of the two men cast by the guttering torch—tall, distorted silhouettes that played like malformed giants across the stone walls of the circular dead end. Kadian shrugged the odd feeling aside. Wasn't he a bit too old to be unnerved by shadows? He affected a cheerful tone and gestured with the knife.

"Hand it over, milord. That's right. Your purse. Don't feign surprise. What else would a cutthroat be interested in? Now don't let that disturb you, milord. 'Cutthroat' is simply a name, my title if you will. I don't actually cut throats—usually." Kadian dropped his voice to a low growl with that last word.

"Here! Take it!" the foppish man squealed in a choked voice. "Take all of it. I don't care. I won it only tonight playing at Dragon's Eyes."

The petty lord clumsily fumbled with the plump leather purse and heaved it at Kadian's feet. Kadian casually stooped to retrieve the heavy purse and stood, tucking it under his belt. The nobleman eyed the curved dagger in Kadian's hand fearfully. "You aren't . . . you aren't going to use that, are you?"

"As a matter of fact, I think I am," Kadian replied jovially. The petty lord let out a small whimper as Kadian slowly lifted the dagger. Then, with a deft motion, Kadian turned the blade and began using it to clean his fingernails. He chuckled to himself and looked up to see what the lord had thought of his little joke.

The nobleman was gaping, his beady eyes wide with terror.

Kadian sighed in annoyance. "Oh, stop it," he growled. "I told you, I'm not going to kill you, so—" He realized then that the petty lord's eyes were not fixed on the dagger. The man's gaze was focused above Kadian, and behind him. Taking in a hissing breath, Kadian spun around. At first, all he saw was his oversized shadow sprawled across the stone wall. Then he noticed something odd. Kadian was standing still, but Kadian's shadow was—

"By all the gods of midnight, it's moving!" Kadian gasped.

The shadow—*his* shadow, cast by the torchlight— undulated on the rough surface of the wall. The dark silhouette rippled, remolding itself. For a moment it coalesced into an amorphous blob, like a great stain on the stone. Then, with malevolent speed, the dark blotch spread, outlining talon, fang, and horn—the shape of a beast. Two pinpricks of crimson light flared to life like feral eyes. For a moment, those eyes seemed to burn directly into Kadian's chest. Then the shadow stepped off the wall.

The petty lord screamed. Reflexively, Kadian swung his head around and stared in dull astonishment. Another black, monstrous form, that moments before had been the nobleman's shadow, had also separated itself from the stone wall, opening its gigantic maw in a silent howl. Kadian blinked dizzily. Was that starlight he saw

through the shadowbeast's mouth, or the glint of sharp
teeth? When he turned back, his own shadowbeast
advanced on him.

"We have to run!" Kadian shouted impulsively, grab-
bing the lord's arm. The petrified nobleman did not move.
He stared at the two approaching shadowbeasts, his
pasty face a mask of horror. "Run, blast you!" Kadian
cried, jerking the man's arm. Still he did not move. By
then it was too late.

Something dark lashed out at Kadian, and his thief's
instinct took over. He dove for the ground, though not
fast enough to entirely avoid the shadowbeast as it
struck. A hot line of fire traced itself across his cheek.
Rolling to a crouch, he pressed his back against the wall.
The hand he touched to his burning cheek came away
dark and sticky. His mind reeled. How could a shadow
draw blood?

Kadian looked up. The two bestial shapes were circling
around the paralyzed petty lord, moving with eerie
silence. Swiftly they closed in. Kadian's eyes noticed the
flickering torch in its iron sconce, and he was moving
before the idea was fully formed in his head. Behind him,
a piercing scream of agony shattered the air. Kadian
could no longer see the petty lord for the dark bulk of the
shadowbeasts. He lunged toward the iron sconce, grabbed
the torch, and beat it against the stone wall. Sparks flew.
As if realizing what he was doing, the shadowbeasts
turned and flew toward him with terrifying speed.
Kadian could see the crumpled form of the nobleman
lying on the cobbles, the yellow doublet now dark and
wet. He beat the torch more fiercely. Dark arms stretched
outward; curved talons reached for his heart. The torchlight flickered, dimmed . . . and was snuffed out.

Darkness descended on the cul-de-sac like a shroud.
Kadian braced himself, waiting to feel the claws of the

shadowbeasts plunge into his chest and rip out his wildly beating heart. The death blow did not come. Gradually his thief's eyes adjusted to the faint starlight that filtered down from above. The small stone circle was empty save for the motionless heap that had been the petty lord. Kadian's hunch had proved right. The shadowbeasts had been extinguished along with the light source that had spawned them. Numbly, still clutching the knife in one hand, he shuffled toward the fallen lord. Kneeling, he placed a hand on the nobleman's chest. Quickly he snatched his hand back, dripping gore. The man's body had been ripped to shreds. Shuddering, Kadian stood. He had to flee this accursed place.

Abruptly, brilliant light flared to life in the cul-de-sac, causing Kadian to blink against the searing brightness. When his vision cleared, a new fear stabbed at his guts. Three uniformed men stood in the archway, bearing torches. The city guards stared at him with hard eyes.

"Caught in the act, eh, thief?" one of the guards snarled in disgust.

Kadian looked down at his hand, still dripping with the dead lord's blood. Sick coldness filled his stomach. He looked up, slowly shaking his head. "No," he whispered. "The shadows . . . " But the guards were already upon him. Gripping his arms brutally, they hauled Kadian roughly through the stone archway.

That was when he caught a glimpse of the man. For a fractured second, a flickering beam of torchlight pierced the darkness of a corner near the archway. The man stood within. His black attire blended seamlessly with the night, but his face hovered clearly in the dimness. Almost against his will, Kadian met the other's eyes. They were impossibly deep, and filled with a rage and a sorrow so vast they did not seem human. Kadian thought those eyes would rend his soul.

The torchlight wavered. Once more the corner fell dark. The man vanished. Kadian struggled against the hands that gripped him, shouting to the guards, trying to tell them about the man who lurked in the corner. But all his protests bought him was a sharp blow to the back of his head, and Kadian was lost in darkness.

One

It was the cold that woke the boy.

Kellen Caldorien opened his eyes and found himself gazing up at the slanted ceiling of the attic room where he slept. Faint illumination filled the small chamber, the steely light that comes before the dawn and that casts no shadows. When he breathed out, his breath hung on the frigid air above him like the pale ghost of a bird. The inn was quiet at this hour, and the silence seemed heavy with portent. Kellen had the feeling that something was going to happen today. He didn't know what it would be, nor when exactly it would occur, nor whether it would be for good or ill—only that *something* would happen. Something important.

As quickly as it came, the odd feeling of prescience vanished, and the last vestiges of dreaminess with it. Wide awake now, Kellen slipped from his bed, shuddering with the cold, and realized at once the source of the fierce chill. The chamber's round window hung open, and a steady wind blew in. Even this early in the month of Uktar, when the days could still be fine and golden, the nights were sharp with the promise of winter. The window must have blown open during the night.

Kellen padded barefoot across the cold wooden floor and reached out to shut the window. Abruptly he paused, his eyes glowing with curiosity in the half-light. The surface of the glass bore a patch of pearly frost. Being autumn, this was not unusual. That the patch of frost was shaped exactly like a human hand was far more peculiar. It appeared as if some terribly cold being had pressed its fingers against the glass for a moment, leaving behind pale crystals of ice. Slowly, Kellen reached out his own hand and placed it over the frosty print. His hand was much smaller, but the heat of it melted the frost, and in moments the mysterious handprint was gone. He wondered if this was the *something* he had felt was going to happen today. After a moment he decided that this mysterious occurrence wasn't the awaited event, but that it might be related.

"I will simply have to wait and see," he whispered. Unlike most children, Kellen knew how to be patient.

Turning from the window, he shrugged off his night-shirt and in its place pulled on woolen breeches, a wine-colored tunic, and soft deerskin boots. He combed his almost-black hair with a wooden comb. Fine boned and slight of build, Kellen was often mistaken for a child of seven or eight years rather than the eleven he was. Strangers often found this discrepancy unsettling, for he spoke with uncanny precision, and a wisdom in his gray-green eyes that no eleven-year-old boy should have possessed.

When he had finished dressing, Kellen knelt to open a battered trunk beside his bed. Gently he took out his greatest treasure, a bone flute that his father had carved for him. Kellen slipped the instrument into a leather pouch at his belt. He left his room—shutting the door quietly, as it was still early—and made his way down two winding flights of stairs to the inn's common room.

A halfling woman with nut-brown eyes looked up from the fieldstone hearth. She was stirring the coals that had been banked beneath the ashes for the night. "You're up early, Kellen," she said merrily.

"Yes, Estah," he replied seriously. "I am."

Estah was the proprietor of the Sign of the Dreaming Dragon, the inn where Kellen lived with his father, Caledan Caldorien. The halfling innkeeper stood, dusting her hands against her homespun apron. Grown woman though she was, she stood only as high as Kellen's shoulder. A curious look crossed her broad face.

"And may I ask what roused you from your bed before the sun has even climbed from his own?"

Kellen considered whether he should tell Estah about the frosty handprint he had seen on his bedchamber window. He knew that Estah, unlike many adults, would listen to a young boy's words. However, she tended to worry unduly, and he didn't want to distract her from her tasks about the inn, which were considerable. After a moment he decided against telling her. He could wait until his father was awake, if he must tell somebody.

"I thought I would help you knead the bread dough today," he said instead.

Estah studied him for a moment. Then she laughed, eyes crinkling. "Very well, then. To the kitchen with you."

Kellen liked kneading dough. He leaned over a halfling-sized wooden table in the center of the warm kitchen, rolling up the sleeves of his tunic so he could stick his arms deep into the floury mass. Mountains, castles, and dragons all took shape under his deft hands before he squashed them, laughing, like a careless giant.

When the dough and Kellen's arms needed a rest, Estah sat him down in front of the kitchen's massive stone fireplace with a breakfast of oat porridge, honey, and sausages. The first red-gold glow of dawn was gilding the kitchen's windows when Jolle, Estah's husband, tramped inside with a load of firewood. As the halfling man went back out to the courtyard for more, Kellen got up and neatly stacked the wood he had brought in.

"It looks as if someone's in a helpful mood today," Jolle observed with a broad grin as he returned, setting down a second armful of wood. Like his wife, the halfling man was not even as tall as Kellen, but he was sturdily built.

"More so than usual, actually," Estah commented with a sharp glance at Kellen.

Kellen just smiled mysteriously, returning to his breakfast. Sometimes it was fun to make adults wonder if you had done something wrong.

Soon Jolle had a summer-fattened piglet roasting over a steady fire in the gigantic fireplace. Kellen finished his breakfast and returned to the bread dough, this time shaping it into loaves instead of unicorns and wyverns. Before long these were baking in the ovens next to the fireplace, filling the kitchen with their warm fragrance. Kellen was wiping excess flour off the table when two voices drifted from the inn's back hallway.

"I told you I would take care of the problem, Caledan." The first voice was rich, like wine and smoke, but there was a sharp edge of annoyance to it.

"What's the difference, Mari?" This voice was rougher than the first, almost a growl, but with a note of musicality to it all the same. "You wanted the problem taken care of, and I took care of it. It doesn't really matter whether it was my knife or yours."

The first voice was blistering. "For your information, Caledan, 'take care of the problem' does not universally mean 'put a dagger in its heart.' "

Kellen looked up to see a man and a woman enter the kitchen. The woman was not pretty. She was tall and rawboned—though not at all ungainly—wearing doeskin breeches and a green velvet jacket over a billowing white shirt. She tossed her thick, darkfire hair over a shoulder like a horse tossing its mane; indeed there was something rather horsey about her large features and too-square jaw, though in a pleasing way.

If the woman was equine, the man was wolfish. He was lean and broad shouldered, and moved with a stiff, predatory grace. Gray flecked his dark hair, and his eyebrows were shaggy above gray-green eyes. His slate-colored doublet was well kept, but over it he wore a travel-stained cloak of midnight blue.

Kellen knew the pair well. The wolfish man was his father, Caledan Caldorien, while the square-jawed woman was Caledan's companion, Mari Al'maren. The two of them were more than lovers; they were partners as well, for both Caledan and Mari were Harpers. As a team, they embarked on dangerous and invariably secretive missions for the mysterious, benevolent organization known as the Harpers. Kellen's mother had died over two years ago. As his father's constant companion, Mari might have filled the void. However, Estah was more than enough mother for everybody who lived at the inn. Thus, over time, Mari had become more like an aunt to Kellen, and a very special friend. Together they made up stories, practiced at archery—for Mari was a master of the longbow—and went for long treks in the rolling hills outside the city, hunting for lizards, interesting stones, and buried treasure. For a time, Kellen had imagined that Mari and his father might get married one day. Now he was not so certain. The two had always been contentious in their relationship. However, these days arguing was all they seemed to accomplish.

"Good morning, Kellen," Caledan said, his grin cheerful if a bit haggard. Apparently, Harper work had kept
the pair out all night, as it often did. He flopped into a
chair and started to put his boots up on the table, but a
sharp glare from Estah made him think twice. He lowered his mud-spattered boots to the floor. Mari paced
tensely in front of the fire, arms crossed. She cast a smile
at Kellen, but it was thin and fleeting. Kellen shot her
his warmest smile in return, for which she gave him a
grateful look.

"The spy we discovered in the High Tower could well
have been Zhentarim, Caledan," Mari went on in a low
voice. "If so, he would have known if there are others of
his kind in Iriaebor, and whether it's the Black Network
that's behind the unexplained murders in the city. I
really would have liked to have kept him alive long
enough to ask him a few questions."

Caledan gave a rough snort of laughter. "Answering
questions *is* difficult when one has a dagger in one's
back. It's very distracting to one's concentration. At least
so I've heard."

Estah scowled at this. "Well, that's fine talk for present
company," she said sharply, giving a meaningful nod in
Kellen's direction.

Caledan seemed not to hear the halfling's reproving
words. As happened increasingly often of late, his gaze
had gone suddenly distant, as if he stared into some far-
off place that the others could not fathom. It was just one
of several peculiarities Caledan had been exhibiting
recently. At times he seemed terribly far away, while on
other occasions his temper would flare hotly at the most
minor of annoyances, and he might laugh loudly—almost
too loudly—at unlikely things such as a coal bursting on
the hearth or a dropped plate shattering against the

floor. Shadows hung beneath his eyes, gathering in the hollows of his cheeks. He had not been eating much lately, to Estah's great concern. Kellen was beginning to wonder if his father might be ill.

Caledan's gaze came back to his surroundings. "I don't see why you're so mad at me, Mari," he went on as if there had been no pause. "I was having some fun and got a little carried away, that's all."

Mari stared at him in shock. "It isn't like you to be so cavalier about Zhentarim, Caledan. If the Black Network could find a way to get Iriaebor under its yoke again, it'd do it in a second. And these murders may be the beginning of some plan to do just that."

Caledan and Mari didn't usually speak to Kellen of their work for the Harpers. Despite this, he gleaned much from what they let slip in his presence. For instance, he knew the Zhentarim were a sort of cult. They followed no god in particular, though they cultivated many of the darker ones to gain magic, but instead worshiped gold and power, stopping at nothing to win these. The Harpers worked against all evils in the Heartlands, but the Zhentarim were their time-honored enemies.

Several years ago, the Black Network had taken control of Iriaebor, enslaving the populace and bleeding the city dry. It was Caledan and Mari, on a mission for the Harpers, who finally had ousted the Zhents from Iriaebor. The Black Network was still furious at losing its grip on the wealthy city and would do anything to regain control.

If Mari's suspicions were right, now the Zhentarim were trying to do just that. Since Higharvestide, there had been over a dozen murders in Iriaebor. Each of the murders shared the same grisly details: All occurred at night, with the corpses horribly mauled. In each case the victim was a less-than-savory individual, ranging from back-alley hoodlums to corrupt petty nobles. The

Harpers feared the deaths were part of some Zhentarim plot—perhaps sacrifices for a ritual magic of dark and unknown purpose—and that the Black Network was preying on the dregs of society for some mysterious reason. Mari and Caledan had been given orders to investigate. However, it looked as if they had no answer to these strange occurrences.

Kellen thought of his intention to tell his father about the curious handprint he had seen on his window. He looked at Caledan, then Mari. Both seemed weary from their night's travails, and from their argument. After a moment, he decided he would have to figure out for himself what the handprint signified.

Mari took her leave then. "It was a long night," she said with a deep sigh before heading upstairs to her chamber.

Caledan did not follow her. "I have some things to do down in the New City," he explained gruffly. "I'll be back before sundown."

Estah only nodded, her lips pursed in a frown of disapproval. Caledan paused to ruffle Kellen's hair affectionately, then disappeared out the inn's back door.

Midday arrived dim and dreary. A storm had gathered over the city, and the failing light forced Jolle to light candles throughout the inn. The threatening cloudburst kept customers away; the inn's long main room stayed empty. Kellen sat in a corner, playing a gentle melody on his bone flute while two very small people sprawled on the floor before him. These were Estah's children, Pog and Nog. The girl, Pog, was the elder of the two; she was red-cheeked and impish. The boy, Nog, was quieter; he seemed to subscribe to the theory that actions spoke more strongly than words. Being the eldest, Kellen often found himself taking care of the two young halflings.

"Today I'm going to tell you the story of the Shadowking,"

Kellen told them in a low voice.

"The Shadowking?" Pog gasped, her eyes wide. Nog let out a squeal of terror and delight.

"That's right," Kellen said mysteriously. "A long age ago, in a land called Ebenfar, there lived a king. This king was a great sorcerer, and his name was Verraketh." Lifting the flute to his lips, Kellen played a few wild notes. He gestured to the shadows on the wall, cast by a flickering candle. Pog and Nog stared, wide-eyed. In time with Kellen's music, the shadows swirled, silently reshaping themselves into jagged shapes that suggested a craggy landscape. Atop the highest peak stood the silhouette of a man, his cloak blowing behind him.

This was shadow magic. It was a rare talent that ran in Caldorien blood and that always appeared in a family member at least once in a generation. Caledan possessed it, and so did Kellen.

Kellen lowered his flute. "Although he was powerful beyond all others, Verraketh's magic was dark at heart. In time it transformed him, until at last he was a man no longer, but an awful creature of evil—the Shadowking." He played a dissonant melody on his pipes, and the shadows on the wall responded. The silhouette of the man expanded, twisting into a new form: a bestial shape crowned by pointed antlers. Pog and Nog let out small cries, clutching each other, but they did not take their eyes off the shadows.

Kellen went on in an eerie whisper. "For centuries, the Shadowking ruled from his dark throne in Ebenfar, laying waste to the land all around, for he drew strength and power from the destruction of living things. Eventually, the Shadowking decided to bring all the world of Toril under his dark dominion. Deep in a mountain cave, he forged a stone. The magic of the stone was that it could control the shadows that reside in a man's heart—

for all men have a dark aspect within—and thus control the man himself. It was called the Nightstone, and with it the Shadowking would have the power to rule the world."

"But the Shadowking didn't, did he?" Pog asked in a quavering voice. "Rule the world, I mean."

Kellen shook his head. Pog and Nog knew the familiar tale almost by heart. "No, he didn't. When the Shadowking tried to use the Nightstone, the troll who had worked the bellows of the forge threw off his disguise. He wasn't a troll at all, but a man. His name was Talek Talembar, and he was a great bard. Unknown to the Shadowking, Talembar had bound an enchantment into the Nightstone as it was being forged. This was the shadow song. When Talembar played the song on his pipes, the Nightstone listened and would not obey the Shadowking. In fury, the Shadowking attacked Talek Talembar, and the two fought night and day for a year."

Kellen played a stirring air on his flute, and the shadows reshaped themselves into the two titanic figures, caught in the throes of battle. Pog and Nog were mesmerized. "In the end, Talek Talembar used the shadow song to wrest the Nightstone from his foe, and thus the Shadowking was defeated. Talembar raised a great cairn over the crypt of the sorcerer-king of Ebenfar, so the evils of the Shadowking and his Nightstone were hidden away." Kellen played a triumphant melody, and the outline of a mountain rose over the fallen silhouette of the Shadowking.

"But what happened to Talek Talembar?" Pog asked.

"Like many heroes, he met an unheroic end," Kellen said quietly. "He was slain by a goblin's arrow, in a land that is now lost under the Fields of the Dead, far to the west." He played one last wistful note on the bone flute, and the shadows swirled like mist before a wind. When they coalesced again, it was in the shape of those mundane objects standing between candle and wall: chairs and tables and small halfling children. The shadowplay was over.

Pog's forehead crinkled in a frown. "That's not a good enough ending," she protested. "Talek Talembar ought to live happily ever after." Nog nodded emphatically in agreement.

"But that's not what happened," Kellen said softly. He cast a sad look toward the door of the kitchen. "Sometimes people don't live happily ever after, and that's just the way it is."

Before Pog and Nog could protest further, Estah poked her head into the common room, calling her children to their chores. They groaned but obeyed, dragging their feet as they shuffled into the kitchen.

Alone, Kellen ran his fingers over the smooth bone flute. He thought about the part of the tale he had never told Pog and Nog. A thousand years after the time of Talek Talembar, the crypt of the Shadowking was found once more, and the Nightstone with it, and the Shadowking almost came to life again. It was a story Kellen knew all too well, for he himself had been a part of it.

It was Kellen's own mother, the Zhentarim lord Ravendas, who discovered the crypt beneath the Tor—the crag upon which perched Iriaebor's many-towered Old City. With the Nightstone, she aspired to rule all the Zhentarim. However, to remove the stone from its resting place, she needed someone with shadow magic, such as Talek Talembar himself had possessed. Kellen wasn't entirely certain of the details—adults could be infuriatingly vague about certain subjects when they knew children were listening—but Ravendas tricked Caledan into thinking she was someone else, someone he loved, and thereby used him to create a baby. That

baby was Kellen, who like Caledan possessed the
shadow magic. Ravendas had what she needed.

Though Kellen didn't know it at the time—his mother
had kept him locked in a room in Iriaebor's High Tower—
the Harpers had sent Caledan and Mari to stop Ravendas. Helping them was the renowned Fellowship of the
Dreaming Dragon, including Estah, the mage Morhion, a
monk named Tyveris, and a thief called Ferret, who was
lost forever in the destruction of the Shadowking's crypt.

For indeed, it was destroyed in the end, as was Kellen's
mother, and by her own evil plan. When Ravendas seized
the Nightstone, its magic consumed her. From her body
burst a dark, monstrous shape: the Shadowking reborn.
The Shadowking would have walked the face of Toril
once more, but at the last moment Caledan discovered
the long-lost secret of Talek Talembar's shadow song.
When he played the song on his pipes, the Nightstone
burst asunder, and the Shadowking—as well as Ravendas—was no more.

The events in the crypt had taken place two and a half
years ago. Afterward, Kellen went to live with Caledan
and Mari at Estah's inn, and for a time they had all been
happy. For a time. Kellen sighed. Once again, he wondered why Caledan and Mari could not seem to get along.
He supposed that, sometimes, even love wasn't enough to
overcome all differences. Picking up his flute, he played a
melancholy tune. Shadows swirled once more on the
wall, and the dark silhouettes of two birds whirled and
dived gracefully. Kellen concentrated, and the music
changed, growing bolder. Suddenly, the two bird shadows
flew off the wall. Like wisps of dark silk, they swirled
around Kellen's head, flapping their silent wings in time
to the music.

"Your father could never do that."

Kellen jumped out of his chair at the sound of the

voice, nearly dropping the flute. The shadow birds vanished like puffs of smoke. He spun around to see a tall man with eyes like blue ice and hair as long and golden as a lion's mane. Though Kellen had seen the man only a handful of times over the last two years, he recognized him all the same. It was Morhion, the mage who had once belonged to the Fellowship of the Dreaming Dragon.

Morhion took a step closer. He was clad in shirt and breeches of pearl gray, and over these flowed a vest of twilight purple so long it almost reached the ground. The mage spoke again in his resonant voice. "Caledan can make shadows dance with his music, but I have never seen him pipe them right off the wall. How long have you been able to perform this feat, Kellen?"

Kellen thought about this. "Always, I suppose," he said finally. "However, it was only a few months ago that I discovered I could do it. It isn't so hard, really. I just think about the shadows jumping off the wall . . . and they do!"

A musing smile touched the handsome mage's lips. "Something tells me that it is not quite so simple as you present it, Kellen. You have great talent at magic."

Kellen only shrugged, but inwardly he beamed. He barely knew Morhion, but Kellen liked the mage all the same. Morhion was cool, even distant, but there was lightning in his blue eyes, and he wore power comfortably, like a soft cloak. An idea struck Kellen. "I think that we should be friends, Morhion."

Morhion raised a single eyebrow. "Oh? And why is that?"

Kellen thought of the years he had spent locked in a tower room by his mother, so that his power over shadows would remain a secret. He knew Morhion spent most of his time in solitude in his own tower, studying spells. "Because," he said finally, "we both know what it is to be alone with our magic."

After a long moment, Morhion nodded. "I think perhaps you're right. Very well. Come to my tower tomorrow, Kellen. We shall talk of magic, you and I."

Kellen gave the mage a smile. Then, placing his flute in its leather pouch, he dashed off to the kitchen to help Estah and Jolle with the evening meal. Outside, the storm had passed, and by sundown the inn would be crowded with hungry patrons once again.

Caledan returned from his wanderings late in the afternoon. Mari came downstairs just as he stepped through the inn's door. The two exchanged troubled looks but no words. Morhion spoke briefly with each. He had some news concerning their investigation into the unexplained deaths, though Kellen did not learn its precise nature. After that, Morhion left the inn to return to his tower. Belatedly, Kellen realized that the mage would have been the perfect person to tell about the frosty handprint.

"I suppose I can tell Morhion tomorrow," Kellen decided as he cranked the handle of the iron spit, turning the sizzling piglet over the hot flames.

Estah appeared before him. "I need some more sage for the stew, Kellen. Do you think you could pick some in the garden for me?"

Kellen nodded and ran out the back door of the inn. He was glad to escape the heat of the fire; the cool evening air felt good against his glowing cheeks. The inn was perched on the precipitous western edge of the Tor, and Kellen paused to gaze at the distant horizon, watching the sun sink into a sea of clouds as brilliant as molten copper. He hurriedly made his way through the garden. This late in the year, the garden was mostly a tangle of dried brown plants and witchgrass. At last Kellen found a patch of dark green herbs. He knew which was sage by its dusty scent, and he picked a handful. Turning, he started back toward the inn.

That was when he saw them. They glittered on the hard ground, outlined in white crystals of frost. Footprints. Kellen's heart skipped a beat. He took in a deep breath of air—air no longer just cool, but sharp and cold, like steel in the dead of winter. Slowly, he followed the trail of shimmering footprints with his eyes.

The ghost stood on the edge of the Tor.

The last rays of sunlight filtered through the man's translucent body. He seemed to waver in and out of existence—now dim, now bright—like the flickering light of a dying candle. The man was clad in peculiar, ancient clothes, at once more flowing and more angular than modern attire. Although he wasn't certain how, he realized who the spirit was. His father had encountered this same shade once before, though that had been far from here, in the desolate land known as the Fields of the Dead. Kellen's breath fogged on the frigid air as he whispered the words.

"Talek Talembar."

The ghost gazed at Kellen with eyes like emeralds, then stretched out his arms in a plaintive, urgent gesture. The spirit's voice blended eerily with the low moan of the wind.

"The old king hath fallen . . . and a new king doth rise to take his place . . ."

As the last sliver of the sun slipped below the far horizon, the ghost vanished, leaving Kellen to shiver alone in the gathering gloom of the garden.

Two

 Mari Al'maren sat in the common room of the Dreaming Dragon, waiting. Through a window, she watched as the black night sky softened to slate blue, then pearl gray, and at last blazed into scarlet brilliance. She had been up all night. Finally she heard the sounds she had been waiting for outside the inn's door: the grating of a boot heel on stone, the rattling of an iron key in the lock, the creak of hinges as the door swung open. A tall figure wrapped in a tattered midnight blue cloak stepped into the common room. Surprise registered in his faded green eyes.

"You're up early," Caledan said cheerfully.

"No," Mari countered crisply. "I'm up late."

It took a moment for the implication of her words to register on his angular visage. His grin faded. "How about if I told you that I went out for a midnight constitutional and lost track of the time?"

Mari gazed at him steadily. "You can give it a try, but

don't get your hopes up. I'd really hate for you to be disappointed."

Caledan winced. "I was afraid of that." He shrugged off his ragged cloak. Beneath, he wore the old travel-stained black leathers he preferred for night work.

Mari stood, taking a half dozen paces toward the stairs before turning to regard him. "All right, Caledan. Where have you been all night? You can tell me now, or if you'd rather, we can scream at each other first. But either way, you *are* going to tell me."

Caledan opted to cooperate directly. "I went to the Barbed Hook," he said. "It's a tavern down in the New City, on the waterfront."

"I've heard of the place," she said coolly, crossing her arms. "The clientele consists of brawling sailors, besotted dockhands, one-handed cutpurses, and a generous sprinkling of harlots. A little too high class for you, don't you think?"

Caledan grimaced. "I'll be generous and ignore that. Do you remember the spy we discovered in the High Tower?"

"A man dancing around trying to pull a dagger out of his back before he drops dead is a curiously memorable image."

He pretended not to hear the sarcasm in her voice. "I did a little investigating and found out that our spy had been seen down at the Barbed Hook, so I decided to scout things out. Guess what? I noticed a few of our friend's cohorts disappearing down a hidden passage into a back storeroom. One of them bore ritual scars on his cheekbones. There's no question about it. They were definitely Zhentarim."

Mari arched an eyebrow. She had a sinking feeling. "*Were* Zhentarim?"

"You can stop worrying," Caledan snapped in annoyance. "I didn't harm a hair on their evil little heads. Not that I wouldn't have liked to. Whatever you may think, I'm not so impulsive I'd follow three Zhentarim into their hideout without someone to back me up." He shook his head in frustration. "But I still can't understand this overwhelming desire of yours to sit and have a pleasant chat with every member of the Black Network we turn up. That's exactly why I left—"

Caledan halted, swallowing his words. Mari finished for him. "That's exactly why you left me behind last night. Is that what you were going to say?" He stared at her sulkily. Mari felt her wrath building. He had gone too far this time.

"How dare you?" Her voice was low and even, but there was scorching fire in it. "How dare you sneak behind my back, like some cowardly adulterous husband, just so you can indulge your childish impulses? In case you've forgotten, Caledan Caldorien, you are not the only Harper in Iriaebor."

Anger flared in his eyes. "Well, maybe I should be. After all this time, you still don't have the faintest idea how evil the Zhentarim are, do you, Mari? There's only one thing worth doing with a member of the Black Network—and that involves a good sharp blade, not polite questions." His voice rose dangerously. "And by the way, I am *not* your husband."

"Believe me, I'm aware of that fact," Mari replied caustically. All in a rush, harsh words she had been saving up for months poured out of her. "I just don't understand, Caledan. You never would have behaved this rashly a year ago. I'm not sure exactly what is going on, but you . . . you've gotten careless—no, not careless, but *reckless*. You don't give a damn about anything or anyone these days, least of all yourself." She was shouting now. The noise would wake everyone up, but she didn't care.

"You've changed, and I'm not certain I even know who you are anymore, Caledan Caldorien!"

"Maybe you never did," he snarled, clenching a fist in rage. "Maybe you don't have the faintest idea, Mari Al'maren!"

It happened so fast that, afterward, Mari was never certain what really happened. Out of the corner of her eye, she saw Caledan's shadow expand on the wall, growing to monstrous proportions. Like a black serpent, the shadow lashed out an arm, striking at her own shadow. A searing line of fire raced across her cheek. She screamed, reeling backward, falling to her knees. Dazed, she lifted a hand to her cheek. It came away wet with blood.

Suddenly, Caledan was there, kneeling beside her. "By the gods—Mari, are you all right?" His voice was desperate. "Mari, talk to me!" He gripped her shoulders with big hands.

She shrank away from him, casting a furtive glance at the wall. Now their shadows were mundane silhouettes, nothing more. Gradually, she let herself relax into his strong embrace. "I'm all right," she gasped. "It's a scratch, that's all."

"But how did . . . ?"

Mari thought of the way his shadow had moved . . . or had it? She had been angry and distracted. Caledan could make the shadows dance on the wall—that was the nature of his shadow magic—but the shadows he controlled did not have physical substance or the ability to harm. Maybe in her rage she had imagined it. She could have scratched her cheek when she fell in her attempt to back away from him. She realized that her anger had receded, whatever the explanation for her injury. All she felt now was a great weariness.

"Forget it, Caledan." She took a deep breath. "It's nothing. Really."

Mari pulled herself to her feet. She drew a handkerchief from her pocket and blotted her cheek; already the flow of blood had stopped. There were more pressing matters to concern her now. She took her wine-colored cloak from its hook and opened the door.

Quickly, Caledan stood. "Where are you going?" he asked in confusion.

"The Barbed Hook. It might have slipped your mind, but we still have a mission to complete." She gave him a wan smile. "So are you coming or not, Harper?"

His wolfish visage was unreadable. At last he nodded. "Lead the way."

* * * * *

The narrow crag upon which Iriaebor's Old City was built soared a full three hundred feet above the surrounding plains. Leaving the precarious towers and mazelike streets of the Old City behind, Mari and Caledan made their way down a serpentine road to the sprawling New City below. It was nearing midmorning, and the New City's broad avenues were crowded with throngs of cityfolk. Iriaebor was prosperous these days.

And that was precisely why the Zhentarim would love to dig their claws into the city once again. With Iriaebor's gold draining into their own coffers, the Black Network could fuel their evil designs of domination in a dozen other lands. Mari still wasn't certain how the strange murders might benefit a Zhent plot to overthrow the city, but she didn't doubt that they could. The Zhentarim were as insidiously ingenious as they were wicked.

A thought struck her. Kellen had told them about the apparition he witnessed yesterday, and she wondered if this strange occurrence had something to do with the Zhentarim. Mari had no doubt that Kellen had in truth

seen the ghost of Talek Talembar. She had witnessed
Talembar's shade once herself, far away in the Fields of
the Dead, and Kellen's description of the ghost coincided
with her memories. Yet what did the appearance of the
ghost portend? And what of his peculiar message? *The
old king hath fallen . . . and a new king doth rise to take
his place.* Perhaps it was a warning that the Zhentarim
plotted against City Lord Bron. The appearance of the
ghost had left them all shaken, except for Caledan. He
had merely brushed the strange occurrence aside, as he
did everything these days.

As they walked, Mari glanced sidelong at Caledan. For
a time, after the Fellowship defeated Ravendas in the
crypt of the Shadowking, life with Caledan had been joyous. Then, gradually—so gradually she didn't even notice
it at first—they had slipped back into their old habits,
quarreling bitterly as often as they embraced. She sighed
deeply.

Consciously, Mari forced her thoughts to the mission at
hand. Morhion had come to the inn yesterday bearing
news from their old friend, the monk Tyveris. Tyveris
had once been a member of the Fellowship. Now he
served as an advisor to City Lord Bron in the High
Tower. According to Tyveris, the perpetrator of the unexplained murders had finally been apprehended. Two
nights ago, city guards had caught a thief beside the
mangled corpse of a petty nobleman. The mystery,
Tyveris reported, had been solved. Yet for some reason,
Mari did not feel as certain as the monk. It was difficult
to believe that a common thief could be responsible for
over a score of grisly deaths. Mari fully intended to visit
the dungeon, to question the thief before he received
judgment. However, first there was the task at hand.

Mari and Caledan turned from the main avenue and
picked their way down a narrow lane, trying to avoid the

rivulet of foul water that trickled down the middle. The city was not so crowded here. The rank scent of rotting fish hung on the air; gulls cried out raucously above. Between ramshackle warehouses, Mari caught a glimpse of a flat, silvery surface, the Chionthar River. The two reached the end of the lane, finding themselves before a dilapidated building fashioned from the overturned hull of a barnacle-encrusted galleon. The Barbed Hook.

Mari and Caledan exchanged looks. Making an assault on a Zhentarim lair by daylight had its risks, but Zhents tended to do their work under cover of night. They were used to fighting in the dark and to resting during daylight hours. With luck, that would give Mari and Caledan the advantage.

Caledan gestured to the door of the tavern, his grin almost like that of old. "After you, my lady."

"You're too kind," she replied dryly. She sauntered casually toward the door.

And kicked it in.

The two Harpers stepped through a cloud of splinters and dust into the murky interior of the tavern. A dozen coarse faces gaped in surprise at the sudden intrusion. Quickly, surprise gave way to anger. "Harpers!" someone shouted.

"You forgot to take your badge off again," Caledan said in annoyance, jabbing a finger at the silver moon-and-harp brooch pinned to Mari's jacket. "Now they know who we are."

"Oh, bother," she replied with mock exasperation. "I suppose that means we'll have to kill them all."

Caledan bared his teeth in a nasty smile. "Why, I suppose you're right."

A brawny sailor launched himself forward, ready to snap Caledan's neck with his big, callused hands. In one fluid movement, Caledan crouched down, drew a dagger from his boot sheath, and spun inside the sailor's reach. As he rose, he deftly plunged the blade inward just beneath the other's sternum, angling it upward until it pierced the man's heart. The sailor collapsed to the floor like a side of beef falling from a meat hook. Caledan wrenched the dagger free and gestured with its crimson tip. A one-eyed dockhand leapt over a table, bellowing as he unsheathed a rusty short sword.

"Your turn, Mari," Caledan said graciously.

"Why, thank you." She dodged a wild swing of the dockhand's sword, then whirled inside the circle of his arms. "Care to dance?" she asked demurely. She grabbed the wrist of his sword arm and gave it an expert twist. Bones snapped audibly. The dockhand howled in pain as the short sword clattered to the floor. She spun him around in a dizzy circle, then let go. The dockhand careened backward against a wall covered with dusty fishing trophies. He stared down in dull wonder at the serrated snout of a spearfish protruding from his chest, then had the sense to realize he was dead. His eyes rolled up in their sockets as he slumped on the end of the fish's sharp proboscis.

Mari turned around in time to see the bony, hook-nosed man who stood behind the bar reach down and pull something out of a hidden recess. With a quick move, the man threw the object in Caledan's direction. Metal glinted dully. Caledan lifted a black-gloved hand, snatching the thing in midflight.

"I don't recall ordering this, barkeep," Caledan said good-naturedly. "Mind if I return it?"

With a flick of his wrist, he sent the object hurtling back toward the barkeep. A second later, the bony man took a step backward, clutching feebly at the knife embedded in his throat before collapsing over the filthy surface of the bar.

Hands on her hips, Mari gazed at the rest of the tav-

ern's occupants. "All right, who's next?" she asked
sweetly. "No pushing, please. I promise, each of you will
be killed as promptly as possible."

There was a second of silence. Then came a scraping of
chairs and a clattering of boots as the remaining customers departed hastily out the tavern's door. In
moments Mari and Caledan were alone save for three
rapidly cooling corpses.

"I have to admit, you certainly know how to clear a
room," Caledan commented.

Mari shrugged. "It's a talent. Now let's get moving.
This isn't over yet."

Caledan nodded, following her through a dim archway
into the back room. After a few minutes searching, they
spotted the corner of a trapdoor, hastily hidden beneath a
stack of old ale casks. The two pushed the casks aside
and crouched down to examine the iron door. It was
locked.

Caledan looked up at her. "Can you . . . ?"

Mari cut him off. "With my eyes closed." She began
rummaging in a leather pouch.

"I think we're beyond the stage where you need to
show off to impress me," Caledan noted acidly. "With
your eyes open will do just fine."

"As you wish." Mari slipped a pair of thin wires—one
bent, one straight—into the trapdoor lock. Carefully, she
began probing, constructing a mental image of the lock's
interior. The mechanism was of good but not exceptional
construction. Four minutes was all she would need, five
at most. Her brow furrowed in concentration.

It was then that the screams began. The sounds echoed
up from beneath the trapdoor, muffled shrieks of terror
and agony. Mari and Caledan stared at each other. More
screams drifted upward. Something in them made Mari's
blood run cold.

"I won't tell you your business," Caledan said hoarsely, "but you just might want to hurry it a bit."

She nodded silently, bent over her task. After what seemed hours, the lock sprang open. Caledan pulled up the trapdoor. Silence. The screams had ended. All the two could see was a square of perfect blackness.

Mari swallowed hard. "You know, I got to enter the tavern first. I think you should lead the way here. It's only fair."

"How thoughtful of you." Caledan gripped the edges of the trapdoor and lowered himself through, disappearing into darkness. A moment later he whispered, "There's a ladder."

Taking a deep breath, Mari followed. In the blackness, her hands found rusted iron rungs bolted to the rough stone wall. In moments she reached the bottom. They were in some sort of low tunnel. The musty air was cold, and she sensed Caledan's nearness only by the heat of his body. Hunching over, they moved swiftly down the passage. Tomblike silence pressed in from all sides.

The tunnel ended abruptly in a door. A thin line of ruddy light glowed above the sill. Slowly, Mari turned the door handle, which creaked softly. She tensed her body, then threw the door open. Crimson torchlight spilled outward like blood. The two Harpers leapt through the doorway, daggers drawn.

The Zhentarim were all dead.

With caution, Mari and Caledan moved into the long subterranean chamber. It took Mari several moments to count up the corpses, for they were all horribly mangled. Stray body parts were strewn haphazardly across the room, and the floor was slick with blood. She clamped her jaw shut, trying not to retch. Seven, she decided at last. There had been seven agents of the Black Network in the underground lair. And someone had slain them all. Or some*thing*.

Caledan knelt beside one of the corpses and touched a finger to a gory puddle on the floor. "However they died, it happened only a few minutes ago."

"The screams we heard," Mari said with a shudder. "Those were their death cries."

Caledan wiped his hand on the dead man's tunic, then stood. "I can't say that I'm sorry. I wanted the scum dead myself. But I'm more than a little curious to find out who managed to do my job before I had the chance."

Mari shuddered. "Whoever . . . whatever . . . they were, they're gone now." She moved to a table littered with sheaves of parchment. The ones on top were illegible, spattered with blood, but those below were unstained. Several showed schematic drawings of the interior of the High Tower. Mari realized that they were plans for an attack. "Look at these, Caledan. The Zhents *were* plotting to take over the city. These plans prove—"

"Mari."

Caledan's voice was low and quiet, but the tension in it made her freeze.

"Mari, I want you to turn around. But do it very slowly. Do you understand?"

She nodded jerkily. Then, as slowly as she could, she spun around.

They were streaming out of the shadows that filled the far end of the chamber. Dozens of them. Even as they drew near, Mari could not identify them. They reminded her of sea creatures she had once seen off the coast of Amn, far to the south. Raystingers, the creatures were called—flat, boneless animals that floated in the warm tides, trailing whiplike tails barbed with poison. These things that drifted out of the shadows toward the two Harpers were not so different from raystingers, except they were dark as obsidian, and were floating on thin air, not water.

Heart pounding, Mari followed Caledan's lead, backing
slowly toward the door. Suddenly, she felt something cold
and slick brush against her hand. She gasped, looking
down to see one of the dark creatures float past her and
move toward the others. She twisted around. More of the
things rose from a shadowed corner behind her. They
spilled out of the darkness and streamed silently past.
Their touch made her flesh crawl, yet they did not harm
her. She saw that the creature's touch had left a red
smear on her hand. Blood.

"By Milil, what are they?" she gasped.

Caledan's halting reply came from behind her. "I
don't . . . I don't know. Perhaps the Zhentarim conjured
them, but the spell of binding went awry, and the things
turned on the Zhents. I . . ." There was a pause. Then
Caledan's voice came again, a hoarse whisper. "Mari,
help me . . ."

Dozens of the dark creatures had surrounded Caledan.
They drifted around him like a dense black vapor.
Caledan gazed at Mari, face pallid, eyes shining with terror. The creatures circled him slowly, brushing gently
past his hands and letting their long tails slip softly
around his neck in movements that seemed almost like
caresses.

Caledan shuddered uncontrollably. Finally he could
remain still no longer. "Get away from me!" he hissed,
lashing out with an arm.

Like a cloud of smoke, the creatures swirled away from
him. The dark mass drifted apart. Caledan stared in
amazement, then lurched forward. He grabbed Mari's
wrist. "Let's get out of here."

Choked by fear, Mari could barely voice the words.
"The door . . . they're blocking it."

A score of the amorphous black creatures had drifted
before the open portal. The fear in Caledan's eyes was

quickly usurped by rage. He shook a fist at the nameless creatures, snarling. "Let us pass!"

At once, like a curtain of black velvet, the creatures parted before the doorway, leaving room to pass. Caledan pulled Mari's arm. "Come on!"

She froze, staring at him. She was struck by a sudden, inexplicable fear. At that moment, Caledan seemed as alien as the jet-black blobs that floated before them.

"What's wrong with you?" he growled, tugging at her arm.

It was irrational—perhaps even mad—but he frightened her as much as the unnameable creatures. She tried to pull away, but he held her tight. At last she managed to speak. "They . . . they listen to you. They obey your commands." She felt dizzy and ill. "But why . . . ?"

Caledan's eyes were wild with urgency. "What does it matter?" he shouted at her. "The way is open. We have to go!"

This time he pulled her hand so fiercely it seemed to nearly dislocate her shoulder. Brilliant pain flared, but she welcomed it, for it cleared her head. Later she could deal with what had just occurred between Caledan and the things of darkness. Now they had to flee. Hand in hand, she and Caledan dashed between the floating ranks of onyx creatures and careered headlong down the twisting stone tunnel.

* * * * *

To Belhuar Thantarth
Master of Twilight Hall

In Milil's name, greetings!
I am gladdened to report that the Zhentarim threat to Iriaebor has once again been averted. It is now clear

*that the unexplained murders were indeed part of a
Zhentarim plot to assume control of the city. I have
concluded that the unfortunate victims were being fed
to ravenous magical creatures conjured by a group of
Zhentarim sorcerers hidden in the New City. In the
lair of the Zhentarim were found schematic drawings
of Iriaebor's High Tower, suggesting that the magical
creatures were going to be used as a weapon in a
bloody coup attempt. Ironically, it seems that the Zhentarim's own magic turned against them in the end; all
the Zhent sorcerers were found slain in their hideout.
Scores of the strange creatures were discovered in the
Zhent lair. It appears that, in their hunger, the creatures turned upon the evil sorcerers who had conjured
them. However, when I returned later to investigate
with the mage Morhion Gen'dahar, the creatures were
not to be found. Apparently, without victims upon
which to feed, the magical creatures were dispelled.*

*With this mission completed, I am ready to assume
the new task you have described in your latest missive.
I will report again in one moon's time. Until then, may
Milil's music be sweet upon your harp!*

Yours in the fellowship of Harpers
Mari Al'maren

Alone in the chamber she shared with Caledan on the
upstairs floor of the Dreaming Dragon, Mari set down
her quill pen. She sprinkled a dusting of fine sand across
the missive she had written, then tilted the crisp piece of
parchment, shaking off the excess sand. Finally, she
rolled it up with the sketches she had made of the dark
creatures and sealed the scroll with hot wax from the
single candle resting on the writing table. For a time, she
stared at the neatly rolled parchment, thinking how the

eerie creatures had drifted around Caledan in what almost seemed to be reverence; how she and Caledan had fled the Barbed Hook in terror; how only at Morhion's urgent prompting, after they told the mage what they had witnessed, did they return to the Zhent lair and find them vanished.

Why the things had seemed to obey Caledan's commands was a mystery. Perhaps it had something to do with his shadow magic. After all, the creatures had come from the shadows. Morhion had discovered a black, noxious residue in the corners of the underground chamber, and had collected some in a vial in order to perform experiments on it. The mage's research might explain why the creatures had behaved as they did.

The other piece of the puzzle that still did not fit was the thief who had been caught in the act of one of the brutal killings. Of course, it could be that the man had simply committed that murder in imitation of the others. It was unfortunate, but such things did occur.

It had been a long day, and there was still one last task to complete . . . one Mari was not at all looking forward to.

The chamber door opened quietly.

"Mari. You're still awake. I thought . . . I thought you'd be asleep."

Mari regarded Caledan as he shut the door. His face was drawn, his eyes shining with weariness. For a moment her love for him washed over her like a wave. How could she possibly do what she intended? But she had made her decision.

She gestured to the writing desk. "I've just penned my report to the Harpers. They've sent new instructions. We both have new orders. I'm to go to Easting, and you—"

"I know. I'm to travel north to Corm Orp. I received a missive as well."

Mari nodded. Silence reigned between them. At last

Caledan spoke, his voice gruff. "You're going to tell me good-bye, aren't you, Mari?"

It took her a long moment to find the words. "I don't know, Caledan. Perhaps I am. I think we should let this be a parting of ways for us. At least for now."

He swallowed hard. "Have I been so terrible, then?"

Mari turned away, crossing her arms across her chest to hide her trembling. "No," she said hastily. Then she decided to speak her mind. "Yes. Yes, you have, but not in the way that you think. Today, in the Zhentarim hideout . . . what you did with those creatures . . . I . . ." She turned toward him, and only as the words sprang to her lips did she realize how true they were. "I'm afraid of you, Caledan. I think I have been for the last six moons." She lifted an unconscious hand to touch her cheek. "I'm afraid of who you are becoming."

A mirthless smile touched his lips. "It's funny you should say that, Mari. You see, I'm afraid, too." He approached, enfolding her in his strong, lean arms. She stiffened for a moment, then melted into his embrace. His whisper was fierce now. "I know I've been acting strangely lately. I do feel . . . different somehow. And the truth is, I don't know why. Perhaps it's something I'll be able to find out on my next mission. But whatever is happening between us, believe me when I tell you this, Mari. I would never harm you. Do you understand me? *Never.*"

"I know that, Caledan." She held on to him, feeling his hard, muscular body beneath her hands. Yet she could not shake the disturbing sensation that this was not *her* Caledan she held in her arms, but a stranger. "Perhaps, after we've been apart for a while . . ."

He pressed a finger softly to her lips, silencing further words. Slowly, he ran his finger down her chin, her throat, to the leather laces that bound her green jacket. He bent down and kissed her. She returned the kiss urgently. Their clothes slipped softly to the floor as he bent to blow out the single candle. For a time, fear was lost in the familiar warmth of each other's touch.

Later, when she floated drowsily in the misty realm between sleep and waking, she thought she heard him rise from the bed. A softness touched her cheek, a low voice whispered in her ear.

"Fare thee well, Harper."

Perhaps it was just a dream. But in the morning, when she woke to gray daylight, Mari found herself alone and shivering beneath the bed covers.

Three

 The boy sat at a table high in the mage's tower, chin on hands, gazing into the multicolored center of a small, pyramid-shaped gem.

"Tell me, Kellen, what do you see within the crystal?"

Morhion spoke softly as he paced around the table. His long vest of dusky purple rippled gently as he moved, causing the runes embroidered on its edges to undulate like silver serpents.

"I see the light of the candles, refracted by the crystal's facets," Kellen answered solemnly.

"Are you certain that is all?" Morhion's voice was almost hypnotic. "Look deeper, Kellen. Do not be so certain you already know what you will see. Open your mind to unexpected possibilities."

Kellen frowned skeptically but leaned over the crystal once more, furrowing his forehead in concentration. "I see . . . I see . . ." Suddenly his green eyes widened. His voice became a whisper of wonderment. "I see stars, Morhion! Shining against the deepest sea of black. And there are bright moons, fiery comets with glowing tails, and . . . and a strange orange ball with striped rings around its middle. I don't know what it is, but I can tell that it is very large. Larger than I could even imagine."

A fierce spark glinted in Morhion's ice-blue eyes. "Yes!" he said quietly, more to himself than to the child. "Well done, Kellen."

"It is all so beautiful," the boy said dreamily. He was swaying in his chair now.

"Do not lose yourself in the crystal!" Morhion warned sharply. He gave Kellen's shoulder a hard squeeze, snapping the boy out of his trance. Kellen gave a shudder, then with great effort turned away from the gem. "You must always maintain control of your senses when gazing into the crystal," Morhion told the boy sternly. "Once lost in its depths, you might find it is not so easy to return."

Kellen nodded, apprehension written on his round face. Morhion reminded himself that, despite Kellen's remarkable perceptiveness, he was still only a boy of eleven winters. The mage's expression softened. "Fear not, Kellen. You will never become lost in the crystal so long as I am near."

Kellen smiled at the mage. "I know, Morhion." He touched the smooth surface of the crystal. "It is magic, then, isn't it?"

Morhion nodded. "There are some small magics bound into the crystal, yes. But they merely provide the catalyst, that is all. True magic comes from within."

Kellen thought about this for a long moment. Then he asked, "What is the world I perceived in the crystal, Morhion?"

"I cannot say, Kellen. There exist many worlds beside

our own. There are mages who believe that some of these worlds are the wells from which we are able to draw our magic. Perhaps just such a world you saw."

Outside the arched window, the full orb of the moon was rising above Iriaebor's spires. The autumn evening was chilly, although Morhion's study was warm and comfortable. Most people thought mages live in drafty old towers littered with musty tomes and rotting scrolls. Morhion enjoyed living against stereotype. Vibrant tapestries hung from the circular chamber's stone walls; the floor was thick with expensive Amnian carpets. Books, parchments, and all manner of magical paraphernalia were arranged neatly in dark wood cases, and a fire burned brightly in a copper brazier in the room's center.

Morhion poured two cups of spiced wine. As he handed one of the silver cups to Kellen, he watched the boy. The mage found he was curious to discover the limits of Kellen's abilities. True, such inquiries would be premature. Most youths did not test their magic until their fifteenth year, or even later. And yet . . .

Morhion moved to a glass cabinet and took out a small wooden box. He set the box on the table before Kellen, opening the lid. Inside, resting on a cushion of purple velvet, was a small, dark stone. Carved into the pebble was an arcane sigil, the rune that symbolized *magic*.

"I want you to pick up the stone, Kellen," Morhion said, gazing at the boy intently.

Kellen bit his lip in thought, studying the pebble for a long time as if trying to unlock its mysteries. Finally he shrugged. Reaching out, he picked up the stone. It lay small and dark in the palm of his hand. Morhion leaned forward, eyes glittering. Now, he thought. It should come now!

Nothing happened. Kellen opened his mouth as if to say something. The words were never uttered. The dark stone flared with brilliant green light, shards of emerald illumination spraying outward, dancing crazily across the walls and ceiling. There was a sizzling sound, and the smell of burning flesh. Kellen cried out, dropping the stone. Abruptly, the blinding green light dimmed.

Morhion blinked, clearing his vision. The stone lay on the mahogany table, dark and ordinary-looking once more. Kellen clutched his left hand. His face was pale and drawn. Morhion reached out and gently unclenched Kellen's fingers. Branded on the boy's palm was a mirror image of the symbol that was carved into the pebble—the rune of magic.

Kellen looked up at the mage, his pain suddenly forgotten. "What does it mean, Morhion?"

Morhion did not answer. Instead, he slowly raised his own left hand. In the center of his palm was an old, puckered scar—a duplicate of the blistered mark on Kellen's hand. Kellen was bursting with questions, but before he could voice any, Morhion shook his head, silencing him. This had been enough for tonight. He drew a silk handkerchief from a pocket and tied it loosely about the boy's wounded hand.

"Go to the inn, Kellen, and find Estah," Morhion instructed. "She will heal your hand. But the burn will scar. You will bear the mark of magic all your life."

Kellen nodded gravely. "I know."

"And if Caledan is angered at what I have done, send him to me and I will speak to him."

Kellen shook his head. "My father isn't in the city, Morhion. He left last night on a journey for the Harpers. He'll be gone for a tenday at least, if not more."

"I see. I didn't know Caledan and Mari had a new mission."

"Mari didn't go with him. She has her own assignment for the Harpers." While Kellen's voice was always solemn, now it seemed strangely sad as well. "I think it's better this way. They were getting tired of arguing all the time."

Morhion stiffened, a peculiar tightness in his chest. Was there trouble between Mari and Caledan?

As if reading the mage's thoughts, Kellen went on. "Mari and my father have said good-bye to each other, Morhion. I think that, when they return from their current missions, she will leave Iriaebor forever." He sighed deeply. "I don't want her to go, but I suppose she has to."

"I see." They were the only words he could manage. Mari and Caledan parting ways? The mage could hardly imagine such a thing. Yet that was not quite true, was it? For he *had* dared to imagine it—he, Morhion the traitor. A spike of shame pierced his heart.

Kellen pushed himself from his chair and walked softly to where Morhion sat. He did a surprising thing then, putting his arms around Morhion's neck and leaning against the mage's shoulder. Morhion froze. He was not accustomed to such intimacy. You have dwelt too long in the cold isolation of magic, Morhion, he admonished himself. Tentatively, he enfolded the boy in his arms, returning the innocent embrace.

For a time, after Kellen had left, Morhion sat gazing out the window, sipping spiced wine. Finally he rose and picked up the dark pebble, shutting it once more in its box. He knew that he had taken a risk in asking Kellen to touch the magestone. Yet, after the ease with which the boy had used the crystal to scry other worlds, Morhion's curiosity had overwhelmed him. The stone had proven undeniably that Kellen was mageborn. Had he not been, the stone would have wounded him terribly or might even have struck him dead. Not only born to magecraft, Kellen also had shadow magic in his blood. Each was a great power—and a great burden. Had the two talents ever combined before in one individual? And what would be the effects of their coexistence? Morhion did not know, but something told him the world of Toril had never before seen the likes of Kellen.

Morhion returned the wooden box to its cabinet, then moved to a long table laden with neatly arranged rows of clay jars, glass vials, and copper crucibles. He had promised Mari he would examine a dark substance they had discovered in the Zhentarim hideout. He bent to his task and soon found himself caught up in the search for knowledge—mixing potions, weighing out bits of colored powder, heating ingredients over a candle flame. Magic was a pastime of which he never tired.

Morhion paused, lifting a glass vial of the tarlike substance. So far, his tests had revealed that the substance was not magical itself, but that a faint residue of magic clung to it, as was typical of conjured matter. It was necessary to test the effects of the substance on a living creature.

He reached into a wicker basket and drew out a wriggling white mouse. It blinked its red eyes fearfully. Morhion stroked its snowy fur, calming it with soft words, and slipped it inside a large glass bottle. The mouse scurried around the bottom of the bottle. Carefully, Morhion opened the vial and poured a single drop of the dark fluid into the bottle. Then he corked both vial and bottle. The mouse avoided the dark, sticky spot but otherwise seemed to suffer no harm. Apparently, the substance did not exude a poisonous humour.

At last, Morhion turned his gaze from the bottle. It was time for another experiment. He wanted to try to ignite some of the dark substance. He lit a candle, and with a murmured spell caused the flame to flare up brightly.

There was a muffled squeal of terror. Startled, he turned and stared at the glass bottle, now bathed in the brilliant light of the candle. Inside, the white mouse scrabbled frantically at the glass. The dark spot on the bottom of the bottle had started to undulate. Even as he watched, the small blob expanded, molded itself into a new shape, and rose off the glass. Morhion took in a sharp breath. The thing was shaped exactly like the dark creatures Mari had described, only in miniature. Spreading its winglike appendages, the thing floated toward the frantic mouse. The mouse stopped scrabbling and cringed against the glass.

The attack happened so quickly that Morhion almost didn't see it. With startling swiftness, the creature dove at the mouse, engulfing the animal. The mouse squealed, struggling violently inside the inky folds of the creature. Abruptly the struggling ceased. The dark creature floated away from the mouse. All that was left were a few gobbets of bloody pulp plastered to the inside of the glass. Morhion stared in fascination and revulsion. Behind him, the minor spell he had used to light the candle expired, and the brilliant flame dimmed. As it did, the floating creature inside the bottle dropped suddenly to the bottom and melted once more into a small splotch of dark fluid.

Morhion raised his eyebrows in surprise. So it was the light, he realized. The bright light had caused the black fluid to form itself into one of the strange creatures, and after the light was extinguished, the creature reverted to liquid. The things the Zhentarim sorcerers had conjured were creatures of both darkness and light. For a moment, Morhion hesitated, thinking of the poor, doomed mouse. Then he did what he knew he must.

He destroyed the vial of dark fluid with a spell of disintegration. That seemed the safest and the most conclusive thing to do. He did save one tiny drop of the dark substance, and this he bound magically in the center of a small ruby pendant around which he wove a strong enchantment. He slipped the pendant's chain over his head and tucked the cold gem beneath his robes. Now he would be able to sense the magic that had conjured the dark substance, if he ever chanced to draw near its source.

Midnight found the mage in the bedchamber below his study. He sat in a velvet chair, gazing into the flames dancing in a stone fireplace, thinking of all this day had wrought. On a small table beside him, seven runestones lay scattered in an intricate pattern. The runecast had upset Morhion at first. The pattern was one of chaos and upheaval. It worried him, yet there was a dangerous feeling of exhilaration in his chest as well. He dared to admit the truth to himself: There was a part of him that longed for catastrophe, even craved the excitement of it.

These last two years had been years of calm and peace for Morhion. They had proven a welcome respite from the dark turmoil of his life, and he had even known something of a mild joy. Yet of late he had grown complacent. He no longer pushed his magic to the limits of its power; he no longer sought knowledge with the same voracity and hunger as a stag pawing through the snows of winter in search of sustenance. He needed to face adversity once more, to meet a challenge of both mind and magic. Otherwise, he might one day wake up and find himself nothing more than a court magician, conjuring petty magics to entertain simpleminded nobles, and content with that. On that day, Morhion knew that he would be as good as dead.

He glanced once more at the runecast scattered across the silver tray. The runes spoke clearly. Some great change was coming, and with it risk and hardship. A sharp smile touched his lips. Let the upheaval come, he thought. I shall welcome it.

Morhion leaned over the table to gather up the runestones. A chill gust of air rushed past him, and the fire flared brightly. Sparks flew crackling into the air, but the flames died down as quickly, leaving the chamber eerily darkened. Morhion shivered, his breath fogging. He rose, his long golden hair flying wildly behind him, and turned to shut the window. It was closed. The cold light of the full moon spilled through the glass, gilding the room's furnishings with frosty light. Though Morhion half guessed what he would see, the horror of it was not lessened.

Like strands of pure silver thread, the moonlight wove itself into a recognizable shape. Glistening tendrils spun faster and faster in midair, outlining the form of a tall man clad in ornate, archaic armor. The glowing threads plunged into a pair of black pits where the figure's eyes should have been, and two pinpricks of crimson light flared to life. The last silvery tendrils spun themselves into nothingness; the apparition was complete. The spectral knight, surrounded by a corona of pale light, took a step toward the mage.

Old, familiar dread gripped Morhion's heart. He managed to whisper a single word. "Serafi."

The ghostly knight bowed, but the gesture was one of mockery, not respect. "The orb of Selune rises full into the night sky. It is time once again for you to fulfill our bargain, Morhion Gen'dahar." Serafi's voice seemed to echo eerily from all directions.

A mirthless smile touched Morhion's lips. "Do you truly believe that I could have forgotten?"

"Perhaps," Serafi intoned indifferently. "The memories of the living are fleeting. But the dead never forget."

"I do not forget my vows," Morhion said.

The knight drifted menacingly closer. "Then give to me the blood that is my due. The pact is binding."

Though he had done this once each month for the past ten years, Morhion trembled involuntarily as he went through the ritual of lifting an arm and drawing back the

sleeve of his night robe. Beneath the cloth, his forearm
was crisscrossed with thin, white scars—the legacy of a
pact he had once forged to save Caledan's life, an act for
which he was later branded a traitor.

It had begun ten years before, in the darkest hour of
the old Fellowship of the Dreaming Dragon. The Harper
Kera, a member of the Fellowship and Caledan's beloved,
lay dead—murdered at the hands of their foe, the Zhentarim warrior Ravendas. Blaming himself for Kera's
death, Caledan journeyed to the Zhentarim fortress of
Darkhold to exact his revenge. Confronting Ravendas in
her lair would mean his own demise, but Caledan cared
not, for he meant to join Kera in death. Morhion's
betrayal was this: He had forced Caledan to choose life.

Against Caledan's wishes, Morhion too went to Darkhold, and revealed Caledan's plans to Ravendas. Without
the advantage of surprise, Caledan's attempt to slay
Ravendas was foiled, as was his own suicidal objective.
Caledan would have been captured, then executed, but
Morhion engineered their escape from the catacombs
beneath Darkhold—doing so at terrible cost.

It happened that in ancient times Darkhold had been a
keep of the lost Empire of Netheril. Morhion had learned
of a dark spirit that haunted the caverns beneath the
keep—the usurper Serafi, who two thousand years before
had schemed to seize the throne of Netheril and been
executed for treason. The spectral knight agreed to show
Morhion a secret way out of the catacombs, demanding a
dark vow in exchange. Morhion had no choice but to
accept.

With Serafi's help, Caledan and Morhion escaped
Darkhold, surviving to defeat Ravendas later in the crypt
of the Shadowking. For years afterward, Caledan
despised Morhion as a traitor. However, Caledan eventually came to understand that Morhion had betrayed him

in order to save his life, and thus the two renewed their friendship. To this day, Caledan did not know of the pact Morhion had forged to save his life.

And he never will, Morhion thought fiercely.

The mage drew a small knife from the sheath at his hip. Slowly, carefully, he used the sharp tip to trace a thin red line into the flesh of his arm. Crimson blood oozed forth.

"The pact is binding," Morhion whispered hoarsely.

With menacing speed, Serafi knelt and caught Morhion's arm in a freezing grip. "Ah, the sweet substance of life!" the spirit cried exultantly in his sepulchral voice. "How I long to taste it again . . ."

A low moan of fear escaped Morhion's lips as the spectral knight bent over the mage's bleeding arm and began to drink.

Four

 The autumn moon rose full and bright in the dark sky, casting its golden light over the little village of Corm Orp. Tam Acorn threw open the blue wooden door of his burrow and hurried outside. Tonight was the annual Harvest Festival, and he didn't want to be late for the dancing, the merrymaking, and—most important—the sugarberry pies. Hastily, he locked the door to his tidy underground home with a brass key and scurried down the winding path that led toward the center of the village.

Tam arrived red cheeked and breathless at the village commons just in time to see Pel Baker pull his first batch of bubbling sugarberry pies out of a brick oven. Moments later, Tam was two silver coins poorer and two steaming pies richer. Slipping one pie into a pocket, he began happily munching the other. He burned his tongue, and dark syrup ran down his chin, dribbling onto his green jacket and yellow waistcoat. Tam did not care. Sugarberry pies were his favorite part of the Harvest Festival.

Villagers were streaming into the open greensward
now. While most of Corm Orp's residents were halflings
like Tam, there were a few big folk as well. They lived in
the stone houses that surrounded the village commons,
while the diminutive halflings preferred to dwell in snug
underground burrows. A bonfire flared to life in the center of the commons, chasing away the night. Laughter
rang out, along with the clinking of cider-filled mugs.
Tiny halfling children scurried about in an ongoing game
of hide-and-seek. The rich scents of hot sausages, honey
bread, and baked apples filled the air.

A call went up for the dancing to begin. "Somebody
fetch old Quince Piper!" called out a plump, middle-aged
halfling named Rin Miller.

Shouts of happy agreement rang out, but one voice
rose above the others.

"I'm afraid my grandfather is ill," Ali Bramble said
sadly to the faces turned toward her. "He won't be able to
play for you tonight."

A collective groan of despair came from the throng.
Tam sighed in disappointment. True, sugarberry pies
were the best part of the Harvest Festival, but things
wouldn't be complete without dancing to the music of
Quince Piper's flute.

Rin Miller frowned gloomily. "I don't suppose there's
anyone else who can play music as well as old Quince?"
he asked without much hope.

"I can," a voice replied.

The crowd gasped with surprise, and the crowd hastily
parted.

The stranger was a striking fellow. He was dressed all
in black, except for his cloak of midnight blue, and he
rode a horse as pale as a ghost. Dismounting, the
stranger approached the bonfire. Tam thought there was

something odd about the man. He seemed pale and haggard, though perhaps it was simply a trick of the flickering shadows. The man drew something from a pouch at his belt. It was a set of polished bone pipes.

"Well, now, I don't know," Rin said suspiciously. "This is all highly irregular, and—"

Rin stopped short as the stranger lifted the pipes to his lips and began to play. The most beautiful music Tam had ever heard drifted on the air. The villagers listened in rapt silence as the stranger's haunting melody filled the night. When at last he lowered his pipes, tears shone in more than one set of eyes. Someone called out for another song, and the crowd echoed the request.

"Make it something we can dance to, piper!" Rin shouted, now enthusiastic.

The stranger seemed to hesitate, then lifted the pipes once more. This time the music was fast and rollicking, almost wild. Whoops of joy rang out as the crowd leapt into a brisk dance. In moments, Tam found himself being breathlessly spun from one partner to another as the villagers danced merrily around the blazing bonfire.

That was when Tam noticed something peculiar. He blinked, wondering if it was simply his imagination.

The shadows around the bonfire seemed to be moving quite independently of the flow of the dancers. Even as he watched, they stretched out, forming themselves into shapeless blobs that began to whirl slowly around the bonfire. Then, impossibly, the shadows separated themselves from the ground and rose into the air. Tam untangled himself from his dancing partner and stared up in horror. Before he could shout a warning, Ali Bramble's scream shattered the air.

"The shadows! Look at the shadows!"

In shock, the villagers looked upward, other screams echoing Ali's. Now the stranger's music was fey and dissonant. It seemed to pierce Tam's ears and numb his brain. The shadows began to whirl faster and faster above the bonfire. One of them spun away from the whirling ring of darkness. It stretched outward, engulfing a stone house close to the commons.

When the shadow rose once more into the air, the house had changed. Now the stone walls were hideously warped and distorted, as though they had melted partway under some fierce heat, only to resolidify into something more grotesque. More screams rang out. The dance descended into panic as humans and halflings alike fled in all directions.

Still the stranger continued to play, his eyes staring blankly as if he did not notice the mayhem all around. More shadows spun away from the bonfire. Everything they touched became horribly disfigured. Cottages, sheds, fences, wells, and signposts—all were reshaped by the dark embrace of the shadows.

A cry of animal pain rent the night, and Tam turned to see a hideous form stumble toward him. In horror, he realized it had once been a milk cow. One of the shadows had brushed it in passing, and somehow the beast had been turned inside out. White bones and glistening muscles clung to the outside of its body. Its still-beating heart dangled from its chest. A moment later, the tortured beast collapsed and died, its agony blessedly ended. Tam stared in horror. If one of those shadows were to touch a villager . . .

In desperation, he wondered what he should do. Suddenly, an idea struck him.

"The bonfire!" he shouted above the din. "We have to put out the bonfire!"

At first, he thought no one had heard his words amid the tumult. Moments later, Ali Bramble and a pair of humans pushed their way to his side. They had had the same idea. Dodging fleeing villagers and the horrible shadow creatures, they grabbed buckets of water and heaved their contents onto the bonfire. There was a terrible hissing noise as clouds of steam rose into the air. The flames flickered and died out. Night closed about the commons like a dark hand. With it came a deep silence.

The music had stopped.

Tam held his breath. Gradually, his eyes adjusted to the pale moonlight. The shadows were gone. So too was the stranger.

Exhausted, Tam sank to the ground, only to feel something damp and sticky beneath him. He reached into his pocket and pulled out the remains of a sugarberry pie, smashed but still edible. As he gazed at the destruction that had minutes ago been a happy and prosperous village, Tam found he no longer had much of an appetite for sugarberry pie.

* * * * *

The sun was dying on the western horizon when Mari crested a rise and caught her first glimpse of Iriaebor shining in the distance. The big chestnut gelding beneath her nickered excitedly, sensing a stable and a meal of oats were near, and quickened into a canter.

Mari laughed aloud. "Oh, come now, Farenth. Must you risk our necks just because you can't wait to have a feed bag strapped to your nose?" As was his custom, Farenth pointedly ignored her. There was nothing for Mari to do but grip a handful of dark mane and hold on as he raced across the gray-green moor. Not that she really minded. She too was ready for this journey to end.

It had begun a tenday ago, in the small but lively trading town of Easting. Here the dwarven smiths that dwelt in the southern Sunset Mountains came to sell the exquisite metalwork they fashioned in their subterranean forges.

However, over the last several months, fewer and fewer dwarves had journeyed to Easting. Without the trade, Easting was failing. The Harpers had sent Mari to investigate.

At first she had been frustrated. No one in Easting knew what had happened to the dwarven smiths, so she undertook a journey into the mountains to scout the dwarven clanlands themselves. As it turned out, she didn't need to go that far. While traveling a road that wound deep into the rocky crags, she espied a hapless dwarf being ambushed by a band of orcs. As she watched, the hairy, pig-faced creatures knocked the dwarf on the skull and hauled him into the mouth of a cave. Keeping a safe distance behind, Mari followed and soon discovered the fate of the missing dwarven smiths.

They were being held prisoner by the orcs. An orc prince named Gtharn was behind the kidnappings. Gtharn was forcing the dwarves to forge weapons—swords, axes, and arrowheads—for an all-out assault on the dwarven clans. Mari prowled unseen through the orc warrens—the brutes always made bad sentries—and discovered that over fifty dwarves were being held captive. However, each was imprisoned in isolation, without realizing so many other dwarves were nearby, and so believed escape was impossible.

Mari took it upon herself to rectify this. She stole a set of keys from a guard and freed the dwarves. When the dwarven smiths saw the number of their kinsmen, they banded together and attacked their captors. The cowardly orcs were no match for fifty furious dwarves all swinging bright, newly forged weapons. It was a rout. Mari herself slew Gtharn as he tried to flee. Freed from the filthy orc warrens, the joyous dwarves had tried to reward her with gold and silver. She had refused, telling them instead to return to Easting and renew their trading there. This they did, and so both dwarves and town were saved.

As ever when she completed one of her missions successfully, Mari had ridden away with a warm sense of accomplishment and pride. However, the three-day ride from the mountains across the plains grew tedious, and she soon found her thoughts turning to other, less cheerful matters. Even now, as Iriaebor rose higher on the horizon with each passing moment, Mari found herself wondering if Caledan's mission was going equally well, and whether she had been right to bid him such a definite farewell. She was resolved to stay true to her decision, but she thought she might come back to Iriaebor in a year or two. Perhaps Caledan would have sorted out his problems by then. But for now, wasn't it best that she make her good-byes and leave?

She was jolted from her reverie as Farenth skidded to a snorting halt, bridle jingling and leather creaking. Mari had long ago learned to trust the horse's instincts. Her hand strayed to the knife at her hip. "What is it, friend?" she whispered. They had stopped in a low hollow at the base of a round hill. Atop the hill was a circle of wind-worn standing stones, raised by some forgotten folk. A soft mist was slowly rising from the ground, and Mari's spine tingled with a preternatural chill.

"All right, show yourself!" she called out sharply, suddenly certain she was not alone. The mist swirled, and seemed to take on human form.

The first things Mari noticed about the woman were that she was very beautiful and very pale. Her skin, her hair, her clothes—all were as gray as the rising fog. The second thing—and this Mari noticed with surprise—was that the woman was not standing on the ground. Rather, she drifted atop the mist as if she were no more solid than the vapor itself. Mari's arms broke out in gooseflesh.

This was no living person, but an apparition. Farenth
pranced skittishly, and Mari tightened her grip on the
reins.

"Who are you?" she dared to ask in a quavering voice.

The ghostly woman's words floated eerily on the wind.
"Do you not know me by this?" She lifted a hand to her
breast. There Mari caught a glint of light and a silvery
shape: a harp surrounded by a crescent moon. Mari's
breath caught in her throat. Finally she managed to
whisper the word, her voice trembling with awe.

"Kera?"

The spectral woman smiled wistfully. "I was certain
you would know me, Mari Al'maren. Though we have
never met, it is as if we were sisters."

Mari shook her head, choking back a sob. Once, long
before Mari had ever met Caledan, he and Kera had been
lovers. They had worked together as Harpers and were
betrothed. All their plans were shattered when Ravendas
murdered Kera, an act made all the more loathsome by
the fact that the two women were sisters. All these years,
Mari had felt a sort of kinship with the Harper woman
she had never known. Now she found herself face-to-face
with her. It was wondrous, and bitterly sad as well.

"Weep not, Mari," the ghost intoned. "I have never
begrudged you Caledan's love. I am joyous he found one
to make his heart whole once more. And do not be sad
that you have parted ways, for you came to each other
wounded, and now you each leave with those old wounds
healed."

Mari bowed her head.

"I have but one thing to ask of you, Mari."

She looked up, her cheeks damp with tears. "Anything," Mari said fiercely, and meant it. "I will do anything you ask, Kera."

The ghostly woman smiled fondly. Then her smile van-

ished, and there was an urgency in her colorless eyes.
"Though you have parted with Caledan, do not turn your
back on him. He needs your help, Mari, now more than ever."

Mari shook her head in confusion. "I don't understand.
Is Caledan in some sort of danger?"

"All of Toril is in danger." The spirit was fading, her
edges blurring with the mist. Her voice echoed faintly on
the wind. "Beware the king, Mari. He must not ascend
the throne . . ." The tendrils of fog swirled, the ghostly
woman faded.

"No, Kera, don't go!" Mari reached out a hand. "What
do you mean?"

It was too late. An evening zephyr stirred the mist.
When it cleared, the ghost of the beautiful Harper was
gone. Mari gazed for a time into the gloaming, hardly
able to believe what she had just witnessed. Finally she
nudged Farenth's flanks, and the big horse started into a
trot, his hoofbeats muffled by the moist grass. Mari huddled inside her cloak, but all the rest of the way to Iriaebor she could not stop shivering.

It was full dark when she reached the Sign of the
Dreaming Dragon, where a missive from the Harpers
was waiting for her.

"It arrived earlier this evening," Estah explained. "I
told the messenger I wasn't certain when you'd return."

Shaken by her encounter with the ghost of Kera, Mari
was glad to have something mundane to concentrate on.
She sat by the fire in the common room and let Estah
bring her a cup of chamomile tea. She drank down the
hot tea and finally managed to control her shivering.

Breaking the wax seal on the scroll, she unrolled the
parchment and began to read. In moments, it was clear
that this was no routine directive. By the time she finished reading, her shivering had commenced anew.

Estah returned and noticed Mari's pallid face. "Dear

one, you look as if you'd seen a ghost!"

Mari smiled ironically. "I'm afraid that's only half of it, Estah."

Estah drew up a chair and listened raptly as Mari spoke of her encounter with Kera's shade. At some point, Mari looked up and noticed Kellen was there, sitting on the floor and watching her intently. For a moment, the Harper realized how much he looked like his aunt Kera— far more so than he resembled his mother, Ravendas.

"First Talek Talembar, now Kera," Estah said in soft amazement. "What can these appearances mean, Mari?"

"I'm not sure. But I don't think this is a mere coincidence." She gestured to the parchment before her. In it, she explained, were two disturbing pieces of news. The first concerned a strange occurrence in the village of Corm Orp. Apparently, some local harvest festival had descended into a riot in which several people were hurt. The details were unknown, but the villagers whispered of how shadows had come to life and attacked them. "Sound familiar?" Mari asked.

"It sounds like the creatures you and Caledan saw in the Zhentarim hideout," Estah agreed. She frowned in puzzlement. "But you said the creatures were dispelled. And there hasn't been another murder in Iriaebor since you and Caledan left."

Mari took a deep breath. "I know. That brings me to the second report. Caledan was supposed to meet with a Harper operative in Corm Orp on the same day as the festival, to receive his orders. But Caledan never showed up at the appointed meeting place."

Estah clutched her apron worriedly. "What are you saying?"

Mari gazed directly at the halfling innkeeper, her expression grim. "Caledan is missing."

It took a moment for the implication of this to register

on the halfling. Then she gasped. "But you don't . . . you
don't think the strange happenings in Corm Orp have
anything to do with Caledan?"

"I'm not sure what to think, Estah." Mari squared her
shoulders. She recalled Kera's urgent words. *Do not turn
your back on him, Mari.* "It's time I paid a visit to someone I should have spoken to a long time ago. There's only
one person in Iriaebor who ever witnessed one of the
murders and lived to tell about. I'm going to find out
what he saw." She pulled her cloak about her shoulders.
"If he hasn't been executed yet, that is."

An hour later, Mari picked her way down the slimy
stone steps that led to the gaol beneath Iriaebor's High
Tower. Behind her came Morhion; she had fetched the
mage on her way to the tower and filled him in on all she
knew. Leading the way down the steps to the dungeon
was another draftee—a big, bespectacled man with dark,
coppery skin.

"I hope you know I'm doing you an enormous favor,
Mari," the big man grumbled. He was as powerfully muscled as a warrior—in fact, he had been a warrior once—
but now he wore the plain brown robe of a monk. Or, to
be more exact, a Loremaster of Oghma. "It would be
decidedly awkward if City Lord Bron's chief advisor were
to be caught sneaking around the dungeon at night to
talk with murderers on death row." He turned to glare at
Mari. "In fact, I have half a mind to go back right now."

"Shall I cast that charm spell so he'll be forced to do
our bidding, Mari?" Morhion asked with a musing smile.

She blinked at the taciturn mage's rare display of
humor, then laughed. Reaching up, she patted Tyveris's
cheek affectionately. Despite his dusky skin, the big
man's blush was clear to see. "No, thank you, Morhion,"
she replied lightly. "I think I have our good monk suit-
ably charmed already."

Tyveris scowled darkly, though his brown eyes glowed with devotion. "You never did play fair, Mari."

Of all the old members of the Fellowship of the Dreaming Dragon, Tyveris was the biggest and strongest, but he also had the softest heart. Years ago, the big Chultan gave up the sword he had never enjoyed wielding and became a man of learning—though, when necessity required, he could still bring down a running horse with his bare fists. Mari was awfully fond of him.

The stairs ended, and the trio made their way down a dank, torchlit corridor. "Why do you want to talk to this thief, Mari?" Tyveris asked quietly. "I thought you and Caledan solved the mystery of the murders. It was the Zhentarim, right? You yourself told me the one we caught in the act was probably just a madman killing in imitation."

"I thought so, too," Mari said grimly, then filled Tyveris in on what she had learned concerning the strange happenings in Corm Orp and Caledan's disappearance.

When she finished, Tyveris swore a rather colorful oath.

Morhion raised a single eyebrow. "That didn't sound like any prayer to Oghma I'm familiar with," he noted dryly.

Tyveris shot the mage a black look. "It's a new one. I just made it up." His expression became somber. "So Caledan's in trouble again. The sages aren't kidding when they say old habits die hard. Come on, then."

Moments later they came to an iron-barred cell at the end of the corridor. "Wake up, Kadian!" Tyveris called out in a booming voice.

A haggard voice spoke out of the darkness. "I am awake."

Tyveris took a torch from a bracket and held it aloft. Flickering light spilled through the bars to illuminate the cell. A man sitting on a bed of clean straw rose stiffly to his feet. The thief Kadian was a large man—taller than Tyveris, though not so broad—but his pale hair and round face gave him a boyish look.

"Is it time for the hanging?" Kadian asked. There was no fear in his colorless eyes, only grim resignation.

"No," Tyveris said huskily. "The next hanging will be in three days' time, on the Feast of the Moon."

Mari stepped forward. "We've come to ask you some questions, Kadian."

At this, the thief let out a mirthless snort. "Questions? Now that's a novelty. No one's bothered to ask me any questions before."

She cast a scathing look at Tyveris, who shrugged sheepishly. Well, better too late than not at all, Mari thought. "Tell me, Kadian, did you kill that nobleman?"

Kadian laughed ruefully. "That foppish sot? He wouldn't have been worth the trouble it would take to stick a knife in and pull it back out."

"Just answer the question," Mari instructed caustically.

Kadian locked eyes with her. "No," he said flatly. "I did not kill the petty lord. I wanted to steal his gold, and that was all. I was probably doing him a favor. No doubt he would have lost it all gambling at dice the next night, and those who can't pay their gambling debts have a habit of taking long midnight swims at the bottom of the Chionthar. The last thing I wanted was for anyone to die."

Mari kept her voice cool and emotionless. "If you didn't kill the petty lord, then who did?"

While there had been no fear in the thief's eyes at the talk of his own hanging, suddenly they were filled with a stark terror so strong Mari was taken aback. Kadian gripped the rusting iron bars; he was shaking visibly.

"What did you see, Kadian?" she asked intently. "Who killed the nobleman that night?"

He opened his mouth, but it took a long moment for the words to finally come out. "The shadows," he choked. "It was the shadows . . ."

Mari exchanged a startled glance with Morhion, then leaned closer to the thief. "Tell me, Kadian . . ."

In halting words, the thief told what had happened that night. When he finished, the three friends gazed silently at each other. None of them doubted the truth of the thief's story. The finest Cormyrean actor could not have feigned so genuine a terror.

"I don't understand, Mari," an obviously shaken Tyveris said softly. "Does this have something to do with the weird shadows in Corm Orp?"

Mari ran a hand nervously through her thick auburn hair. "I'm not sure, Tyveris. I'm afraid it does." She added grimly, "I trust that you will let Kadian go—"

"Wait!"

It was Kadian. Mari regarded the thief in surprise. The fear had not left his gaze. "I haven't told about the man," he said hoarsely.

"The man?" Mari asked.

Kadian nodded. "I saw him as the guards were dragging me away. He was standing in a dark corner, but the torchlight fell on him for a moment."

Morhion moved forward. "Describe this man," he demanded.

"He was tall, I think, with dark hair. His face reminded me of a wolf's, and he was wearing a cloak"—Kadian's brow furrowed in concentration—"a dark blue cloak, the color of a midnight sky."

Mari gazed at Morhion in shock. As ever, the mage's expression was emotionless, but a strange light glittered in his cold eyes. He turned to her and asked, "Mari, have you anything with you that belonged to Caledan?"

The mage's question caught her off guard. "Yes," she

answered after a moment. "I have this." She showed him the braided copper bracelet she wore on her left wrist. Years ago, Kera had given it to Caledan, and later he had given it to Mari as a symbol of their love.

"May I borrow it?"

Mari nodded, hastily slipping off the bracelet and handing it to the mage. He set the bracelet on the stone floor, and within the circle of metal he placed a small bit of white fleece drawn from one of the myriad pouches at his belt. Standing, he held out his arms and chanted in a guttural tongue. The bracelet flared brightly, and the fleece vanished in a puff of smoke.

Mari gasped. Before her stood Caledan. Had the mage summoned him with his magic? After a moment, she realized it was not Caledan at all. The figure did not move in the slightest, and if she concentrated she found she could see right through his body. An illusion.

"It is he!" Kadian hissed, reaching through the bars to point at the phantasmal Caledan.

Mari stared at the thief in shock. "This is the man you saw in the darkened corner? Are you certain?"

Kadian nodded frantically. "I will never forget his face as long as I live. It's him, all right. Except the eyes aren't right. They were deeper, and ancient . . . so terribly ancient, I thought they would drive me mad."

Morhion said nothing, but banished the illusion with a wave of his hand. He retrieved the bracelet and handed it to Mari. The metal felt nauseatingly warm as she slipped it on her wrist once more. "I think we have what we came here for," she said huskily. "Tyveris, call the gaoler. Tell him to release Kadian."

"No!" the thief cried desperately. "Ask him to wait until the dawn. I beg you. Let me stay here tonight, where it's safe." He shuddered, gripping the iron bars with white-knuckled hands. "Don't you see? The shadows come out at night . . ."

Mari nodded in sad understanding. Kadian would never be a thief again. She led the way out of the dungeon, finding that she herself was not so eager to face the night.

* * * * *

Midnight found Mari and Morhion sitting by the fire in the Dreaming Dragon's deserted common room, piecing together what they knew. Though the Zhentarim beneath the Barbed Hook had indeed been plotting to take over the city, they had not masterminded the brutal murders. The Zhents had simply been victims like all the others. And Mari was beginning to suspect that she knew who their killer was, though it was a conclusion so terrible she could not bring herself to consciously consider it.

Morhion regarded her with piercing eyes. "You are thinking the same thing that I am, aren't you, Mari? There is only one answer to our mystery."

She shook her head fiercely. "It *can't* be," she said hoarsely.

"Can't it?" Morhion's quiet words pierced her like knives. He reached beneath his shirt and drew out something hanging on the end of a silver chain. It was a small ruby. A faint light flickered erratically in the center of the gem.

"What is it?" Mari asked in fascination.

"I fashioned this pendant with a drop of the dark substance I discovered in the Zhentarim hideout," he explained. "Its enchantment is such that it will glow if it comes near to the source of magic that conjured the shadow creatures."

"But it's glowing now!" Mari protested.

"It has been glowing ever since I entered the inn," Morhion replied, "though only weakly. However, the meaning is clear. The source of the magic that conjured the shadow creatures was here in this inn, but now it has gone." His eyes bored into her. "There are only two who have ever dwelt in this place who have power over shadows, Mari. One is still here, but the other is not. There is only one conclusion. The person responsible for the murders is . . ."

At last, Mari whispered the word she had feared.

"Caledan."

Morhion nodded gravely. "He had ample opportunity. And consider the victims. Each was despicable in some way. Perhaps, unaware that he was even doing it, Caledan was passing judgment and sentencing them to death with his shadow magic."

Mari gripped the arms of her chair. She felt ill. "But what does it mean, Morhion? What is happening to Caledan?"

"I think that the ghosts know," a voice said quietly.

Both Mari and Morhion turned in surprise to see a slight form standing on the edge of the firelight. "Kellen," Mari said after a moment. "You should be in bed."

"I know," he replied. "But this is more important."

Mari studied his serious face. Kellen had a way of listening to conversations without being noticed. She wondered how much he had heard.

As if he had somehow intercepted her unspoken question, he said, "I heard enough, Mari. I know that my father's shadow magic is . . . changing."

Morhion peered intently at the boy. "What did you mean about the ghosts, Kellen?"

"I think Talek Talembar and Kera knew what was happening to my father and were trying to warn us."

Mari tried to swallow the cold lump of dread in her throat. "Warn us? Warn us of what?"

Kellen gazed at her with his calm, intelligent eyes.

"My father is becoming a shadowking."

Five

 It was the dead of the night.

High in his tower, Morhion pored over the time-darkened book lying open on the table before him. He took a pinch of silvery dust from a clay jar and sprinkled it over the yellowed parchment. The faded ink began to glimmer with an unearthly blue light.

Quickly, before the spell dissipated, Morhion read the spidery runes written in a long-dead tongue. As the glowing runes dimmed, Morhion sighed and leaned back in his chair.

"Worthless," he murmured in disgust.

In the hours since he had left the Dreaming Dragon, Morhion had researched all he could concerning the history of the Shadowking, hoping to find something that might refute Kellen's terrible conclusion. So far he had found nothing.

In a silver dish, Morhion burned an incense of mint, hyacinth, and sage. He breathed in the fragrant smoke—

it would help keep him alert—and turned back to the book. It was a copy of an ancient tome, called *Mal'eb'dala* in the lost language Talfir; this translated into common-speak as *The Book of the Shadows*. The original book had been destroyed in a battle between two powerful mages an eon ago. This volume was an old replica. It contained passages that had been miscopied in or entirely omitted from the more recent copy in which Morhion had first read about the myth of the Shadowking. The book Morhion now held had been stolen by the Zhentarim warrior Ravendas from the library in Elversult when she began her search for the Shadowking's crypt. Morhion had discovered it in the High Tower after Ravendas was defeated by the Fellowship.

Summoning the discipline for which mages were renowned, he bent again over the timeworn text. After a moment of painful effort, he swore softly. His weary eyes would no longer focus on the intricate runes. He knew he should shut the book for the night. It was all too easy to miss a crucial passage when exhausted, and he had hundreds and hundreds of pages yet to peruse.

"But I must learn what is happening to you, Caledan," he whispered fiercely.

He stood and paced around the table, pondering the problem. Unfortunately, there was no magic he knew that could compel a book to read itself. If only there were someone else who could read the words to him . . .

Suddenly he knew the answer. With the ashes left from the incense, he traced an intricate pattern on the mahogany table. In the center of the pattern he placed a beeswax candle, lighting this with a minor cantrip. Lastly, he picked up a bronze hand-bell and rang it three times with a small mallet.

"*Maharanzu kai Umaruk!*" he intoned in the language of magic. "Come to me, Small One!"

The candle flared brightly, as if touched by some other-worldly wind, and purple magic sparked around the magical symbol drawn on the table. There was a great cracking sound, like a clap of thunder, and a dark rift opened in the air above the candle—a tear in the very fabric of the universe. A small, gray shape tumbled out. As quickly as it had opened, the rift mended itself.

"*Youch!* That's hot!" the little creature shouted, barely avoiding the candle flame as it fell to the table with a *plop!*

Morhion watched with guarded amusement as the small being picked itself up and dusted itself off. It was shaped vaguely like a man but stood no higher than the length of Morhion's hand; its skin was as rough and gray as stone. It was an imp, a denizen of one of those nebulous worlds that could be glimpsed through the facets of the crystal. They were small and devious beings, of minor importance at best, but they did have their uses.

The imp glared at Morhion with hot-ruby eyes, flapping its leathery wings in agitation. "Was it really necessary to put the gateway right above the candle, mage?" the creature complained in a raspy voice. "I singed my tail. I have a half a mind to turn around and go back to my own plane of existence right this second . . ."

"I wouldn't advise that," Morhion said ominously. "Attempt to leave, and you will find your tail more than merely singed. Do not forget—the symbol binds you to do my bidding."

The imp glowered at him. "Details, details," it grumbled. "You wizards certainly are a persnickety lot, aren't you?"

"Don't forget 'short-tempered,' " Morhion added.

"Believe me, I haven't," the imp replied acidly. The scaly creature let out a resigned sigh, then sat on the edge of the table, crossing its legs and twirling its barbed

tail impatiently in one hand. "All right, wizard. Excuse
my lack of enthusiasm, but this makes ten thousand and
two summonings so far this millennium, and the eon's
not even half over yet. Let's just get this over with as
quickly as possible. My name's Qip. So what disgusting,
nauseating, and onerous task will I be performing for you
today, completely against my will?"

"I want you to read this book," Morhion said, pointing
to *The Book of the Shadows*.

The imp's expression was incredulous. "A book? You
want me to read a book?" The creature hopped to its feet
and began pacing back and forth on the table. "Let me
get this straight. You mean you don't want me to collect
the sweat of an ogre for one of your spells? Or find a lost
treasure in the Forest of Prickly Rashes? Or"—the imp
shuddered at some unbidden memory—"retrieve an
enchanted ring you dropped down the privy by accident?"

"No," Morhion said with growing impatience. "I only
want you to read the book."

"Just the book? You're quite certain?"

"Unless I'm entirely mistaken, that's what I said."

The imp clapped its hands together jubilantly. "Finally!
A simple task. And one that doesn't even smell bad!"

"You can do it, then?" Morhion asked in relief.

The imp stared flatly. "Of course not. Imps can't read,
you nincompoop."

Morhion restrained himself from throttling the impu-
dent imp. With a sigh, he raised a hand to banish the
wretched creature back to its wretched plane of existence. Abruptly he halted. An idea had occurred to him.

"Qip, you can't understand the runes in the book, but
you could recognize a specific pattern of lines, couldn't
you?"

The imp rolled his eyes. "I said I couldn't read, wizard.
I didn't say I was a moron."

With great effort, Morhion ignored the imp's insolence. There might be a way to make things work yet. He retrieved pen and parchment from his desk and carefully wrote down the specific runes that signified "shadowking." He showed the parchment to Qip.

"I want you to find every occurrence of these runes, in this exact sequence, in the book," Morhion instructed. "Can you do that, Qip? Or is that beyond the limited capabilities of an imp?"

"There's no need to be insulting!" Qip complained. The imp grabbed the parchment, scanned it, then tossed it aside. The creature sidled to the book and began flipping pages with its gnarled hands. Morhion allowed himself a smile. All he would have to do was read the few pages on which the imp found the word "shadowking."

Morhion soon realized the job was going to take as long as it would have taken for him to read every word of the whole book himself. Qip required several minutes to scan each page, and there were hundred and hundreds of pages. It seemed pointless.

"I have a solution," Qip said cheerily when Morhion expressed his impatience.

Morhion regarded the imp cautiously. Why was the devious little creature suddenly being so helpful?

"All I have to do is invite a hundred or so of my cousins to drop by this backwater plane of existence," the imp elaborated. "Divide all the pages up among us, and we'll find your precious runes like that." Qip snapped a pair of clawed fingers for emphasis.

"Yes," Morhion said. "It could work."

"Er, and you don't even have to bother with that silly sigil of yours," Qip added hastily, gesturing to the magical symbol on the table. "I can just bring my friends through the gateway myself . . ."

So that's the little cretin's plan, Morhion thought. Any

imps summoned by Qip outside the sigil would not be bound by the symbol's magic. Imps were capricious and maleficent creatures. Freed of the mage's binding magic, they would be all too happy to turn on Morhion and tear him to bits.

A musing smile touched Morhion's lips. "I like your plan, Qip," he began. The imp's ruby eyes flared with victory. "But," Morhion added quickly, "you will open the rift *within* the sigil, not without."

Hatred burned in the imp's gaze. "And what if I don't?"

Morhion's smile broadened nastily. "With a single spell, Qip, I can ignite your tail with a fire so hot you'll think the candle's flame a cold winter wind by comparison." He lifted a hand menacingly.

Qip's crimson eyes bulged out of his skull. "Now, there's no need to for that," the imp said hastily. "Did I say to ignore the sigil?" He thumped his forehead with a fist. "What was I thinking? Of course I'll use the sigil. Why, I would never think of *not* using the—"

"Just open the rift, Qip," Morhion said testily.

The imp gulped, then clambered back inside the glowing magical symbol on the table. The creature rang the bell three times, and the dark rift in the air opened once more. At once, dozens of imps began to pour out, swearing colorfully when they found themselves bound by the mage's spell. Morhion allowed himself a satisfied smile. This was going to be fun.

Morhion was reluctant to tear the pages out of the ancient book, but there was no other solution. Besides, the old binding was cracking, and he could have the pages resewn. Soon the mage's study was littered with imps. The little creatures perched on every available surface—shelves, ledges, chairs—some even hanging from the rafters like bats. Each clutched several pages of the book, scanning furiously. Whenever one of them came upon the rune-words that Morhion had specified, the imp would flutter crazily through the air to deliver the parchment excerpts to the mage. Within a quarter hour the imps were finished, and Morhion had a dozen such pages, each bearing a reference to the ancient being of shadow magic. Some were pages he recognized from past readings, but a few contained passages he had never seen before.

"You and your kin have done well, Qip," Morhion told the imp.

"Oh, thank you, Great One," Qip replied with mock adulation. "You know your approval means everything to me. I crave nothing else."

The imp's tone was sarcastic, but Morhion was surprised to see a glint of sadness in the creature's crimson eyes. He realized what a difficult existence it must be, constantly being summoned and forced to do another's bidding. Then Morhion made an unusual decision. He moved to the magical sigil, erased some of the lines, and redrew them.

"What's the meaning of that?" Qip asked suspiciously.

"It means," Morhion explained, "that once I send you back to your plane of existence, no one—not even the most powerful wizard—will be able to summon you or your kindred for three hundred years."

Qip's eyes went wide. "You'd really do that for us?" the creature asked in astonishment.

Morhion shrugged indifferently. "I just want to make certain you don't come back to pester me in my lifetime."

Qip grinned, displaying countless needlelike teeth. "Thanks, wizard. You're not so bad after all." The imp gestured elaborately to the others. "Come on, everyone! No summonings for three centuries. It's vacation time!"

Morhion rang the bronze bell once, and the imps vanished in a puff of acrid smoke. He found himself laughing

softly at the curious creatures. Then he picked up the
pages that the imps had brought him, and his laughter
halted. Instinct told him that what he was about to read
would not give him cause for mirth.

He was right. He read the crackling pages once quickly,
then again slowly, making certain that he did not misin-
terpret the ancient runes. What he read chilled him to
the core. At last he set down the sheaves of parchment.
There could be no doubt about it. Caledan was indeed
undergoing the same terrible transformation that the
sorcerer Verraketh had experienced a thousand years
ago. He was becoming an inhuman creature of utter
evil—a shadowking.

Morhion collected all the loose pages of the *Mal'eb'dala*.
Dawn was still a few hours away. He was exhausted, but
he knew there would be no sleep for him that night. The
upheaval foretold by the runestones approached. Morhion
was filled with dread, yet also with renewed exhilaration.
This was what it felt like to be alive. Gathering the book
pages into a neat stack, he set them on the table and
turned to leave his study.

Before he could open the door, a cold wind blew through
the chamber. Morhion turned to see the gale rip through
the stack of papers, filling the air with hundreds of
swirling pages. A piece of yellowed paper slapped itself
against Morhion's face, blinding him. He clawed it away,
then gasped. The whirling pages were coalescing into a
small cyclone in the center of room. They spun faster,
until they were little more than a blur. The noise of the
gale rose to a keening howl. Abruptly, the wind ceased.
The loose parchments fluttered to the floor. The dark figure of a knight, surrounded by an eerie corona of light,
hovered where the pages had spun.

"Serafi," Morhion hissed in trepidation and loathing.
"Why have you come to me? It is not the full moon. You

have had your blood for this month."

The spectral knight drifted slowly toward Morhion, his eyes glowing with unearthly blood-red fire. "I have come to help you, Morhion," the spirit intoned.

"I do not think I can afford any more of your help," Morhion said bitterly. He gestured to the myriad scars that covered his arms.

"Oh, but you can, Morhion," Serafi countered in his chilling voice. "You can, and you will."

Morhion's eyes narrowed in suspicion. "What makes you so certain I'd be interested?" His tone was bold, but he could not quite disguise the trembling in his voice.

"I know you, Morhion," Serafi said, drifting closer. "I know you as no other possibly could."

Morhion choked down the panic rising in his throat. "What do you want, usurper?"

The ghostly knight's eyes flashed. "Do not taunt me with that name, Morhion. You will only regret it. For I have something that you would pay dearly to possess."

"What?"

"Knowledge. The power to save or damn Caledan Caldorien once and for all."

Morhion found himself sinking weakly into a velvet chair, gripping the smooth wood of the arms. Serafi hovered behind him. Morhion could feel the spirit's chill, dusty breath on the back of his neck.

"What do you seek in return for this knowledge, Serafi?" the mage asked in disgust. "Do you wish to drink my blood *twice* each moon?"

The spirit's laughter curdled Morhion's blood. "Nay. Knowledge this great is worth far more than a mere sip of blood."

"Then what?"

The spectral knight's voice became a chantlike whisper. "I do not think you realize, mage, how cold it is to be dead. How cold, how dry, how hollow. I long to experience again all the sensations of life. You cannot imagine how deep and vast my hunger is, Morhion. To feel again—that is what I crave beyond all. To see with living eyes, to taste with fleshly tongue, to touch with warm fingers. I want these things, and all the other delicious sensations that living flesh has to offer."

Morhion was sweating. "But life brings pain as well as pleasure, Serafi."

"Yes, and I want to experience that as well," Serafi spoke exultantly. "After the numbing cold of death, even the fiercest agony would be sweet awakening."

"But how can I give you what you want?" Morhion demanded, fearing the answer. Suddenly he stiffened. A chill caress ran down his neck, his shoulders, his chest, traveling over his body, touching him in places where he had not been touched by another in long years. He wanted to cry out, to leap from the chair, but he sat as if frozen to the spot. A low moan escaped his throat, a mixture of fear and strangled pleasure.

"You have kept your body well." Serafi's voice burned in his brain like poison. "You are older than I would like, yet you are strong, and handsome of face. I think that, with a body such as yours, I could seek out and enjoy all the sensations I desire . . ."

At last, Morhion managed to wrest himself from the ghostly embrace, lurching from the chair. Gasping for breath, he spun around to stare at the spectral knight. "I don't understand," he choked. But even as he spoke the words, he knew he was lying—that he did understand, and had already made his choice.

Serafi's sinister voice echoed all around him. "I would live again, Morhion. And I require your body to do so. I will give to you the knowledge you need to save Caledan. I will grant you the time you need to pursue him and halt his metamorphosis. But, when the quest is over, my payment will be due." The spirit's eyes burned into Morhion. "And your body will become mine."

"What . . . what then will become of my spirit?" Morhion managed to gasp.

Serafi waved a translucent hand, as if this were a matter of no importance. "You will be dead, Morhion. Nothing more, nothing less. Simply dead." Drifting through the chair, the spectral knight approached. "Tell me your answer, mage. Do you accept my bargain?"

Terror clenched Morhion's heart. He could not do this. Even he, who had sacrificed so much in his life for what he believed was the larger good. Or could he? Once before, he had destroyed his friendship with Caledan in order to save Caledan's life. Now that friendship had grown anew, stronger than ever. Once again, was there anything he would not do for Caledan's sake? All at once, the terror melted from Morhion's chest. A strange peace descended on him. As if in a dream, he heard himself speak the words.

"I accept."

Six

The sending from Master Harper Belhuar Thantarth came to Mari in the shadowless hour before dawn.

She had not slept. Kellen lay curled inside a patchwork quilt before the common room's fieldstone hearth, sleeping the untroubled sleep of a child. Mari sighed, longing for such innocence. However, she was no child.

A crackling sound shattered the still air. Mari jerked her head up, gripping the arms of her chair with white-knuckled hands. A shining azure sphere hovered in midair before her. White-hot tendrils snaked around the sphere, sizzling and popping brightly. The acrid stench of lightning filled her lungs. Abruptly an image appeared in the center of the glowing orb—the face of a man. His eyes were kind, but his graying beard and hard expression lent a sternness to his visage. Mari took in a sharp breath.

"Master Thantarth!" she exclaimed.

She was shocked anew when the image in the sphere spoke to her in return.

"Greetings, Mari Al'maren."

Mari's mind raced. She had heard rumors that, among the Harpers, there were one or two mages capable of sending messages over vast distances. However, the power required for a feat like this was immeasurable. Messages were relayed in this manner in only the direst of circumstances. Slowly, Mari rose from the chair, her muscles stiff from sitting all night.

"How may I serve the Harpers, Master Thantarth?" Her tone was formal. She had spoken face-to-face with Belhuar Thantarth only once before, when she had first joined the Harpers. He was the Master of Twilight Hall, the western stronghold of the Harpers, located in the city of Berdusk. His duties kept him too preoccupied with great affairs to deal directly with all the Harpers under him. Orders from Thantarth were usually relayed by the high-ranking Harpers who served as his assistants. Thantarth was reputed to be a stern but benevolent man who was not afraid to anger others in pursuit of what he believed was right.

"I have a new task for you, Al'maren," said the image of Thantarth in the glowing sphere. His deep voice reverberated in the still air of the common room. "And I will tell you now that it will be the most difficult mission you have ever undertaken."

Mari's heart skipped wildly in her chest. "On my oath as a Harper, I will do my best, Master Thantarth."

Thantarth nodded somberly. "That is well, Al'maren, for this task will require all your strength, and far more." His steely eyes seemed to search her heart, piercing it as they scanned for something. "I have dire news, Mari. We have reason to believe that Caledan Caldorien is undergoing a terrible transformation—the same transformation that, a thousand years ago, resulted in the creation of the magical creature of darkness known as the Shadowking."

Despite her years of training, Mari could not conceal the anguish on her face. She had not thought the Harpers would come to this realization themselves. Yet why shouldn't they? There was little that surpassed the reach or understanding of the Harpers.

"I see you have reached the same conclusion," Thantarth said grimly.

"Just last night," Mari answered hoarsely.

"After Caledan's disappearance and the happenings in Corm Orp, there can be no other explanation," the Master Harper said.

Mari gathered her will. "What is to be my mission, Master Thantarth?"

It took him a long moment to speak. When he did, there was no longer a hint of sorrow in his voice. Cold authority spoke. "You know Caledan better than any in the Harpers, Al'maren. That is why I am giving this task to you. Your mission is to track Caledan Caldorien. And when you find him, your orders are"—Thantarth hesitated only a fraction of a heartbeat—"to destroy him."

It was as if someone had yanked the ground out from beneath Mari's feet. She managed to grab the edge of a table and hold on, and only by this means did she manage to keep her footing. Finally she gasped a single word.

"*What?*"

"You heard my orders, Al'maren." Thantarth's voice was cold, hard stone.

She shook her head dully. Gradually, anger flared to life inside her. She welcomed it, letting the fire burn away the vast sickness in her gut. Slowly she straightened, locking gazes with the image of Thantarth in the shining sphere. "With all due respect, Master Thantarth,

I cannot believe what I have just heard," she said incredulously. "Caledan is one of the greatest Harpers alive. Perhaps *the* greatest. And you would simply have him disposed of like some broken tool that is no longer needed?"

"I am well aware of Caldorien's accomplishments as a Harper, Al'maren," Thantarth thundered angrily. "I hardly need a mere journeyman to instruct *me*. It is tragic that a hero of Caldorien's caliber must be destroyed. But the Harpers cannot allow the evil of a shadowking to be loosed upon the world once more. We have no choice. Caledan Caldorien must die. And you have been chosen to perform the deed."

Thantarth would not be swayed. Mari's rage melted into numbness. "I . . . *can't* do it."

"I know of your feelings for Caldorien, Al'maren. I do not envy your position. However, you must put your feelings aside in favor of the oath you swore to the Harpers."

She shook her head in disbelief. "You don't know what you're asking of me. I can't . . . I can't destroy the man I . . . I . . ."

Thantarth's booming voice shook the timbers of the inn. "You are wrong, Al'maren. You *will* do it, because I command you to do so. Your vow to the Harpers stands above all. You have no choice!"

That was his mistake. Mari realized she did have a choice. A thrill of fear coursed through her as she thought about what she must do, but it was quickly replaced by cool calm. She raised a hand to the silver moon-and-harp pin on her green jacket—the badge of the Harpers. When she spoke, her voice was steady.

"If as a Harper I must obey you, Thantarth, then this day I am a Harper no longer."

She tore the silver badge from her jacket.

Thantarth's expression was livid. "You cannot do this,

Mari Al'maren!"

"It's too late. I already have."

His voice became a growl. "Do you understand what this means, Al'maren? You will be branded a renegade. Every Harper will have the right to hunt you down and slay you. And by all the gods, they will be obliged to do it!"

"I know," she said sadly. "I know."

Within the glowing sphere, Thantarth shook a fist at her, his face crimson. "Stop this foolishness now, Al'maren. Stop it, or I swear you will—"

Mari did not wait to hear what awful fate he intended for her. In one swift motion, she picked up the chair and hurled it at the shimmering sphere. There was a brilliant flash and a sound like shattering glass as the orb burst into a thousand azure shards. Mari shut her eyes against the blinding glare. When she dared open them again, the magical sphere was gone. All that was left of the chair were a few charred sticks of wood scattered on the floor. They looked like nothing so much as burnt bones.

I never believed it would come to this, Mari thought with a mixture of apprehension and peculiar exultation. I never believed that I, Mari Al'maren, would become a renegade Harper.

Yet that was exactly what she was now. A renegade, a fugitive, and an outlaw. The full realization of what she had done crashed down upon her, and she slumped down into a chair. She had just given up everything she had ever fought for, everything she had ever believed in. But she could not destroy Caledan, and she would not let anyone else destroy him. There had to be a way to stop Caledan's dark metamorphosis. I promised you, Kera. I told him good-bye, but I will be damned to the Abyss if I'll turn my back on him.

"Are they going to kill my father, Mari?"

She had forgotten Kellen. He stood beside her chair, his green eyes overly large in his pale face. He had overheard everything.

"No, Kellen," she said quietly. "No one will hurt your father. We won't let that happen."

He nodded gravely, then threw his arms around her neck. She returned his hug fiercely. At last she pushed him gently away and stood up. There was no time to waste.

When Morhion arrived at the Dreaming Dragon an hour later, he found her packing her saddlebags. He raised a single golden eyebrow. "Going somewhere, Mari?"

She firmly buckled the last leather strap and dusted off her hands. "You might say that."

"Haven't you forgotten something?" He eyed the small rip on the collar of her green jacket meaningfully.

"No," she replied crisply. "I haven't."

Interest flickered in Morhion's icy eyes. "I see."

They sat at one of the common room's long trestle tables. Estah brought hot tea, brown bread, and honey for their breakfast. The halfling innkeeper eyed Mari curiously. She had heard the commotion in the common room this morning, but Mari had not yet had the courage to tell Estah about her disturbing conversation with Belhuar Thantarth. There was no more putting it off. By the time she finished, Estah's usually gentle expression had been replaced by one of flinty outrage.

"They have no right," the halfling said harshly. "Caledan has devoted the best part of his life to serving the Harpers, and in his darkest hour of need they turn against him. How dare they!"

Mari sighed. "The Harpers always work for the greater good, Estah. If sacrificing one man can save a hundred, then in their minds it's a fair bargain."

"Yet sometimes," Morhion countered, "when one stone is taken out, an entire wall can come tumbling down. That is something the Harpers have never understood—if you'll forgive me, Mari."

She shot him an ironic look. "Believe me, Morhion, no apology is necessary."

"What do you intend to do?" he asked.

"Follow him," she said fiercely. "And find him."

"And then?"

"I don't know," she said impatiently. "I'll think of something."

"I can see you've really thought this out," he noted dryly.

"Well, do you have any better ideas?"

"As a matter of fact, I do."

Mari groaned. Why would mages never come out and *say* what they were thinking? "All right, Morhion. What's on your mind?"

A faintly smug smile touched his lips. "I thought you'd never ask."

As a brilliant square of morning sunlight crept across the wooden floor, Mari and Estah listened with growing fascination—and growing dread—to the knowledge Morhion had gleaned from the ancient copy of *The Book of the Shadows*. First he told them about the Shadowking. Mari knew the myth—how the ancient sorcerer Verraketh was transformed by his own dark magic into a bestial creature of evil, and how he was defeated by the legendary bard Talek Talembar. Yet, as Morhion now explained, all that was only the first part of the tale. The prelude, as it were.

"In ancient days," the mage began, "a blazing star fell to Toril. The only one to see it fall was a wandering minstrel. Curious, he journeyed in the direction of the falling star and came upon a smoking crater. In the center of the steaming pit, the minstrel found a hot piece of metal shaped like a star. Thinking it beautiful, the minstrel quenched the piece of metal in a pool of water and fastened it to a silver chain, making it into a medallion. The minstrel donned the medallion, and from that day on his fortune changed. First he became a renowned musician, then a noble lord, and finally the ruler of his own land. The medallion was called the Shadowstar. The minstrel's name was Verraketh—Verraketh Talembar."

Mari and Estah exchanged startled looks, but they said nothing, not wishing to interrupt the mage's narrative.

"In time," Morhion went on, "the medallion granted Verraketh not only great fortune, but great magic as well. It infused him with awesome power—power over the substance of shadows. It was a magic that was passed on to his only son, Talek Talembar, who became a bard and a sorcerer in his own right. As the years went by and Verraketh aged not, he became known as the Shadowmage; his kingdom was called Ebenfar.

"The years turned into centuries, and the magic of the Shadowstar began to transform Verraketh until he was a man and a mage no longer, but a thing of pure and evil magic, which folk in fear named the Shadowking." Morhion regarded his two listeners solemnly. "I think you both know the rest of the tale. Seeking dominion over all men, the Shadowking forged the Nightstone. But Talek Talembar defeated his father and sealed both Shadowking and Nightstone inside the crag upon which, an eon later, Iriaebor was raised."

"So it was from his father that Talek Talembar inherited his shadow magic?" Mari asked.

"That is so," Morhion replied. "There is something else I learned, though not directly from the *Mal'eb'dala*." He turned to the halfling innkeeper. "Estah, what was the name of Caledan's father?"

She scowled, obviously wondering at the purpose of this question. "It was Caledan Caldorien."

"And the name of *his* father."

"Why, Caledan Caldorien, of course," Estah replied in consternation. "Morhion, you know as well as I that it's a family name. It's been passed down from father to son for centuries."

"Yes," the mage replied gravely. "Just like the shadow magic."

Chill fingers danced up Mari's spine. "Get to the point, Morhion."

The mage pulled a sheaf of parchment from his belt and unrolled it on the table. He pointed to a series of runes. "This is the name Talek Talembar. It is written in Talfir, the language spoken in these lands a thousand years ago. Later, when folk came from the east, crossing the Sunset Mountains to settle the Western Heartlands, they brought their own language with them. Many of the old names, of both people and places, were still used, but the tongue of the easterners contained different sounds than the speech of the Talfirc. As a result, the old names were bastardized—their pronunciations changed—so they could be written in the new language."

Morhion pointed to another line of writing on the parchment. The letters looked vaguely familiar, but Mari couldn't quite read them.

"This is 'Talek Talembar' as it was written in the language of the easterners," Morhion explained. "Only it wouldn't have been pronounced the same as in Talfir. It would have sounded something more like 'Calen Calendir.' A few centuries ago, a new wave of immigrants came over the Sunset Mountains from the kingdoms of Cormyr and Sembia. These were our direct ancestors, Mari. They brought yet another language—the one we now speak—and the names of people and places in the

Western Heartlands were changed once again, this time
to conform to Cormyrean writing and pronunciation."
The mage pointed to the final line of writing on the
parchment. "This is the Cormyrean version of the name
'Calen Calendir.'"

Mari read the words, then looked at the mage.
"Caledan Caldorien?" she whispered.

Morhion's chill blue gaze locked on her own. "The very
same."

"But that means that Caledan is a direct descendant of
Talek Talembar!" Estah exclaimed.

Mari spoke, half in a daze. "And a descendant of the
Shadowking as well. Of course! It all makes sense now.
That's why Caledan's shadow magic had the power to
defeat the Shadowking. It came from the Shadowking
himself!"

"It must be so," Morhion replied grimly. "The same
magic that flowed in the veins of Verraketh flows in
Caledan's."

Mari grappled for understanding. "But if that's true,
why didn't any of Caledan's other ancestors become shadowkings?"

"I believe I know the answer to that," Morhion
explained. "Talek Talembar had many descendants, and
all possessed the shadow magic, though many to only a
slight degree. In them, the power of the shadow magic
was diffused. None inherited enough of the magic to
undergo the dark metamorphosis. Then Ravendas's Lord
Steward, Snake—who in truth served the Shadowking—
summoned a shadevar, one of thirteen ancient beings of
mayhem banished from the world by Azuth the High
One. The shadevar's orders were to hunt down and slay
all in the Realms who possessed the shadow magic. This
it did before we destroyed it."

"Save for Caledan and Kellen," Mari said in amazement.

"Yes. And in them, the shadow magic is concentrated as never before. I think that is why Caledan's transformation seems to be progressing so quickly, while Verraketh's took centuries."

A terrible thought occurred to her. "Then will . . . will Kellen become a shadowking, too?"

Morhion shook his head. "I do not know. However, I suspect there can be but one Shadowking at a time. For now, let us concern ourselves with Caledan." He rolled up the parchment and replaced it in his belt. "Oh, there is one more thing that I learned. The Shadowstar has the power to halt Caledan's metamorphosis . . . or complete it."

Mari pondered the implications. "You think Caledan is searching for the Shadowstar, don't you?"

He nodded in affirmation. "Long ago, the Shadowstar was buried in the crypt of the Shadowking beneath Iriaebor, but at some point it was stolen by a tomb robber. I have discovered that it is presently in the possession of a mysterious personage known only as Stiletto."

A thought struck Mari. "You couldn't possibly have read that in the *Mal'eb'dala,* Morhion. Where did you learn about this Stiletto?"

For the first time in this grim conversation, Mari saw a troubled look cross Morhion's impassive visage. "I dare not reveal my source," the mage said coolly. "Suffice it to say that I know, and leave it at that."

Mari did not press the point. Regardless of how Morhion had come by the knowledge, the important thing was that the Shadowstar had the power to save Caledan. The three agreed that they had to find the medallion before Caledan did.

"Do you have any idea who this Stiletto person is, Morhion?" Estah asked. "Or where we could find him?"

Morhion regained his composure. "I am afraid that knowledge has eluded even me."

Mari tapped a cheek thoughtfully. "Stiletto . . . Too bad Ferret isn't around to lend a hand."

Ferret had once been a member of the Fellowship of the Dreaming Dragon. The weasely thief had helped the others escape the crypt of the Shadowking as it crumbled, while he himself was lost in the destruction. Despite his wily and greedy exterior, Mari had met few in her life as truly selfless as the thief Ferret. She wished he were here now, but it was a vain thought.

Morhion offered a suggestion. "We do need to find someone like Ferret, someone who deals in information and who casts a wide enough net that he may have heard of this Stiletto."

A crooked smile curled about Mari's lips. "On second thought, I think I know just the person. And he adores me."

Seven

Mari groaned. Why did these things always seem to happen to her?

"I thought Cormik *adored* you," Morhion said coldly.

"I thought he did, too," she said through clenched teeth.

"Well, if you don't mind my saying, he has a rather peculiar manner of expressing his affection."

For emphasis, Morhion rattled the heavy iron shackles that bound his wrists. He and Mari were chained to a rough stone wall in a dank underground chamber. The muffled sounds of raucous laughter and clinking coins drifted down from above. They were somewhere in the basement of the Prince and Pauper, the seamiest gambling house in Iriaebor.

"In case you're wondering, you really aren't being helpful, Morhion," Mari replied in a surly tone. "Can't you get us out of here with a spell?"

"No, I can't. Casting a spell requires ritual gestures as

well as magical words"—he cast a rueful look at the thick
bands of iron that held his hands immobile—"a fact of
which your dear friend Cormik seems well aware."

"Everyone's entitled to a few mistakes," Mari grumbled. She seemed to remember Caledan saying that exact
phrase once when the two of them were caught in a similar predicament. Things were worse than she thought if
she was starting to sound like Caldorien.

Mari racked her brain, trying to think of what she
might have done to get on Cormik's bad side. Cormik was
the proprietor of the Prince and Pauper, but he was also
one of the most powerful underworld lords in Iriaebor.
Officially, Mari could not condone Cormik's illicit prac-
tices, but he had helped the Fellowship to defeat Ravendas. Besides, she had always liked his daggerlike wit and
impeccable sense of taste.

It must have been that incident a year ago, she decided.
Cormik had wanted her help in prying some compromis-
ing secrets out of a particularly wealthy nobleman. Mari
had haughtily told Cormik to go ask one of the painted
ladies on the Street of Lanterns instead, and had run
him out of the Dreaming Dragon. She had not spoken to
him since that day. Well, if he was still holding a grudge,
she was going to have to find a way to—

The chamber's ironbound door flew open. Mari blinked
against the glare of crimson torchlight that gushed
through the opening. When her vision cleared, a figure
stood before her. Cormik. He was a corpulent man with a
florid, pockmarked complexion and a jewel-encrusted
patch over one eye. As ever, he was clad in gaudy finery
that involved voluminous quantities of blue silk, wine-
colored velvet, and gold brocade. Flanking him were two
hulking bodyguards, each bearing a jeweled sword.

Mari licked her lips. "Cormik, if you'll let me explain—"

He cut her off with a wave of a chubby, ring-laden

hand. "Haven't we been through this once before, Harper?" he said impatiently. "I didn't want to hear Caledan's explanation then, and I don't want to hear yours now. I'm a busy man, you know." He made a sharp gesture to his bodyguards. "Jad, Kevrek—deal with these two for me."

Cormik strode from the chamber. His two bull-necked servants stepped forward, grinning fiercely as they reached into leather pouches on their belts. Mari's eyes widened as she caught a glint of silver and a wisp of steam. She shut her eyes, bracing herself against the coming attack.

"A mirror and a hot towel?" Morhion's incredulous voice said beside her.

Mari's eyes fluttered open. She gaped in surprise. Sure enough, each of the bodyguards held a small silver mirror and a steaming cloth towel.

"Of course," one of the muscle-bound men said in a surprisingly cultured voice. "You'll both need to freshen up before your audience with the Master."

"Dungeons can be so messy," the other hulk added in an equally genteel tone. "Don't you agree?"

Jad and Kevrek held up the silver mirrors while Mari and Morhion wiped themselves clean of dust and cobwebs. The towels were deliciously hot and scented faintly with ginger. Mari was forced to admit that she felt refreshed. However, she was still furious with Cormik.

A few minutes later, Cormik's bodyguards led Mari and Morhion into a brightly lit chamber richly appointed with Sembian tapestries and Calishite statuary.

"So, did you like my little ruse, Al'maren?" Cormik inquired coyly. The rotund man was sprawled across a pile of embroidered cushions, a glass of pale wine held loosely in one stubby hand. "I can't believe you fell for it a second time!"

"In case you hadn't noticed, I'm not laughing," Mari
griped. "Are you laughing, Morhion?"

An ironic smile touched the corners of the mage's lips.
"Actually, I think I am."

Mari flopped sulkily onto a pile of cushions and treated
Cormik to her best scathing look. It was an expression
she had perfected in her years working with Caledan.
After a moment, Cormik squirmed uncomfortably.

"Oh, stop looking at me like that," he said testily. "I'm
sorry I had to have you thrown in chains, but you really
should have given me some warning before you stopped
by the Prince and Pauper."

"So this is all my fault?" Mari inquired dubiously.

"Everyone in Iriaebor knows you're good friends with
the monk Tyveris. And everyone also knows Tyveris is
City Lord Bron's closest advisor. I couldn't very well have
acted as if we were the best of chums when you walked
through my front door. If my clients thought I was in
cahoots with Bron, I wouldn't have a customer left. I'd be
ruined."

Mari was forced to admit, she could see the logic of his
actions. However, she wasn't about to concede the argument that easily. "Couldn't you have thought of something besides throwing us in your dungeon?"

Cormik shrugged noncommittally. "I was rushed. It's
hard to be creative under pressure, you know."

"All right, Cormik. I'll forgive you this once. But you
owe me a favor."

The corpulent man gave her a sardonic wink. "Why, I'll
do anything you desire, my sweet."

"I'm sure you would," she noted dryly. "But don't get
your hopes up. It's your mind I need, Cormik, not the rest
of you." Mari drained her wine, gathering strength, then
proceeded to tell Cormik all they had learned concerning
Caledan, the Shadowstar, and Stiletto.

When she finished, Cormik seemed visibly shaken. "Caledan is becoming a shadowking?" he murmured in disbelief. "I always knew the man had a dark side, but this is ridiculous."

"So, do you know anything about this Stiletto character or not?" Mari asked impatiently.

A calculating gleam appeared in his one good eye. "I'm afraid that's an answer that will cost the Harpers a good amount of gold, Al'maren."

"I'm not asking for the Harpers," she said quietly. "I'm asking for myself."

"Is there a difference?"

"There is now." Mari swallowed hard. She might as well get used to telling people. "I've resigned from the Harpers, Cormik."

His reaction surprised her. "Good for you, Mari! It's high time you left behind that meddling bunch of do-gooders. And don't worry about money. You can always come work for me."

Mari smiled wistfully. "I just might take you up on that offer when this is all over."

"What of Mari's question?" Morhion asked grimly.

Cormik shot him an annoyed look. "Don't worry, my good, repressed mage. I hadn't forgotten." His gaze returned to Mari. "Because the information is for you, my dear, I'll waive the usual fee."

"So you know where we can find this Stiletto?" she asked excitedly.

"No, I don't. However," he added in response to her crestfallen look, "I think I know someone who might."

* * * * *

The sun was shining overhead as Mari and Morhion followed Cormik along a precarious stone bridge high

above the streets of the Old City. Over the centuries, Iriaebor's myriad towers had been connected by a tangled
web work of bridges, stone arches, and midair causeways.
Many of the bridges were crumbling and in ill repair, and
a few were trod only at great risk, but it was still possible
to travel from one end of the Tor to the other without
ever descending to the streets below. Some of the larger
causeways were broad enough to accommodate merchants' stalls, and vendors hawked food and drink.
Everything one needed to survive was available on the
heights, and some folk who lived high in the towers never
bothered to venture down to the ground.

The three passed through an open turret atop a dilapidated tower and proceeded onto another bridge. It was a
spindly arch, its stones cracked and pitted with age. Mari
could feel the span shudder beneath her with every step.
Nervously, she clutched the stone balustrade to steady
herself. A chunk of the railing broke off in her hand. She
swallowed hard, casting a look at Cormik.

"Are you certain this bridge is safe?" she asked in a
quavering voice.

"Oh, the bridge is sturdy enough," Cormik replied, "but
I wish someone would clean up after the pigeons." With a
sound of disgust, he hiked up the hem of his rich velvet
robe and picked his way delicately around the piles of
bird droppings.

To Mari's relief, they soon turned onto an intersecting
causeway that was in better repair. After that, they followed a confusing succession of bridges until the city
seemed to spin beneath her.

"Do watch where you're going, Mari," Cormik complained.

Mari blinked. The rotund man had stopped on the
bridge, and she had run right into him. She gasped, seeing why he had halted.

The bridge ended in midair. The stones trailed off raggedly, as if half the bridge had collapsed and the other half had remained, hanging unsupported over the city below. In panic, she clutched Cormik's hand and hauled him backward.

"We have to get off!" she shouted urgently. "The rest of the bridge could collapse at any second."

To her astonishment, he shook off her hand. "Calm down, Mari," he said in a perturbed voice. "You're rumpling my silk shirt." He fussed with the soft material, smoothing out wrinkles that would have been imperceptible to less fastidious eyes. "Now, follow me. And whatever you do, don't look down."

With that he turned and stepped off the end of the bridge. Mari screamed. She lunged forward, trying to grab him, but he had already vanished from sight. Frantically, she peered over the edge of the bridge. She could see the labyrinthine streets of the Old City far below, but she caught no glimpse of Cormik. His body must have already landed.

"Why, Morhion? Why did he do it?"

"Indeed, why?" Morhion echoed her, but Mari had the distinct impression he was mocking her. "Cormik was hardly the suicidal type. In fact, I've never met a man as obsessed with staying alive."

Mari shook her head in disbelief. Yet she had seen Cormik step off the edge of the bridge.

"Oh, stop this nonsense," a voice said impatiently. "We haven't got all day."

A chubby hand shot out of thin air and grabbed Mari's green jacket, yanking her off the end of the bridge. This time she was too surprised to cry out. She braced for the shock of the plunge, but she wasn't falling. In fact, she could feel a hard surface beneath her deerskin boots.

Cormik was glaring at her. She looked down. That was

a mistake. Though it felt as if she were standing on solid rock, all she could see beneath her feet was clear air and the twisting streets a hundred feet below. A wave of nausea crashed through her, and she clutched Cormik's arm for support.

"Didn't I tell you not to look down?" he chided her.

"Invisible," Morhion murmured with interest. "The bridge doesn't end at all. It merely becomes invisible. And when we stand upon it, we are invisible as well." He turned to Cormik. "This was wrought with powerful magic. Who are we going to find at the other end of the bridge?"

"You'll see," Cormik replied mysteriously.

Cormik was right, Mari realized. It was definitely better if she did not look down. Her feet were content to believe they trod upon hard stone, and she didn't want to give them any other notions. She kept her gaze fixed ahead. Far below was a dark and seamy section of the Old City. They continued to walk.

"We're here," Cormik announced.

"Er, where's here?" Mari asked hesitantly. "I don't see anything."

"Must you always be so negative, my dear?" Cormik asked in exasperation. "I know it's difficult for you, but just trust me."

He moved forward and vanished from sight. Mari knew there was little point in protesting. "Here goes nothing," she grumbled, stepping forward.

The tower was invisible as well, at least from the outside. Once within, Mari found herself surrounded by comfortable, solid stone walls. The three passed through an arch and into a circular chamber with a domed ceiling. Instantly, Mari was dazzled by a shimmering spectrum of ruby, emerald, sapphire, and diamond-white light.

"Welcome, Cormik," a husky voice said. "This is a surprise. And I see you've brought friends. Well, don't just stand there. Come in."

After several moments, Mari's eyes adjusted to the dazzling illumination. The chamber's walls were encrusted with precious stones, and the gems refracted the light of countless candles. The effect was breathtaking. In the middle of the chamber, on a chaise of crimson velvet, reclined the figure of an incredibly beautiful woman. Her short hair was like a wave of polished onyx, her skin as lustrous as burnished amber, her eyes as bright as violet sapphires.

"Hello, Jewel," Cormik said, his bow surprisingly graceful for a man of his girth.

"Greetings, my dear, doddering coot," she replied sharply.

"Ah, my sweet, hideous hag—I see you're still grating on the nerves."

Mari frowned at this curious exchange. Cormik had called the woman "Jewel." The name seemed vaguely familiar, but Mari couldn't remember where she had heard it. Certainly she had never seen the exotic woman before. At first she had thought Jewel to be about her own age, but now she wasn't so certain. There was something strangely old about Jewel's sharp violet eyes and smoky voice.

"Now, let me see," Jewel mused, turning her attention to Cormik's companions. "This must be the Harper Mari Al'maren and the mage Morhion Gen'dahar. Cormik has told me much about you. But don't worry yourselves, loves, for I seldom believe anything Cormik tells me." She smiled warmly, and Mari returned the expression despite herself. She found she liked this mysterious woman.

Jewel bade her guests sit on crushed velvet lounges. Servants clad in black leather jerkins and black silk

masks appeared with glasses of ruby-colored wine. Each
of them wore a long knife at the hip. Mari drained her
glass quickly in an effort to settle her nerves.

"I'm so glad you brought your friends, Cormik," Jewel
said in her throaty voice. "It is good to finally meet some
of those who journeyed with my grandson."

Mari blinked in confusion. "I'm sorry," she sputtered. "I
didn't realize I knew any of your kin."

Cormik set down his glass with a frown. "Haven't you
been paying attention, Mari? Of course you knew her
grandson. This is Jewel Talondim, Ferret's grandmother."

This was too much for Mari to absorb. "Ferret's grandmother?" she said incredulously. "But she's so . . . young.
Ferret was a good ten years older than me, and Jewel
can't be a day over—"

"Ninety-three," Jewel interrupted with a laugh. "Oh, I
know what you're thinking, but I can assure you there's
no magic involved. Just good blood. The women of the
Talondim clan have always aged gracefully."

"I believe that qualifies as an understatement,"
Morhion commented matter-of-factly. Jewel gave him a
solemn nod.

Mari had learned a little about Jewel from her grandson, Ferret. The Talondim clan were independent thieves,
not allied with any guild. Normally, such free-lancers
were eradicated by the fiercely territorial thieves' guilds,
but the Talondim family was unusually powerful—due in
no small part to the strong hand and keen mind of the
clan's matriarch. As a result, instead of attacking the
Talondim family, the thieving guilds of Iriaebor more
often sought to forge alliances with Jewel. Thus the
Talondim family prospered.

Mari was suddenly filled with sadness at the memories
of Ferret. "Your grandson was a good thief, Jewel," she
said quietly. "I can't tell you how much he helped us

when we were fighting Ravendas. But more than that, he was a good man. I miss him."

Jewel reached out and gave Mari's hand a squeeze. "I know, love. We all do." She sighed wistfully. "For the longest time I was furious with the Harpers and the Fellowship of the Dreaming Dragon, for taking Ferret away from me. But now that we've met at last, I can see why he risked everything to help you."

Mari wanted to say how sorry she was, but the words would not come, so she settled for gripping Jewel's hand fiercely. Jewel laughed and caught Mari in a maternal embrace. "There's no need to cry, Mari. Don't you see? We've already become friends."

Despite a flood of tears, Mari couldn't help laughing, for it was true.

It was Cormik who politely reminded them all why they had come to Jewel's invisible tower, and they got down to business. It took some time to recount all they knew concerning Caledan's transformation, yet Mari was amazed that Jewel absorbed it so quickly and with such aplomb.

"I have heard of this Stiletto," Jewel confessed when Mari finally finished. "But I'm afraid I know very little about him."

"Very little would be more than I know at the moment," Cormik replied gruffly.

"Why doesn't that surprise me in your case, Cormik?" Jewel asked smartly. "As far as my sources have been able to determine, Stiletto is a new underworld power in the Western Heartlands. He—or she, for no one really knows—appeared about two years ago, and since then has quickly risen to power in the world of thievery. Each day, more and more underworld operations fall under Stiletto's control. Every thieves' guild west of the Sunset Mountains has felt Stiletto's bite, and I'm afraid the

Talondim clan is no different. We're all losing obscene amounts of money, so you can imagine that the location of Stiletto's base of operations is something every guild-master and crime lord in the Western Heartlands would give his pickpocketing hand to know. Despite all our efforts, Stiletto has managed to keep his lair—and his identity—a secret."

Mari chewed her lip in thought. "Well, at least now we know that Stiletto is somewhere in the Western Heart-lands. That narrows it down a bit."

"Oh, indeed," Cormik replied drolly. "Now we have only a quarter of a continent to search rather than the whole thing."

Mari scowled at him. "I was just trying to look on the bright side."

"I think you'll have to look harder," Morhion advised gloomily. "I fear we have little chance of finding Stiletto before Caledan does. I have no doubt that the Shadow-star beckons Caledan. It may take time, but eventually its call will lead him to Stiletto."

Jewel gave the mage an appraising look. "At the risk of uttering the obvious, why don't you just let Caledan do the work for you?" Mari, Morhion, and Cormik stared at her, uncomprehending. "Think of it, loves. If Caledan is going to try to get the Shadowstar from this Stiletto, then why don't you simply follow Caledan for now, and ask questions about Stiletto along the way? You might get lucky and learn where Stiletto is in time to beat Caledan there. And if not, at least you won't be far behind."

New hope flooded Mari's chest. It wasn't perfect, but it was a plan. "Jewel, you're brilliant!"

The matriarch of the Talondim clan shrugged modestly. "It's a gift."

Eight

The gateway was ready. Morhion stepped back and regarded the stone arch.

With red ochre, for power, he had outlined the runes carved into the rock. In front of the arch he had laid down a pathway of willow branches to symbolize travel. At present, the archway opened onto only a wall of rough-hewn stone. But when he spoke the word of opening . . .

The gateway stood in a chamber beneath Morhion's tower. It had been placed here by the powerful mage who had first raised the spire, three centuries ago. Yet the gateway was an artifact whose age was better measured in eons. It had taken Morhion long years of study to unlock the gateway's secrets. Even now, he was not certain that he truly understood the arch's ancient, alien magic.

"You risk great peril by using the gateway, Morhion," a sepulchral voice spoke behind him.

Morhion spun around, breathing in air suddenly turned chill. The hateful word escaped his lips with a hiss. "Serafi."

The spectral knight drifted closer, bringing with him the scent of dry dust and rot. His eyes glowed like drops of molten iron, smoldering with contempt—and desire. "It is folly for you to use the gateway, mage. Its magic is far more vast than your puny, mortal mind could possibly imagine."

Forcibly, Morhion willed away the fear and loathing that clouded his mind. "I cannot imagine that you care," he said flatly.

"Oh, but I do care." Serafi's hollow voice oozed mock sympathy. "Have you forgotten our bargain already, Morhion? How like a mortal!" The ghostly knight floated closer still. "Allow me to remind you, then. Your body belongs to me now. I am concerned what happens to it. I want to be certain it comes to me in the same excellent condition in which it stands now."

Morhion felt his head being tilted back. He resisted, the cords of his neck standing out with the strain, but it was no use. Icy, invisible hands tangled through his long golden hair, then moved to stroke the warm flesh of his throat. Suddenly the bodiless fingers tightened. Morhion choked, unable to breathe. His hands scrabbled at his neck, but they found no purchase against the incorporeal grip that strangled him. A roaring noise filled his ears. Everything grew dim . . .

"No, not yet," Serafi whispered.

The freezing hands released Morhion's throat. He staggered backward, drawing in shuddering breaths while brilliant sparks of light exploded before his eyes.

Serafi's voice reverberated with menace. "Do not think that you can escape your vow through death, Morhion. Your body is my property, and I will be watching over it."

Morhion wanted to shout, to hurl some curse at the spectral knight, but Serafi melted into the air and was gone.

Mari arrived a short while later. She stepped through the tower's door along with a flood of late afternoon sunlight. It was time to begin their search for Caledan and the Shadowstar.

When she saw Morhion, concern lit Mari's eyes. "Are you all right, Morhion? Your neck . . . it's been bruised."

Hastily, Morhion turned up the collar of his purple vest, concealing the livid marks. "It is of no importance," he said, more sharply than he intended. But she had caught him off guard.

Mari looked unconvinced, but when she opened her mouth to ask another question, a slight figure stepped from behind her.

"Hello, Morhion."

Mari looked surprised, but amusement flickered across Morhion's usually impassive visage. This was unexpected . . . or had it been prearranged?

"Hello, Kellen," the mage said.

"Kellen, what are you doing here?" Mari asked sternly. "You should be back at the inn with Estah."

Though the halfling healer had wanted to join the search for Caledan, Morhion and Mari had convinced her that someone needed to stay at the Dreaming Dragon in case Caledan returned. Reluctantly, Estah had agreed to remain behind, though she was not pleased about it.

"It's all right," Kellen said gravely. "I left her a note so she wouldn't wonder where I went."

Morhion gave the boy a speculative look. "And just where is it that you *are* going, Kellen?"

"With you, of course. You're going to need someone with the shadow magic on your journey."

Morhion glanced at Mari. "The boy is right, you know."

"I don't care if he's right," Mari countered crossly. "Right has absolutely nothing to do with it. He's only eleven years old, and he's not coming with us."

Morhion made a decision. "Listen to me, Mari," he urged quietly. "You know as well as I do that Caledan's power over shadows has become chaotic and dangerous. We may have to face shadow creatures like those in the Zhentarim lair. And if we do, we may indeed need Kellen's shadow magic."

Mari wasn't budging. "I packed supplies for only the two of us. And we don't have a horse for him."

"I'm small," Kellen offered. "I could ride with you or Morhion. And I don't eat much."

Mari let out a resigned sigh. She knelt and gripped Kellen's shoulders. "All right, Kellen. This is going to be a hard journey, and a dangerous one. Once we've left, there can be no complaining or begging to turn back. And you must do everything that I or Morhion ask you to do, quickly and without question. Do you promise?"

He nodded earnestly. "I promise, Mari."

She studied him for a moment, then smiled in spite of herself. "All right, then. Let's get going."

"Wait a minute!" a huffing voice shouted. "Not so fast!"

What now? Morhion wondered. He and Mari looked up in surprise to see a rotund figure stumble through the doorway before collapsing to the floor, wheezing. A willowy form stepped lithely over the prostrate bulk.

"I didn't know you could actually run, Cormik," Jewel said in sincere amazement. "Did you burst something, you silly goat?"

"I'm quite fine—no thanks to you, old witch," he grumbled, hauling himself to his feet. He wore a voluminous pearl-gray traveling cloak over his usual opulent finery.

Mari thrust her hands against her hips. "What now?"

Cormik pointed a chubby, accusing finger at Jewel.

"This crafty wench thought she would tag along with you on your quest, in hopes of learning the location of Stiletto's hideout." He glowered darkly at the matriarch of the Talondim clan. "Information she could then sell to other thieves for a profit."

Jewel let out a trilling laugh. She had clad her lean form in supple riding leathers dyed the same dusky violet color as her eyes. "You're angry only because I thought of the idea first."

"Actually, *I* thought of it first," Cormik grumbled. "You just run faster."

"Enough!" Mari shouted, holding up her hands. "It doesn't matter who thought of the idea first, because neither of you is coming with us." She looked to Morhion for support. "Am I right?"

"Actually, Mari, both Cormik and Jewel have many connections in the underworld—connections that may prove useful in our search for Stiletto."

She shot the mage a withering look. "Can't you be on my side just once, Morhion?"

He gave her a mysterious smile. "Perhaps I'll surprise you some day."

It was decided. Their plan was simple enough. They would attempt to follow Caledan's trail, asking questions about Stiletto along the way. Morhion had discovered an incantation in *The Book of the Shadows*, an incantation that could be spoken only by one with shadow magic who held the Shadowstar. If they gained the Shadowstar first, Kellen could recite the spell and reverse Caledan's transformation. At least, so Morhion believed.

But if Caledan reached the Shadowstar before them . . .

Well, it was best not to consider that possibility, for if Caledan completed his metamorphosis, Morhion was not certain anything could stop him.

Soon the five gathered before the gateway. The horses

had balked at being led down the stone staircase, prompting Mari to scold her chestnut gelding, Farenth. He was a prideful beast and, thus insulted, decided to prove his mettle. When Farenth pranced down the steps, the other horses followed willingly: Morhion's jet-black stallion, Tenebrous; Jewel's fine-boned mare, Pearl, named for the white mark on her forehead; and Cormik's sturdy brown destrier, Plinth. Jewel and Cormik had brought a shaggy pony with them for extra supplies, and this provided a perfect mount for Kellen. The pony was a quick and lively creature that Kellen named Flash.

Morhion guided Tenebrous toward the blank stone archway and spread his hands. He concentrated, then spoke a single word, "*Avarra!*," which meant "open" in the language of magic.

The rough stone within the arch rippled, blurred, then seemed to melt away like mist. A series of rolling hills beneath a sharp azure sky appeared beyond the arch. Sunlight spilled thick and golden as honey over the dun-colored landscape. Faintly, Morhion heard the soft hiss of wind through dry autumn grass.

"Quickly," he said through clenched teeth. "I cannot hold the gateway open for long."

Hastily, the others rode under the arch. Sweat pouring down his brow, Morhion was the last, spurring Tenebrous through the magical portal. As he passed through, a thin curtain of cold washed over him, momentarily taking his breath away. He found the others on the other side, looking vaguely ill. It was disconcerting to ride a few dozen feet yet find oneself over sixty leagues away. By horse, the village of Corm Orp lay seven days north of Iriaebor. Vast distances were nothing to the gateway. There were still many of these scattered across the Realms. A man could travel instantly between any of them if he knew the right spells. And if he was lucky, Morhion added to himself.

"It worked," Morhion murmured in relief.

Cormik gaped at him. "You mean there was a chance it wouldn't?" he asked. "What might have happened?"

"I really don't think you want to know," Morhion replied acerbically. Looking decidedly queasy, Cormik didn't push the point.

Morhion turned his horse around to face the gateway hovering in the air between two wind-worn standing stones. Through the arch, Morhion could see the chamber beneath his tower.

"*Bahadra!*" he spoke, adding a sharp gesture—"close" in the tongue of magic. With a flash, the gateway shut. Now, all that could be seen between the standing stones were wave after wave of hills marching toward a distant line of jagged purple peaks. The Sunset Mountains.

"Let's go," Morhion said, turning his back to the mountains. He spurred Tenebrous into a gallop, and the others followed behind.

The five rode into Corm Orp with the long shadows of sunset. At first glance, the village seemed pitifully small, no more than a score of stone buildings clustered around a wide place in the Dusk Road, which led from Iriaebor in the south all the way to the city of Elturel to the west. However, a closer look showed that the low hills bordering the vale were dotted with numerous brightly painted doors. Most of Corm Orp's residents were halflings, and the diminutive folk preferred to dwell in their snug underground burrows rather than in drafty aboveground houses like the big folk.

As they rode into town, the companions noticed what seemed to be signs of a bad fire. Broad swaths of the village commons were blackened and barren, and several stone houses had been twisted into grotesque lumps as if they had been melted by a terrible heat. The five travelers

made for the village inn, a blocky, comfortable stone building that leaned against a steep slope. Inside, the Green
Door was much larger than it appeared, for it extended
back into the hillside and thus had rooms that would
appeal to halfling as well as human patrons.

The companions stepped into the common room and
were treated to several dozen suspicious stares. The barkeeper was the only human in the establishment; all of
the patrons were stout, broad-faced halflings.

"I suppose this rules out appearing inconspicuous and
mingling, loves," Jewel murmured.

"What ever gave you that idea?" Cormik replied acidly.

The halflings whispered to each other nervously, casting sideways glances at the newcomers. The barkeeper
glared at them as he slammed several pots of ale onto the
table where they had sat. It was clear that strangers
were not welcome.

"I wish Estah were here," Mari sighed in exasperation.
"She could tell us what we're doing wrong."

A halfling man at the next table looked up in surprise.
"Estah?" he said in amazement. "You know Estah of the
Dreaming Dragon?"

Almost instantly, the atmosphere in the common room
changed. Numerous questions were flung out excitedly,
and when the patrons learned that Mari and Morhion
were in fact part of the legendary Fellowship of the
Dreaming Dragon, the occasion turned into something of
a celebration. Estah, it seemed, was a local hero. Morhion
had forgotten that the halfling woman had grown up in
Corm Orp. Within minutes, he and the others had been
introduced to a dozen smiling halflings, each claiming to
be Estah's cousin. However, when Mari asked about the
strange happenings at the recent Harvest Festival,
things turned somber once again.

The halfling who had first spoken to them finally

answered Mari's question. His name was Tam Acorn, and he was one of Estah's multitudinous cousins.

"It was the stranger," Tam said grimly. "He was the cause of all the dark happenings. A man in black on a pale horse."

The companions exchanged glances. There was no need say the name aloud.

"Can you tell us what happened?" Mari asked urgently.

Tam scratched his chin in thought, then began to describe the mayhem that had resulted from the stranger's wild music, and from the shadows.

Tam took his time, drawing out the tale. "We were lucky none of the village folk were touched by the shadowbeasts," he said finally, his voice hoarse with freshly remembered fear.

There was a long moment of silence. Finally, Mari leaned toward the halfling man. "How long ago?" she asked fiercely. "How long ago did all this happen?"

"Why, the festival was only five nights ago."

Mari looked at Morhion. He nodded in understanding. They had found Caledan's trail, and he was only five days ahead of them.

The following morning, they rode north out of Corm Orp in the pearly light of dawn, hoping to pick up Caledan's trail along the Dusk Road. The morning was bright and cold. Frost glittered on the ground like a sprinkling of crushed glass, and the dome of the sky was as hard and blue as a cobalt porcelain bowl. Periodically, they dismounted to search for any trace of Caledan's passing—all except Cormik, who stayed on his horse.

After this pattern was repeated a few times, Jewel made a disparaging remark to the patch-eyed man. "Tell me, my dear, bloated whale, are you afraid that if you get off your horse, you might not be able to get back on?"

"Not in the least, my sweet, witless strumpet," he said

indignantly. "Unlike some of us, who in their senescence have become as nearsighted as a geriatric bat, I can see just fine from up here."

Jewel looked unconvinced. Indeed, getting Cormik onto Plinth's back that morning had been an arduous ordeal involving a fair amount of pushing, grunting, cursing, and—on the part of Morhion—a minor spell of levitation.

"Let's move on," Mari said in frustration. "There's nothing here."

"Many people travel the Dusk Road," Morhion said grimly. "In five days, all traces of Caledan's passage could have been obliterated."

Mari gave a tight-lipped nod but said nothing as she climbed back into the saddle. They nudged their horses into a trot, starting once more down the road.

It was midmorning, and the autumn day was turning fine, when Morhion noticed that only four horses were trotting down the dirt road. Kellen was missing.

"He must have fallen back," Mari said worriedly after Morhion called the others to a halt.

"Then we'd better go find him, and fast," Cormik said darkly. "I wouldn't be surprised if there were thieves on the road. Other than ourselves, I mean."

They wheeled their horses around and thundered back down the road. As they rounded a bend and skidded to an abrupt stop, Kellen's pony let out a whinny and trotted toward them, trailing his reins. Flash's saddle was empty. Mari shot Morhion a fearful look. Unpleasant possibilities were numerous. Thieves were not the only perils in the wilderness. Morhion swore inwardly. If Kellen was hurt—or worse—he would never . . .

Jewel called out, "Over here, loves!" and the others hastily spurred their mounts in her direction. They found Kellen kneeling by the side of the dirt road, peering at something amid a tangle of brambles and witchgrass.

Morhion allowed himself a sigh of relief. "What are you doing, Kellen?" he asked sternly.

"I've found something," Kellen indicated solemnly.

The others exchanged curious glances, then dismounted and approached, pushing aside the underbrush to get a glimpse of Kellen's discovery.

By the looks of it, the milestone was very old. It was cracked and sunk halfway into the ground. Centuries of wind and rain had almost completely worn away the words carved into its surface. Yet it was not the basalt monolith's sense of age that made the companions stare. It was the face. The milestone had been grotesquely distorted, much like the stone houses in Corm Orp. One of its four surfaces bore a human visage. The image was crude and half-formed, as though it had melted before resolidifying. Yet its expression was vivid, a look of utter sorrow.

It was Cormik who finally spoke. In a low voice he said, "Well, at least now we know Caledan came this way."

Morhion drew out the ruby amulet he had forged. A spark flickered deep in the heart of the gem. Cormik was right.

Mari shook her head. "By the gods—look at it. The face is so unspeakably sad. He knows what's happening to him, doesn't he? He knows what he's becoming . . ." Her words trailed off.

"We should try to reach Hill's Edge before nightfall," Morhion said finally. "If Caledan continues to follow the road, people there will notice him."

Somberly, the others agreed. They thundered down the Dusk Road, leaving the eerie face of sorrow far behind.

Nine

The rolling landscape slipped by in a blur of russet, brown, and burnished copper. As the afternoon wore on, dark clouds moved in from the west, accompanied by the low drumming of thunder. Soon the light began to fail, turning a dusky green. A storm was coming. Morhion tilted his head back, letting the wind tangle through his long hair. He loved storms. Like all wizards, he had a passion for gaudy displays of power.

Eventually the travelers realized they were not going to make Hill's Edge before dark. Morhion raised a hand, signaling the party to a halt. "We had better find shelter for the night," he advised.

They dismounted and began scouting to either side of the Dusk Road. It was almost dark when Jewel called out over the rising gale. The thief led the others into a nearby aspen grove where slender, leafless trees danced in the wind. In the center of the grove, in a massive granite outcrop, was the dim mouth of a cave. Just then, a bolt of lightning rent the sky, and the first cold drops of rain began to fall.

"I checked it out," Jewel shouted above the roar of the storm. "It's dry and goes back only a dozen paces. Plus," she added with a grin, "it doesn't appear to be inhabited."

Tethering the horses under the shelter of a tall pine, they headed into the cave. They spread their bedrolls on the sandy floor and soon had a cheerful fire burning, making the place warm and almost snug. Mari volunteered to cook and was soon stirring a bubbling pot.

Cormik rubbed his chubby hands gleefully. "So, what are we having for supper, Mari? Poached pheasant eggs seasoned with saffron? Braised fillet of young wyvern? Or perhaps"—he shivered with anticipation—"hummingbird tongues in a reduction of white wine and cloves?"

"Stew," Mari replied flatly. "We're having stew."

"*Stew?*" Cormik repeated the word distastefully. "I'm not sure what that is, but I must say I really don't care for the sound of it."

Apparently he didn't care for the taste of it either. While everyone else ate heartily, Cormik picked at the contents of the wooden bowl in his lap, periodically letting out a despondent sigh. He clutched his expansive stomach. "I'm going to waste away to nothing, you know."

As usual, everyone ignored him.

The fire was burning low and they had just lain down to sleep when the whinnies of frightened horses drifted through the mouth of the cave.

"It's probably just the storm," Mari whispered, "but they sound really upset."

Morhion stood up. "I'll go." Wrapping his cloak tightly around himself, he headed out into the stormy night.

Cold rain lashed at Morhion, and in moments he was soaked to the skin. Every few seconds, a white flash of lightning tore apart the darkness. He struggled against the violent wind, finally reaching the tree where they had tethered the horses. The animals were pawing at the ground, snorting and rolling their eyes. Morhion peered into the night but could see nothing save the wildly swaying trees. He stroked the horses, calming them, and led them around the tree where they would be more protected. Instructing his onyx stallion, Tenebrous, to keep an eye on the other beasts, Morhion headed back.

He stepped inside the cave and instantly knew that something was wrong.

The cave was silent and dark, the air acrid with the stench of smoke, as if the fire had been hastily kicked out. With a whispered word, Morhion conjured a pale sphere of magelight in his hand. Even before its faint, purple glow filled the cave, he knew what he would see.

Mari, Kellen, Cormik, and Jewel were gone.

The cave's sandy floor was churned up, as if there had been some sort of struggle. Yet where had the assailants come from? And to where had his friends disappeared?

Cautiously, Morhion moved deeper into the cave. Then he saw it—a thin crack in the rear wall. He approached, examining the fissure more closely. It was the outline of a door. Something was jammed into the crack. He reached down to pluck out the tuft of dark fur that had kept the portal from shutting completely.

There was only one possible conclusion. Some sort of creature—or creatures—had abducted his companions. Without hesitating, Morhion pushed against the door. The ponderous slab of rock did not budge. He threw all his weight against it, but to no avail.

Morhion glowered at the door. He was a wizard, not a warrior. He was trained to use his mind, not his body. Kneeling, he examined the floor in front of the portal. A half-circle had been scratched into the sand. Blue eyes glittering, he rose. He studied the door for a moment more, then placed his hand precisely along the center of the slab's left edge. He pressed lightly. The door pivoted smoothly on a central axis, revealing a dark opening beyond. He allowed himself a brief smile of victory, then plunged into the passageway. Magelight bobbing before him, Morhion moved swiftly down a twisting stone tunnel. Soon he realized he was traveling at a downward angle, deep into the bones of the world.

In his haste, he nearly tripped over the corpse. He bent down in dread, fearing the body might be that of one of his friends. It was not. Whatever the creature was, it had been dead for several days. The sweet scent of decay rose from the corpse in sickening waves. The being's form was so twisted—a grotesque melange of dark fur, sharp teeth, and rippling flesh—that it could not possibly have lived and functioned like this. Morhion did not know what sort of beast this had once been, but something had distorted its body, molding it into this hideous shape as it died.

The mage drew the ruby amulet out from beneath his shirt. As he moved the amulet toward the corpse, a faint spark flickered in the heart of the gem. He whispered a single grim word.

"Caledan . . ."

Quickly, Morhion leapt over the rotting corpse and continued down the tunnel. Soon he came upon another horribly twisted creature. Then another, and another, until he lost count. As the ruby amulet proved, all had been metamorphosed by Caledan's chaotic shadow magic. Without doubt, Caldorien had come this way several days ago. But was he still here? Heart pounding, the mage ran on.

The walls dropped away to either side, and Morhion sensed a vast space extending before him. Abruptly, he ducked behind the cover of a sharp stalagmite. While his magelight reached only a dozen feet in each direction, he could see farther. Much farther.

A livid green phosphorescence glowed in the air, emanating from a feathery moss that clung to the stones all around. In the faint light, Morhion saw that he was on the edge of a vast cavern. A jagged chasm ran across the cavern, and on the other side of the defile was a writhing sea of furred flesh and sharp teeth.

Gibberlings.

Morhion had never before laid eyes on the beasts, but he had read about them. Gibberlings were not sophisticated creatures. Their gaping maws and huge teeth left little room for brains in their doglike skulls. They walked on two legs and, although they were no more than four feet tall, their furry bodies were stocky and thick with muscle. Even so, two or three gibberlings were no match for a skilled warrior or a trained mage. On the other hand, gibberlings rarely attacked in twos or threes. Their strength was in numbers, and when they attacked, they did so in a growling, slavering horde that consumed everything in its path.

Morhion scanned the mass of gibberlings on the other side of the chasm. It was difficult to get a fix on their number, but there had to be at least a hundred of the creatures. They cavorted around a raised slab of stone. Swearing softly, Morhion saw the reason. Cormik lay sprawled upon the slab, trussed like a piglet ready for roasting. Beyond Cormik, inside a natural cage formed of stalactites and stalagmites, Morhion glimpsed three other pale faces. Mari, Kellen, and Jewel. No doubt the gibberlings intended to feast on all their victims, with Cormik, the juiciest of the lot, as the first course.

As Morhion watched, a gibberling stuffed an apple into Cormik's mouth, silencing the rotund thief's colorful swearing. Cormik struggled uselessly against the crude bonds of twisted fur that encircled his wrists and ankles.

Morhion knew he had little time to act. A natural stone bridge spanned the deep chasm. However, crossing it would leave Morhion utterly exposed; the gibberlings would see him coming. There had to be another way.

An idea struck him. On his stomach, he crept to the near end of the stone bridge. He whispered the words of a spell, and his hands began to glow with a magical purple aura. Leaning over the precipice, Morhion reached down, stretching his hands toward the rough underside of the bridge. All of a sudden he lost his balance and slid over the edge. Cracking his body like a whip, he thrust his hands upward. His fingers brushed the underside of the bridge . . . and dug into the stone as if it were soft clay.

Hanging from his arms beneath the bridge, Morhion gritted his teeth and—thanks to the spell of rock-gripping he had cast—dug his fingers deeper into the stone. Hand over hand he edged forward, first plunging one hand into the stone, then pulling the other out and swinging forward under the narrow stone arch. The chasm yawned darkly beneath his dangling boots, and he forced himself to keep his gaze fixed ahead. His arms began to ache fiercely, and by the time he was halfway across, his shoulders seemed on fire. Over and over in his mind, he recited an old litany of concentration he had learned as an apprentice mage. He did not dare think what would happen if he let go of the stone.

Morhion was startled when he brushed up against a rough cliff face. He had reached the far end of the bridge. Vicious snarls echoed on the dank air. Forcing his throbbing arms to work, Morhion pulled himself upward, heaving his body onto the bridge. Gasping, he leapt to his feet. A trio of gibberlings stood mere paces away. Pointed ears pricking up, the stocky beasts heard him and turned around, their maws gaping ravenously.

Morhion was already moving. He kicked out, planting a boot squarely on one gibberling's canine face. Short limbs flailing, it tumbled over the side of the bridge and vanished into the gloom below. Another beast lunged for him, only to find the mage's knife buried in its throat. Morhion pulled the blade free. Squealing, the creature stumbled backward into its companion. In a snarling collision of fur and claws, the two gibberlings fell off the bridge and plunged into the defile.

Morhion looked up. The remaining gibberlings had closed in on Cormik, ready to begin their feast. One beast held his chubby leg in front of its open mouth, preparing to take a big bite. Desperate, Morhion let out a whooping battle cry. Startled by the sound, the creatures turned around, and Morhion found himself facing a hundred long-muzzled faces. For a frozen moment, nothing moved. Then, as one, the gibberlings sprang toward their new prey.

Morhion was way ahead of them.

"Darakka!" he shouted, thrusting his arms out before him. Crackling bolts of purple lightning sprang from Morhion's fingertips. Yips and howls of agony filled the air, along with the reek of singed fur. The magical lightning dissipated, leaving in its wake a wide swath of dead gibberlings. Morhion wasted no time. He pick·d his way over the heaps of smoldering bodies and leapt onto the slab beside the quivering Cormik. Those gibberlings scorched but not slain by the spell ran around in circles, snarling and snapping at others in pain and fear. The mayhem gave Morhion a chance to cut Cormik's bonds.

Cormik lurched to his feet, pulling the apple from his mouth and flinging it away. "I do like food," he gasped, "but not when I'm the main course."

Already the gibberlings were recovering from the blast, and some recalled their prey. Morhion slashed out with his knife, keeping several of the beasts from leaping onto the platform. Cormik drew a jeweled dagger long enough to serve as a short sword and plunged it into the belly of another gibberling. It fell howling into the crowd. Instantly, several other gibberlings set upon the creature and tore it apart in a gory feast.

"We've got to free the others," Morhion said urgently, waving his knife at an advancing gibberling.

"I suppose you want me to go," Cormik complained as he eviscerated another of the creatures. "Very well, but do cover me. And remember, gibberlings don't like bright lights."

One of the disgusting creatures clambered onto the slab right in front of Morhion, its open maw dripping saliva. The mage kicked out, shattering its jaw and throwing it backward. Concentrating for a moment, he muttered the arcane words of a spell. A spark shot up from his hand, bursting overhead in a ball of radiance that hovered in the air like a tiny sun.

Immediately, the gibberlings descended into bedlam. The creatures cowered against the light, yowling and whining piteously, frantically running around in small circles. Cormik wasted no time. He hiked up his robe in distaste, stepping on the flat heads of some of the sniveling, prostrate creatures, knocking others aside as he made his way toward the stone cage where Mari, Kellen, and Jewel were imprisoned.

A huge boulder covered the only exit from the prison. "It took a score of them to push the boulder into place," Mari shouted through a gap in the stones. "We'll never be able to move it!"

"I wasn't thinking of moving it," Cormik replied. Grunting, he picked up a large rock and hurled it against the cage's stalagmite bars. The thin columns of stone cracked. Face puffed and red with effort, Cormik hefted

another rock and heaved it at the cage. This time two of
the stalagmites shattered, creating an opening wide
enough for the three to scramble through.

"Thanks for getting the door, Cormik," Jewel said
brightly as she climbed out of the cage. "You're a perfect
gentleman."

"I think I've given myself a hernia," Cormik groaned.

The gibberlings still cowered under the brilliant magical light, and Morhion took the opportunity to climb off
the platform. Something crunched beneath his boot. He
looked down and saw that it was an old skull. A human
skull. Bones were strewn around the stone slab, along
with bits of armor and rusted weapons—the remains of
past meals. A glint of silver caught Morhion's eye. Bend-
ing down, he picked up a metal cylinder. A wax seal covered one end of the silver tube. Morhion broke the seal,
and a curled piece of parchment slipped out. Carefully
unrolling the paper, he saw that it was covered with the
spidery writing of magic. A wizard's scroll. The spell
inscribed there was not one that Morhion recognized. It
seemed to have something to do with . . . feathers.

"Morhion!" Mari cried out. "The gibberlings are getting
used to the light."

Morhion looked up, shoving the scroll into a pocket of
his vest. Mari was right. Shading their beady eyes with
clawed hands, some of the furry creatures were climbing
to their feet. Others were already shambling forward.
Their hunger was stronger than their fear. A few of the
braver gibberlings advanced on Mari and the others,
gnashing yellow fangs. Hastily, Morhion cast another
spell, and a flurry of blazing purple sparks whirled in the
air. The sparks quickly sizzled through fur to the creatures' tender flesh. The gibberlings snarled and rolled,
batting their paws against their smoldering pelts.
Morhion quickly moved toward the others.

"Duck!" Mari shouted as he drew near.

Without hesitating, he crouched down. Mari swung her short sword, neatly decapitating two gibberlings who had been just about to pounce on the mage's back.

"We have to get back to the bridge!" Jewel exclaimed, waving a curved dagger to keep a slavering gibberling away from a wide-eyed Kellen.

Morhion concurred, but now dozens of the creatures were braving the light to close in around the companions, and more joined them every second. He slashed his knife at one of the creatures, cutting a mortal gash in its side. In moments the things would overwhelm them with sheer numbers.

"We've got to do something!" Mari grunted as she brought her sword down in a slashing arc. Her blow cleaved a gibberling in two, revealing the creature's inner anatomy, which consisted largely of stomach. Mari slashed again, and Morhion noticed something interesting. Chittering with terror, several gibberlings had scrambled away from a shadow on the cavern wall—Mari's shadow, cast by the magical sphere of light. He wondered . . .

"Kellen, can you bring our shadows on the wall to life?" he asked quickly. "Make them large, and turn them into frightening shapes?"

Kellen nodded gravely.

"But there's no need to bother with Cormik's shadow, love," Jewel added glibly as she yanked her dagger out of a dying gibberling. "It's already frighteningly large as it is."

Cormik glowered at the impertinent thief, but before he could utter a biting retort, Kellen had lifted his flute and begun to play a haunting melody. Their shadows moved on the cavern's rough stone wall. The five silhouettes expanded, looming like twisted giants as they stretched out long, menacing arms.

Instantly, howls of fear rose from the army of gibberlings. The creatures abandoned their prey as they bit and clawed each other in a frantic effort to escape the undulating shadows.

"Keep playing, Kellen!" Morhion shouted above the cacophony. "It's working!"

"They're not very intelligent creatures," he called out, "but they do remember what they're afraid of. I think they encountered Caledan a few days ago, and now they are terrified of shadows. For good reason."

The gibberlings were dispersing, scurrying into tunnels and crevices.

"Come on!" Morhion shouted. "I think we can make it to the bridge now."

As they pushed their way through the panicked horde toward the stone arch, a stray claw sliced a shallow gouge in Mari's leg. Kellen's face was gray and strained, but he did not stop playing. The shadows continued to writhe threateningly on the cavern wall.

At last they reached the bridge. The narrow span of stone was swarming with fleeing gibberlings, all snarling and scratching in an effort to climb over each other.

"We'll never make it across *that*," Cormik said in disgust.

"Allow me to clear the way," Morhion replied with mock congeniality. Fluid words of magic tumbled from his lips, and a small crimson sphere appeared in his hand. As Morhion finished the incantation, he hurled the sphere at the bridge. It sped through the air, expanding rapidly into a huge, blazing ball of fire.

The creatures never knew what hit them. The fireball raced along the length of the bridge, igniting everything in its path and exploding in searing flame when it hit the far end. Engulfed in fire, scores of the creatures careened off the bridge, plunging into the chasm like shooting stars. When the smoke cleared, the bridge was empty. Only a thin layer of ashes covered its scorched surface.

"After you, Cormik," Morhion said graciously.

"You're too kind," he replied with a nasty grin as he stepped onto the bridge.

A sharp *crack!* resounded on the air. The bridge shook violently as a jagged line snaked across its surface. As they watched in horror, more cracks spread out from the fissure. Chunks of stone broke off the edges of the arch, dropping into the void. The bridge was collapsing. Jewel grabbed Cormik's belt and pulled the crime lord backward just as the rock beneath his boots crumbled. There was another sharp, rending sound. All at once, the bridge disintegrated, collapsing into the darkness below.

"The fireball," Mari murmured, gazing at the now-impassable chasm. "The heat of it must have weakened the bridge."

Morhion scratched his chin, giving the others a sheepish look. "Everyone makes mistakes now and then."

"This one was a doozy, love," Jewel commented smartly.

"Thanks," the mage replied.

Kellen lowered his flute for a moment. "Morhion," he said breathlessly. "The orb of light, it's fading." He raised his flute and resumed playing.

The others looked up. Sure enough, the ball of magical light Morhion had conjured was beginning to flicker. The shadows on the wall were growing dim. Already some of the gibberlings were creeping back out of their hiding places, eyeing the receding shadows warily as they edged toward the companions. Soon there would be nothing to hold back the horde.

"Hurry, Morhion," Mari said. "You've got to cast the light spell again."

"And I presume you're going to rewrite the rules of

magic so I can do this?" he replied acidly. "Once a mage has cast a spell, he cannot cast it again until he has relearned the incantation. And something tells me I don't have the time."

The globe of light flickered alarmingly. The shadows were barely visible on the wall now. More gibberlings crept from their holes and crevices, then still more. With grim expressions, the humans backed slowly toward the edge of the precipice, weapons raised. The drooling horde closed in.

Kellen lowered his flute. "There goes the light!" he cried.

Above them, the glowing sphere flickered erratically. In seconds the spell would expire. It was hopeless.

Or was it? Morhion sheathed his knife and drew out the scroll he had found. He didn't know exactly what the spell did—that would take hours of study to learn—but he had a hunch.

"Everybody, sheathe your weapons and hold on to me!" he shouted.

The others just stared at him.

"Do it!" he commanded fiercely.

Startled, they did as they were told. Morhion wasted no time. He lifted the scroll and began to read the arcane incantation in the fading light. Just as he was speaking the final words, the hovering sphere of magical light vanished in a puff of smoke, plunging the cavern into darkness. Chittering with glee, the gibberlings rushed forward, ready to gobble up their prey.

"Now jump!" Morhion cried.

He leapt backward off the cliff. The others were too surprised to stop him. Clutching the mage, they toppled over the precipice with him, screaming as they plummeted into the darkness below. Above, the thwarted gibberlings howled in dismay.

It will be now or never, Morhion thought in panic.

For a split second, as they fell through the chill dark, speeding toward a bloody death on sharp stones below, it seemed as if they would all die. Suddenly, the scroll in Morhion's hand burst into flame and was consumed as the magic of the spell was released. A heartbeat later, the five reached the bottom of the chasm. However, instead of being dashed upon jagged stone teeth, they found themselves cushioned by a blast of warm air that came from nowhere. The gust of air dissipated as quickly as it had appeared, lowering the five safely—if not gently—to the hard ground.

Slowly, Morhion got to his feet, smiling. His hunch had proved right.

Dazed, the others pulled themselves to their feet, blinking as their eyes adjusted once more to the dim green phosphorescence that filled the cavern, trying to understand what had happened.

A dark shape dropped down from on high, striking the bottom of the defile with a loud *plop!* Moments later, another shape fell from above, and then another, all landing disconcertingly close to the companions.

"It's the gibberlings," Mari breathed in amazement. "They're jumping after us!"

"Remarkable," Cormik muttered in awe. "They're even more stupid than I thought."

In seconds, it was raining gibberlings. The creatures shrieked and snarled as they fell, striking the ground with wet *thud*s and dying instantly. Dodging the deadly rain of doomed gibberlings, the five picked their way along the bottom of the chasm.

At last they left the grisly cascade of furry creatures behind. Before long, Jewel caught a faint whiff of fresh air. They ducked into a side tunnel and soon stumbled out of the granite hill and into the night. The storm had

ended; now tatters of clouds raced across a moonlit sky.
The companions leaned against the rain-slick rocks,
catching their breath.

"You know, Jewel," Cormik grumbled, "that was without
doubt the worst campsite at which I have ever had
the displeasure of spending a night."

"Well, you can pick the next one if you think it's so
easy, love," Jewel replied tartly.

Cormik opened his mouth for a scathing retort, but
Morhion held up a hand. He had had enough for one
night.

"Let's just go find the horses," he said wearily, and that
was what they did.

Ten

K'shar had always loved the night.
The golden moon of midnight hovered above the low stone buildings of Twilight Hall, its pale-wine illumination conjuring as many purple shadows as it banished. Somewhere in the distance, a nightingale sang in sweet mourning. And despite the lateness of the year, the wild perfume of nightflowers wafted on the wind. Silent and wraithlike, K'shar moved from one pool of darkness to the next, piercing the gloom easily with eyes as brilliant and golden as the moon above. He was at home in the dark; but then, darkness was in his blood.

Twilight Hall, which stood on a green hill in the center of the city of Berdusk, was the western stronghold of the Harpers. It was not, as its name implied, merely a large meadhall or gathering place, but rather consisted of a number of stone buildings clustered around a central courtyard. Yet there was more to Twilight Hall than even this, for much of the compound lay beneath the ground—

including the dusky meeting hall for which the Harper
fortress was named. Though K'shar had joined the
Harpers more than twenty years earlier, he had spent
little of that time in Twilight Hall itself. Most of his days
were spent traveling the Heartlands, hunting down such
prey—be it Zhentarim, Red Wizards, or goblin lords—as
the Harpers commanded. K'shar was the best Hunter the
Harpers had. This was not a matter of pride, just fact.

Tonight, K'shar was to learn the details of his latest
assignment. He could only hope that his new quarry
would prove more interesting than the last several. It
had been long since he felt challenged by one of his
adversaries. The Red Wizards of Thay were always over-
confident and thus easily tracked; the Zhentarim were
simply stupid. Again and again, the fugitives were too
easily caught, too easily slain. When they lay dead at his
feet, his blood had only just begun to surge with the passion of the chase, and he was left feeling hollow and
unfulfilled. Perhaps, he thought—and not for the first
time—he should leave the Harpers. Perhaps he should
seek out challenges more worthy of his talents.

K'shar pushed aside these foolish, discontented
thoughts. He was bored, that was all. As soon as he
began the chase again, he would feel better.

K'shar approached the compound's central building
and stepped into the pool of torchlight by the main door.
Two young Harpers stood guard at the portal, and by the
surprise on their faces, he knew they had not heard his
soft approach. He bared white teeth in a feral smile.
Apprentices! he thought wryly.

The young Harpers did not recognize him—this was
not surprising, given the rarity of his visits to Twilight
Hall—but after examining his letter of summons from
Belhuar Thantarth they let him enter, their eyes wide
and respectful. K'shar wound his way down through a

dim labyrinth of corridors and staircases until he reached a pair of gilded doors. Without hesitating, he pushed them open, striding into the Great Hall beyond.

Instantly, a dozen pairs of eyes riveted upon him. K'shar was striking to look at. He knew this, even as he dismissed it as meaningless. His skin was a deep, burnished color, like ancient bronze; his golden eyes were eerily at odds with his colorless, close-cropped hair. He was unusually tall and thin, a fact accentuated by the tight-fitting black leather he wore, but he showed none of the awkward gangliness that usually afflicted such individuals. Rather, his leanly muscled limbs seemed like supple whips. His slightly pointed ears, tilted eyes, and uncanny grace betrayed the elven blood that mingled with the human in his veins.

The cavernous Great Hall was of ingenious construction. Hewn by dwarven stonesmiths out of the surrounding rock, it seemed not a cavern at all, but a dusky, primeval forest. Countless columns were carved to resemble trees, their stone branches stretching to support the high ceiling. The walls were covered with lifelike leaves of copper and gold that seemed to flutter in the flickering illumination of the rushlights scattered about the hall. The floor, of mottled green-and-brown marble, added to the illusion.

Belhuar Thantarth looked up as K'shar approached. The Master Harper was holding council—hence the presence of so many Harpers in the hall—but when he spotted K'shar, he quickly dismissed the others with a wave of his hand. In moments, Thantarth and K'shar were alone in the stone forest.

"K'shar, I am glad you could come." Thantarth's deep voice echoed in the now-empty hall.

K'shar inclined his head slightly. "It is my duty to serve the Harpers," he said formally, even as a part of

him wondered if this was truly so. Was his duty to the
Harpers, or simply to the chase?

"It is with a heavy heart that I set this task before you,
K'shar," Thantarth said somberly. "For both of those
whom we ask you to seek are—or at least *were,* until
recently—among the most exalted of Harpers."

While K'shar listened with growing interest, Thantarth
explained what had transpired. There wasn't a Harper
alive who had not heard the tale of the Shadowking in
Iriaebor. The deeds of Caledan Caldorien and Mari
Al'maren were heroic folklore passed down to all Harper
apprentices. Thus it was all the more shocking—and
intriguing—that K'shar's new prey were none other than
these two legendary figures, now turned renegade.

"Caledan's transformation must be stopped at any
cost," Thantarth finished firmly. "Whatever his deeds of
the past, the Harpers cannot allow a shadowking to walk
the Heartlands once more. Mari Al'maren has forsworn
her vow as a Harper, and we can assume she will attempt
to protect Caledan. While your mission is to find and
destroy Caldorien, you are also authorized to . . . dispose
of Al'maren should she block your way." Thantarth
appeared troubled, but his expression was resolute. "Do
you accept this mission, K'shar?"

"I accept it, Master Thantarth." K'shar spoke the
words without emotion, but inwardly his heart soared.
He could not believe his luck! He had longed for a mission that would test his skills, and now Thantarth had
ordered him to hunt down two of the greatest heroes the
Harpers had ever known. While it was regrettable that
two such extraordinary individuals must die, K'shar felt
no personal sorrow. Such decisions were beyond him. He
was simply a Hunter.

Thantarth handed K'shar a scroll containing details of
the mission. The half-elf scanned it quickly with his

sharp, golden eyes. Rumors placed Caldorien in Corm
Orp five days ago, and a Harper agent dispatched to Iriaebor reported that Al'maren had vanished. No doubt
she had already gone to pursue Caldorien. Last on the
parchment was a warning of the perils of Caldorien's
mysterious shadow magic. This part K'shar read hastily.
What did he, a creature so at home in the night, have to
fear from shadows? He handed the parchment back to
Thantarth.

"When will you leave?" the Master Harper asked.
"With the dawn?"

"No," K'shar said softly. "Now."

"Very well. I'll see to a horse and provisions for—"

But K'shar had already turned, moving swiftly from
the Great Hall. He needed no mount, no food, no weapons.
There was no horse that could run faster or farther than
K'shar, no sustenance he needed that the land would not
provide, and no weapon deadlier than his own two hands.
He headed outside, quickly leaving behind Twilight Hall
and the city of Berdusk. Soon the dark wall of the Reaching Woods loomed before him in the gloom. He stood on
the edge of a vast, ancient forest that stretched all the
way from Berdusk to the village of Corm Orp, sixty
leagues to the northeast. He would be in Corm Orp by
sunrise two days hence.

K'shar glanced once at the stars to fix his bearings.
Then, like a stag taking flight, he plunged into the trees,
running swiftly, tirelessly, and without sound. Something
told him that this was going to be the hunt of a lifetime.

* * * * *

It was twilight on the day after their battle with the
gibberlings when the companions reached the trading
town of Hill's Edge. They crested a rise and saw a small

cluster of lights shining in the gloom below, next to a sinuous strip of onyx that Morhion said was the River
Reaching.

"You might want to take off your Harper badge, Mari,"
Cormik advised. "Hill's Edge is near the west end of Yellow
Snake Pass, which means it's crawling with Zhentarim.
The Black Network seems to think the pass is their own
personal highway through the Sunset Mountains."

Mari gave the patch-eyed man a sharp look. "Thanks,
Cormik, but aren't you forgetting something?" She gestured to the collar of her jacket, where in the past she
had proudly worn the badge of the Harpers.

Cormik gave her a sheepish grin. "Sorry, my dear. I'm
afraid I forgot."

"Are we growing senile already?" Jewel inquired conde-
scendingly.

He gritted his teeth. "No, we aren't. But we *are* growing a trifle irritable."

"Speak for yourself," Jewel said with a bright laugh.
"Personally, I'm having fun."

They guided their mounts into town, searching for a
place to stay the night. Cormik was right. They scouted
out five inns, and each showed signs of Zhentarim occu-
pation. While Mari no longer wore the moon-and-harp
symbol, her face was known among the Zhentarim. The
last thing they needed was to be delayed by an encounter
with the Black Network. It looked as though they were
going to have to spend the night outdoors.

"Oh, good," Cormik grumbled. "I simply adore sleeping
on the ground. I can't tell you how much I love getting all
those dry, prickly bits of moss stuck down my shirt."

Everyone ignored him.

They rode out to the western edge of town, toward the
bridge over the River Reaching. On the way, they passed
one last inn—the Five Rings, according to the brightly

painted sign. They almost rode by without examining the place, then stopped, more out of a sense of duty than any hope that this establishment would prove different than the others.

Mari suddenly gave an abrupt laugh. "This place will do just fine," she told the others.

"Let me guess," Cormik said dryly. "Either you know something we don't, or you've suddenly been blessed by magical powers of prescience."

"Er, the first one," Mari replied glibly. She pointed to the upper left corner of the inn's front door, where a small symbol had been scratched into the green paint. "It's a Harper sigil," she explained. "It means 'friend.' Harpers have stayed at this inn recently, which means . . ."

"No Zhentarim," Morhion concluded for her.

"No mossy ground!" Cormik countered firmly.

"No more whining," Jewel sighed thankfully.

The proprietor of the Five Rings was a red-faced man by the name of Faladar, and it was clear from the outset that he was no friend to the Zhentarim. He greeted the companions in the common room, though 'confronted' might have been a better word. "I hope you'll forgive the impertinence," he said in a tone that was anything but apologetic. "These days I like to ask my guests where they've journeyed from."

"We came from Iriaebor to the south," Morhion replied smoothly. "We're traveling the Dusk Road."

Faladar fixed Morhion with a piercing look. "You didn't come over Yellow Snake Pass, then?"

"No," Mari said, "we aren't from . . . the east." The significance of her words was not lost on Faladar. She could as easily have said, "We aren't from Zhentil Keep."

At this he grinned, apparently satisfied. "Come in, then, come in," he said merrily. "You look like honest folk—er, except for that one." He shot a questioning look at Cormik. "Are you certain he's in your group?"

"I'm afraid so," Mari said with an air of resignation.

Cormik gave her a wounded look.

The Five Rings was bustling, but Faladar saw to their needs quickly and with good humor. Soon their horses were stabled, their gear was stowed in a large suite on the second floor, and their bellies were filled with a repast of meat pie and barley beer.

After supper, Jewel and Cormik decided to delve into the underworld of Hill's Edge in hopes of learning something about Stiletto. The two could have covered more territory if they had split up. However, neither trusted the other to reveal all he or she might learn, and so they went off together. Mari talked with Faladar after Kellen and Morhion headed upstairs.

In their chamber, Kellen watched thoughtfully while Morhion studied his leather-bound spellbook. As Morhion had explained, once a mage used a spell, the memory of it was wiped clean from his or her mind and had to be learned anew. Endless study was one of the many prices of magic. Kellen wondered when he would be allowed to learn spells, but he knew better than to ask. When the time was right, Morhion would let him know.

The door opened and Mari came in. Morhion looked up from his book, and for a moment a smile flickered across his usually impassive face.

"Faladar remembers Caledan," Mari said, her brown eyes glowing. She sat down and recounted her conversation with the innkeeper. Faladar had been sweeping the front step of his inn when a striking man with dark hair and a blue cloak passed by on a white mare, heading for the bridge across the River Reaching.

Morhion closed his spellbook. "So Caledan is still following the road. How long ago did Faladar see him?"

"Four days ago. We've gained a day on him."

Morhion nodded thoughtfully. "The Shadowstar draws him onward, but he is not certain where he's being led. I imagine he must pause often, trying to determine in which direction the call is strongest. If we ride hard, we may catch up to him in a few more days."

"I hope you're right," Mari said earnestly. "We can't let him get to the Shadowstar before us."

Kellen was just climbing into bed when Jewel and Cormik returned after paying a visit to the local thieves' guild. The complicated etiquette of the underworld required that local thieves welcome their traveling brethren for a single night. After that, wandering thieves were fair game. Unfortunately, the two had not learned anything specific about Stiletto.

"However, I think we may be getting warm," Jewel said, her dusky violet eyes sparkling. "Cormik and I got the impression that the thieves in Hill's Edge started feeling Stiletto's bite several months before we did in Iriaebor. That may mean they're closer to his base of operations."

"That's something," Mari said, then explained what she had learned from Faladar. Feeling optimistic, they went to bed. Tomorrow was going to be another long day.

Kellen woke in the middle of the night, with the same strange feeling as he had on the day when he saw the ghost of Talek Talembar. Something was going to happen. Something important. He sat up in bed. Cool moonlight spilled through the chamber's round glass window. The mark of magic on his left hand throbbed fiercely.

Kellen rose quietly from his bed. The others were sound asleep. He could move very quietly when he wished, and Cormik's steady snoring helped mask any noise. He slipped out the chamber door and moved down the corridor. As he went, he hummed a soft melody under his breath. The shadows to either side of him swirled, gathering around his slight form in a soft cloak of darkness. He smiled in satisfaction. To passing glances, he would be all but invisible.

Kellen crept down the stairwell, halting when he heard whispered voices below. The first voice he recognized as belonging to Faladar, the innkeeper. The second was unfamiliar, a grating hiss that jarred Kellen's nerves. Cautiously, he peered between two slats in the stairway railing, into the common room below.

Faladar was arguing with someone. "I'm sure I wouldn't know any friend of *yours,*" the innkeeper said indignantly.

"Ah, but you might have seen him," the other countered in his sibilant voice. He was swathed entirely in a heavy black robe, his face lost in the shadows of a deep cowl. "I am certain you would remember, for he is a memorable individual—a tall man with green eyes. He wears a blue cloak and plays the pipes. Or perhaps you've seen his companions—a woman with dark red hair, a handsome mage, and a young boy."

Kellen bit his tongue to keep from gasping aloud.

Faladar was growing angry now. "I've told you that I don't know your friends. I won't tell you again."

"I think you lie, innkeeper," the black-robed stranger hissed menacingly. "I think you *have* seen them."

"Get out of my inn now," Faladar growled. He raised a meaty fist threateningly. "Get out, or I'll—"

It happened with eerie swiftness. The stranger snaked out a gloved hand and gripped Faladar's throat. The innkeeper didn't even have time to scream. The black-robed man squeezed his hand shut. There was a terrible crunching sound, and a spray of blood splattered against the whitewashed wall. The stranger opened his fist, and the innkeeper crashed to the floor.

Kellen clamped a hand to his mouth to keep from screaming. Fear propelled him up the stairs. Quickly, he slipped back into the chamber where the others were sleeping. He woke Mari first.

"Who's there?" she asked in sleepy confusion. Kellen realized he still wore his concealing cloak of shadows. He whistled a sharp note, and the dark aura vanished. The others were awake now. Mari gazed at him in surprise. "Kellen, what is it?"

He explained in quick, breathless words. Two minutes later they were ready to go. They didn't know who was following Caledan, but considering the importance of their mission, and given the stranger's actions, it would be best to escape first and speculate later. It was a tragedy that poor Faladar had paid for his hospitality with his life, but there was nothing they could do for the innkeeper now.

Morhion opened the round window. "It's about a dozen feet to the ground below. We'll have to jump."

Cormik eyed the window skeptically. "You can't be serious."

The mage gave him a flat, unfriendly stare. "I've never been more serious in my life."

"I was afraid of that."

Jewel went first, leaping nimbly out the window. Morhion followed. It took a good bit of shoving on Mari's part, but she got Cormik and his paunch through the window. He landed below with an audible *thud!*, but from his whispered cursing he was quite all right. Kellen was next. He scrambled easily down a vine that was too weak to support the others. Mari came last, landing on her feet as gracefully as a cat.

At first Kellen thought they had made their escape undetected. They retrieved their horses from the stable and rode hard away from the inn; no outcry followed

them. Soon he heard the rushing sound of water. They
were close to the river now. But then a piercing shriek
shattered the chill night air. Wide-eyed, Kellen glanced
over his shoulder and saw a dark form running toward
them with unnatural speed.

"It's him," he gasped. "The stranger I saw."

"Keep riding," Morhion instructed. "I'll stop him."

The others pressed on while the mage whirled Tenebrous around. He raised his hands over his head, shouting a harsh word. Blazing purple magic crackled between
his hands. With all his strength, Morhion hurled the sizzling orb of magic toward their pursuer. The orb struck
its target and exploded in a sizzling spray of violet
sparks. The stranger was thrown violently backward,
tumbling to the ground.

The others reined their horses to a halt and returned
to Morhion. The mage smiled sharply in victory. "I think
our pursuer will follow us no longer."

Cormik spoke then, his voice filled with awe and fear.
"I think you should have knocked on wood when you said
that, Morhion." He pointed with a chubby finger. "Look!"

Slowly, the stranger rose to his feet.

"That's impossible . . ." Mari started to say.

As the moon broke from behind a cloud, they could see
that the stranger's robe had been ripped to shreds by the
force of Morhion's magic. Now for the first time, in the
pale light, they could see their pursuer clearly. It was not
human.

Jewel swore. "By Shar in all her darkness, what is it?"

Morhion answered her grimly. "It is a shadevar."

The creature took a halting step toward them. Kellen
stared with terror and fascination. He had never seen anything like the shadevar. Its hide was gray and rough like
stone. Onyx barbs protruded from the backs of its arms
and from its sternum, while more dark spikes rose along

its backbone in a razor-sharp crest. Its face was feature-
less, with two small pits for a nose and two small depres-
sions where its eyes should have been. Its slit of a mouth
opened to reveal countless needle teeth, and it let out a
snuffling sound as it began moving deliberately forward.

"But this can't be," Mari protested. "We killed the
shadevar. I saw it die . . ."

"We killed one shadevar," Morhion countered. "But in
ancient times there were thirteen of them."

"Might I suggest we continue this argument later?"
Cormik said with a note of hysteria. "Perhaps sometime
when we're not about to be gruesomely dismembered?"
The shadevar was gaining speed.

"Make for the bridge," Morhion said quickly. "The
shadevari cannot cross large bodies of water. Their
nature prevents it."

The horses required little urging. They galloped wildly
toward the bridge. Kellen gripped Flash's mane tightly;
he had given up even attempting to control the little
pony. The sound of the river grew louder. The stone arch
of the bridge loomed before them in the gloom. Without
warning, Mari reined Farenth to a halt. The other horses
skidded to a stop.

"Have you gone mad, Al'maren?" Cormik demanded.
"Don't stop now. The thing is gaining on us!"

"No, she is not mad," Morhion said hoarsely.

The others followed his gaze. In the faint light, they
could just make out two figures standing in front of the
bridge, blocking the way. Both wore thick black robes.

"By Azuth on High," Mari swore in a mixture of horror
and amazement. "More of them!"

Once, the Fellowship had managed to defeat a single
shadevar. Just barely. Now they faced three of the
ancient, evil creatures. Morhion looked over his shoulder.
The first shadevar loped toward them swiftly. It would be

upon them in moments. The other two stood firm before the bridge, and a river too deep to ford. The companions were trapped.

"This way!" Morhion shouted, turning to the left and spurring his mount away from the road. "The edge of the Reaching Woods is less than a mile away. It's our only chance!"

The others did not stop to argue. They spurred their mounts, leaving the road behind and thundering toward the dark wall of the forest. A cry of inhuman rage rose on the cold night air. Yet, when Kellen dared to glance back a few moments later, the creatures had vanished. Perhaps they had given up. The shadevari were swift, but even they could not outrun a galloping horse.

Jewel spoke up, her smoky voice tinged with fear. "I really hate to be negative, loves, but you might want to look up."

The shadevari had not abandoned their pursuit after all. Three dark shapes whirled in the air above the riders, soaring on broad wings. The outlines of the creatures were hazy and indistinct, almost as if they were formed of smoke. They looked like some malformed mixture of lizard and bat, only far larger. Riding on the back of each of the flying creatures was one of the shadevari. The shadowsteeds folded their wings and began to dive, stretching out curved talons.

"Don't look up!" Morhion shouted. "Keep riding!"

Kellen tore his eyes away from the horrible scene in the sky. Fixing his gaze on the approaching line of trees, he braced himself as his horse sped up, fearing that at any moment he would feel sharp claws rake deep into his back, peeling flesh from bone.

Then Flash crashed through a low wall of undergrowth into the forest. Through the lattice of branches, Kellen looked up to see the three shadowsteeds pull up sharply, barely avoiding a collision with the treetops. Screams of pure fury pierced the night, but the terrible cries faded as the horses pushed onward. The winged shadowsteeds could not pursue them into the forest. They had escaped the shadevari. At least for now.

Kellen let out a sigh of relief as they wound their way deeper into the safety of the trees. Then Mari uttered something that made their hearts sink.

"We've lost Caledan's trail," she said quietly.

After that, they rode for a long time in silence.

Eleven

 The wanderer came to the gates of Triel on a gloomy day late in the month of Uktar.

Even from a distance, Beris thought there was something strange about the fellow, a man clad all in black riding a mist-gray horse. Beris shivered inside his beaten-steel breastplate, chalking it up to the clammy air as he gripped his spear tightly. An unsettling thought drifted through his mind. Didn't one of Lord Elvar's priests say that sometimes the King of the Dead appeared in the guise of a dark man riding a pale horse? Like all soldiers, Beris was a superstitious man. Under his breath, he muttered a charm against evil spirits.

"What are you mumbling about now, Beris?" asked the grizzled soldier who stood with him before the open gate.

"I was just wondering who that rider is, Sarig," Beris answered hastily. Beris was the youngest of the twenty mercenaries Lord Elvar paid to guard Triel, and he took enough abuse from the older men as it was. He didn't want Sarig to think he was afraid of a lone horseman. Which he wasn't, of course. "Who do you suppose it is?"

"Looks like some beggar to me," Sarig grunted in disgust.

Beris nodded. "I suppose he'll be seeking hospitality, then."

Sarig gave a harsh snort of laughter. "Lord Elvar isn't very hospitable!"

While the lord was not an evil man, his distrust of strangers was nearly as legendary as his propensity for switching religions. Elvar ruled a small district, of which Triel was the center. Triel itself was more of a fort than a proper town. Here the Dusk Road met up with the larger Trade Way, which continued on all the way to the great city of Waterdeep to the west. Triel served mostly as a way station for traveling merchants. Its small cluster of cottages and storehouses was surrounded by a sturdy stockade of stone and wood.

When the rider finally came to a halt before the gates, Beris breathed a relieved sigh. The man's skin was mushroom pale, and dark half-moons hung beneath his faded green eyes, but he looked far more like a sick beggar than an incarnation of Death. His midnight blue cloak was spattered with mud. Despite the wanderer's ragged appearance, the gray mare he rode was an exceptional animal.

"State your business!" Sarig barked, brandishing his spear.

The wanderer blinked, as if he had just waked from a deep slumber and was surprised to find himself in some new time and place. "Can you help me?" he asked hoarsely. "I'm so tired. And hungry."

Sarig gave a derisive snort. "I told you, Beris—a beggar."

Beris ignored him. There was something about the

man—perhaps the deep sorrow in his eyes—that made Beris think he was more than a simple vagabond seeking alms. "I'd best take you to Lord Elvar," he told the wanderer. "If you'll dismount, I'll lead your horse for you." He reached out to grip the gray mare's bridle, but she bared her big yellow teeth menacingly. Beris was forced to snatch his hand back quickly.

The ghost of a smile touched the wanderer's lips. "I'd better lead her," he said quietly. "She bites."

"So I noticed," Beris said dryly.

The wanderer dismounted. Beris gestured for him to follow, and they entered the stockade to seek out Lord Elvar. They soon found him standing before the open door of the stockade's large stone granary. Elvar was having a fit. Again.

"Look at that!" he shouted, jowls waggling. Elvar was an overlarge man with beady eyes and an upturned nose that gave him a distinctly piggish look. His expansive gut was stuffed into a too-tight waistcoat of food-stained green velvet. He thrust a torch into the darkened doorway of the granary. A squealing gray form scurried out, vanishing down a nearby drainpipe. "There's another!" Elvar raged. "Rats—they're everywhere!"

A small group of townsfolk, merchants, and soldiers had gathered around the irate lord. "The rats will eat all the grain," he continued his tirade. "And with winter coming, we're all going to starve!" Elvar looked like a man who had never wanted for food in his life, but his eyes were wide with fear all the same. He bore down on a thin-faced man clad in the drab brown robe of a priest.

"You!" Elvar growled angrily. "You told me that if I prayed to Malar, Lord of All Beasts, he would keep the rats away from the grain. But Malar has done nothing!"

"It is not for us to question the actions of the gods," the priest said pompously.

"I've had enough of you and your foolish prattling, priest!" Elvar roared. He turned to a pair of soldiers. "Take this charlatan and throw him out of my town. I am a disciple of Malar no longer."

The priest looked shocked as the mercenaries grabbed his arms and hauled him away. Elvar had converted to worship of the god Malar nearly a moon ago. By Beris's calculations, that actually made this one of Elvar's longer religious commitments. Most gods didn't last a tenday in the lord of Triel's chapel.

When Elvar continued to rant about how they were all doomed to die of hunger this winter, Beris decided this was not the best time for a stranger to beg for hospitality. He turned to tell the wanderer they might do better to wait until later, then stared in alarm. Leading his pale mare, the stranger approached Elvar. Beris made a grab for the man but was too late.

Elvar glared at the wanderer in annoyance. "What do you want?"

"I am hungry," the strange man said quietly.

"And I suppose you want me to feed you," Elvar said in disgust. He rested his chubby hands on his broad hips. "I suppose you think we should be happy to give a cretin like yourself food when we haven't enough to make it through the winter ourselves."

The wanderer gestured to the storehouse. "You have plenty of grain."

"Don't tell me what I have or don't have," Elvar snapped. He studied the wanderer. Suspicion gleamed in his beady eyes. "Tell me, beggar, where did one so wretched get such a fine horse?"

"She's mine."

"Liar," Elvar hissed. "I say you stole it."

Beris pressed forward. "Excuse me, milord, but I think that the horse does belong to him. She seems to obey his—"

"Shut up!" Elvar commanded. "If I say he is a thief, then he is a thief." He gestured to a trio of mercenaries. "Lead the horse to my stable, then take this man and cut off his hands so everyone will know him for the thief he is." With that, Elvar waddled toward the large stone manor house in the center of the stockade.

Beris tried to protest, but the other soldiers pushed him roughly aside. Two grappled the wanderer, ruthlessly twisting his arms behind his back. Another grabbed the gray mare's reins. She let out a defiant whinny, rearing back on her hind legs.

"Stop!" a commanding voice thundered.

Everyone froze—the townspeople, the soldiers, even Lord Elvar—staring in amazement. An aura of power surrounded the wanderer, who now looked more like a king than a vagabond. The pale horse quieted and let out a soft nicker.

The wanderer fixed Elvar with his pale green gaze. "If there were no rats in your granary, would you have given me something to eat?"

Elvar licked his lips. "Of course," he lied hastily.

Reaching into a leather pouch at his belt, the wanderer produced a set of bone pipes. He lifted them to his lips and began to play. The throng stared in trancelike wonder. Beris had never before heard such music—mournful, vaguely threatening, yet so achingly beautiful he thought it would break his heart. As the man continued to play, a gasp rose from the crowd. From a dozen dim corners and shadowed alleyways emerged countless small, dark, lithe forms.

Cats.

In moments there were a hundred of them, as black and silent as smoke. The wraithlike felines padded swiftly toward the granary, emerald eyes winking mysteriously,

before disappearing through the open door. The hideous
cacophony that followed nearly drowned out the piper's
music. People clapped hands over their ears against the
horrible din of squealing and yowling. Abruptly, the noise
ceased. The dark cats streamed out of the granary now,
each bearing a gray bundle in its mouth. As they passed
the stunned Elvar, each of the cats dropped its grisly burden at the lord's feet. In moments there was a furry
mound of dead rats heaped before the lord of Triel. The
wanderer lowered his pipes; the strange music faded into
the air. The dusky cats melted once more into pools of
darkness.

"Now may I have something to eat?" the wanderer
asked solemnly.

Elvar gaped at him, then nodded emphatically. "Of
course! You shall have my very finest!" This time, Beris
noted, sincerity was written across the lord's porcine face.
"But please, stranger," Elvar implored, "tell me your name,
so that I can know who has saved Triel from disaster."

The wanderer hesitated a moment, as if he did not
quite remember his name. When at last he spoke, he
seemed a figure of majesty no longer, but simply a weary
traveler.

"Cal," he said haggardly. "You can call me Cal."

                    * * * * *

The statue watched over the ancient crossroads with
deep, moss-filled eyes. A cool wind rushed through the
sentinel trees, and the misty forest air was filled with
cast-off leaves of copper red and burnished gold. Mari
reached out and touched the timeworn stone.

"I've found another one!" she called out.

There was a crashing in the underbrush as the others
approached, leading their horses among the trees.

"It is indeed a Talfirian Watcher," Morhion agreed after a moment of study. "You have found the path again."

Whether the statue had once represented man, woman, or god, Mari could not tell. An eternity of wind and rain had worn away all features except the staring pits of the eyes. They had come upon a dozen of the mysterious stone figures over the last two days as they wended their way southward, deeper into the Reaching Woods.

It was Jewel who had first discovered the path, the morning after their harrowing flight from the three shadevari in Hill's Edge. At first they thought it was a game trail that paralleled the river. Here and there they turned up what seemed to be cracked paving stones. Then they came upon the first of the Watchers. Morhion instantly realized the significance of the crumbling statue.

"This was a road, once," he explained, "built by the Talfirc, the people who dwelt in this land a thousand years ago. They set the Watchers here to guard the way."

They had decided to follow the ancient road southward. Again and again they had lost the faint tracks in the underbrush and were forced to stop and make a laborious search. The loss of time worried Mari.

"This path divides in several directions," Kellen noted in his grave manner. "Which way do you think we should go?"

"Whichever way leads fastest toward something to eat, besides hardtack and acorns," Cormik said forlornly. He picked futilely at the dried leaves and burrs that clung to his once-elegant attire.

Jewel parted her ruby lips in a wicked smile. "Personally, I think our strict regimen is doing you good, my sweet, expansive elephant. Sparing amounts of food and generous amounts of exercise are exactly what you need."

With his one good eye, Cormik glared darkly at her. "If

I had wanted your opinion, my dear geriatric tart, I most certainly would have requested it. I know exactly what I need, and it involves large and plentiful quantities of roasted pheasant, sweet subtleties, and red Amnian wine. And soon!"

"This path has gradually veered east, away from the River Reaching," Morhion said. "Let us try west. Perhaps that way leads to a ford. We have to get across the river if we're going to pick up Caledan's trail again."

The green forest light was fading to dusk when the narrow path broadened, and they came upon the ruined city. The endless wall of trees parted before them, and the voice of the river roared like thunder on the air. Here the paving stones were intact, though late wildflowers and sweet herbs pushed their way up between the cobbles. Most of the city's structures were little more than jumbled heaps of stone, tangled with vines and crowned by stands of oak and ash. However, in the center of the city was a circular plaza, in the middle of which rose a tapering, step-sided building.

"I think this was a city of the Talfirc," Morhion said, raising his voice above the rushing river.

"What happened to them?" Mari asked in wonder. "Why did they leave?"

Morhion shook his head. "It is a mystery. The Talfirc dwelt in this land for a long age. However, by the time our ancestors came westward over the mountains, the Talfirc were already centuries vanished. No one knows where they went, or why."

"They built this city awfully close to the river," Cormik noted. "I wonder if they built a bridge as well."

Morhion's eyes gleamed brightly. "Let us find out if you're right."

The Talfirc had indeed built a bridge. Unfortunately, the river had shifted in its course over the centuries. The ancient yet solid span of stones now arched over the verdant floodplain. The river came nowhere near it.

"Well, that's about as useful as a rowboat in the desert," Jewel said drolly.

"Not even that," Cormik chimed in.

They made their way back to the central plaza. The light was failing rapidly.

"We might as well camp here," Mari said, though she shivered as she did. The years rested heavily on this place.

"What's that boy doing?" Cormik asked with a scowl.

Mari followed Cormik's gaze, then gasped. Kellen was climbing nimbly up one side of the stone pyramid. "Kellen!" she cried out in alarm. "Come back down!" He seemed not to have heard her over the roar of the river, for he kept climbing. It was unlike him to behave so rashly, but she could see now what had attracted his attention. Atop the pyramid was a gleaming golden orb.

Morhion was the first to the pyramid. He leapt from the saddle and swiftly scrambled up the side after Kellen. Seconds later, Mari, Jewel, and Cormik dismounted and started up the stone steps after the mage. These three were perhaps a quarter of the way up the pyramid when Kellen reached the summit. Glancing over his shoulder, he grinned when he spotted Morhion right behind him. But there was something wrong with Kellen's eyes, Mari realized. They were dull, vacant. And Kellen never grinned, Mari remembered. Sometimes he smiled, but he never bared his teeth and *grinned*.

"Look at it, Morhion," Kellen said in a strangely flat voice. "Isn't it beautiful?"

Morhion also sensed something was wrong. He reached a hand out toward the boy. "Kellen, don't touch the—" But the mage was too late. Kellen had already laid his left hand on the orb.

Green lightning split the sky. A bolt of sizzling energy
shot down from the angry clouds and struck the golden
orb. Both Kellen and Morhion were thrown backward by
the blazing force of the strike, tumbling down a dozen
steps before coming to a halt. Kellen staggered to his
feet, dazed, but Morhion lay still, sprawled upon the
stones. Mari could see a red stain spreading across his
forehead.

Mari scrambled up the side of the pyramid, quickly
outpacing Jewel and Cormik, who followed behind her. A
heartbeat later, the golden orb flashed. There was a hissing noise, like air escaping through a crack, and a grating of rock on rock. Mari cried out as the stones beneath
her shifted. In moments they no longer formed a staircase, but instead a smooth, steep ramp down which she
slid backward. Over her shoulder, she could hear screams.
She twisted her neck just in time to see Cormik and
Jewel disappear into a dark pit that had opened at the
base of the pyramid. Mari clawed at the stone to slow her
descent. Then she heard Kellen's frightened cry.

"Mari, look out!"

She looked up in time to see Kellen and Morhion sliding rapidly toward her. She tried to twist out of the way,
but she was too slow. Child and mage struck her at the
same time. She lost her grip on the stone, and they all
went tumbling down into darkness.

* * * * *

Surprisingly, it was Cormik who took charge. The corpulent crime lord was accustomed to a life of luxury;
nonetheless, he reacted to their predicament with cool-
ness and aplomb.

The five had fallen through an opening into a perfectly
spherical chamber formed of seamless black stone.

Moments after they struck the bottom, there came a low grinding noise. The entire hollow globe seemed to rotate. Mari scrambled on all fours, trying to keep from tumbling end-over-end like a rat trapped inside a spinning ball. When the sphere's movement came to a halt, the opening through which they had fallen was no longer above them, but was instead situated halfway down one of the curved walls. A second stone wall now lay beyond the opening; apparently this sphere was contained within another, larger stone globe. Only a small slit breached the outer wall at this point, a narrow window through which came the faint gray-green light of dusk.

Kellen remembered nothing of what had occurred outside. Whatever power had compelled him to climb the pyramid seemed to have no influence here. He was back to normal, as dazed as the rest.

Cormik began issuing orders. "Jewel, examine that opening in the far wall and see if there's some way out of here. Kellen, please assist her. You have smaller hands and may be able to reach things she cannot. Mari, we're going to need more light—can you do something about that? I'll see to Morhion." The mage had not stirred. He lay on the ground, unmoving, his skin like alabaster against the black marble floor. The wound on his forehead had blossomed into a grisly crimson flower.

Numbly, Mari set to her task. She rummaged in her pockets until she found a stump of candle, flint, and tinder. Creating fire was no simple feat. She struck the flint repeatedly against the edge of her steel eating knife. After many failed attempts, a glowing spark landed directly on the tinder. Quickly, she blew on the bit of fluff. There was a wisp of smoke, and suddenly a bright flame curled out of the tinder. She held the candle's wick to the flame. The candle caught, golden light filling the dark sphere. Mari took a deep breath. Concentrating on the mundane chore had calmed her nerves. She realized that this was probably one of the reasons Cormik had assigned her the task.

She approached Cormik, who bent over the still-unconscious mage. He had placed his velvet cloak under Morhion's head for a pillow, and the crime lord was deftly binding a bandage over the wound on the mage's brow.

"I didn't realize you were so adept at healing," Mari said softly.

"I'm not," Cormik replied. "But in my line of work, unwanted holes have a nasty way of appearing in one's self and one's co-workers, and so one gets accustomed to plugging them up." He tied the bandage and leaned back, sighing. "I'm afraid that's all I can do."

Mari reached out and gripped the mage's chill hand. Don't leave me Morhion, she thought fiercely. Don't you dare leave me. Not now. I can't do this alone.

Kellen and Jewel moved back from the window in the outer sphere.

"Did you see anything near the opening that might help us?" Cormik asked eagerly.

Jewel ran a hand through her short, dark hair. "Do you want some inane but optimistic possibilities calculated solely to keep our spirits up? Or do you want the truth?"

"You make it seem like such an attractive choice," Cormik commented acidly.

"Sorry," Jewel apologized. "I suppose that's why I'm a thief, not a politician. Not that there's much difference in what we do, just how we present it afterward." She went on. "There's only the thinnest crack between this sphere and the one that surrounds it. The window is too small to climb through, and I couldn't so much as scratch the stone with my knife. If our taciturn friend the mage were awake, I think he would tell us the sphere is enchanted. In other words, we're trapped quite nicely."

"Unless we could rotate the sphere again," Kellen went on. "Then we could realign the opening in the inner sphere with the hole we fell through in the outer sphere. Maybe we could boost ourselves up and get through."

"I hadn't thought of that," Cormik admitted with an impressed look. However, they could find no trace of a mechanism by which the globe might be rotated. If any of them could unlock this mystery, it would be Morhion.

"How is he?" Jewel asked quietly.

Cormik shook his head. "I'm not sure, really. The truth is, the blow to his forehead really isn't all that serious. It's enough to give him a good headache, but that's all. I don't know why his breathing is so shallow, or his heart-beats are so fluttery."

"It was the lightning," spoke a cracked voice. "The power of the bolt has confused the life energy that commands his heart to beat."

They looked up in shock to see a face hovering outside the narrow window. The light of the flickering candle revealed the speaker for a wizened woman with straggly gray hair. Her face looked as tough as old leather, and her bright obsidian eyes were nearly lost in masses of wrinkled skin.

"Who are you?" Mari asked breathlessly.

The ancient woman laughed, a sound like the call of a crow. "No one and nothing," she replied hoarsely. "A bad memory, and one best forgotten. That's all. And who are you?"

The old woman seemed more than half mad, but she might be able to help them. "We're on a quest," Mari replied.

"Truly?" the old woman said caustically. "Well, if you were searching for a bad end, then your quest is over, for you've found that here."

Mari winced. That reply hardly showed a helpful

attitude.

"My friend has been hurt," Kellen said gravely.

"And what makes you think I can do anything about it?" the old woman snapped.

Kellen didn't even blink. "I imagine that you're very wise, that's all."

The old woman grunted at this. "Well, you'd be right to imagine so," she said in a surly tone. "And my wisdom tells me that I am too old and far too weary to concern myself with a lot of meddlers and troublemakers. I would say farewell, but I suppose it would be wasted on you, so I'll say nothing at all." She started to draw away.

"Wait!" Kellen cried, reaching his hand toward the window.

The old woman froze. A hissing sound escaped her lips. At last she whispered in a voice filled with wonder and dread. "The child wizard . . ."

With swiftness surprising in one so old, she reached through the narrow opening and clutched Kellen's hand before he could pull away. She ran a gnarled finger over the puckered scar on his left palm. "So young, yet already marked by magic," she murmured in awe. "Of course. After all this time, I had dared to let myself forget. I waited so long, you see, but you never came. Finally I dismissed the prophecy as foolishness. And now, in the dark winter of my life, you have come at last." Her voice became a moan of despair. "But why have you waited all these years? Why have you come when I am so old, so weak, so tired?"

Kellen managed to pull his hand out of her gnarled grasp. He gave her a frightened look. "I don't know what you're talking about. I'm not a wizard. Not yet, anyway."

The old woman laughed at this, an eerie sound. "But you will be. You will be a wizard the likes of which this world has never known. Ah, but do I have the strength to do what I must?" She fell silent.

Mari stepped forward. "Please, listen to me," she said earnestly. "You seem to know much I don't pretend to understand. Won't you help us, so we can talk with you more about . . . about this prophecy?"

The old woman hesitated, then vanished from the window. Mari groaned in despair. Abruptly the old woman reappeared and thrust a hand through the window. "Here, place this on the mage's chest," she ordered.

Mari took the proffered object. It was a small black seed. She thought to question the old woman, then bit her tongue. This was not the time to annoy the stranger. She knelt before Morhion and unlaced his shirt, then placed the tiny seed on the pale flesh above his heart.

At first nothing happened. She traded skeptical looks with Cormik and Jewel. Perhaps the old woman was mad after all. Then Kellen whispered softly, "Look."

The seed was sprouting. As they watched in wonder, a small, dark purple leaf unfurled itself from the seed, and a root tendril snaked outward, plunging into the flesh of Morhion's chest. More leaves uncurled themselves, and the strange purple plant grew larger as its roots sank deeper into Morhion's body. The mage trembled, and his back arched off the stone beneath him.

"It's hurting him!" Mari cried out in horror, reaching to pull the magical plant from his body.

"Stop!" the old woman commanded. Something in her voice made Mari freeze. "If you pluck the heartroot out now, your friend will surely perish."

Mari forced herself to remain still. There was nothing to do now but watch. The plant grew fuller, more lush. Its roots writhed like snakes beneath Morhion's skin. Its deep purple leaves began to throb in time to the mage's erratically beating heart. Morhion convulsed, his hands scratching reflexively against the black marble.

Suddenly his entire body went limp.

For a terrified moment Mari thought he was dead. She clasped a hand to Morhion's wrist. His pulse was strong and even.

Abruptly, the plant began to wither. Its purple leaves turned black and curled upon themselves. The stem broke, and the brittle plant crumbled as it fell to the floor. The only trace it left on Morhion's flesh was a tiny violet circle, and even this began to fade. The mage took in a deep, shuddering breath and sat up, eyes open wide. Immediately he grimaced, touching a hand tentatively to his wounded brow.

"What happened?" he asked in a dazed voice, and the others let out a collective sigh of relief.

* * * * *

The witch's name was Isela, and as far as they could tell from the bits and fragments she told them, she had dwelt in the ruined city—she called it Talis—all her life. She left them for a brief time, only to return to the window with dried fruit, nuts, and a leather jug of water. The others accepted these gratefully, and thanked Isela when she told them she had retrieved and picketed their horses.

"Though I suppose we'll have little need of them if we cannot find a way to escape this trap," Morhion said darkly. Thanks to Isela's magic, the mage had largely recovered from the lightning strike. "I wonder what this prison was originally for. And the pyramid. Do you know, Isela?"

"I think I did once," she said wistfully. "I've forgotten so much . . . so much I wonder how I ever knew it all. It seems to me that the wizards who dwelt here long ago used the pyramid and the orb to defend Talis from its enemies. The orb remembered the touch of magic, and when the boy laid a hand upon it, it called down the lightning to protect the city. But you had no idea what was coming, and so were caught by the trap that would have served to guard the wizards of long ago." She paused, licking her thin lips. "There is a way to rotate the sphere, you know."

"How?" Mari asked intently.

"A wizard could do it." She gave Morhion a piercing look. "But you are too weak from the heartroot."

Morhion took a deep breath. "I'll try it," he said solemnly. "Tell me how."

"It would kill you," Isela said flatly.

"That is not important." Anger flashed in his icy eyes. "We dare not delay our quest any longer. If the price is death, then I will pay it."

Isela gave a derisive snort. "A lot of good that would do your friends. Especially when there is one other who has the power." Her sharp gaze drifted toward Kellen.

"He's only a child," Mari said scornfully. "You would truly have him attempt something so perilous?"

"He has already faced grave peril once." Isela's gaze flickered back toward Morhion. The mage fell silent.

"What do I need to do?" Kellen asked quietly.

Mari started to protest, then halted. What choice did they have? All she could do was watch Kellen closely, and stop him if he appeared to be in danger.

"Close your eyes," Isela instructed in a low voice. "Imagine that you are not inside the sphere, but rather that the sphere is a small black orb you hold in your hand."

Kellen sat cross-legged and shut his eyes. After a moment, he spoke in a dreamy voice. "I can see it." He cupped his hand as if holding a ball.

"Now, you must turn the orb a half-turn to the left."

"It's *hard*," Kellen protested, his brow furrowing.

"Try!" Isela hissed. "You must try!"

Kellen shook his head slowly. "No, it's too heavy," he said with a moan. "It's . . . it's crushing me . . ."

Alarmed, Mari started forward, but Morhion was faster. He knelt beside the boy and whispered in his ear. "Do not fight the weight of the sphere, Kellen. That is its magic you feel. Let that magic fill you."

"I can't," Kellen gasped. "It hurts . . ."

"Do not resist it," Morhion said in a chantlike voice. "Clear your mind. Imagine your body an empty vessel. Then let the magic fill you. It will not harm you if you do not fight it."

A spasm crossed Kellen's face, then his visage relaxed. "Yes . . . ," he whispered. He moved his hands, and the sphere lurched into motion. The window—and Isela with it—vanished as the opening in the wall rotated. After a moment the sphere ground to a halt. Kellen's eyes flew open. "Did it work?" he asked breathlessly.

"Yes, it did," Mari said in amazement.

The opening in the inner sphere was now aligned with a similar-sized opening in the outer sphere. Beyond was moonlight. Without warning, Isela's wizened face appeared in the opening. "Well, what are you waiting for?" she snapped. "An invitation?"

Twelve

Isela served them soup as they huddled around a dancing fire. The night was cold, and Isela's dwelling offered scant protection from the frosty autumn air. The witch made her home in a chamber of what Morhion supposed was once a palace. Only three of the chamber's walls still stood, and the roof had collapsed in one corner.

The witch shoved a rudely carved wooden bowl into Morhion's hands. "Eat, wizard," she said curtly. "You will need your strength for what lies ahead."

The mage gave Isela a curious look. She made a peculiar figure, with her straggly gray hair, her craggy face, her bony form huddled inside a shapeless mass of dirty rags. Yet the keen light of intelligence in her eyes was unmistakable. Whatever the witch Isela was, she was not crazy. Morhion did not feel hungry—his head ached fiercely from the wound on his brow—but he did his best to eat some of the soup, so as not to offend Isela. The broth was flavored with strange herbs and contained the meat of an animal he did not recognize.

Cormik cautiously stirred his own bowl. "I really hate to complain—"

"Then I suggest you don't," Jewel interrupted, digging an elbow into his side as she glanced at Isela.

He shot her a perturbed look. "It's only a figure of speech, Jewel. You know perfectly well that I actually love to complain."

"Really, Cormik," she chided him, "you have no idea what you're missing." She scooped up a large spoonful of soup, including the scaly foot of some nameless creature, and ate it with relish. After that, Cormik made only gagging noises, and the others were able to eat in peace.

It was Kellen who broke the silence. "Isela, why do you think I'm the one mentioned in the prophecy?"

Isela fixed him with her piercing gaze. "I do not *think* you are the one, child. You *are* the one." She shook her head wearily, passing a gnarled hand before her eyes. "But I had no idea you would be so long in coming. How I have longed to lie down upon the forest floor, to let my bones sink deep into the ground and nourish my beloved trees. Still I waited, as I was pledged to do." She lifted her gaze once more to Kellen's face. "And now my waiting is over at last. The prophecy has come to pass."

"But what *is* the prophecy?" Kellen asked.

When Isela finally spoke, it was in an eerie whisper. "Long, long ago, in an age now lost in the mists of time, there was a great oracle who was a leader of his people, a tribe of the Talfirc. The oracle journeyed to this place and said that, one day, there would come a child marked by magic, in whose hands would lie the fate of all the Talfirc. The child would come on a quest to stop a great darkness. Someone must await his coming, to aid him when he was in need. So the Talfirc built a city here, and they called it Talis. They remembered the prophecy and awaited the coming of the child wizard." Isela sighed heavily. "But the child never came, the city fell to ruin, and the prophecy was forgotten."

"Except by you," Kellen said, reaching out to touch her crooked hand.

Isela stared at Kellen in surprise, then her expression darkened. "Aye, I remembered. But what does it matter now if the child wizard holds the fate of all the Talfirc in his hands? There are no more Talfirc. They vanished long ago. They are all gone now. All gone."

"Except for you, Isela?" Morhion asked softly.

The witch only laughed her dry, cackling laugh and gazed at him with hard obsidian eyes. After that, Isela seemed unwilling to talk. She curled up in a corner and was still and silent. The companions retrieved their bedrolls from the horses outside and readied themselves for sleep.

"Do you really think she's a thousand years old, Morhion?" Mari whispered as they lay down by the fire. "I know it's impossible, but I almost believe she has lived in Talis since its destruction, awaiting the fulfillment of the prophecy. She does seem to know a great deal about what happened here a thousand years ago. What do you think?"

Morhion met her gaze. "I think, Mari, that you have answered your own question." With that he shut his eyes and swiftly passed into sleep.

"Morhion."

The whisper jolted him awake. His eyes fluttered open. It was Isela. She held a finger to her lips, then gestured for him to follow. He slipped silently from his blanket and padded after her in the sooty predawn light. She led him through twisting corridors until they came to another room. He guessed it might once have been a library, though the wooden shelves had rotted to splinters, and the books had long ago become mulch for the fragrant wild mint that carpeted the floor.

Isela moved to a rusted iron chest and threw back the lid. She drew out two objects and handed them to Morhion. One was a book, its crackling yellow pages still protected by a cover of oiled leather. The second was a silver ring set with a violet gem.

Morhion raised an eyebrow. "What are these things, Isela?"

She placed her gnarled hands on her hips. "That is for you to discover, wizard. But I will tell you this—you will have need of them on your quest."

His eyes narrowed. "How is it you know what we seek to do?"

She waved this away as if it were an unimportant detail. "How I know matters not. But heed me, wizard. You seek to destroy a great shadow. Yet shadows can exist only when there is light to cast them. To destroy the shadow, you must destroy the light as well. Do not forget that."

"I won't," he promised solemnly, though he was not sure what she meant.

She nodded and, without a word, turned to leave. By the time they made it back to the sleeping chamber, the others were waking. They ate a breakfast of hardtack and leftover soup—ignoring more of Cormik's grumbling—and discussed their plans. They had to cross the River Reaching and return to the Dusk Road to search for Caledan's trail. Isela claimed to know a way across the river, though she remained deliberately mysterious.

"You shall see," was all she said.

They gathered on the damp green bank of the river in the misty light of dawn.

"You have *got* to be joking," Cormik said in blatant disbelief. "How, by all the gold of Ghaethluntar, are we going to get a horse across the river in *that?*"

Jewel gave Cormik's paunch an appraising look. "I'm not certain it's the horses that will be the problem."

Cormik treated her to a withering glare. "You actually enjoy being unpleasant, don't you?"

"Just to you, love," she said, parting her ruby lips in a winning smile.

Morhion studied the contraption Isela had rigged for crossing the frothing torrent of the river. He had the distinct impression that the entire thing had not been built, but had rather been *grown*. A thick vine hung across the river, attached to a stout oak tree on each bank. Suspended from the braided vine was a large basket woven from green saplings. Attached to the basket was another, thinner cord that could be used to pull the craft along the main vine.

"Can it truly hold one of the horses, Isela?" Mari asked.

The witch nodded. "Once each fall I kill a stag for winter food. Often I hunt on the far side of the river, and bring the stag across in the basket. It will hold a horse."

Despite Cormik's skepticism, Isela was right. Mari and Jewel crossed first, easily pulling the basket along the vine to the far bank. The others pulled the basket back and began sending the horses across the river to the two women. It wasn't easy getting the horses into the curious conveyance, but with a cloth sack covering their eyes, the animals stayed reasonably calm. It took a great deal of grunting and heaving on the part of Mari and Jewel, but soon all the horses stood on the far bank.

Cormik and Kellen climbed into the basket next, the crime lord somewhat reassured after the favorable performance with the horses. Before joining them, Morhion turned to bid Isela farewell.

That was when the baying started.

It echoed through the forest, distant at first, yet rapidly drawing nearer. This was not the baying of mundane hounds. It was an eerie noise; the snarls and barking sounded strangely like voices speaking in an unknown evil language.

Bloodthirsty cries pierced the foggy air. These came from above, and the companions recognized the source instantly: the bellowing of the winged shadowsteeds conjured by the shadevari. In moments the baying and bellowing grew frighteningly near. Morhion thought he saw shadowy shapes moving swiftly toward them through the ruins of the city.

"Yes, these hounds are creatures of shadow," Isela hissed, as if reading his thoughts. She shoved him into the basket with Cormik and Kellen. "You must go. Now."

"What of yourself?" Morhion demanded.

"I am staying."

Morhion stared at her. "But the beasts—they'll be here in moments."

"I know, you fool," she snapped. Then her dark eyes softened a fraction. "You must guard the child wizard. Now go." She tugged the smaller vine twice. In response to the signal, Mari and Jewel began hauling on the cord. The basket swung out over the river.

The baying of the shadowhounds shattered the air. "Isela!" Morhion shouted, but the witch was already lost in the mist of the far bank. He thought he saw a dozen dark forms slinking through the swirling fog, but he could not be certain. Abruptly the basket came to rest on the western bank of the river. Jewel and Mari helped Cormik and Kellen out, but Morhion gripped the vine. "I'm going back," he said hoarsely.

Before the others could protest, the cord suddenly went slack. The main vine crashed down into the turbulent surface of the river and was swept away. Isela had sev-

ered the cords. There was no going back. The snarling of
the shadowhounds rose to a frenzied pitch. Across the
river, brilliant green light flickered in the mist, and
howls of pain mingled with the snarls. Somewhere in the
fog overhead the shadowsteeds shrieked again.

"Come on," Mari said, tugging at Morhion's hand.

"But Isela . . . ," he protested.

"I know," she replied angrily. "She is sacrificing herself
so that we can escape. Will you have that sacrifice be for
nothing?"

It was like a cold slap. Morhion, of all people, understood sacrifice. "You are right," he said coolly. They
mounted their horses and soon left behind the eerie baying and flashes of light.

*   *   *   *   *

Late the next day, they stumbled out of the northern
edge of the Reaching Woods and once again found themselves traveling west on the Dusk Road. This time it was
Jewel who spotted the sign of Caledan's passing. Near
the road, a dead tree had been twisted into an agonized
shape that looked uncannily like a dying man raising his
arms toward the sky. The crimson light of sunset dripped
down the tree's bark like blood.

"He has been this way," Mari said, visibly shaken.

"But how long ago?" Cormik wondered. No one could
answer his question.

They rode on, glancing frequently at the sky above,
searching for signs of the shadevari. While they did not
know who had summoned the ancient creatures of evil,
or why, by now it was clear that the shadevari were
tracking Caledan, just as the companions were. To their
relief, the winged shadowsteeds did not appear.

Two days later, they halted at a fork in the road. Here

the Dusk Road continued on west, while a lesser-used track branched off to the north, winding its way into the rocky Trielta Hills. There seemed no way of knowing for certain which direction Caledan had gone.

"Nothing," Cormik said darkly, scrambling out of the hedgerow he had been searching. "I can't see any signs that Caledan came this way at all."

Jewel appraised the rotund crime lord critically. "Let me guess—it's all the rage in the royal court of Cormyr to wear a bird's nest on one's head, and as usual you're just a pawn of fashion?"

Cormik hastily snatched at the abandoned nest that had gotten tangled in his dark hair. He glowered at her. "You're evil, aren't you?"

Her only answer was a disturbingly sweet smile.

Mari sighed in frustration. "I suppose we'll just have to make our best guess as to which way Caledan went."

"I have an idea."

The others turned to Kellen in surprise. He had not spoken much since the ruined city. Whether or not Kellen was in truth the one foretold in Isela's prophecy, something strange had happened to him in Talis. What had been going on in his mind since, Morhion could only guess.

Jewel knelt, regarding Kellen with curious eyes. "What did you have in mind, love?"

"I'll show you," he said mysteriously.

From the leather pouch at his belt, Kellen drew out the polished bone flute his father had made for him. Sitting cross-legged at the fork in the road, he began to play a stirring air, almost like a marching song. Morhion felt a prickling on the back of his neck. Then the magic began. Dark shapes coalesced on the surface of the dirt road and slipped silently past Kellen to either side. More and more of the dark blobs drifted down the road, most turning left at the fork, a few turning right, before continuing on.

Cormik let out a booming laugh. "Clever lad!" he said, clapping his stubby hands together. "We can't know which way Caledan took, but you'll show us the way his shadow went."

"And it's safe to assume that the rest of him went along," Jewel said brightly.

Kellen smiled as he continued to play the flute.

The shapes moving on the ground were the shadows cast by travelers who had passed this way recently. Raptly, the companions watched the shadows go by: the silhouette of a peasant man bent under a load of firewood, a trio of mounted soldiers, a farmer's ox-drawn wagon, and a nobleman's coach-and-six. At last the silhouette of a lone rider came into view. All of them recognized the horse's graceful head and the rider's wolfish profile.

Propelled by the magic of Kellen's song, the shadows of Caledan and his horse, Mista, approached the fork in the road, hesitated a moment, then took the left-hand track. Caledan had continued west, down the Dusk Road. Kellen lowered his flute. As the haunting music faded away, so did the silent procession of shadows. He looked tired but pleased.

"That's a fine trick, lad," Cormik said, impressed.

Morhion approached the boy. Kellen's shadow magic was powerful indeed. He wondered what other unknown abilities the boy possessed. "I did not know that you could summon shadows of the past, Kellen."

Kellen shrugged, putting away his bone flute. "I didn't know either, until I tried."

They mounted their horses and cantered down the broad swath of the Dusk Road. The full moon was rising when they made camp in a copse of beech trees. This time, Jewel made certain there were no caves in the

vicinity. While Kellen piped a gentle tune on his flute,
Cormik and Mari fashioned what supper they could from
dried meat and such wild roots, mushrooms, and herbs as
they could find.

From his saddlebag, Morhion pulled out the two gifts
the witch Isela had given him. The book, which was certainly ancient, was written in the dead language Talfir,
which meant Morhion would have to spend long hours of
translation to understand its contents. He was eager to
begin; he knew enough Talfir to read the book's title. It
was *K'sai'eb'mal,* or in the common tongue, *On the
Nature of Shadows.* Morhion carefully set down the tome
and picked up the ring, a simple silver band set with a
large stone the purple hue of a twilight sky.

"I've never seen a gem like that," Jewel said, sitting
down next to the mage. She winked at him slyly. "And
you might consider me an expert on the topic."

"I think it is forged of magic," Morhion said. "But as to
its precise nature, I cannot guess."

Jewel studied the stone, an intent expression on her
ageless face. "The facets refract the firelight beautifully,
but the center of the gem is dark. That's strange. Given
this type of cut, the center of the stone should be alive
with light."

Morhion thought about this. "Thank you, Jewel," he
said finally. "I'm not certain how, but I think that's
important."

"Always glad to be of help, love."

They ate dinner in silence, each of them wondering the
same thing: How far ahead of them was Caledan? As the
others readied themselves for sleep, Morhion took the
chance to slip away.

The mage circled around a jagged rock outcropping to
be certain he was out of earshot of the others. He did not
need to call out. A blast of cold air whipped the leaf litter

into a miniature cyclone, and out of the swirling leaves drifted a vaporous, armor-clad figure Morhion knew well.

"You are wise to come to me, mage," Serafi intoned in his sepulchral voice. "Just because we have forged a new pact, it does not mean that our old pact is binding no longer."

"A fact of which I am well aware," Morhion said bitterly.

Serafi drifted closer. Pale frost tinged nearby leaves of gold and crimson. "I am angry with you, mage. You risked yourself foolishly in the ruined city. You nearly perished. Have you forgotten that your body belongs to *me?*"

Morhion shrugged indifferently. "And what if I die, Serafi? There is nothing you can do then."

The spectral knight's laughter echoed malevolently from all directions. "Oh, you are wrong about that, mage. I have dwelt long in the twilight world of the dead, and I am powerful here. Die without granting me your body, and I will make every moment of your eternal after-existence one of pure and utter torment."

Morhion shuddered despite himself. He drew out a small knife and made a cut on his forearm. Dark blood welled forth. He was glad for the pain; it cleared his head. "Get on with it, spirit," he snapped. "I cannot be long. The others will wonder where I've gone."

Serafi knelt and began to drink rapturously. "Ah, yes . . . ," he moaned. "Exquisite. But soon I will no longer need to drink to feel the sweet warmth of blood. Soon it will flow in my own veins. Your body will be mine, Morhion. Then, perhaps, that of the woman you call Mari will be mine as well . . ."

"*What?*" Morhion hissed.

"Do not play the innocent with me, Morhion," Serafi said mockingly. "I know you desire her." The knight's laughter echoed again on the cold air. "Ah, but you have this perverse need to torture yourself, don't you? Yes, you must always deny yourself that for which you long. Well, be certain of this, Morhion—if you are too foolish to claim her, then once your body is mine, I will."

Crimson rage flared before Morhion's eyes. He snatched his arm from the spirit's chill grip. "Get away from me," he snarled. "Your drink is done. Our pact is fulfilled for this moon. Now begone."

Serafi rose, eyes glowing hotly. "As you wish, mage. But I will not go very far."

Before Morhion could spit a curse at the spectral knight, the frigid wind gusted again, and Serafi was gone. For a long moment the mage stood still, breathing deeply, trying to regain his composure. The spirit's mocking words echoed in his mind, words made all the more horrible because there was a shard of truth in them. However, those were feelings Morhion had banished long ago. It is a mage's lot to dwell in solitude, he told himself. He repeated the words again, and again, until at last his heart quieted. Then he made his way through the grove, hurrying back to camp before the others noticed his absence.

Two days later they reached the small trading town of Triel.

It was more of a fortified stockade than a proper town, but they were able to buy fresh supplies, and at least there was one inn where they could spend a night indoors. As in every town, there were thieves in Triel, and it didn't take Cormik and Jewel long to ferret them out. The two returned to their rendezvous point in the town square.

"We're getting closer to Stiletto's base of operations," Cormik told Morhion and Kellen.

Jewel nodded in agreement. "The thieves here were extorted into paying tribute to Stiletto months before anyone had even so much as heard the name in Hill's Edge. We're definitely not far away now."

"Then perhaps there is a chance we may yet reach the Shadowstar before Caledan," Morhion said.

Mari returned then. She had gone to discuss news with the local lord.

"How did it go?" Cormik inquired.

"Strangely," Mari said, rolling her eyes. "Lord Elvar's the most paranoid man I've ever met. He makes you look as svelte as a willow switch, Cormik, yet he's convinced he's going to starve to death. However, he's less worried now than he was a few days ago."

"Why is that?" Jewel asked.

Mari went on excitedly. "It seems rats were plaguing Elvar's granary. Then a stranger came to town—a stranger who got rid of the rats by conjuring dark cats with the music of his pipes. What's more, the stranger stayed on for a while at Elvar's insistence. He left just two days ago." Her eyes flashed brilliantly. "Caledan's been here."

"I know," Kellen said quietly.

He pointed to an object in a dim corner. It was a hand of stone, reaching out of the cobbles from which it had been forged. It was clenched in agony and despair, like the hand of a drowning man.

Mari shook her head in sorrow. "Caledan," she whispered. "It's almost as if he's leaving us these signs deliberately."

"Yes," Morhion echoed quietly. "But if so, what do they mean?"

* * * * *

K'shar pushed aside the tangled witchgrass and gazed upon the half-metamorphosed milestone with curious golden eyes. Without doubt, this was the work of Caldorien's twisted shadow magic. For three nights and two days, the half-elf had been running swiftly through the Reaching Woods, stopping a mere half-dozen times, and then only long enough to sip water from a clear brook or to swallow a handful of acorns or late berries. Now blood surged hotly in his veins. He had found the trail.

Quickly, he examined the footprints pressed into the soft earth around the milestone. Five people had gathered here: a strong yet graceful woman, a tall man, a child, a heavy man, and a small woman who walked lithely but with a slight foot drag—perhaps due to age or injury. K'shar could guess the identities of at least three of them. The strong woman was Mari Al'maren; the tall man was the mage Morhion Gen'dahar; the child was Caldorien's son, Kellen. The renegade Al'maren was indeed trying to find Caldorien, and it appeared she had help. K'shar regretted that she had a child with her— children were blameless creatures, and far too often paid for the crimes of their elders—but that did not matter. He would let nothing stand between himself and his prey.

As the autumn day wore on, K'shar loped easily down the Dusk Road, stretching out his long legs. From time to time, spying a traveler approaching, he would plunge into the thickets beside the highway, moving silently until it was safe to return to the road once more. K'shar preferred to make his way through the world unseen.

While he felt no hunger, by midday he knew he needed sustenance, or the swiftness of his pace would suffer. Halting, he scanned a hedgerow with keen eyes. Suddenly he plunged a hand into the bracken with uncanny speed. When he withdrew his hand, a fawn-colored rabbit struggled in his grip. K'shar spoke a gentle word, passing a hand before the creature's face. The animal fell still, gazing at him with trusting brown eyes. It felt nothing when he snapped its neck with a precise twist of his hand. There was no time for a fire, so K'shar ate the rabbit raw. While the half-elf respected all animals, he felt no regret in killing the rabbit. It was the lot of the hunted to sustain the hunter. And one day, when he died, his own body would feed the grass that the rabbit ate. Such was the nature of the chase.

Stars were beginning to appear in a dusky sky when K'shar reached Hill's Edge. The trading settlement was in a stir; something had transpired here recently. Curious, the half-elf prowled undetected through town, catching snippets of conversations. At last he overheard something of interest. Sinking into a shadowed corner, he listened to two people talking on the front steps of an inn.

"I told Faladar that I didn't like the looks of them," lamented a red-faced woman—a cook by her stained apron and the large wooden spoon she clutched. "But he wouldn't listen to me. Not that he ever did."

"You saw them then?" a man in merchant's garb asked in fascination.

"Aye, I did," the woman replied dramatically. It was clear this was not the first time she had told this tale. "They came here at dusk two nights ago, and a strange-looking bunch they were. The red-haired woman, she wore a sword at her hip. And the tall one, he had the air of a wizard about him. Had a gaze to freeze your blood, he did. They killed poor Faladar, I'm certain of it." She let out an overwrought sigh. "And now it's up to me to run the Five Rings all by myself."

Something made K'shar think that the woman was not truly sorry to be in charge of the inn. Silent as a wraith, he slipped away. He needed to hear no more. Al'maren and her companions had been here just two nights ago, and evidently they had murdered a man. The renegade was sinking low indeed. Quickly, he made his way out of town.

It was full dark, and the moon had not yet risen when K'shar came to the stone bridge over the River Reaching, but his golden eyes required only the faintest of light. He knew it was for abilities such as this that his grandmother's people had been—and still were—persecuted. Some thought that the ability to see in the dark could come only from evil magic. K'shar knew that the darkvision came from generations of his ancestors living in lightless underground caverns. Regardless of its origin, the darkvision was best kept secret, K'shar knew, even from the Harpers. Those who walked the daylight world would not understand his dark heritage.

As he set foot on the bridge, something caught his sharp eyes. He knelt to examine the moist dirt in front of the stone span.

"By all the stars of midnight," he swore softly.

The tracks had been trampled by booted feet and iron-shod hooves. But K'shar could see enough to know they were like no tracks he had seen in all his years as a Hunter. They were shaped like the prints of a barefoot man, but the toes were unusually long, and there were only three of them, and these ended in curved talons. No man had left these tracks. Nor had any beast that K'shar was familiar with.

Fascinated, he followed the strange tracks. There had been two of the creatures. They had stood before the bridge for a time before heading southward. The tracks were clearer once they left the heavily traveled road, and after a short way they were joined by the prints of a third, similar creature. K'shar halted. He had come to a place where the tracks of the unknown creatures were superimposed on a different set of prints—prints he recognized.

"Al'maren," he said in amazement.

He squatted down and studied the myriad shapes pressed into the ground. Whatever the three creatures were, they had chased Al'maren and her friends toward the edge of the Reaching Woods. Had Caldorien ventured into the Reaching Woods as well? Or had he continued westward down the Dusk Road? The half-elf mulled over this dilemma. He could not be certain which way Caldorien had gone. On the other hand, he *was* certain about Al'maren. He made his decision.

"A Harper in the hand is worth two in the bush," he noted wryly, before plunging soundlessly into the shadowed forest.

Thirteen

 The lone traveler had been following the broad swath of the Trade Way for three days now, ever since leaving the strange little town of Triel behind. The traveler did not know his destination, but that did not matter. For he would certainly know it when he arrived there; he dreaded that time, even as it drew him onward.

Occasionally he passed other travelers on the road—merchants, soldiers, or wanderers on pilgrimage—and these drew away, clutching cloths to their mouths and noses as they hurried by, as though they feared he might have some disease. He knew that he looked strange. That morning he had caught a glimpse of himself in a pool of water as he bent to drink. His flesh was mushroom-pale, and half-moons of shadow hung beneath his green eyes. Given this, and his midnight blue cloak that was caked with mud and dried leaves from sleeping on the ground, he supposed people feared him for a dead man risen from the grave. It was ironic, for a shambling corpse was nothing compared to the horror he was in truth becoming. He laughed, knowing it was a terrible sound.

The mist-gray mare he rode nickered questioningly, shattering his dark reverie.

"It's all right, Mista," Caledan murmured, leaning forward to stroke the smooth arch of her neck. "It's just me here now, not . . . the *other*."

Mista let out a soft whinny.

"Let's stop a moment," he said, trying to sound more cheerful. "We've been on the road all day, and you must be tired."

At this, Mista gave an emphatic and slightly indignant snort. She hadn't planned to mention it, but since he brought it up, she was indeed overdue for a rest stop. They came to a halt at the side of the road, and Caledan dismounted. He ran his hand over the pale velvet of her nose. While this would have been a perfect opportunity to bite his fingers, as she was wont to do, she only nibbled at them halfheartedly. Mista knew this was a dark time for her friend.

"I don't know what I'd do without you, Mista," Caledan said quietly. "I think I'm starting to forget myself, to forget who I am. I try to remember things from my life, and all I see are shadows. I can hardly remember what Mari looks like now, or Kellen, or Morhion." He leaned his cheek against Mista's flat forehead. "But you're my oldest friend of all, aren't you? And you're here with me, so I can't forget you."

The opportunity was simply too much for her to resist. She bared her big yellow teeth and chomped his ear.

"You wench!" he roared, slapping her flank. She threw her ears back and gave him a distinctly self-satisfied look. "So much for tender moments," he grumbled, and went to find some water for them to drink.

A clear brook ran beside the road. Next to it was a bush laden with autumn blackberries. He wasn't hungry, but he knew he should eat. Plucking a handful of the berries, he popped them into his mouth one by one. Then he picked another handful for Mista. He started to rise, then halted. Now was the perfect chance, while the *other* slumbered.

Caledan reached his free hand toward the blackberry bush, whistling a dissonant melody. All he had to do was relax his will for a heartbeat, and the shadow magic welled forth like dark water gushing from an underground spring. Still, he usually played his pipes or at least hummed a tune when he worked the transformations. It helped him concentrate. And somehow it made him seem less of a monster.

Caledan's hand began to tremble, calling tendrils of darkness from nearby shadows. They coiled like onyx serpents around the bush, molding the plant, reshaping it. After a moment, he whistled a sharp note of dismissal. The dark tendrils slipped silently back into their pools of shadow. Caledan never knew what form the metamorphosis would take, but the new shape was always a reflection of his soul. This time, the bush's branches had been molded into two, intertwining figures. They were human forms, but whether they were embracing each other in a sensuous expression of love or were fighting to strangle each other in their loathing, it was impossible to tell.

Caledan scrambled away from the bush. It was dangerous to linger too long. The *other* was sleeping now, but when it woke it would know all that he knew. If the *other* learned what the metamorphosed objects meant, it would surely try to stop him from creating more.

The dark presence had been growing within Caledan for months now, perhaps years. For a long time it had

kept its existence hidden. He knew now—as he did not
know before—that he had been the cause of the murders
in Iriaebor. The *other* had used his shadow magic to perform the deeds without his knowledge, but Caledan was
not blameless. The victims—men of violence, corrupt
nobles, agents of the Zhentarim—all had been people
Caledan himself despised. The hatred had been his own.

In the village of Corm Orp, he had finally realized the
truth about himself. He had been powerless to halt the
destruction he had wreaked there with his shadow
magic. The incident had nearly driven him mad. It would
have, except afterward the darkness had retreated deep
within him, as if to rest there, and regroup.

Since then, he had battled constantly to control the dark
chaos raging inside him. Yet with each passing day, the
other woke more often and stayed awake longer. During
those times, he felt that his own consciousness was simply
a spark awash in a sea of darkness. It was only a matter of
time until the spark was extinguished. When that happened, he would cease to be Caledan entirely. All that
would remain would be the *other* . . . the shadowking.

Caledan returned to Mista, offering her the blackberries. She ate the proffered treat delicately, "accidentally"
nipping his fingers only once.

The next day they came to the sprawling tent city of
Soubar, and he sensed that he had reached his destination.

Ever since leaving Corm Orp, the thing had called to
him, like a ringing in his ears, drawing him onward. The
Shadowstar. He wasn't certain when the name had
drifted into his mind. It had come to him unbidden, like
so many things did these days. He did not even know
what the Shadowstar might be, only that it was the key
to his salvation . . . or his damnation.

Now it was close. Perilously close.

"We're almost there, Mista," he murmured. The pale

mare gave an uncertain nicker, then began wending her way through the disordered cluster of tents and shanties.

Soubar was a seasonal trading town situated on the harsh plains south of the Forest of Wyrms. It boasted only thirty or so permanent structures in winter, but in summer its population swelled a hundredfold as merchants, caravaners, and traders from a dozen lands journeyed there, setting up tents to trade all manner of goods. This late in the season, however, most of the wealthier merchants had departed, leaving only the dregs behind—swindlers, charlatans, and thieves.

Mista picked her way disdainfully through the town's makeshift streets, a twisting maze of foul, churned mud that would freeze solid in another tenday or two. Caledan knew the Shadowstar was near, but it was difficult to hear its call amid all the noise and confusion.

Rickety wagons rattled past. Two traders engaged in a shouting match over the price of a cart of moldy turnips. Bawdy music and coarse laughter drifted from dozens of canvas tents. It would take time for him to determine the direction of the Shadowstar's call. It was growing dark, and Caledan decided to see if he could find food and rest.

After some searching, he discovered a makeshift tavern set up inside a rank-smelling tent. There was a small corral out back. Caledan managed to find a bit of musty hay and a trough with an inch of scummy water at the bottom. Mista was not impressed.

"Well, it's the best I can do," Caledan griped. "Besides, I have a feeling I'm not going to fare much better inside."

He was right.

It took his eyes a long moment to adjust to the murky interior of the tent. When they did, all he could see were a dozen unfriendly faces glaring at him. Hastily, he sat at a filthy table in one corner. After a while a surly barmaid brought him a cup of sour beer, some stale black bread, and a bit of moldy cheese. The cost was exorbitant—an entire gold coin—but he needed the food. The fare tasted foul, but he gagged it down.

Finished, he decided it would be best not to linger here. He stood and made his way toward the tent's canvas door. Three burly men—traders of some sort—blocked his way. They grinned evilly, displaying no more than a dozen yellowed teeth among the lot of them.

"Pardon me," Caledan muttered, trying to move past them to the door.

One of the men stuck out a muddy boot, tripping him. The three men laughed heartily, as if the sight of Caledan sprawling on the floor were a great joke.

"This fellow thinks he's too good for our establishment," one of the traders said coarsely.

"I think you're right, Goris," another agreed.

"Maybe if he had a little less gold in his purse, he wouldn't feel so damn superior," the third trader growled.

The three men advanced, clenching their meaty hands into fists. The other patrons in the tavern studiously looked away. Caledan would get no help from them.

"I'm warning you," he said hoarsely. "Leave me alone. For your own good."

The trader called Goris let out a mirthful bellow. "You hear that, men? He's concerned for our well-being." He loomed over Caledan. "I'll tell you the best thing for my own good, worm. It would be to take all your gold, and then smash your ugly face to a pulp. How's that sound?"

Rage blossomed in Caledan's chest. Desperately, he tried to suppress it, but it was already too late. He felt the first dark stirring deep inside. The *other* had sensed his anger. It was waking.

"Please," Caledan whispered urgently. "Please listen to me. Your lives are in danger. You've got to go. Now."

Goris spat in disgust. He gestured to the other two.

"Come on, men! Hold him down while I break a few of his fingers for fun."

The three men lunged for Caledan, but their hands never reached their target.

"I warned you," Caledan whispered sadly.

Suddenly, he felt himself swept away on a surging flood of power. Shadowy, bestial shapes sprang from the dim corners of the tent. The air was filled with the sounds of ripping canvas and splintering wood—or were they the sounds of ripping flesh and splintering bone? Caledan was only dimly aware of the bedlam. The hysterical shrieks of the three men seemed to come from a far distance before they were abruptly cut off. As the dark storm swirled around him, Caledan huddled on the ground, curling himself into a tight ball. He rocked back and forth, muttering four words again and again, as if they were a charm that could keep him from drowning.

"I will not forget. I will not forget. *I will not forget . . .*"

* * * * *

"He's been here, all right," Cormik said with a low whistle of amazement.

Mari could only nod. There was little left of the tent besides a shallow crater littered with a few tatters of greasy canvas and a handful of wood scraps. According to the rumors Jewel and Cormik had overheard, seven people had been slain in the tent's destruction two nights before. Most versions of the story claimed that the cause had been a bolt of lightning or a freak cyclone. The companions knew better. The tent's main pole still stood in the center of the blasted crater, the thick shaft grotesquely twisted. Seared into the wood were the shapes of a hundred bulbous, staring eyes. Mari wondered how the local folk explained *that*.

"I think we've seen enough," she said finally. "Let's find out if there's still a market in this town. We need supplies."

It was three days since the companions had left Triel behind. Outside Lord Elvar's walled town, Kellen had once again conjured shadows of the past, and they learned Caledan had ventured north, following the Trade Way. They rode hard on his trail, trying to make up for lost time.

As they traveled down the road they twice heard blood-thirsty cries above and glanced up to see three dark specks circling high in the sky. The shadevari. Both times the companions had plunged into the thick bracken beside the road, and Morhion had cast a spell that concealed them with a magical dome. The dome acted as a mirror, reflecting the surrounding trees and brush. Twice they waited in terror for the claws of the shadowsteeds to pierce the magical dome and slice them to ribbons. And twice, after what seemed an agonizing eternity, the hideous cries receded.

Now they guided their mounts through the twisting, muddy warren of makeshift tents and shacks. The population of Soubar had been dwindling with the waning days of autumn, and the violent incident two nights ago had begun a mass exodus. Everywhere merchants and traders were packing their wagons and heading for winter bases. Still, there were hundreds of tents in the squalid encampment, and soon they discovered a bustling market in the town's center.

"We may be able to uncover a few more tidbits about Stiletto here," Jewel suggested. She turned to Cormik. "Shall we do a little scouting, love?"

The big crime lord frowned. "Why are you being so nice to me all of a sudden?"

"What's the matter with a little niceness now and then?" Jewel replied a bit too sweetly.

"Nothing," Cormik grumbled, "except when it's used to draw attention away from the dagger one's holding behind one's back."

"Really, Cormik," she scolded him. "Have I ever given you cause to be so suspicious of me?"

"Frankly, yes."

"Oh, very well!" she said, throwing up her arms in exasperation. "I'll promise to dispense with all semblance of niceness, you mistrustful old walrus. Will that make you happy?"

He grinned at her. "Very happy."

The two tied their horses to a hitching post and quickly disappeared into the throng. Mari, Morhion, and Kellen hitched their horses as well.

"I am going to see if there is an herbalist in the market," Morhion said. "I require some ingredients for my spells. Kellen, would you like to accompany me?"

"Yes," the boy replied earnestly.

"I'll go see if I can buy some supplies for the road," Mari told them. "Let's meet back here in an hour." She whispered into her mount's ear. "Farenth, keep an eye on the other horses, will you?" The chestnut gelding nickered softly, and by that she knew he understood.

Mari watched as Morhion and Kellen wended their way through the market. It was clear from the way he gazed up at the taller man that Kellen worshiped the mage. Why should he not? Morhion was intelligent, powerful, and of noble bearing. Mari supposed she worshiped him a bit herself. Not for the first time, she thought how grateful she was that he had accompanied her on this journey. She could not have done all this without him. True, the mage could be distant at times, even cold. Yet Mari considered him a close friend, ever since the night he had told her of the terrible pact he had forged to save Caledan's life—a secret he had never shared with anyone

else. Mari realized that she and Morhion had something
else in common now, for she had made her own sacrifice
for Caledan by becoming a renegade Harper.

Oddly buoyed by this thought, Mari set off to complete
her tasks. She returned to the horses an hour later to
find Morhion and Kellen waiting for her. They helped her
pack the foodstuffs she had bought—in small quantities
at outrageous prices—into their saddlebags. Just as they
finished, Jewel and Cormik reappeared. The two seemed
both excited and agitated.

"What is it?" Mari asked. "Did you find out something
about Stiletto?"

"As a matter of fact, we did," Cormik replied, glancing
around nervously.

"More than we expected," Jewel added. "Er, we may
want to get going and talk about this elsewhere."

"Why?" Morhion asked darkly. "What is wrong?"

"Nothing, really," Cormik replied, fidgeting with his
numerous rings. "It's just that we finally learned where
Stiletto's base of operations is located, and—"

"Where?" Mari interrupted him excitedly.

Before Cormik could answer, the crowd suddenly
parted around them. Out of nowhere, a dozen figures
materialized, each clad in black and bearing a brightly
polished saber. With astonishing swiftness, the men in
black encircled the companions. Mari swore. They were
surrounded.

"Let me guess," she whispered harshly. "Stiletto's hideout is here in Soubar?"

"However did you guess?" Cormik replied as the
thieves closed in.

Fourteen

"Look on the bright side," Cormik offered with forced cheer. "At least we finally found this Stiletto character."

"Actually, Cormik," Jewel countered acerbically, "I think he found us first."

Cormik rolled his eyes in annoyance. "Well, if you're going to get technical about it, Jewel . . ."

Morhion ignored the two fractious crime lords as he paced around the octagonal chamber in which they were imprisoned. Earlier, the thieves had led the companions at sword point through Soubar's muddy streets. Folk had scurried out of their path with averted eyes, which suggested that Stiletto's thugs were well known—and well feared—in the settlement. The thieves had stopped before a rude tent. Inside, under a pile of refuse, was a trapdoor. The companions were forced down a spiral staircase and pushed through dim passages. At last they came to a chamber, and the thieves had sealed them inside.

The air in the chamber was chill. The room lay deep in the ground, where frost never loosened its cold grip on the soil, even in the warm months of summer. Walls, floor, and ceiling were all lined with seamless black marble flecked with crimson and gold. The door through which they had entered had vanished. Morhion ran a hand across one wall. The stone was so slick it felt almost oily, though it left no residue on his fingers.

"Can't you cast some spell to get us out of here, Morhion?" Mari asked, her face drawn.

"I am afraid not. The walls have been infused with a powerful ward against magic." Morhion frowned thoughtfully. "This stone seems familiar to me, but I can't remember where I've seen it before."

"Beneath Iriaebor, in the crypt of the Shadowking."

Morhion turned to gaze sharply at Kellen. The boy ran a small hand over a dark column that looked as if it had been poured rather than carved. "There was stone just like this in the tomb below the city. I remember."

Kellen was right. That was where Morhion had noticed the strangely slick marble before. It explained the aura of magical resistance that emanated from the stone. The crypt of the Shadowking had been permeated by just such an aura. But why was the same stone in this chamber?

The mage drew in a sharp breath. "Stiletto has been using the Shadowstar."

The others stared at him. Before they could reply, a sharp sound shattered the silence. Cracks appeared in one wall, outlining the hidden door. The portal flew open. A dozen thieves slipped into the chamber, as dark and seemingly fluid as the strange marble, positioning themselves around the perimeter of the room. A figure clad from head to toe in a robe of flowing black silk stepped through the doorway. His shadow, cast by wavering torchlight, loomed larger than life on the wall behind him.

Morhion whispered the word. "Stiletto."

"I see introductions will not be necessary," the one called Stiletto said, his raspy voice muffled by the dark cowl that concealed his face. "For I certainly know the great mage Morhion Gen'dahar." The dark cowl regarded each of the others in turn. "And here with him is Mari Al'maren, lately of the Harpers—but no longer I hear. And Kellen Caldorien, son of renowned Harper Caledan Caldorien. And Cormik One-Eye, proprietor of the Prince and Pauper in Iriaebor. And of course Jewel Talondim, the enchanting matriarch of the illustrious Talondim clan."

Morhion had not expected Stiletto to know them. It seemed the underworld lord was omniscient as well as all-powerful.

"Why have you journeyed here seeking me?" Stiletto demanded.

The mage allowed himself a grim smile. "You know so much about us, Stiletto. Surely you know that as well?"

"Perhaps I already do, and merely wish to see if you will lie to me," the dark-robed man snapped, but his words came too hastily, suggesting that in truth he did not know their purpose.

"Wait a minute," Mari said suspiciously, her eyes narrowing as she studied Stiletto. "I can see how an underworld lord might know his rivals, like Cormik One-Eye and Jewel Talondim. And I can even see how he might keep track of Harper agents and those who work with them, which would explain why you know me and Morhion." She took a step forward. "But it doesn't make any sense that you would know the identity of an eleven-year-old boy."

At those words, Morhion forgot the armed thieves surrounding them. Mari was right. Curiosity burned in his brain as he advanced on Stiletto. "Who are you?" he demanded in a low voice.

Stiletto began an indignant reply, but he never finished it. Kellen whistled three sharp notes of music and stretched out an arm. On the wall, the silhouette of his hand touched the shadow cast by Stiletto. Kellen flexed his fingers and Stiletto's cowl was jerked back, revealing his startled visage. The crime lord was a small, weasely man with close-cropped brown hair, darting eyes, and crooked teeth. He grinned sheepishly as the companions stared in astonishment. At last, it was Jewel's scathing voice that spoke.

"You have quite a bit of explaining to do, Ferret Talondim!"

* * * * *

"You've hurt her feelings terribly, you know," Cormik murmured.

"I know," Ferret replied sadly.

They were alone now; the little thief had sent his masked servants away. He cast a fleeting look at his grandmother. She stood on the far side of the octagonal chamber, where Mari and Kellen were doing their best to calm her. Jewel stalked lithely back and forth, looking almost like a dangerous violet panther in her dusk-purple leathers.

"Honor doesn't mean much to thieves," Ferret went on, "but blood does. I suppose my operations have been cutting into Grandmother's business."

Morhion gave the thief a hard look. "I think you err in judging the source of your grandmother's ire, Ferret. Whatever she might say, I imagine she cares little enough for any gold you have cost her. I would say she is angry at the grief you have caused her by letting her believe that you were dead." Mari cast a furious look in their direction. "And I suspect Jewel may not be the only one to feel that way," the mage added meaningfully.

Ferret swallowed hard. "Perhaps I acted recklessly. I suppose, now that Grandmother knows I'm not really dead, she'll go ahead and kill me anyway."

Across the room, Jewel let out a particularly blistering array of expletives. Cormik raised an eyebrow, clearly impressed. "You may be right." He laid a ring-laden hand on Ferret's bony shoulder. "Unless, of course, you go over right now and speak to her. You *are* her grandson, after all. And her favorite, from everything I've heard. That might still count for something."

Ferret nodded uneasily. "I suppose it's worth a try. If nothing else, maybe if I beg for mercy she'll make my demise a little less painful."

Morhion poked a finger against Ferret's chest. "And when you've finished explaining things to Jewel, you can start explaining them to the rest of us. Last we knew, you were lost in the destruction of the Shadowking's crypt beneath Iriaebor. I'm very interested to learn how you got from there to here, and you're going to satisfy my curiosity. Understood?"

Ferret's eyes bulged out. "I hope you're not expecting me to say I'm looking forward to it."

"Frankly," Morhion countered, "I'd be happier if you were dreading it."

"You would, Morhion," Ferret said with a grimace and scurried across the room.

Morhion allowed himself the bare suggestion of a smile. It was good to see the little thief again. The world had been a duller place without him.

Mari approached, gripping Kellen's hand. "Let's give Jewel and Ferret a little space," she suggested, and they withdrew to the far side of the room. It was only a short while later that Jewel and Ferret strode toward them.

The weasely thief was grinning his crooked-toothed grin, and now the matriarch of the Talondim clan was smiling as well, though there was a slightly perturbed light in her eyes.

"It's all right," Ferret pronounced in his raspy voice. "We've made up."

"That was quick," Morhion noted dubiously.

"He didn't play fair," Jewel complained.

"What do you mean?" Mari asked.

"He kissed my cheek and told me that he loved me," Jewel said, as if this were a tremendous outrage.

Ferret beamed. "Even a grandmother as remarkable as my Jewel can't resist kisses from her favorite grandchild."

A scowl cast a shadow across Jewel's ageless face. "You always were the slyest scion of my clan," she muttered.

Cormik adjusted his jewel-encrusted eyepatch. "I hate to interrupt this sweet but twisted family reunion, but perhaps it's time we told Ferret why we were searching for 'Stiletto' in the first place."

Minutes later, they gathered in a sumptuously appointed chamber deep in the underground warrens that were Ferret's—or Stiletto's—hideout.

"Not bad," Cormik said with grudging approval as he eyed the room's mahogany furniture and thick tapestries. "Not bad at all, for an amateur." Cormik, of course, was an expert on luxury.

Soon the companions were seated in comfortable chairs, sipping rich red wine. Morhion savored his glass. It had been a long time since he had drunk such an exquisite vintage. He wondered when, if ever, he would have such an opportunity again. Despite himself, he cast a fleeting glance at Mari. Her eyes were intent on Ferret as the thief began recounting what had befallen him after they defeated the Shadowking in the tomb beneath

Iriaebor.

"It was only last year, Mari, that I finally learned you had survived the bolt of magic that Lord Snake struck you with in the Shadowking's tomb," Ferret explained in his raspy voice. "I was glad to hear it. When Caledan and Morhion and the others ran from the crypt with you in their arms, I thought you were dead. Of course, when those stone doors shut, trapping me inside the tomb, I thought I was dead, too. The entire place was coming down around my ears. I was certain I was a goner. So I said to myself, 'All right, Ferret, my boy—if you're about to cough up the ghost and head to that big dungeon in the sky, you might as well go in style.'"

He rubbed his nimble hands together. "I dodged the falling stones and grabbed all the burial treasure—gold and silver and jewels—that I could find, making a big pile. Then I sat on the pile, thinking that at least I had everything I ever wanted in life, and waited for the rock that would bash my brains." Ferret paused, his beady eyes glowing. "That was when I saw it."

Morhion murmured two words. "The Shadowstar."

"So *that's* what it's called," Ferret said softly. "Of course—what else would it be named?" After a pause, he went on. "I looked down, I don't know why, and saw a strange medallion half-buried in the heap of treasure. It was dark and shining at the same time, and without even thinking, I picked it up." Ferret's pointed noise crinkled in thought. "I'm not sure if it really used words, but it talked to me. At first I wasn't certain what it was saying. It's a little hard to concentrate when one is caught in a shower of boulders and is expecting to get flattened like a bug at any second. After a few moments, I realized that it—the medallion, the Shadowstar—was asking me something." His beady eyes went distant. "It was asking me if I wanted it to take me away from the crumbling tomb. Needless to say, I answered yes." He shook his head in wonder. "The next thing I knew, the crypt was gone, and I was sitting on a hill north of Soubar. What was more, the medallion had brought the pile of treasure along."

"How thoughtful of it," Cormik muttered darkly. "So that's where you found the capital to set yourself up as a crime lord. That really wasn't fair, you know. It took me years to get to that point in my career."

Ferret gave an unimpressed shrug. "I never knew thieving was about fairness, Cormik," he said dryly. "It's a fascinating theory. You'll have to convene a council of guildmasters and tell them all about it. I'm sure they'll be quite receptive to the idea."

"Oh, quit rubbing it in," Cormik said petulantly. "I'm just jealous, of course. You needn't chastise me for it. It's perfectly natural, after all."

"You're right, Cormik," Ferret conceded. "The gold did give me the foundation for building up quite a profitable business. Of course, all the money in the world is nothing if you don't have a natural talent for the illicit and illegal, which fortunately I do."

"You come by it honestly," Jewel said proudly. "Or *dis*honestly, as the case may be."

Ferret flashed a crooked smile at her. "But that wasn't all." His smile faded into an uncharacteristically solemn expression. "I think the Shadowstar had a hand in things. For one, the local master thief conveniently dropped dead the day I strolled into Soubar. Nothing completely impossible ever happened. It just seemed that every time there was a chancy situation that could go for or against me, it always went *for* me. And, well"—he gestured to the opulent furnishings around them—"this is the result."

"Why didn't you let us know you were alive?" Mari

asked in exasperation.

Ferret scratched his chin nervously. "I was going to, really. It's just that I started to realize being dead has its advantages. It was like being given a completely fresh start. Everyone thought the thief Ferret had met his demise, and no one knew anything at all about the man Stiletto. The fact is, I've found that an aura of mystery is a great weapon. No one knows what to expect from you, so they always expect the worst. That tends to make them a little more . . . er, pliable." He sighed. "I suppose that's all over now." Ferret shook his head, dispelling his momentary melancholy. "But you still haven't told me why you've been searching for me. And by the way, where's Caledan?"

Morhion exchanged grim looks with the others. "You might wish to pour yourself another glass of wine before we explain . . ."

When at last Morhion had finished recounting all that had befallen, Ferret appeared visibly shaken. "Poor Caledan," he whispered sadly.

"You can understand why we are glad to have reached you before Caledan did," Morhion said. "The Shadowstar is the key to halting or completing his metamorphosis. With it, we should be able to—"

"You can't have it!" Ferret snapped suddenly. As if by dark magic, the little thief's usually cheerful face was transformed into a pale mask of suspicion. He retreated into a corner, crossing his arms and glaring at them with calculating eyes. "I should have known all along that was what you wanted, to come here and rob me. Well I won't allow it! I'll call my servants before I let you touch any of my treasure." A look of pure greed crossed his face. "I found the medallion. I rescued it from the tomb. The Shadowstar is mine!" His hand strayed to the jeweled dagger at his belt as the others stared in shock. None had ever seen Ferret behave this way.

There was a tense moment of silence. At last, Jewel
stepped forward. "That's not like you, Ferret," she said
quietly, her violet eyes intent. He gripped the hilt of the
dagger more tightly, staring at her with a mixture of fear
and hatred, like a cornered animal. Jewel continued to
approach him, speaking calmly.

"Greed is a thief's worst enemy, Ferret. You know that.
It was the first lesson I ever taught you. A covetous thief
is a dead thief. We commit thievery for our livelihood,
and that's all. As soon as the objects we steal become
dearer to us than life, it is our own lives that are stolen."
Slowly, she reached out to touch his hand.

Ferret stared at her with a look of utter terror and
loathing. For a moment he gripped the knife with white-
knuckled hands. Then he shuddered violently and let go
of the dagger. He passed his hand before his face. The
look of violence vanished.

"I'm . . . I'm so sorry, Grandmother," he said haggardly.
"I don't know what came over me. I must be tired, that's
all." He turned toward Morhion. "Of course you can have
the Shadowstar, Morhion, if you think it might help
Caledan."

Morhion only nodded. He watched the little thief
thoughtfully. Once, a thousand years ago, the Shadowstar had transformed a simple minstrel into the Shadowking. Ferret had possessed the medallion only a short
time, but the thief had not gone untouched by its dark
influence.

Ferret led them out of the chamber and through the
twisting labyrinth of his hideout. Soon they came to a
door hewn of a single massive slab of the same strangely
slick black marble they had seen before. "I keep all my
greatest treasures in here," Ferret explained. "The Shadowstar created the door for me. It will open only at my

touch."

He placed his hand in a circular depression in the center of the marble slab. There was a hissing of air. Then the door parted along an unseen crack and swung silently open. Ferret took a torch from a nearby sconce and led the way. Inside the circular chamber were chests filled with glittering gems, stacks of priceless antique furniture, and heaps of ornate weapons forged from precious metals. In the center of the chamber was a pedestal upon which rested a black velvet cushion, and on the cushion rested . . .

Nothing.

"By Shar!" Ferret swore in disbelief. "It's gone! The Shadowstar!"

"But how?" Mari demanded. "I thought you said that only you could open the door."

"A door created by shadow magic," Morhion added pointedly. From beneath his shirt, he drew out the ruby amulet. It glowed a brilliant crimson. "Caledan was here," he said grimly.

"I don't think we really need your amulet to tell us that," Jewel replied, pointing to the far wall. A patch of stone looked as if it had melted and resolidified, forming the shape of a grotesque mouth that gaped open in a silent, frozen scream.

"In which case," Cormik added soberly, "he now has the Shadowstar."

Kellen bowed his head in sorrow. "Then we've lost."

Fifteen

"So where will he go now?"

Mari asked the question as she paced restlessly back and forth across a thick Amnian rug. They had regrouped in Ferret's luxurious receiving chamber.

"Ebenfar," Morhion said after a moment.

The others looked at him in puzzlement.

"Ebenfar was the ancient kingdom ruled by Verraketh, the Shadowking," the mage explained. "Think of the words spoken by the two ghosts. The shade of Talek Talembar warned that a new king would rise to take the place of the old. And Kera's ghost warned Mari not to let Caledan ascend a throne." He smoothed a wrinkle from his long purple vest. "Now that he has the Shadowstar, Caledan will journey to Ebenfar, to rule as the new shadowking from Verraketh's throne."

Mari shivered. "If Caledan's transformation won't be complete until he sits upon Verraketh's throne, then he

isn't a shadowking yet," she said fiercely. "I'm going after
him, to stop him before he reaches Ebenfar."

"You will not go alone," Morhion said solemnly. "But
there is a problem." He took a deep breath. "I do not
know where Ebenfar is. We can follow Caledan's trail, as
we have been doing, but we have little chance of reaching
Ebenfar before him."

Mari's heart sank. Morhion knew so much—she had
simply assumed he would also know the location of Verraketh's ancient kingdom. She shook her head in despair.
Now what were they to do?

A chill gust of air blew through the chamber, ruffling
the tapestries and causing the chamber's oil lamps to
gutter crazily. In the center of the room, a dark figure
materialized out of thin air. It was a man, clad in ornate
armor as black as polished onyx. Clearly, he was not
alive. His eyes smoldered like hot cinders, and Mari
could see dimly through the vaporous substance of his
body.

"Serafi!" Morhion choked on the word.

Mari stared at Morhion. Serafi—that was the name of
the dark spirit with whom, years ago, the mage had
forged a pact to save Caledan's life. The others gaped at
the dusky spirit in horror, except for Kellen, whose gaze
was calm and interested.

"Why have you come to me?" Morhion said hoarsely.
"Why here, and why now?"

The spectral knight seemed to absorb all the light in
the room. "I have come because it is clear you are far too
stupid to complete your quest without my help," Serafi
hissed. "And complete it you must, so that I can claim my
due."

"How can I possibly afford any more of your *help*, Serafi?" Morhion sneered.

"Oh, indeed, you cannot," the spirit intoned with sinis-

ter mirth. "So, in my generosity, I will give it to you
freely. The lost kingdom of Ebenfar lies in the center of
the High Moor. Journey there. I will come to you from
time to time, to guide you. Now go. And remember, I will
always be near." With a blast of charnel house air, the
spirit vanished.

At last, a rattled Cormik spoke. "What, in the name of
all that's holy, was *that?*"

"The spirit Serafi has little to do with holiness,"
Morhion replied darkly. He cast a glance at Mari. For a
moment, she thought she detected fear in his eyes. Then
his face grew cool and impassive, his mask in place once
more. "I will explain later," he went on. "Right now, we
must ready ourselves for our journey to the High Moor."

Purple dusk was upon them as they gathered with
their horses outside a tent-stable on the edge of Soubar.
They dared not wait until morning to leave. Ferret had
seen the Shadowstar in his treasure room yesterday.
That meant Caledan was only a single day ahead of
them. With the help of the eerie Serafi, they might have
a chance of beating him to Ebenfar. Once there, Mari was
not certain how they would get the Shadowstar away
from Caledan. But get it they must, so Kellen could cast
the spell Morhion had discovered in the *Mal'eb'dala* and
stop Caledan's horrible transformation.

Ferret threw a saddlebag and bedroll onto the back of a
skittish roan stallion and mounted alongside the others.
Morhion gave him a piercing look. "Just what do you
think you're doing?"

"Going with you," Ferret replied nonchalantly.
"Caledan is my friend, too, you know." A sharp light
glinted in his beady eyes. "Besides, I imagine there's all
sorts of lost treasure in Ebenfar."

Both Cormik and Jewel were flabbergasted.

"But you can't simply leave your business like this!"

Jewel protested. "An underworld empire doesn't run itself, love. Surely you know that."

"I truly hate to say this, but Jewel is right," Cormik added. "Who's going to take care of all your operations while you're gone?"

"Actually," Ferret said matter-of-factly, "I was rather hoping you two would."

The effect this had on the two crime lords was astonishing. Mari had never before seen either of them at a loss for words. When at last they found their tongues, it was to protest vehemently, but Ferret refused to take no for an answer. At last the two agreed, not entirely with reluctance. Clearly they were more than a little excited by the notion of running someone else's thieving empire.

"Think of it," Cormik said with relish. "All the fun without any of the responsibility!"

"Don't get carried away, love," Jewel said dryly. "I'm sure Ferret would like it if some of his empire actually remained intact by the time he returns."

"Oh, bother!" Cormik said petulantly. "I can see you're going to be a stick-in-the-mud. Well, my dear, sour shrew, I'm not going to let you spoil my fun."

"We'll have lots of fun," Jewel countered dangerously. "As long as we do things *my* way, my sweet, bloated simpleton."

The two fell to eager scheming about which duties would be whose. Ferret guided his horse toward Mari, nodding toward Jewel and Cormik. "So how long have they been in love?" he asked softly.

Mari gaped at him. *Love?* What was Ferret talking about? Yet even as she was about to dismiss this as an impossibility, she realized the truth of it. She had been so caught up in the search for Caledan that she had been blind to what was happening in front of her eyes. Now, as she looked at the two crime lords, it seemed comically obvious. They bent their heads near as they spoke, touching hands, and even as they hurled caustic insults at each other, their eyes glowed with affectionate mischief.

"I'm not certain," Mari murmured. "But I'm glad they found each other."

It was time to go. They bid a warm farewell to Jewel and Cormik, then turned to ride into the gathering gloom. Suddenly Mari raised a hand. The hair on the back of her neck prickled. "Get back into the tent," she hissed. Such was her tone that the others did not argue.

Mari watched through a thin gap in the canvas as a lone figure appeared on a distant rise, moving toward the sprawling tent city. Even before she saw his face, she guessed who he was. When he drew near enough for her to catch a glint of two glowing amber eyes, there could be no doubt. Her heart contracted in terror when the tall, lean man paused. He seemed to sniff the air. Then, swiftly, he loped toward the heart of town, disappearing from view. Mari breathed a sigh of relief.

"I was afraid this would happen," she whispered.

"You were afraid *what* would happen?" Morhion asked.

She swallowed hard. "The Harpers have sent one of their Hunters after us. Or perhaps after Caledan. It doesn't really make a difference."

"A hunter?" Ferret asked. "Maybe he can catch a few pheasants for our stew pot."

"He's not that kind of hunter, Ferret," Mari replied darkly. "People are his usual prey, not animals. I've heard of this particular Hunter. His name is K'shar, and he's a half-elf. I've also heard that no quarry has ever escaped him."

"And just what does he do when he catches his quarry?" Ferret asked nervously.

"Use your imagination."

"Oh. I was afraid you would say that."

"It looks as though this K'shar is just arriving in Soubar," Cormik said. He turned to Jewel. "What do you say we arrange a few interesting diversions for him, to make certain that he doesn't leave town quickly?"

"A wonderful idea, love," Jewel purred. "I have a few ideas you might find interesting . . ."

Despite her new worries, Mari managed to smile. It was clear that the rotund crime lord and the older, sultry masterthief were going to make an effective—and deadly—duo.

"Let's go find Caledan," she said.

Morhion, Ferret, and Kellen followed her out of the tent, into the deepening night.

* * * * *

Hooves clattering against loose scree, Mista scrambled the last few feet out of the rocky defile and onto a windswept ridge. Caledan pulled gently on the reins, bringing her to a halt.

"There it is, Mista," he said quietly. "The High Moor."

The mare snorted softly. A vast wasteland stretched before them, marching toward the distant horizon in endless gray waves. Pale mist pooled in low hollows, and here and there jagged spurs of rock thrust upward toward the leaden sky like beckoning fingers. A few wind-twisted plants clung precariously to the barren landscape, but there was no sign of anything moving. The High Moor was a dying land. How appropriate that somewhere in its heart should be a dead kingdom. Ebenfar.

Caledan nudged Mista into a canter across the damp moor. Almost unconsciously, he lifted a hand to grip the star-shaped medallion resting against his heart. Despite the chill air, the dull silvery metal was curiously warm. It had been strangely easy to take the medallion from the treasure chamber in Soubar. No—it had not been strange at all, for the Shadowstar had *wanted* to be found. The door to the treasure chamber had responded willingly to Caledan's shadow magic, and the medallion had nearly leapt into his hand.

In the instant he hung the medallion around his neck, he had understood his destiny. He was to journey to Ebenfar, to the ancient kingdom of the Shadowking. He sensed that the medallion had the power to whisk him instantly there but did not wish to do this. The journey itself was important. The *other* still needed time to grow. And grow it would. Soon, all that would be left of him would be the shadowking within, and he would leave behind the man Caledan forever.

"I have to hold on, Mista," he whispered hoarsely, gripping her mane tightly in clenched fingers. "I cannot forget who I am. I must not."

For a moment, thoughts of those he loved drifted into his mind. Were the companions following him? Would they understand the signs he had been leaving for them? Quickly, he forced his friends from his mind. It was a mistake to think about them. Now that he had the Shadowstar, the *other* slept less and less, and he had to keep his one fragile hope concealed.

"If there is any hope at all," he murmured.

Suddenly the Shadowstar twitched against his chest, sending a hot, dizzying wave coursing through his body. Caledan brought Mista to a halt. Gripping the medallion, he squeezed his eyes shut. Yes, he could feel the dark ones. They were close now. The shadevari.

Ever since his journey had begun, Caledan had sensed the dark presence following him. As soon as he gained the Shadowstar, his senses had grown remarkably keen, and he had discerned the true nature of the creatures pursuing him. They were shadevari, three of the ancient,

malevolent beings banished beyond the Circle of the
World by the god Azuth—beings who, he now realized,
were somehow inextricably linked with the shadow
magic.

An idea occurred to him. "We don't want the shadevari
to find me too easily, do we, Mista?" he said with a harsh
laugh. "That wouldn't be any fun for them. Maybe there's
a way to make my trail a little harder to follow."

Mista gave a snort.

"Just watch," Caledan replied.

He gripped the Shadowstar more tightly and hummed
a dissonant tune under his breath. Mista pranced skittishly as a patch of shadow near her hooves swirled and
expanded. Like dark serpents, a dozen sinuous forms
sprang from the patch of shadow. The forms wriggled
swiftly away, each in a different direction, snaking across
the High Moor until they were lost in the distance.

"There," Caledan said in grim satisfaction, releasing
the Shadowstar. "The shadevari won't be able to distin-
guish my trail from any of those shadowserpents. That
should keep them guessing which way I've gone, at least
for a little while."

Mista gave an impressed whinny.

"Why, thank you." Caledan patted her neck fondly.
Slowly his eyes rose toward the far-off horizon.

"All right, my friend," he whispered. "Let's go."

* * * * *

Concealed inside a heavy cloak, K'shar watched the
crimson tent from a distance. At last the half-elf's
patience was rewarded. The tent's entrance flap parted a
few scant inches, and he caught a glimpse of a face peering out. After a moment, the face vanished. However, the
glimpse had been more than enough for his sharp golden

eyes. He knew the watcher in the tent from the description given by a soldier he had interrogated in Triel. It was one of Al'maren's companions, the thief Jewel. His quarry must still be in Soubar. Anticipation boiled in K'shar's veins. The chase was nearly over.

For a time, in the tangled depths of the Reaching Woods, he had feared that the unthinkable had happened, that he had lost his prey. The trail had led to a ruined city where he had seen evidence of a battle with some sort of doglike creatures. The signs indicated that the companions had crossed the River Reaching, but by what means K'shar could not discern. For two days he searched for a way across the roiling river and found none. At last he was forced to give up and return to the Dusk Road. Just as he was growing concerned that his quarry had escaped him, he picked up the trail once again in Triel. Running night and day, he had journeyed swiftly to Soubar. Now it appeared that he had caught up with them at last.

"You are a worthy opponent, Harper Al'maren," he murmured, baring his slightly pointed teeth in a feral smile. "But no one can elude me forever."

Soundlessly, he moved to the entrance of the crimson tent and slipped within. His eyes adjusted instantly to the dim interior. But the tent was empty. Alarm flared in his mind. Something was wrong . . .

Too late he realized it was a trap. There was a hissing sound as the floor dropped from beneath him, and he fell through a series of steel hoops to land upright. Then the metal hoops tightened forcefully around his body, clamping his arms to his sides and immobilizing him. From behind, a hand reached out and pressed an acrid-smelling cloth over his mouth and nose. Reflexively, he inhaled.

You fool, K'shar! he chastised himself. You have grown lazy and thoughtless in your arrogance. Never did you

consider that Al'maren might figure out you were following her. Never did you consider that she might lay a
trap . . .

Quickly, the pungent vapors from the cloth did their
work, and K'shar sank into unconsciousness.

After a time, he woke to the sound of voices.

For a moment he listened, eyes closed. The voices were
far-off, so faint that no human ear could possibly hear
them. Fortunately, K'shar's ears were more than merely
human.

"Now that we have him, what do we do with him?" a
smoky, feminine voice said. That could only be the thief,
Jewel.

"Well, how should I know?" a bubbling male voice
replied. K'shar guessed that one belonged to the corpulent crime lord, Cormik.

"I thought you were the one who was always full of
ideas," Jewel said peevishly.

"Even the best of us have our off days," Cormik whined.
"I'd rather not win the undying enmity of the Harpers by
killing their best Hunter. However, we have to make certain K'shar doesn't follow the others into the High Moor.
They've got only a day's jump on him, and they . . ."

K'shar's amber eyes flashed open. He did not bother
listening to the rest of Cormik's words. There was no
need. Al'maren was journeying to the High Moor, only a
single day ahead of him. That was all he needed to know.

Now there was simply the small matter of escaping. He
was in an underground chamber, he guessed by the chill,
musty air. They had left him alone, no doubt expecting
the effect of the drug to last longer than it had. K'shar
knew his metabolism worked more swiftly than that of a
normal human. He was suspended upright from the
chamber's ceiling, still immobilized by the steel bands
bound tightly around ankles, knees, waist, torso, and

shoulders. Shutting his eyes, he concentrated, drifting into a trance.

Focusing on his thrumming heartbeat, he forced his body to relax, willing his muscles to become as soft and malleable as clay. One by one, they responded. Soon it felt as if he were adrift in a warm ocean. He was ready. Gathering his will, he gave a swift, sharp jerk, dislocating his left shoulder. There was a wet popping noise, but almost no pain. Without hesitating he jerked again, dislocating his right shoulder.

Now that his arms dangled loosely, it was easy to fold his shoulders inward, like a severely hunched old man. This created precious inches of space within the three steel rings that bound his upper body. Slowly he inched his left arm out of the rings that encircled his waist, his midriff, and finally his shoulders. This created yet more space within the rings; his right arm was more easily freed. He took a deep breath, then clenched the muscles of his back and shoulders. There was an audible sucking sound as the round ends of his arm bones were drawn once more into the sockets of his shoulder joints. He would be sore tomorrow, but it did not matter. Arms free, he reached up and gripped the iron chain that suspended the steel hoops from the ceiling. He hauled himself upward, his relaxed muscles allowing him to slip out of the rings that bound his legs, and dropped nimbly down to the floor.

Now all he had to do was find a way out of the room.

This presented itself in the form of a ventilation shaft. Clearly, his captors had never imagined he might escape his bonds, else they would have placed him in a more secure chamber. Most men would not have fit into the shaft, but, though tall, K'shar was willow-thin. He pulled himself into the narrow tunnel and wriggled his way upward. Aided by his uncanny flexibility, K'shar passed through several tight turns with little difficulty. He pulled himself out of the mouth of the shaft onto the muddy ground, gazing into the crimson eye of the dawning sun.

K'shar stretched his limbs as the flow of blood returned to his hands and feet. His prey was close now. Very close. He felt a strange sense of kinship with the renegade Harper he had been following. When he met her at last, he imagined he would almost regret killing her. Almost.

"I am coming, Al'maren," he whispered softly.

He broke into a swift run, moving northward out of Soubar.

Sixteen

The four riders picked their way across the bleak expanse of the High Moor. The rough terrain looked as if it had been shattered by a war among giants. Long stretches of treacherous scree gave way suddenly to jagged chasms that sliced across the ground like gaping wounds. More than once they had been forced to travel miles out of their way to find passage. Despite the harshness of the moor, a sprinkling of moss and lichens clung to the rocks, softening the landscape like a gray-green veil. Mari had never before seen such a melancholy land. Yet it was also lovely. She marveled at the stark contrast of sorrow and beauty dwelling side by side, each blending into the other so that she could not possibly have said from which arose the aching in her heart. She sighed, her breath turning to mist in the cold air.

An icy gust of wind snatched the breath from her lips as a spiderweb of glittering frost spread across a nearby heap of stones. A dark blot appeared in the air above the rock. In moments, the swirling patch of darkness resolved itself into a ghostly knight with smoldering eyes.

"In another mile, the walls of this ravine you follow will rise into sheer cliffs," Serafi said in his sepulchral voice. He pointed to one side with an ethereal gauntlet. "Follow this gully to the north. It will take you out of the ravine and up to a ridge where you may ride more swiftly."

Then the spectral knight vanished, a chill gloom lingering in his wake.

"Well, isn't he just a ray of sunshine?" Ferret muttered glumly.

Mari cast a look at Morhion. He sat astride his dark stallion, Tenebrous, head bowed. Over the last several days, as they rode deeper into the High Moor, Serafi had appeared from time to time, warning them of obstacles or steering them toward easier paths. The mage had told the others of the pact he had forged with Serafi to save Caledan's life. Yet Mari could not help thinking there was something else beneath the mage's brooding. Morhion's pact with the spectral knight, forged ten years earlier beneath the fortress of Darkhold, didn't really explain the spirit's presence on this journey.

There was no sunset that day—the iron gray clouds hid all traces of the sun—but gradually the wan daylight faded, until Mari could barely see Ferret, who led the way astride his bony roan stallion. They made camp in a low hollow that offered some protection from the bone-numbing wind. Supper that evening was only dried fruit, nuts, and hardtack, for they dared not light a fire. They had seen no signs of the shadevari since leaving Soubar, but there was no sense in making themselves any more conspicuous than necessary.

Morhion retrieved a leather-bound tome from Tenebrous's saddlebags. "I am going to study my spellbook," he said coolly. With a soft word, the mage conjured a tiny sphere of purple magelight. He sat on a rock, hunching over the book and shielding the faint illumination with his body to conceal it from prying eyes.

"Would you play a song, Mari?" Kellen asked then.

Out of habit, Mari had packed her lute in her saddle-bag, but she had not yet brought the instrument out on this journey. She had not felt like making music. Yet tonight the prospect seemed appealing. It might be good to let her mind drift on the forgetful strains of a song.

She smiled at Kellen as she retrieved her lute. It was a beautiful instrument, fashioned of cherry inlaid with rosewood. Her adopted father, Master Andros, had made it for her. Its surface had been polished to a glowing patina with long years of use.

The ballad she sang told the story of a prince who fell in love with a maiden trapped in a witch's tower. The prince tried to climb the tower but fell into a hedge of thorns. The thorns scratched his face, blinding him, and the prince became a wandering beggar.

Mari paused, her fingers hovering above the strings. Why had she chosen such a mournful song?

Kellen had rested his head on her knee, listening. Now he looked up at her. "The poor prince," he murmured sadly. "If only he had never fallen in love with the maiden."

At this, Mari shook her head fiercely. "Don't say such a thing, Kellen. It is never wrong to feel love. Besides, I have yet to finish the tale."

Strumming softly on the lute, she sang the remaining verses.

After several years the witch died, and the maiden escaped from the tower. In the forest, she came upon a wretched beggar and realized that it was her prince. She cried bitterly, her tears falling on his face. Such is the power of love that her tears healed his eyes and restored his sight. They returned to the tower and lived there together to the end of their days.

Mari played a few final, wistful notes, then let her hands fall from the lute.

"Thank you," Kellen said quietly.

Ferret had finished repacking their supplies. "I'm going to do a little scouting while there's still a shred of daylight," the thief said.

Kellen hopped to his feet. "Can I come along?" he asked eagerly.

Ferret gave him a critical look. "Can you move without making a sound?"

Kellen chewed his lower lip. "I think I can," he decided, "if you show me how."

Ferret laughed at this. "I imagine you could at that. Come on then, if it's all right with Mari."

Mari nodded her assent—the boy could be no safer than with Ferret—and watched the two disappear into the gathering gloom. She turned to see Morhion watching her.

Mari sat down on the smooth rock beside the mage. "He is wise for a child," she said after a moment. "Kellen, I mean."

Morhion stared into the deepening night. "Sometimes I think he is wiser than any of us."

She laughed softly. "You may be right."

At last the mage spoke again, his voice oddly wistful. "Do your truly believe what you told him, Mari? That it is never wrong to feel love?"

This seemed an unusual question for the usually reticent mage. Finally she nodded. "Yes, I do believe it."

A rueful smile touched his lips. "You are fortunate then. Would that I could believe in love so strongly as you."

Mari frowned in puzzlement.

"I mean . . ." The mage began, then shook his head. "But it is foolishness to talk about it. Forgive me." He started to stand.

"Wait," Mari said intently. "Why won't you tell me what you were going to say, Morhion? I thought . . . I thought that we were friends."

His chill blue eyes sent a shiver down her spine. "Are we?" His tone was not mocking; it was as if he were asking a question whose answer he truly did not know. "I am not . . . I am not certain I know what it is to be close to another person, Mari. It is a mage's lot to dwell in solitude."

Mari stared at the mage. What in Milil's name could he possibly mean? All at once, realization washed over her. How could she have been so blind?

"Why, Morhion?" she whispered. "Why have you never told me how you feel?"

The mage shook his head sadly. "How could I? You are the partner of my closest friend. How could I tell you that—" A bitter expression twisted his face into a sneer. Quickly, he rose. "I am sorry. I imagine that I must disgust you now."

Before he could move away, Mari stood and gripped his arm.

"You're wrong," she said fiercely. "Yes, I am surprised at your words. Maybe even shocked. The truth is, I really don't know what to think. But there is one thing I do know, Morhion, and it is this: There can never be anything wicked in feeling love, whatever the priests in the temple might say. If there is one thing in all this world that is truly good, then it is love. And it is wrong to pretend that love does not exist."

He gazed at her, his blue eyes unreadable. "Perhaps

you are right," he said finally. "Or perhaps not. It does not matter now." A shadow crossed his handsome visage. "There is . . . something else I must tell you, Mari."

He spoke for a long time in low, measured words. An icy horror filled Mari's chest as she learned the hideous truth about Morhion's new pact with Serafi. It was the spectral knight who had given the mage knowledge of the Shadowstar and Stiletto, but for the price of Morhion's own body.

"But how could you accept Serafi's offer?" Mari gasped in disbelief.

Morhion shook his head somberly. "How could I refuse it?"

Mari clenched a fist. "Damn him, Morhion!" she choked hoarsely. "Damn him to the Abyss! Why must we always sacrifice everything for Caledan? *Why?*"

"Because we love him," Morhion said quietly.

It was true, and she knew it. As the anger drained out of her, she sank back to the cold stone. Morhion joined her once more. For a time they sat in silence, while somewhere in the distance a pair of mourning doves filled the night with their sweet lament.

*　*　*　*　*

Kellen crept softly among the scattered heaps of rubble toward a dim shape. Night blanketed the moor, but a faint gray glow hovered on the air, giving just enough light to navigate by. Somewhere behind the thick clouds, the moon had risen. Kellen concentrated on moving stealthily, and he was no more than three paces away when the dim form let out a surprised oath.

"Gods, kid—you're pretty good at this moving in shadows stuff," Ferret said in his raspy voice.

Kellen sat down on a rock beside the thief. "I like shadows," he said matter-of-factly.

"Well, I think they like you, too," Ferret replied, his crooked teeth gleaming in the darkness. "You'd make a good thief, Kellen."

With a thumb, Kellen traced the puckered scar on the palm of his left hand. "I think I'm supposed to be a mage someday, Ferret. At least, that's what Morhion says."

Ferret gave a shrug. "Who says you can't do both?"

Kellen considered the possibility. Mages cast powerful spells and used magical wands to conjure lightning and fireballs, but thieves got to prowl about in the dark and steal interesting treasures from ancient tombs. Both professions had their attractive points. "I'll have to think about it," he said finally.

As he spoke, the night wind picked up, whistling mournfully over the jagged rocks. Kellen felt icy pinpricks stinging against his cheeks. It was starting to snow.

"We'd better get back to camp," Ferret said. "Mari and Morhion will be wondering where we are."

Together they moved silently through the chill night toward the hollow where they had left the others. They had gone no more than a dozen paces when the wind suddenly turned into a gale. Another dozen paces and the gale became a hurricane. Kellen stumbled, the fierce wind lifting him bodily off the ground. He would have been blown down a ravine and dashed against the rocks were it not for Ferret's quick reflexes. The thief grabbed the collar of Kellen's tunic and pulled him back. Holding on to each other, they tried to make headway against the wind, but the gale seemed to blow them back nearly as many paces as they stumbled ahead. The sound of the wind rose to a keening wail, and the hard snow felt as if it were scouring the skin off Kellen's face. The scar on his left hand throbbed dully.

"I don't think this is a normal storm, Ferret!" he cried over the shriek of the wind.

"Even I could figure that one out, kid!" Ferret shouted back.

Cloaks flying wildly behind them, the two struggled on. Suddenly, like a dark wound, a rift opened in the clouds that had hung for three days over the High Moor. With impossible speed the rift widened as the violent wind ripped the clouds to ragged tatters. As quickly as it had risen, the gale dwindled and blew itself into stillness. The night was utterly silent. Stars glittered like chips of ice in the perfect black sky, and a gibbous moon frosted the land with crystalline light.

"It's beautiful," Kellen whispered, his breath making ghosts in the motionless air.

"Yeah?" Ferret asked softly. "I was thinking more along the lines of 'weird' myself." The thief's beady eyes glittered warily in the moonlight.

Then a new sound shattered the frozen air—the hunting call of a lone hound. After a moment, the hound's distant cry was echoed by that of another, and another, then dozens like it.

"I think we might want to hurry a little, Ferret," Kellen said gravely.

The thief did not argue. They started into a trot, then a lope, and finally an all-out run. The malevolent baying echoed all around now, and it was getting closer. Hearts pounding, the two reached their encampment to find Mari and Morhion staring wide-eyed into the night.

"What in the name of the Abyss is going on?" Ferret swore, panting.

"The shadevari conjured shadowhounds to pursue us," Mari said grimly.

"We managed to escape them in the Reaching Woods," Morhion added. "However, I fear we have little chance of eluding them on the open moor."

Ferret shuddered. "It was a rhetorical question. You really didn't have to answer it, you know."

More sinister baying splintered the night, closer than before.

"We can stand here and argue semantics, or we can find a place to defend ourselves. Which would you prefer?" Morhion asked.

"What do you think?" Ferret snapped in exasperation.

"There," Mari said, pointing into the moonlit night. "We'll make our stand there."

Less than a quarter of a mile away, a low hill rose against the starry sky. Standing atop the tor was a jagged ring of stones, the ruins of an ancient tower. There was little need to urge the frightened horses into a gallop. In moments, the four reached the crest of the hill and led the horses through a gap into the ruin. The wall of weathered stone stood about shoulder height, and the floor, which was covered with a carpet of moss and witchgrass, was no more than a dozen paces across.

Morhion muttered the words of a spell, and a blue incandescence burst to life between his hands. Slowly, the glow began to spread outward in a widening circle.

"What are you doing?" Mari asked breathlessly.

"This is a spell of protection," Morhion explained. "However, I fear it will do little to ward us against the shadowhounds. But it may give us a few moments to—"

Morhion gasped. The ring he wore on his left hand—the ring given him in Talis by the witch Isela—flashed brilliantly. The magical circle of radiance changed from blue to dark purple and expanded rapidly, striking the wall. There was a sizzling sound, and countless tendrils of purple magic crackled, coiling around the weathered stones and plunging into the cracks between them. In moments the entire wall glowed with a deep purple radiance.

"What was *that?*" Ferret asked. "Er, and that one *wasn't* a rhetorical question."

"I don't know," Morhion said in wonderment. "Somehow the ring altered my spell."

Howls of bloodlust filled the air. At the bottom of the hill, a score of dark forms appeared out of the night. Swiftly, they began loping up the rocky slope.

"Well, we'd better hope the ring knew what it was doing," Mari said somberly as she drew the short sword at her hip.

Ferret followed suit, pulling a long dagger from a leather sheath at his belt. "I suppose it's too late to tell you that I've changed my mind and decided to stay behind in Soubar," he said forlornly.

No one even bothered to reply.

With impossible swiftness, the shadowhounds streamed up the side of the hill. They looked like normal dogs, only they were blacker than midnight and bigger than the largest of mastiffs. Their sharp teeth glowed in the moonlight, their eyes burned with crimson light.

"Stay behind me, Kellen," Morhion ordered, and the boy did as he was told.

For a moment the baying ended, and there was only eerie silence as the shadowhounds closed the last few yards to the ruined tower. Then, as one, they struck. Snarling ravenously, the onyx hounds leapt easily over the ragged wall, long tongues hanging out of gaping muzzles.

Purple radiance crackled brilliantly as snarls of hunger turned to yelps of pain. Like tiny bolts of violet lightning, tendrils of purple magic arced upward from the wall to engulf each of the shadowhounds in midair. The onyx beasts were thrown violently backward. They struck the ground howling and writhing until the purple sparks flickered and dimmed. The hounds regained their feet and padded warily toward the tower, lips curled back from sharp fangs. This time, however, they did not jump over the wall.

"The magic of the ring—it's holding them back!" Mari said in amazement.

"Don't get your hopes up yet," Ferret countered. "We still have a little problem." With his dagger, he pointed to the gap in the wall through which they had entered the ruined tower. Even now the hounds were prowling around the wall.

"Hold out your weapons," Morhion commanded.

Startled, the other two did as they were told. Morhion muttered the words of another spell of protection, conjuring a second sphere of blue light. As before, the ring on his left hand flashed. Blue radiance became purple. The sizzling violet magic coiled around Mari's sword and Ferret's dagger until the two blades glowed with an enchanted light.

A shadow appeared in the gap, along with a pair of burning eyes. Mari and Ferret whirled just in time to face the shadowhound's leap. Maw snapping violently, the monster fell upon Mari as she thrust her sword out before her. She fell to the ground, the beast on top of her. Suddenly it threw back its head, letting out a howl of agony. Searing purple magic radiated from Mari's sword, engulfing the beast; the enchanted blade had pierced its body. The hound stumbled backward, howled again, then collapsed. In seconds its body had dissolved into a puddle of dark sludge. The purple magic faded. Pale-faced and bruised, Mari pulled herself to her feet.

Another shadowhound tried to jump through the breach. Ferret slashed with his blazing dagger, and the beast leapt backward. More of the dark hounds gathered outside the gap, but they had seen the effects of Mari's sword on one of their ilk. They growled menacingly, but none dared try to force its way in. Then, as if in answer to some inaudible signal, the hounds all turned and loped away down the hill. The companions stared at each other in amazement.

Mari lowered her short sword. "They're gone," she said hoarsely. "They've given up."

Kellen moved to the wall. He pulled himself up the rough stones and peered over the edge. "No, they haven't given up," he said quietly. "They're just . . . changing."

Drawn by his strange words, the others approached the wall.

"By all the gods of darkness!" Ferret swore.

The shadowhounds had gathered at the base of the hill, milling around in a growling throng. Two hounds brushed against each other, and, as if made of dark clay, their separate forms merged into one. More shadowhounds pressed themselves against their brethren, merging their bodies into shapeless blobs that oozed fluidly across the ground. Finally, the formless blobs coalesced with the remaining shadowhounds into one gigantic mass, which began to take on a new shape. Wings spread outward like midnight sails, a sinuous neck unfurled like a great serpent. Crimson eyes blinked to life in a huge, wedge-shaped head, and obsidian talons sprang from outstretched claws. The thing tilted its horned head back, its vast roar sundering the night.

"Milil save us," Mari whispered in awe.

It was a dragon. A dragon of shadows.

Seventeen

The shadowdragon spread its vast wings and rose into the sky, blotting out the stars.

Kellen had never seen anything so magnificent—or so terrifying. The shadowdragon soared higher, the surging sound of its pumping wings like that of white-capped waves breaking on a rocky shore. In moments, the gigantic beast circled far above hill and ruined tower, tilting its triangular head back to let out another trumpeting roar.

"All right, now what?" Ferret rasped, his pointed nose twitching furiously. The little thief looked at the mage expectantly.

"I'm open to suggestions," Morhion snapped.

"What about Isela's ring?" Mari shouted over the dragon's roar. "It helped protect us against the shadowhounds."

"It is worth a try," the mage agreed.

"Well, you might want to try soon," Ferret gulped,

pointing upward.

Silhouetted against the starry sky, the shadowdragon folded its wings against its body and dove, stretching out scythelike talons. Morhion crossed his wrists and shouted the guttural words of an incantation. Crackling bolts of blue lightning sprang from his out-turned palms and shot upward. As the bolts sped toward the shadowdragon, the jeweled ring on his left hand blazed brilliantly. The lightning changed from blue to deep violet. The diving dragon spread its sail-like wings, halting impossibly in midair. The beast cocked its neck, then thrust its head forward, jaws gaping open. Some dragons breathed fire, others emitted clouds of poisonous gas or flesh-searing acid. This was a dragon of shadow. Its breath was darkness.

A bolt of onyx streamed from the dragon's mouth and collided with the crackling purple lightning halfway between mage and beast. Tendrils of darkness coiled around the blazing pillar of lightning and spiraled rapidly downward, like black serpents slithering down a glowing column.

"Morhion, let go of the spell!" Kellen cried out.

His face twisting with effort, the mage uncrossed his wrists at the last possible second. The onyx dragonbreath engulfed the magical lightning, and the spell shattered violently, filling the night with hurtling shards of slick darkness and sizzling purple radiance. The force of the explosion threw Morhion backward against the stone wall. He slumped to the ground and Mari ran to him.

"I'm all right," he gasped hoarsely. "But if the ring has the power to help us now, I do not know the key . . ."

"Well, we'd better think of an alternate plan, and on the double," Ferret suggested nervously.

The shadowdragon swooped low over the hilltop, then soared into the sky to ready itself for another dive. As it passed overhead, Ferret hurled his dagger in a precise arc. The knife struck the creature's eye—and passed right through the shadowy substance of its body. The thief swore vehemently. "How can we fight something that's made of shadows?" he shouted.

Ferret helped Mari pull Morhion to his feet. The three gazed upward, faces pale with fear, as the shadowdragon folded its wings against its sinuous body and once more began to dive. Kellen did not join them. Instead, he scrambled nimbly to the top of the wall and drew out his bone flute. He took a deep breath and began to play.

It was a song like no other he had made before. It was wilder, bolder, and far more powerful. It had to be, if there was to be any hope at all. The first notes to rise from the instrument were daring, questioning—almost a challenge. Then Kellen launched into a surging, rhythmic counter-melody. In moments, he felt shadow magic racing through his veins. His left hand itched furiously. It was time. He reached his mind out, calling to the shadows.

They came.

Tendrils of dark mist rose from nearby pools of shadow and drifted toward Kellen. More shadows reached out from an inky patch at the base of the hill, and from the dark depths of a chasm a half mile away. Kellen had never summoned shadows from so far a distance. His song grew fiercer yet as more shadows heeded his call. They rose from distant valleys, floated out of deep caves, and drifted down from the vast reaches of the night sky itself. In moments the entire world was alive with shadows. From all directions they moved swiftly toward Kellen, drawn inexorably by his song.

"By all the gods—" Mari started to swear, but Morhion held up a hand, silencing her. They watched Kellen in wonder.

Kellen concentrated on his music. The shadows above

coalesced into a gigantic shape. The dark mist formed stamping hooves and flowing mane, black armor and pointed lance. In seconds the form was complete. What better foe to face a shadowdragon than a shadowknight?

Half man, half horse, the onyx knight of shadows loomed as tall as five men. The dark champion raised his tree-length lance in salute, two starlike sparks glowing in the slit of his visor. He let out a trumpeting battle cry and launched into a gallop, angling upward into the sky, his hooves beating against the air as if it were hard ground. The shadowdragon let out a shriek of fury and changed the direction of its descent, diving toward its new foe.

Knight and dragon hurtled on a collision course. For a few chilling heartbeats there was eerie silence as the two titanic forms sped toward each other. Then, with a clap of thunder, they met. The knight's lance plunged through the dragon's body at the same moment as the beast's claws punched through the knight's armor. Dragon roared and knight screamed, the vast sounds shaking the very ground. For a second they spun together in midair, as if whirling in an eerily graceful dance. Then, caught in a mortal embrace, dragon and knight plummeted toward the ground.

As they fell, shreds of shadow ripped away from their writhing forms. Then more tatters of darkness peeled away. Before the two creatures could strike the ground, there was nothing left of them except for a few drifting wisps of dark mist. These settled softly to the moor and in moments melded with the night shadows beneath rocks and in dim hollows. Shadowdragon and shadowknight were no more.

Hands trembling, Kellen lowered his flute. The night was silent once more. Mari, Morhion, and Ferret stared at him in amazement. He smiled wanly at them, then collapsed.

* * * * *

They spent all the following day inside the ruins of the old tower, huddling against the cold wind. To Morhion, the delay was maddening. With each passing second, Caledan drew closer to Ebenfar. Yet they had little choice. After defeating the dragon with his shadow magic, Kellen had fallen into deep unconsciousness, and he had not waked since.

Ferret stood atop the ruined wall, keeping watch over the moor. A dreary mist had settled over the landscape once again. Mari knelt beside Kellen, bathing his forehead with a damp cloth dipped in water steeped with willow bark. Despite the chilly air, sweat slicked Kellen's pallid skin. A fever raged inside him, so fiercely that Morhion could feel waves of heat radiating outward from several paces away. The source of the fever seemed to lie in Kellen's left hand, the one marked with the rune of magic.

Morhion had known Kellen's shadow magic was different than Caledan's, and last night's display had demonstrated it was more potent as well. Yet it was not so much the boy's raw power that intrigued the mage. It was Kellen's great control. More than ever, Morhion was convinced that Kellen's special qualities came from being both mageborn and a descendant of Talek Talembar. Even now, it appeared that the two powers—sorcery and shadow magic—were waging a battle within the boy's body.

"Is there any sign of the fever lessening?" Morhion asked quietly.

Mari shook her head grimly. "I'm afraid not. In fact, I think it's getting worse."

He nodded in reply. Rummaging around in his saddlebag, the mage pulled out a book. There was no telling when Kellen would be well enough to travel; he might as well put the time to good use.

Morhion sat on the ground and rested the ancient tome on his knees. It was the book the witch Isela had given him in Talis. Before opening the tome, he paused to examine Isela's ring. Last night, the silver ring's magic had helped protect them against the shadowhounds but not the shadowdragon. Why? Despite the dreary daylight, the ring's purple gem shimmered with light. Yet when Morhion peered deeper into the stone, he saw the center of the gem was dark, just as Jewel had pointed out earlier. He shut his eyes and heard Isela's words once more.

You seek to destroy a great shadow. Yet shadows can exist only when there is light to cast them. To destroy the shadow, you must destroy the light as well . . .

In his mind, Morhion ran over last night's events. The ring had altered his spell of protection so that it harmed the shadowhounds. A protection spell had components that were both light—a visible aura—as well as dark—an invisible barrier. However, he had attempted to attack the dragon with a lightning spell—magic forged solely of light. That time, the ring's magic had failed to have an effect. It seemed that the ring's enchantment required both light and dark to function properly. Just like the creatures that had attacked the Zhentarim in Iriaebor, Morhion realized—creatures conjured by Caledan's shadow magic. He put the ring away and turned his attention to the book.

Morhion had no idea what knowledge the tome contained. It was penned in the dead language Talfir, and so far the mage had not had time to translate anything but the intriguing title: *On the Nature of Shadows.* However, as he bent over the time-darkened pages and began to painstakingly translate the ancient words, he had a hunch he would find something of interest between the cracked leather covers.

When he finally lifted his gaze from the book, he was surprised to see that it was growing dark.

"Hey, you're back," Ferret said with a crooked-toothed grin. "I was beginning to think it was actually possible to drown inside a book. Mari and I were about to draw straws to see who would dive in and pull you out."

The thief squatted beside a small fire built in an alcove in the stone wall, stirring something in an iron pot. Mari had taken Ferret's place atop the wall and was keeping watch. They had moved Kellen's motionless form near the fire; he was still unconscious.

The mage blinked his bleary eyes. "I think you'll both want to hear what I've read in Isela's book."

"Can't it wait until after dinner?" Ferret asked. "I'm famished."

A spicy aroma arose from the pot. Morhion realized he was fiercely hungry. He nodded his assent, and the three gathered around the fire to eat. Miraculously, the thief had turned jerked meat, a handful of dried tomatoes, and a few wild-growing herbs into a delicious stew. When they set aside their wooden bowls, Morhion began explaining what he had read in the book the witch of Talis had given him.

"The book is entitled *On the Nature of Shadows*," Morhion said in his rich voice. "It is penned in the dead tongue Talfir. At first I had a difficult time translating it, until I made a rather intriguing realization. In this particular dialect of Talfir, the word for 'shadow' is the same as the word for 'shadevar.'" Morhion paused. A chill wind moaned softly over the crumbling stone walls of the tower. "This book is a history of the shadevari."

Mari and Ferret exchanged startled glances but did not interrupt.

"I have long known that the thirteen shadevari were ancient beings. But according to this"—Morhion ran a finger over a faded page of runes—"the shadevari are older than the world itself. They are creatures of the dim chaos that existed before the gods forged Toril, in the time before time, before light and dark were separate entities. Instead of a world, as there is now, there existed only a misty realm of shadows, and the shadevari were lords of that realm. Then came the gods—though from where, no one knows—and they separated the shadows into light and dark, and set the world Toril spinning between the two."

Carefully, Morhion turned a brittle page. "For eons, the shadevari prowled the face of Toril, wreaking havoc and seeking ways to shatter the creation of the gods. Their only desire was to find a way to break the world and meld light and dark into shadowy chaos once more. Finally, the god Azuth, the High One, found a way to banish the shadevari. Beyond the edges of the world, he created the illusion of a realm of shadows, and the shadevari were drawn to the image. Once within, the shadevari realized that the illusion in truth masked a prison. Too late they discovered the trick, and Azuth locked the prison with a key forged of shadows by the god Gond, the Wonderbringer. Then, with all his might, Azuth hurled the key into the cosmos, sending it spinning among the stars so that it would be lost forever."

"Something tells me that this cheerful little bedtime story isn't over yet," Ferret said, scratching his chin.

"Something tells you rightly," Morhion replied. "For a long age, the shadevari remained sealed in their prison. In time they were forgotten. However, as fate would have it, one day the key that Azuth threw into the void entered the world once more."

"The Shadowstar," Mari breathed in amazement.

Morhion nodded. "Indeed. What seemed a shooting star to the wandering minstrel Verraketh was in truth the key Azuth had used to imprison the shadevari. The Shadowstar gave the shadevari a small window on the world. Though still imprisoned, through it they were able to exert some influence. As the medallion transformed Verraketh into the Shadowking, the shadevari spoke to him, making him their slave, until at last he vowed that, when he was powerful enough, he would use the Shadowstar to free the shadevari from their prison. Then the thirteen would seek to destroy Toril once and for all. Fortunately, Talek Talembar defeated his father, Verraketh, before this could come to pass, so the shadevari remained sealed in their prison beyond the edges of the world."

"Wait a minute," Ferret protested. "We killed one shadevar in the Fields of the Dead two years ago. Now three more are after us. That means at least four of the shadevari have been freed from their prison. And while they're nasty creatures—and I'll grant you, I'm no expert on theology—they really don't strike me as godlike beings."

"You are correct, Ferret," Morhion agreed. Dusk had fallen. Firelight played mysteriously across the mage's angular visage. "However, from what I have learned, I would conjecture that the creatures that have pursued us now and in the past are merely avatars of the shadevari—limited, corporeal effigies conjured by the Shadowstar to work the will of the shadevari on Toril. They are shadows of shadows, if you will. The real shadevari are not corporeal at all, but are beings of pure chaos. And they are vastly more powerful than the creatures we have faced."

"Oh, lovely," Ferret said without enthusiasm.

Mari shook her head, her forehead wrinkled in puzzlement. "That doesn't make sense, Morhion. If all you've said is true, then when Caledan's metamorphosis is complete and he becomes a shadowking, he'll be able to use the Shadowstar to free the shadevari from their prison."

"That is so."

"Then why are the three shadevari out to destroy him?"

"Maybe they aren't," Morhion offered. "Two years ago, the Shadowking and a shadevar conjured by Lord Snake sought to destroy all in the Heartlands who possessed the shadow magic. The Shadowking knew that only someone with shadow magic could destroy him, and the shadevar wished to protect him from such individuals. This time, Caledan is the Shadowking—or will be soon.

"There can be only one answer," Morhion concluded. "The shadevari aren't after Caledan. They're after *us*. They want to make certain Caledan completes his transformation into a shadowking, so that he can free them from their prison." Morhion took a deep breath. "In fact, there is only one person who could possibly have summoned the avatars of the shadevari . . ."

"Caledan," Ferret whispered hoarsely. "Caledan himself summoned them, deliberately or not."

There was a long silence as the three huddled around the pitiful little fire. A small sound broke the tension. They turned in surprise to see Kellen sitting up in his blankets. The boy's face was pale but no longer deathly so. His fever had broken. He lifted a hand to rub his eyes, then yawned heartily.

"I'm hungry," he said blearily. "What's for dinner?"

Kellen frowned when the only answer he received was a chorus of joyous laughter.

* * * * *

K'shar loped across the desolate landscape. The broken plateau of the High Moor stretched endlessly in all direc-

tions, brooding under an iron-gray sky. The half-elven
Hunter tilted his head back as he ran, breathing in the
sharp air, searching for the scents of man: smoke from a
campfire, the odor of cooked meat. At first he detected
only the metallic traces of stone and snow. Then, faintly,
he discerned a third scent. It was acrid, like the odor that
lingers after a lightning strike. K'shar recognized the
stench of magic.

His gaze was caught by a jagged silhouette standing
against the leaden sky. The Hunter squinted at the crumbling stump of a ruined tower atop a low hill. For leagues
all around, it was the only place that might offer some
protection from the elements. Instinct urged him toward
the tor. Above all else, K'shar trusted his instincts.

As he climbed easily up the steep slope, he noticed
footprints in the damp turf. A smile sliced across his thin
face. He recognized the impression of a woman's boot
with a triangular nick in the instep. Al'maren. Outside
the mostly collapsed stone wall he found tracks like those
he had seen in the ruined city in the Reaching Woods.
The gigantic hounds that had attacked Al'maren and her
companions in the ancient city had found them again,
here on this hilltop. K'shar noticed numerous gouges in
the rocky soil along with dozens of scorch marks. Some
sort of magical battle had been waged here—one or two
days ago by the look of things.

With animal grace, K'shar leapt over the stone wall.
How long had his quarry camped here? And had they
survived their battle with the magical hounds? K'shar
knelt beside the remains of a cookfire, holding his hand
over the ashes. They were still warm. Al'maren and her
friends had been here only that morning. They had
indeed survived the battle. And they were no more than
two hours ahead of him.

Swiftly, K'shar stood. "You have been a worthy opponent,

Al'maren," he whispered to the chill air. "But I have almost caught up with you now. And once you are gone, nothing will stand between me and Caldorien."

Like a stag taking flight, he sprang over the wall and stretched his long legs to run lightly down the hill. His nostrils flared in anticipation. Instinct told him the chase was almost over.

And above all else, K'shar trusted his instincts.

Eighteen

It was midday when they brought their horses to a halt before the onyx bridge.

" 'Beyond lies the Domain of Ebenfar,' " Morhion read, translating the dim runes carved into a timeworn standing stone.

Mari nudged Farenth toward the edge of the yawning defile. She peered down, blinking dizzily. The vast depths tugged at her, as if trying to suck her down to the jagged rocks far below. Hastily, she backed Farenth away from the precipice. The slender bridge that arched over the chasm was made of black stone. Mari did not need Morhion to tell her that it had been forged with magic. On the far side of the bridge stood two colossi—gigantic statues hewn of basalt—forming a sinister gateway with outstretched arms. The towering statues were cracked and pitted, but Mari recognized their eyeless faces and spiny crests. They were shadevari. She shivered, gathering her forest green cloak tightly around her shoulders. There could be no doubt now that the ancient beings were inextricably linked with the Shadowking.

"Do you think Caledan has been here?" she asked, her voice breaking the brooding silence.

"There are no traces of his passing," Morhion answered, "but that means nothing. He has left no sign for a long time—not since the last one in Soubar."

"My father has been here," Kellen said, his voice filled with quiet certainty. "Not long ago."

Mari opened her mouth to question Kellen's statement, then bit her tongue. After their battle with the shadow-dragon at the ruined tower, she knew there was much about Kellen she could not possibly understand. "Then we had better get moving."

"I'll go scout out the bridge and make certain that it's safe," Ferret said. He dismounted, heading for the stone arch. A few minutes later he returned, looking vaguely queasy.

"What's wrong?" Mari asked. "Will the bridge hold us?"

"It shouldn't even be able to hold itself!" Ferret said with a shudder. "By all rights, that spindly excuse for an engineering project should have collapsed into the gorge centuries ago. Some sort of magic is holding it up."

"It will bear us, then," Morhion said in satisfaction.

"I suppose so," Ferret replied grudgingly. "Unless the enchantment that glues it together conveniently decides to come unstuck just as we're crossing." He shot the mage an uneasy look. "Magic doesn't spoil after a few centuries, does it?"

"It can," Morhion said nonchalantly.

"Thanks for the reassurance," Ferret grumbled.

Astride Tenebrous, Morhion volunteered to be the first to cross the ancient bridge. Mari came next, followed by Kellen, while Ferret brought up the rear—muttering something about "demented, suicidal wizards." As she guided Farenth onto the narrow span, Mari noticed a single transparent crystal set among the bridge's black stones. She asked Morhion what it was.

"I think it is a keystone." He rubbed his chin thoughtfully. "It is the magic of such keystones that keeps the arch from collapsing."

Cautiously, they continued across the bridge. The horses snorted nervously, their hooves skidding on the smooth onyx stone. One slip would send horse and rider plummeting into the chasm. As they passed the center of the span, Mari noticed a second crystal embedded in the bridge—another one of the magical keystones.

Suddenly, a blast of cold air snatched at Mari's cloak, and Morhion looked up, his long golden hair flying wildly back from his brow. The horses clattered to a halt. In front of the mage, a dark form coalesced out of thin air. Serafi. Mari's heart froze as she thought of the most recent pact Morhion had forged with the spectral knight.

The mage's voice was a mixture of loathing and revulsion. "What do you want, Serafi?"

The dusky knight bowed mockingly in midair. "Why, as always, I wish to help, Morhion. You are being followed. Your pursuer is a half-elf, a skilled tracker. I know not who he is, but he comes to kill you—which, of course, I cannot allow."

"K'shar." Mari whispered the name of the Harper Hunter. "How far behind us is he?"

"A few minutes at most," the ghostly knight said coolly. "You must prepare yourselves to encounter him."

Morhion clenched a fist in anger. "If you're feeling so benevolent, Serafi, why don't you dispatch him for us?"

The spirit's burning eyes flashed. "Would that I could exert my will so directly upon the world of the living," he hissed. "But my incorporeal form allows it not. You must deal with the Hunter yourselves." With that, the spectral knight blurred into a swirl of dark mist, vanishing on the keening wind.

"Well, he's a big help," Ferret noted acidly.

"Let's get moving," Mari said with urgency. "We have only a few minutes to find a place to confront K'shar."

"At least we have the advantage of surprise," Ferret said hopefully.

"It may be our *only* advantage," Mari replied grimly. "K'shar has been known to single-handedly lay waste to legions of Zhentarim and Red Wizards."

As quickly as they dared, they guided their mounts across the remaining span of the bridge. As they stepped off onto solid ground, Mari noticed a third crystal embedded in the surface of the bridge. An idea struck her.

"All right, I have a plan," she told the others. "It may not be a good one, but I don't think we have a lot of options."

Scant minutes later, the four were hiding behind the gigantic foot of one of the stone colossi. Mari peered cautiously over the statue's clawed toe. Very soon, on the opposite side of the bridge, a tall figure appeared out of the mist. The Hunter was a striking man, his form-fitting black leathers a suitable match for his deep-bronze skin and golden eyes, and a vivid contrast to his close-cropped white hair. Swiftly K'shar started across the span, moving with little thought for his own safety. When he reached the center of the onyx bridge, Mari leapt from behind the statue. She stood at the end of the bridge and raised her short sword high. The blade glowed with brilliant purple magic.

"Greetings, Hunter!" she shouted, her voice ringing out clearly in the cold air.

K'shar halted at the center of the bridge, instantly crouching into a wary stance, a cat ready to pounce. A faint smile touched his lips.

"Greetings, Al'maren," he said in a formal tone, transforming his crouch into a fluid bow. He straightened with a curious expression. "I must thank you, Renegade."

Mari was taken aback by this. "Thank me, Hunter? For what?"

"For providing me with a most excellent chase," the half-elf replied smoothly. "Never before have I had such a worthy opponent. You have given my life new meaning, Al'maren, and for that I will always be in your debt."

Mari laughed harshly. "I don't suppose that means you've decided *not* to kill me."

"I think you know the answer to that, Renegade." K'shar's smile became a feral grin. "What is the chase without the kill?"

"A pleasant walk in the countryside?" Mari offered with mock ingenuousness.

K'shar shook his head. "It is nothing. I know you understand this, Al'maren. You have your duty, even as I have mine." The half-elf tensed, ready to spring across the bridge.

"I wouldn't make a move if I were you," Mari said. "You see this crystal?" Mari gestured with the blade to the nearest of the three clear stones embedded in the bridge. "It's a magical keystone. Without it, the bridge will collapse. My friend is a mage, and he has cast an interesting enchantment on my sword—an enchantment of magical dispelling. Mages can be so terribly handy, can't they? If I strike the keystone with this blade, the crystal will shatter. And I think you're intelligent enough to guess what would happen next, Hunter."

Slow, deliberate applause rang out over the chasm. K'shar was clapping. "I salute you, Renegade," the half-elf said in admiration. "You are more worthy than I had even guessed. Truly, you have given me the chase of a lifetime. And you have given me a new experience as well."

"And what experience is that?" Mari asked, curious despite herself.

"Losing," K'shar replied with a rueful smile. "For it is clear that you have won, Al'maren. I congratulate you."

K'shar's reaction unnerved Mari. Strangely, she felt almost sorry to have to kill the half-elf. In a way she rather liked him. She was surprised to find herself saying so. "You know, I think in a different time and place, we might have been friends, Hunter."

"You may be right, Renegade. However, at present our duties contrive to make enemies of us. We will have to save friendship for another lifetime."

All of a sudden, K'shar lunged into motion. As he did, Mari brought the glowing sword down against the keystone with all her might. Purple magic flashed brilliantly, followed by a sound like breaking glass. The crystal shattered into a thousand glittering shards.

Mari stumbled backward. With a sound like thunder, the graceful arch of the bridge lurched violently. K'shar fell sprawling, sliding across the onyx surface and halfway over the edge. His hands scrabbled against slick stone, searching vainly for purchase. When the other two keystones exploded in sprays of shining splinters, the bridge shuddered. K'shar slid farther over the edge, feet dangling above the chasm. For a moment he looked up, his eyes meeting Mari's. He opened his mouth, but whether to bid her farewell or to curse her to the Abyss, she would never know. The bridge gave one final twitch. Then with a deafening *crack!* the span disintegrated. The stone arch collapsed into a rain of dark rubble, plummeting into the gorge and carrying the half-elf with it.

Mari dashed to the edge, but by the time she looked down, the remains of the bridge were already out of sight in the vast depths below. Footsteps sounded behind her.

"Your plan worked, Mari," Morhion said softly.

She nodded slowly but did not answer. Instead she bowed her head, whispering a brief prayer for the dead. After a moment she turned and faced the others. "Let's get going," she said hoarsely.

The four mounted their horses and rode between the stone colossi into the kingdom of Ebenfar.

While the High Moor had been desolate, it had still displayed small signs of life as well as a kind of raw-edged beauty. In contrast, the realm they passed through now was utterly barren. The broken landscape was a tortuous labyrinth littered with piles of dark slag and pits half-filled with foul water. Except for the steady hoofbeats of the four horses, all was preternaturally silent. There were no birds, nor any other living creature. Even the wind had stopped. The air hung perfectly still under the dour sky, cold and breathless as a winter tomb. If ever there was a land that was truly dead, Ebenfar was one.

"Cheery place," Ferret noted dryly. "I'll be sure to come here for my next vacation." The thief's words seemed uncomfortably loud against the brittle silence. He shivered in his cloak and refrained from making any further comments.

The cold was a hungry, maleficent thing. Mari moved to warm her hands under her jacket, but she could hardly unclench her fingers from the reins. It felt as if the chill had turned her flesh to pale ice. She turned to make certain Kellen was warm enough and saw that the boy rode with Morhion now. He sat in the saddle before the mage, wrapped in a blanket in addition to his cloak. Morhion had tied Flash's reins to Tenebrous's saddle, and the pony followed behind.

Such was the tomblike nature of this land that Mari was only somewhat surprised when they rounded a large slag heap and found themselves facing a ghost.

At first she thought it must be Serafi, but a moment
later she knew it was not so. The spectral knight was a
dark being with eyes like flames. This ghost was as gray
as the leaden sky, so pale his outlines blurred into the
surrounding landscape. He was clad in misty, flowing
robes, like those of a wizard . . . or perhaps a king. His
visage was proud and noble, and with a start Mari realized that she recognized the man's face. She had seen it
once before, carved into the lid of an onyx sarcophagus
far below the city of Iriaebor. In the crypt of the Shadowking. She opened her mouth, but Morhion beat her to
the words.

"Verraketh Talembar . . ."

Floating several feet above the ground, the ghostly
man bowed his regal head. "Yea, wizard, thou doth know
me well." His colorless eyes flickered down to Kellen.
"Greetings, scion of Talembar, child of my blood."

Kellen regarded the ghost with calm, curious eyes.
"Hello, Grandfather," he said simply.

Mari drew in a sharp breath. "Grandfather" was
hardly the proper term to describe Kellen's relationship
to Verraketh. With thirty "greats" in front of the word,
perhaps. Despite her fear and wonder, a thought occurred
to her.

"I don't understand," she said, shivering. "How is it
that you appear to us as a man, Verraketh, and not as
the Shadowking you were when we . . . when you . . . perished beneath Iriaebor?" She swallowed hard, realizing
this might seem a rude question to someone she'd had a
hand in killing. "If you don't mind my asking," she added
hastily.

The ghost shrugged. "Forsooth, why should I care, Mari
Al'maren? The concerns of the dead are not those of the
living. Yet I will tell thee, this form doth mean nothing.

Once, I was a child as Kellen stands now. I couldst as easily have chosen that form over this. It matters not. In death, I shall forever be all that I was in life—babe and child, minstrel and mage, and yea, Shadowking as well. Still, I choose to appear to thee in this manner. Is it well with thee, Mari Al'maren?"

Mari nodded dumbly. Who was she to argue with a ghost about what form he should take?

Ferret cleared his throat nervously. "Excuse me, Verraketh, your . . . er, ghostliness. My friends seem to be a little more accustomed to dealing with spirits than I am. You see, most of the dead people I'm familiar with aren't nearly so *active* as yourself. Anyway, I was just wondering . . ." The thief screwed up his weasely face. "Let's see. How can I put this tactfully? Are you going to be killing us anytime soon?"

The ghost's mirthful laughter echoed from all directions, an eerie but not altogether unpleasant sound. "Fear not, gentle thief. I bear thee no grudge for thy actions in my tomb beneath Iriaebor. Thou and thy companions did free me from the dark thrall of the Shadowstar, and let me at last find peace in death. For that, I thank thee."

Ferret bowed in his saddle. "Don't mention it."

"Then why have you come to us?" Mari asked, emboldened by the spirit's words.

"To help thee," the ghost replied. "So that the metamorphosis that made me into the Shadowking shall not be worked once again upon my scion, Caledan Caldorien. For only thou doth have the power to save him."

"How would you help us?" Morhion asked, his blue eyes gleaming.

"Listen," Verraketh intoned. "On the other side of yon dark ridge doth lie the vale in which I discovered the Shadowstar after it fell from the sky. There also lieth the

heart of Ebenfar—the throne from which I once did rule
as Shadowking. There is a secret to the vale, a secret
unbeknownst even to the shadevari. A secret that, were
it known, doth have the power to defeat the Shadowstar."

"A secret?" Mari repeated. "What do you mean?"

Verraketh explained. "Long ago, there did echo in the
vale a strange and wondrous music. Some claimed that it
was an echo of the song the gods sang at the time of the
forging of the world. If this is so, it is beyond my ken. Yet
one thing I do know. When the Shadowstar fell into the
vale, it was hot and molten, and before it could cool and
grow solid, the music that echoed in the vale did infuse
the Shadowstar, becoming a part of its being. Ever after,
the music of the vale has had the power to quell the
medallion. Thus the song is the key to defeating the
Shadowstar. It was a fragment of that music that my son,
Talek Talembar, wove into the shadow song with which
he did defeat me once."

"Then when Caledan enters the vale, the echo of the
song will nullify the Shadowstar. We'll be able to get it
away from him!"

Verraketh shook his head. "It shall not be so easy as
that, Mari Al'maren. Thou seest, when I was Shadowking,
I feared the music of the vale. I sought to mar it, and alas I
succeeded. By mine own hand, the ancient song of the vale
is flawed, and as long as it is flawed, it is powerless
against the Shadowstar. Therefore, thou must seeketh to
restore the song."

"But how—" Mari began. Her words were interrupted
by a shriek from above. She gave Morhion a startled
glance. He nodded, confirming her fear.

"The shadevari have found us," the mage said grimly.

"Go," the ghost of Verraketh ordered. "I shall find a
way to delay the Eyeless Ones."

"But what about the song in the vale?" Mari protested.

"How are we to restore it?"

"There is not time for me to explain the way," Verraketh said curtly. "If indeed, after all these centuries, I would even remember how. It is up to thee to find a way to restore the Valesong." His voice rose thunderously. "Now go!"

Another bloodcurdling cry rent the air. This time, the companions did not hesitate; they urged their mounts into a wild gallop. As they rode, Mari risked a glance over her shoulder. The ghost of Verraketh had vanished. However, she noticed that the sky had grown darker. Even as she watched, the clouds began to swirl in a spiral, faster and faster. High above, the unseen shadowsteeds screeched again, and this time their cries were not cries of hunger but of anger. Ghost or not, Verraketh was doing something that the winged steeds of the shadevari did not like.

The four horses raced toward the distant ridge that lay between them and the vale of the Shadowstar. Mari gripped Farenth's mane with white-knuckled hands.

"Hold on, Caledan," she whispered urgently. "We're coming as fast as we can. Hold on just a little while longer . . ."

But the cold wind snatched the words from her lips.

* * * * *

Hooves clattering against loose stone, Mista scrambled up the last few feet to the summit of the knife-edged ridge.

"Good girl," Caledan said, leaning forward in the saddle to stroke her neck. Despite the chill, her pale coat was flecked with foam. "I knew you could do it."

Mista nickered uncertainly in reply. She did not like this place. Nor did Caledan. He gazed down into a dark hollow in the blasted landscape. The vale of the Shadowstar.

"Well," he said. "We're here."

Though he had never seen this place before, Caledan had an eerie sense that he was coming home. Perhaps, in a way, he was. A thousand years of shadow magic ran in his veins. This was where it had all begun.

The vale itself was not so much a valley as it was a crater—a circular pit gouged into the surface of the world by a terrible, otherwordly force. The walls of the vale were formed of jagged black stone. Hot steam rose from countless fissures in the crater's floor, creeping around a jagged spire of rock that stood like a sentinel in the vale's center. He shut his eyes, and he could almost see it: the fiery streak plunging down through the sky to strike the ground with a flash as bright as the sun and a sound as deafening as two worlds colliding, leaving in its wake a gaping wound on the face of Toril.

Caledan opened his eyes and studied the steep slope leading down into the vale. Slowly, he dismounted. His joints ached fiercely, and he was horribly dizzy. Somehow he managed to stand upright.

"I'm afraid this is where we part ways, old friend," he said haggardly.

Mista gave a firm snort, stamping her hoof in protest.

Caledan shook his head. "You can't make it down that slope, Mista, and you know it. Frankly, I'm not certain I can, either." He sighed. "But I have to try."

The ghostly gray mare let out a worried nicker.

He encircled her strong neck with his arms. "I swear, I will come back for you, Mista, if it is at all in my power. I think that you're the only one I really remember now. I know that there are others . . . others who were important to me once. But I don't know their names anymore, or their faces." He gave a bitter laugh. "Damn, but I hardly even remember my own name anymore."

Mista nuzzled his cheek. She bared her big yellow teeth and bit his ear, but the gesture was only half-hearted. Caledan slapped her affectionately.

"Good-bye, old friend," he said softly.

With that, he turned and began picking his way down the treacherous wall of the crater.

The going was agonizingly slow. Rocks skidded beneath his boots. Sharp edges sliced his hands when he reached out to steady himself. He was perhaps halfway down when his feet set a whole section of loose scree into motion. The small rocks were as slick as marbles, and there was nothing for Caledan to grab on to. With a cry he fell, tumbling down the slope in a small avalanche of loose rock. When he came to a stop at the bottom, he was surprised to find he was still alive. Groaning, he pulled himself from beneath a pile of rubble and staggered to his feet. He was bruised and bloodied, his clothes rent in a score of places.

"Well, that was the quick way down," he said with a manic laugh, but there was no one to hear his words.

Taking a deep breath, he stumbled onward, skirting a dozen crevices. Hissing steam rose from the fissures along with a dull red glow, filling the air with a sulfurous reek that seared his lungs. Only after several minutes did he consciously hear the throbbing sound that thrummed in his chest in time to his rapidly pounding heart.

It was music.

So this was the Valesong. Exactly how he knew about the Valesong, Caledan was not certain. The knowledge had simply come to him, like knowledge of the Shadow-star and Ebenfar. He cocked his head to listen. The music echoed all around. It was chaotic and dissonant, and he could make out no melody. That was because the music was flawed. He knew that, just as he knew everything else. Long ago the music had been marred.

"And now I must restore it," he whispered, the words hurting his parched throat. If the Valesong were complete, he would be free of the Shadowstar, free of the dark turmoil that raged within him.

Gripping the Shadowstar, Caledan lurched on. As he went, he racked his spinning brain, trying to figure out what he had to do to make the ancient Valesong whole once more. The knowledge was there, somewhere. It had to be. Then, like one groping blindly in the dark for a flint with which to light a candle, he found the answer.

The acrid smoke swirled. Caledan stumbled to a halt. Before him rose a massive pillar of solid basalt. Carved into its tapering surface were irregular stone steps. His gaze was drawn up the beckoning stairway that spiraled around the towering pinnacle all the way to the top. There, carved into the very summit of the pillar, was a gigantic chair. The throne of the Shadowking.

Even as Caledan gazed upon the onyx throne, he knew that he must sit upon it.

Desperately, he tried to cling to his plan of restoring the Valesong, of freeing himself from the dark power that raged within him, but those thoughts were brutally ripped away by a surging wave of desire. All he could think of was how good it would be to stop resisting, to finally let himself be swept away on that dark, turbulent sea. The *other* woke within him, and for the first time he was not frightened by its presence. At last, here was an end to his battle. He stepped forward, placing his boot upon the stairway.

As he did, one last fragment of the man who had been called Caledan Caldorien bubbled to the surface. He no longer remembered why he had created the myriad signs as he journeyed, or what they had meant. Yet an image drifted in his mind, of one last sign he intended to create.

For a moment, the forces inside him struggled. Then, with a shudder, he reached out and pressed his hand against the pinnacle. Beneath his fingers, dark stone melted, flowed, resolidified. He pulled his hand back, not even bothering to look at the object he had forged. It did not matter now. All that mattered was the throne.

It drew him upward. No longer feeling pain or weariness, he climbed the spiral staircase. At last he reached the top and gazed at the tortured landscape that stretched in all directions. Soon, he thought, all this will be mine. A smile twisted his face. He ascended the final step and sat upon the throne.

Out of thin air, shadows appeared, coiling around him like a royal robe of black satin. He shut his eyes and curled up in the chair, knees to chest, like a child in its mother's womb. It felt so sweet to rest, and finally to forget. More dusky tendrils swirled about him, cocooning him in the soft stuff of shadows. In moments, his body was completely covered by a dark, sticky sheath bound securely to the onyx throne. Swiftly, the jet-black sheath dried, becoming hard and glossy, sealing its contents safely within.

It was a chrysalis.

Nineteen

"There it is," Morhion said solemnly. "The heart of Ebenfar."

They dismounted and gazed into the smoking crater. A bitter wind whistled over the saw-toothed ridge, but clouds of warm mist rose up from the desolate vale. The acrid steam burned in their lungs.

Ferret scratched his stubbled chin nervously. "Let me guess—the Shadowking did his own decorating, am I right? The gloomy neo-gothic overtones highlighted by the retro-apocalyptic blasted rock are a dead giveaway." He clapped his hands together. "It simply screams 'Shadowking.'"

Kellen gave the weasely thief a curious look. "You're a silly man, Uncle Ferret."

Ferret shot Kellen a crooked-toothed grin. "I know. But don't underestimate silliness, Kellen. It's a surprisingly good self-defense mechanism, and a whole lot more fun than panicking."

Kellen reached out and gently patted the thief's hand. "If you say so, Uncle Ferret."

A high-pitched whinny rang out on the frigid air. The companions turned in surprise to see a riderless horse trot toward them across the windswept ridgetop. It was Mista, Caledan's gray mare. When Mari grabbed Mista's bridle, the horse snorted nervously, rolling her eyes. Mari stroked the smooth arch of the horse's neck, trying to calm her.

"Caledan," she said hoarsely. "He's already here. We're too late."

"Perhaps," Morhion replied. "But perhaps not. We must believe that there is yet time to save him."

Mari's shoulders trembled. She clutched at Mista's mane. "I don't know if I can do it, Morhion," she whispered, shaking her head.

"Do what, Mari?"

"Look at him," she answered in anguish. "I don't know if I can face him if he's . . . changed. To see him, turned into a . . . a thing of evil. I'm not sure I have the strength to bear it."

Morhion took a deep breath. He was not certain he could bear it either. Yet maybe he did not need to be so strong. Maybe none of them did. He reached out and gripped Mari's shoulder. "We can all do it together, Mari," he said softly. "Together, we will be strong enough."

A fragile smile touched her lips. "Promise?"

He nodded solemnly. "I promise." Abruptly, a low laugh escaped him. "Did I not warn you that one day, when you least expected it, I would be on your side?"

"Well," she said with mock indignation, "it's about time."

Morhion smiled at her. Then his gaze was drawn downward, into the mist-shrouded vale.

"We'll leave the horses here," he said.

Traversing the steep slope down into the crater was an ordeal. At first, Morhion worried about Kellen's ability to climb the jagged cliffs. Then he realized his fears were unfounded. Kellen moved as nimbly down the treacherous slope as did Ferret. Boy and thief picked their way lightly over sharp rock outcrops and across expanses of slick scree. Mari and Morhion followed more carefully. At one point, the mage's boot slipped on a patch of loose rubble, and he lost his balance altogether. He would have gone sailing over the edge if Serafi had not materialized before him. The spectral knight raised his ethereal gauntlets, and a blast of frigid air blew Morhion backward. Serafi said nothing. He did not have to. Morhion knew the knight had saved his life for one reason only: to protect the body that the dark spirit would soon possess for his own. With a flash of his burning eyes, Serafi vanished. Mari and Morhion exchanged grim looks.

At last they reached the bottom of the crater.

Ferret let out a low whistle. "So this is what the Abyss looks like. Not that I can say I was really all that curious to know."

The vale of the Shadowstar did indeed look like some dismal limbo for the damned. Perhaps it was, at that, Morhion thought with a bitter, silent laugh. Serafi, Caledan, Morhion himself—who were they but lost souls one and all?

Cautiously, the four made their way toward the center of the blasted vale. The sulfurous reek was almost overpowering. Tatters of steam scudded across the rocky ground, and a dull red glow hung on the air like a bloody miasma. Acrid steam rose from countless fissures in the dark rock, and it was from some of these crevices that the ruddy light emanated.

Morhion wasn't exactly certain when he noticed the low thrumming. Abruptly he halted, cocking his head. By the expressions of the others, they had heard it as well. It was a vast sound, and incomprehensibly complex. Countless different tones and pitches blended together to forge a single throbbing voice that was almost like—

"Music," Morhion finished the thought aloud.

"The Valesong," Mari said in amazement. Gradually her expression became a frown. "But there's something wrong with the music. I'm not certain exactly what—this is like no harmony I've ever heard before. It's almost alien. Still, I can't help but feel there's something wrong. It's almost as though some part of it were . . . missing."

Morhion trusted Mari's knowledge of music. "Verraketh said that he marred the Valesong long ago." He gazed around at the rocky landscape. "But what is the source of the music? We cannot restore it if we do not know how it is formed. Does it truly echo here from the dawning of the world?"

"That would be some echo," Ferret commented skeptically. The thief began to look around, exploring. Morhion wondered what he was doing. "Doesn't this music seem familiar?" Ferret muttered. The thief hopped aside to avoid a blast of hot steam shooting from a nearby fissure. At the same moment, another tone was added to the music that throbbed in the vale.

Kellen looked at the fissure, his green eyes curious. "It's almost like a pipe organ," he said thoughtfully.

Ferret snapped his fingers. "That's it!" He tousled Kellen's dark hair. "Good work, kid!" Kellen grimaced, smoothing his hair with a hand.

Morhion gazed at the little thief. "What are you thinking, Ferret?"

"Just a minute," Ferret said hastily. The thief continued to explore the vale in ever-widening circles, climbing atop heaps of rubble and peering into dark pits. At last he let out a hoot of victory. He waved an arm wildly, gesturing for the others.

"What have you found?" Mari asked as they reached the thief.

Ferret perched atop a blocky outcropping. Three jagged holes gaped in the rock beneath him. "Look at these fissures," the thief directed.

"Are we supposed to be impressed?" Morhion asked dubiously.

Ferret hopped down. "Don't you notice something strange about these holes, something that makes them different from all the other crevices in the vale?"

"There's no steam," Mari said after a moment.

"Exactly." He peered into one of the fissures; it was large enough to crawl into. "As far as I can tell, these three holes join together a little way down. Unlike all the other fissures in the vale, no steam is blowing out of these. Something must be blocking them from below."

Morhion suddenly understood what the clever thief was getting at. "Now I see, Ferret. The music doesn't echo in the vale. The vale itself is making the music."

"You got it," Ferret beamed. "It was Kellen who made me understand. The steam blowing through all these crevices acts like a giant pipe organ. Each fissure makes one note, and all the notes blend together to make the Valesong."

Mari nodded excitedly. "But something below ground is blocking these fissures, which means the Valesong is missing three notes. That's how Verraketh marred it."

Morhion bent to examine the rough-edged holes. He could see only darkness beyond. "We have to find a way to unblock these fissures. If we can restore the Valesong, we just might have a chance to—"

"Morhion! Mari! Ferret!"

The cry rang out over the vale. Kellen. Swiftly the three turned, peering into the swirling steam, trying to catch a glimpse of the boy. He must have wandered off.

Mari's sharp eyes found him first. "There!" she said, pointing. As they approached, they saw what had caused him to call out.

"Kellen," Morhion said gravely. "I want you to take a step back. Carefully."

The boy stood on the edge of a wide pit. Crimson light rose out of the pit, along with wisps of hot yellow smoke. Four yards below the rim of the pit was a bubbling pool of lava. When Kellen did as he was told, Morhion reached out and snatched the boy safely away from the edge.

Mari gazed down at the pool of molten rock, her face bathed in the ruddy glow. "The lava must be heating a source of underground water, and the resultant steam is forced up through the fissures in the rock, making the Valesong."

"Hey, guys," Ferret said with a gulp. "You may want to look up for a second."

The others did as the thief bid. Morhion swore softly. On the far side of the pit stood a sharp-edged pinnacle of basalt. Carved into the jagged surface of the spire were stairs spiraling upward, leading to the pointed summit. There was something up there, a dark shape at the very top of the stone spire, but Morhion could not make it out.

Carefully, the four skirted the lava pit and approached the pinnacle. They found the beginning of the stone staircase on the far side of the spire, opposite the pit. They found something else as well: A patch of stone had been molded into a new shape. It was a human hand, reaching out of the surface of the pinnacle. An object rested in the outstretched hand, a set of pipes. They looked like the reed pipes a forest satyr might play to enchant a nymph, but they were made of smooth onyx stone.

"Caledan," Mari whispered.

Kellen approached the stone hand and reached out to

touch the onyx pipes. The instrument parted from the hand with a faint *snick!* and came away in Kellen's grip. He stared at the pipes in wonder. They were beautiful, as smooth and fluid as midnight water.

"Thank you, Father," he said softly. He tucked the pipes into the pouch at his belt, where he kept his bone flute.

"Anyone else curious to find out what's up there?" Ferret said, beady eyes shining. He pointed to the staircase with a thumb.

Cautiously, the four ascended the rough-hewn staircase. The steps were narrow and uneven, and one slip could send them plummeting to the rocky ground far below. Finally they climbed the last steps to the summit and found themselves on a half-moon-shaped stone platform. Before them, hewn from the dark bones of the pinnacle itself, was a gigantic chair.

No, not a chair, Morhion realized. A throne.

"In Milil's name, what is *that?*" Mari gasped.

The thing on the throne was about the size and shape of a barrel, but it was jet black and glossy, and tapered smoothly at one end. The object was attached to the throne by a sticky mass of dark strands. Only after a moment did Morhion realize that the thing's hard surface was slightly translucent. He could just glimpse something within, something dark and pulsating. Whatever it was, it was alive.

"It's almost like some sort of cocoon," Ferret said with awe and revulsion.

"No, not a cocoon," Morhion countered in sudden realization. "Not a cocoon, but a chrysalis, like that which encases a caterpillar while it completes its metamorphosis into a butterfly."

"While it completes its metamorphosis?" Mari repeated. Her voice became an anguished moan. "Oh, by all the gods of light. It's Caledan!"

Instantly Morhion knew she was right. He took a step
toward the chrysalis, reaching out a hand. "Caledan, my
friend—"

His words were cut short by a shriek of pure and
ancient malevolence. A form uncoiled itself from a jagged
outcrop behind the throne. The thing's gray, scaly hide
had blended seamlessly with the dull stone, concealing it
even as it had lain before their eyes. Now the creature
sprang down to stand protectively before the chrysalis on
the throne. It extended spiny arms ending in obsidian
talons; its spiked tail flicked menacingly. The thing's eyeless face was utterly inhuman.

A shadevar.

The creature opened its lipless mouth, revealing dark
needle teeth. "The king sleeps," it hissed in a voice like a
serpent's. "You shall not harm him."

"Get back!" Morhion shouted at the others. They
retreated toward the staircase, but they knew they could
not outrun the shadevar. The mage stretched out his left
hand. Isela's ring glittered on his finger.

Rapidly, Morhion spoke the words of an incantation. It
was the same spell of protection he had cast against the
shadowhounds on the High Moor. Once again, a ring of
shimmering blue magic spread outward from the mage.
The ring's violet gem flared, and the expanding circle of
magic changed from ice blue to brilliant purple. The
glowing circle struck the shadevar and expanded beyond.
Blazing tendrils of magic crackled around the creature's
form, engulfing it in purple fire.

The shadevar only grinned.

As though removing a burning cloak, it shrugged its
spiny shoulders. The glowing tendrils of magic fell to the
ground. There they sizzled for a moment, then went
dark. Morhion stared in horror. The spell had not worked!

He had been certain that the key to the ring's power lay in using a spell that contained elements of both light and dark. Yet he had been terribly wrong.

"Run!" Morhion screamed. "I'll try to hold it off as long as I can!"

The others only stood behind him, frozen in terror. In his mind, Morhion prepared a spell of lightning, though it would likely be useless against the powerful creature. Spiked tail twitching, the shadevar advanced.

"You would defile the king," it hissed poisonously, raising a clawed hand to tear Morhion's throat out. "Now you will die."

Morhion shouted his incantation, knowing he did not have time to finish it properly. The shadevar brought its curved talons down in a slashing arc.

The blow never landed.

So swift it was nearly a blur, a lithe form heaved itself up over the edge of the pinnacle's summit and launched itself at the shadevar. The blur collided with the spiny creature, knocking it off balance so that the shadevar's strike went wide. One sharp talon just grazed Morhion's face, tracing a stinging line along his cheekbone. The mage stumbled backward into the others.

The shadevar's assailant backed away. It was the Harper Hunter, K'shar. The half-elf's clothes were all but shredded. His dusky bronze skin was bruised and torn. Blood matted his pale hair. Yet his golden eyes blazed with light. He had survived the destruction of the onyx bridge.

The shadevar recovered its balance, digging clawed feet into the stone on the very edge of the pinnacle's summit. It turned its eyeless face toward K'shar, slit-shaped nostrils flaring. "Fool!" it shrieked. "Defiler! You cannot harm me. I will rend your flesh to liquid with that of these other mortals."

"Truly?" K'shar mocked. There was no fear in his expression, only a feral eagerness. "Very well, creature. I will make it easier for you. I will not try to escape. On the contrary, I will come directly to you."

Before the shadevar could react, K'shar dove, curling his lean form into a tight ball and rolling toward the creature. The half-elf struck the thing's legs forcefully, knocking the shadevar off balance. The creature's obsidian talons made a hideous screeching noise as they scrabbled against the edge of the precipice. The thing nearly caught itself. Then the rock crumbled under the terrible force of its clawed grip. With a piercing shriek, the creature toppled backward.

They watched as the shadevar fell through the air and plunged into the center of the glowing lava pit far below. The ancient creature's cries were cut short as it sank into the pool of magma. A roiling cloud of crimson fire burst out of the pit, then dissipated. After that, there was no sign of the creature. Even shadevari were not proof against the hellish fire of molten rock.

K'shar rose to his feet.

"How did you survive the fall into the chasm?" the mage demanded.

The half-elf shrugged. "I did not fall. I managed to grab a ledge a few yards down, then pulled myself up the cliff face to follow you."

"You saved us from the shadevar," Mari said in amazement, approaching with Ferret and Kellen.

The Hunter regarded her with his startling eyes. "You are wrong, Al'maren. I killed the creature because it was in my way, that is all." A wistful smile touched his lips. "Would that I could be as free as you, Renegade. Perhaps one day I will be. But at this moment, duty to the Harpers binds me still."

In a single fluid motion, K'shar reached out and pulled

Mari's sword from the sheath at her hip, then lunged toward the basalt throne. The Hunter moved so swiftly that the others had no time to react. They could only watch in horror as K'shar pulled the sword back, then plunged the sharp blade deep into the heart of the jet-black chrysalis.

Twenty

Mari screamed.

She tried to move, tried to dive for K'shar and wrest the gleaming sword from his hands. The half-elf might as well have stood a dozen leagues away instead of a dozen steps. A single agonizing thought pierced Mari's brain, as if it were she whom the Hunter had stabbed.

I have failed you, Caledan!

Smoothly, K'shar pulled the sword from the black chrysalis. A thin stream of dark vitriol spilled out of the slit, pooling before the throne. The chrysalis gave one final twitch, then lay still. The stream of dark fluid slowed to a trickle before ceasing. Whatever had pulsated inside the glossy shell moved no longer. Slowly, his golden eyes unreadable, K'shar turned away from the throne.

"You've killed my father," Kellen said quietly.

The sword slipped from K'shar's hands, clattering to

the stone. "I know," he replied solemnly. "Yet whatever
you think of me, do not think that I feel no sorrow. I
watched my mother die at the hands of men who feared
her for the blood that ran in her veins. Your father has
died for no better reason. And for no worse." A bitter
smile twisted his lips. "Now we are like kin, you and I."

"Damn you to the Abyss!" Morhion snarled. "You are
nothing to him, save his father's murderer!"

Ferret sprang forward, pressing a dagger against
K'shar's throat. The half-elf did not resist. "I'm sure you
want to kill this bastard yourself, Morhion," the thief
rasped, "but I'm afraid I'm going to do it first. Sorry—you
know how selfish we thieving types can be."

"Stop!"

The others looked up in shock as Mari stepped forward, raising a hand in protest. She would not allow further conflict. There had been enough death in this
blasted place.

Morhion's eyes blazed. "What is wrong with you, Mari?
Let the thief do his work."

Ferret pressed the knife harder against the bronzed
flesh of K'shar's throat. A bead of dark blood ran down
the half-elf's neck. K'shar did not even blink.

"Yes," the Hunter whispered. "Let him."

"No, I will not." Mari was surprised at the icy authority
in her voice. "It was not K'shar who killed Caledan. It
was the Harpers. The half-elf was simply their tool,
something with which I am well familiar. Murdering
K'shar will not change anything. It will merely spill more
blood." She glared at Ferret. "Do you want that blood to
be on your hands, Ferret Talondim?" She turned to face
Morhion. "How about on yours, Morhion Gen'dahar?"

The two men stared at her in silence while K'shar
watched with curious eyes. At last Morhion opened his
mouth to say something. His words were cut off by

Kellen's frightened cry.

"Look at the throne!"

Ferret lowered his dagger as all turned to gaze at the throne. Something moved inside the black chrysalis. It pressed against the glossy sheath, distorting it. Then the husk rocked violently, once, and a dark shape began to push through the slit cut by the sword. Something was hatching out of the chrysalis.

They watched in a mixture of fascination and revulsion as, slick with black mucous, a tightly coiled form struggled weakly through the rip in the glossy shell. With one final, spasmodic jerk, the thing heaved itself free, falling with a wet *smack!* to the stone platform. It lay curled before the throne, flexing feebly, rhythmically, like a newborn creature still damp with fetal liquid.

That was exactly what it was, Mari realized with a nauseating feeling. They were witnessing the birth of a shadowking.

The thing was curled tightly, so sticky with black ichor they could make out little of its form, save that it had long, supple limbs and two pulsating protrusions on its back that could only be stubby wings. A dull, spiky lump of metal rested against its chest. The Shadowstar. The creature was shuddering.

"There's something wrong with it," Ferret choked.

"It was born too soon," Morhion said grimly. "K'shar's blow released it from the chrysalis before its metamorphosis was complete."

Mari shivered. "Will it . . ." She forced herself to rephrase her words. "Will he die?"

Morhion shook his head. "No. It's growing stronger every moment. I think it will live. But it is vulnerable now, while it is still taking shape."

"Then Milil save me," Mari whispered. She picked up her short sword, then took a step toward the still-forming shadowking. They had been too late to prevent Caledan's metamorphosis. Now there was only one thing she could do. *Forgive me, Caledan!* she cried silently. She lifted the sword, ready to end his misery.

A shriek of ancient hatred shattered the air as a dark shape swooped down from the leaden sky. Mari stumbled backward barely in time to avoid scythelike talons. With a rush of jet-black wings, the shadowy blur sped once more toward the clouds. Mari craned her neck, gazing up to see a shadowsteed whirling high above the throne. Another malevolent cry echoed off hard stone. Another shadowsteed rapidly approached the pinnacle.

Morhion pulled Mari to her feet. "The remaining two shadevari will protect the shadowking while it is taking form," he warned.

Mari gripped her sword. "Then we have to try to kill him." She gazed at the alien creature that struggled before the throne. Its wings were continuing to grow. They pulsated more strongly now. Each throb squeezed dark fluid into the appendages, stretching them like the expanding wings of a newly hatched butterfly. Was there anything at all of Caledan left inside that hideous form?

Morhion snatched the sword from her hand. "This will not avail you." He heaved the weapon off the pinnacle. "The only thing that can destroy the shadowking now is the Valesong. We must restore the song, while the shadowking is still taking shape."

"Somehow we have to try to unblock the fissure," Mari responded.

Morhion nodded in agreement. "You must do it, Mari. I will try to distract the shadevari, to give you time to reach the fissure."

Mari paled, biting her lip fiercely. The mage intended to buy her time with his own life. Yet, could it be a worse bargain than the one he had already forged with Serafi?

Ferret cleared his throat nervously. "If we're going to do something, we might want to do it soon." He pointed toward the sky. The second shadowsteed had reached the first, and the creatures were circling menacingly.

Morhion moved toward the thief. "Ferret, find a place to hide with Kellen. You must protect the boy at all costs. Do you understand?"

Ferret nodded. "I understand, Morhion. I won't say good-bye, but I will say good luck." He laid a hand on Kellen's shoulder. "Come on, kid. Let's get out of here."

"No," Kellen said crossly. "I want to help Morhion. I'm a mage, too."

"Not now, you're not," Ferret countered. "Right now you're a thief, and a good thief always knows when to get his head under cover. Got it?"

Kellen gave Morhion a hurt look, then hung his head. "Very well, Uncle Ferret."

K'shar approached Mari. "You will need help in the caves beneath the vale. I will go with you, Al'maren."

She looked at the half-elf in surprise. "Why?"

He shrugged. "You said once that in a different time and place we might have been friends." A grin crossed his striking visage. "Perhaps this is that time and place."

After a moment she nodded. "Perhaps it is at that."

Morhion gave K'shar an appraising look. "And those eyes of yours are made for seeing in the dark of underground tunnels, aren't they half-elf? Or should I say, half-drow?"

Only the faintest ripple of emotion crossed the Hunter's calm visage. "I am only one quarter drow, mage. My mother's mother was a dark elf. Though it meant her death, she dared to love a green elf of the forest, and bore him a daughter. As a half-breed, my mother was cast from the underground city of the drow and was forced to live above ground. In the end, she was slain by humans who feared her dark elven blood."

Mari stared at K'shar. Legend told that dark elves
were creatures of cunning and evil, and that this was
why they had been driven underground. Yet she had also
heard rumors of a great drow hero in the Northlands.
She found herself wondering if the dark elves were long
ago forced underground, not because they were wicked,
but simply because they were different.

There was no time to consider such matters. Two
hideous shrieks rang out over the vale. The shadowsteeds were diving.

"Go!" Morhion shouted, blue eyes blazing, his voice
cold and commanding.

Ferret caught Kellen in his arms and dashed down the
pinnacle's spiraling steps. Mari and K'shar followed close
behind. At the base of the pinnacle they spotted a narrow
crevice that led to a small cave.

"This is where we get off," Ferret announced. He
helped Kellen slip into the cave, then turned to give Mari
one last wink. "If I don't see you again in this life, I'll see
you in the next."

Despite herself, Mari grinned. "I'm beginning to think
you have nine lives, Ferret." Impulsively, she kissed the
thief. He gave her a bemused look, then disappeared into
the cave after Kellen.

Mari turned to K'shar. "Let's go."

The two started off across the vale at a run. Mari could
not keep up with the fleet half-elf, but the blocked fissures were not far. She reached the outcrop a few seconds
after him. The shadevari had ignored them. Whatever
Morhion was doing, it seemed to be working.

"What do you think we'll find down there?" Mari wondered, peering into one of the lightless crevices.

"There is but one way to find out," K'shar replied.
Pulling a coil of rope from his belt, he looped an end

around a rocky protrusion, then tossed the rope through the largest of the three holes. "I'll go first." Without waiting for an answer, he slid into the fissure and vanished from sight.

Mari took a deep breath, then followed the half-elf through the gap. Hand over hand, she lowered herself through pitch blackness until she wondered if she would run out of rope before she ran out of shaft. Without warning, a pair of hands gripped her waist, steadying her as her feet struck hard rock. She turned to see K'shar's golden eyes glowing in the darkness. They had reached the bottom of the shaft.

After a moment, Mari realized she could see more than just the half-elf's uncanny eyes. Here and there, spurs of rock defined the mouth of a horizontal passageway. A faint, crimson illumination hung on air that was uncomfortably warm and acrid with the stench of sulfur.

"This way," K'shar said, moving into the tunnel.

Mari followed on his heels. The passage was large enough for her to stand upright, but K'shar was forced to stoop. The walls of the tunnel were formed of irregular yet strangely smooth black stone. After they had walked for a few minutes, the passage forked.

K'shar squinted his sensitive eyes. "The glow is stronger in the left-hand tunnel."

Mari peered that way. "It seems to lead down a bit, too. That could be a good sign."

K'shar gave her a curious look. "How do you know that, Renegade?"

She wiped a sheen of sweat from her brow with the back of a hand. "We all have our talents. You have sensitive eyes, and I happen to have an excellent sense of direction. By the way, K'shar—you're helping me, so that makes you a renegade Harper yourself. Don't you think you should quit calling me Renegade and start calling me

Mari?"

K'shar grinned but said nothing. They plunged into the left-hand tunnel. After that, the path forked numerous times, and once they came to a natural rock chamber into which a half-dozen passages opened. At each diverging of the ways, K'shar used his sensitive drow eyes to determine in which direction the ruddy light was strongest. In turn, Mari made certain they were not backtracking or moving in circles in the underground labyrinth. Neither questioned the judgment of the other.

As they went, the crimson illumination grew brighter and the stifling heat fiercer. They shed their cloaks. Soon after, Mari tossed aside her green velvet jacket; her thin white shirt clung to her body, soaked with sweat. K'shar stripped down to his black leather breeches. Ruddy light gleamed off his sinewy arms and chest. Each breath seared Mari's lungs. She wondered if they could survive much deeper.

Abruptly, they rounded a corner and found themselves staring into a gigantic cavern that was a nightmarish fantasy of dark stalactites and stalagmites, all half-melted into grotesque shapes eerily resembling tortured souls. Crossing the center of the cavern floor, like a huge, fiery serpent, was a stream of molten rock. Wisps of yellow smoke rose hissing from the river of lava.

Mari and K'shar stood on the jagged edge of the passageway. From here it was a sheer drop of thirty feet to the hard floor of the cavern.

"I don't suppose you have another rope with you," Mari choked out.

"I fear not, Mari. But perhaps there is another way to—"

The half-elf's words became a cry of alarm. Weakened by countless years of exposure to the heat, the edge of the tunnel crumbled under their feet. Mari screamed as she and K'shar pitched forward. Desperately, she flailed for balance. K'shar arched his back, stretching his legs out and pushing against the crumbling precipice. This action cast him even farther from the edge of the tunnel, out into midair, yet it also had the effect of throwing Mari away from him, backward into the tunnel.

She fell hard inside the passageway, air rushing painfully from her chest. Gasping and spitting, she pulled herself to her hands and knees and crawled to the precipice. Carefully, she peered over the edge, dreading what she might see.

"Are you well . . . Mari?"

K'shar's voice rose thinly from below. Mari blinked against the fierce glow of the lava. Then she saw him directly below her. She choked back a cry of despair. The half-elf looked like a broken doll dashed against a rock by an angry child. One leg was bent beneath him at a hideous angle, and his right arm dangled limply from his shoulder. Blood smeared his face. She thought she could see exposed bone on his cheek and brow.

"I'm . . . I'm fine, K'shar," she managed to call out.

"I am glad." His words bubbled wetly in his throat. The Hunter turned his gaze away from her. With his one good arm, he began pulling himself across the rough floor of the cavern toward the wall, leaving a wide smear of dark blood behind him. He vanished from sight beneath a rock overhang.

"K'shar!" Mari called out in anguish.

For a moment there was no answer. Then she heard his voice, weak but oddly triumphant. "I have found something, Mari!"

"What is it?"

"There is a door set into the wall. It is fashioned of some sort of metal, but like none I've ever seen. There is a small trickle of water seeping from beneath the door.

And I can hear a rushing sound on the other side. There must be an underground river behind it." There was a long pause. "I think I can open the door, Mari. There is a lever."

It was exactly what they had been searching for, a way to bring a source of water in contact with the lava. Yet if K'shar opened the portal while he was down there . . .

"K'shar," she called out in a quavering voice. "Are you sure?"

"I want to do this, Mari."

She swallowed hard, then shouted as loudly as her parched throat allowed. "I am glad we could be friends, K'shar."

The half-elf's reply echoed faintly back to her. "As am I, Mari. Now please go. I will count to one thousand, then pull the lever. You must be out of the tunnel before then."

There was a pause, and she heard his voice echoing up from the furnace of the cavern. "One . . . two . . . three . . ."

Mari climbed to her feet. "Farewell, Hunter," she whispered. Then she turned and broke into a run, careening down the tunnel. As she went, she began to count desperately under her breath.

" . . . four . . . five . . . six . . ."

* * * * *

Morhion spread his arms as the shadowsteeds dove toward him, claws extended. The two shadevari, each sitting astride one of the winged beasts, opened their fanged maws in screams of depthless hunger. Dissonant words of magic flew from Morhion's tongue. The shadowsteeds were so close he could smell their fetid breath. With a final, shouted word, he brought his hands together, releasing the spell.

A cloud of thick smoke expanded rapidly outward.

Morhion dove to the ground and rolled. There was a deafening whir of wings and a terrible rending sound as sharp talons dug into bare stone inches from his head. The shadevari shrieked in rage; the sound of wings receded. The mage climbed to his feet. Already the magical smoke screen that had hidden him was dissipating.

Cold dread trickled down Morhion's throat. In the minutes since he had last looked, the shadowking had grown. Its midnight wings had spread wider, and it had raised itself slightly off the platform, leaning on a long, muscular arm that looked as if it had been carved from polished onyx. He could not see the shadowking's visage, but curving obsidian horns sprang from its brow. In time with the creature's throbbing wings, the Shadowstar pulsated against the creature's torso, glowing brightly one moment, fading to dark the next. Soon the shadowking would be whole.

The last tatters of magical smoke evaporated. High above, the shadowsteeds cried out as they caught sight of their enemy again. They folded their wings and dove once more. Morhion had no more offensive spells left. He could only watch.

Suddenly a dark form appeared before him. Two burning eyes bore into his chest. "The shadevari will slay you, mage," Serafi hissed. "Why do you not do something?"

"I have no magic that will stop them."

"What of the witch's ring?"

The mage shook his head ruefully. "Would that I understood its magic. It might indeed help me. But I do not." What did it matter now? He had done what he had intended; he had bought Mari and K'shar time enough to reach the blocked fissure. "I will die now."

"You are wrong, mage!" Serafi shrieked. "I will not let you!" He stretched a translucent gauntlet toward Morhion's chest. "I need some of your life force. Give it to me!"

Before Morhion could answer yea or nay, the spectral knight took what he wanted. The mage cried out as crackling green energy leapt from his chest toward Serafi's outstretched fingers.

"Ah, yes!" Serafi whispered exultantly.

The shadowsteeds were nearly upon them. Serafi withdrew his hand as Morhion sank to the ground with a moan. Serafi turned and thrust his clenched gauntlet toward the descending creatures. This time the magic was blood-red, and it crackled away from the spectral knight's hand. Crimson energy engulfed the shadowsteeds, sizzling as it plunged into their dark bodies. They screamed in agony, winging high into the sky to circle warily above the pinnacle.

"Your magic—it harmed them," Morhion gasped in amazement.

Serafi shook an ethereal fist in anger. "It was not enough."

Weakly, Morhion struggled to his feet. "Then do it again," he croaked. "Use more of my life force to destroy them."

"It would kill you," Serafi said flatly. "And in case you have forgotten, preserving your body is the sole purpose of this exercise."

Morhion gave a grim laugh. "Then I think you have failed, Serafi." He pointed weakly. High above, the two shadowsteeds separated, winging away from each other. They were going to dive at the pinnacle from opposite directions.

With effort, Morhion straightened his frame to his full height and brushed his flowing hair from his brow. He would meet his death with dignity. As he lowered his hand, his eye caught a glint of violet. Isela's ring. Once again he was struck by the contrast of brilliance and blackness contained within the ring's purple gem. It was almost as if the jewel did not simply reflect the world around, but rather separated that reflection into the basic components of light and dark.

Morhion let out a gasp. In that moment, he understood the key to the ring's magic.

He jerked his head up; the shadowsteeds were mere seconds away. At the ruined tower, his spell of protection had worked against the shadowhounds. Yet he knew now that it had not been the spell itself. It was because of the wall. Morhion cast his memory back to that night, picturing the ancient stone wall: the light of the rising moon glowed brilliantly on one side, while on the other side night reigned pure and perfect. It was the same separation that had marked the beginning of the world, when the song of the gods had split the shadowy chaos into two ordered elements, light and dark.

Could he forge a similar wall now? Perhaps. The spells were simple, and Morhion knew them. He began with a spell of light, conjuring a sphere of brilliant white radiance, then stretching and shaping it into a sheet that covered the summit of the spire. Then he cast a second spell, one of darkness, conjuring a sphere of perfect blackness. By force of will, he stretched this one into a dark plane next to the glowing sheet of white light.

He blinked. There it was, stretching across the pinnacle before him: a wall as thin as a hair, blazing white on one side, as black as pitch on the other. The whir of wings filled the air. Astride the shadowsteeds, the shadevari closed in from either side of the spire. They cried out in triumph, unafraid of the two petty magics that formed the wall. That was their mistake.

He plunged his left hand into the wall.

The ring exploded in purple brilliance. Violet sparks crackled on both sides of the magical wall. One of the shadowsteeds was slightly closer than the other. It spread its wings, trying to change course, but too late. Together, beast and shadevar collided with the wall.

For a fractured moment, twin shadevari writhed in midair—one black as midnight, the other blazing as the sun. Creatures of shadow, the shadevar and its steed had both been separated into elements of light and dark, and it was their death. Their combined screams shook the rock beneath Morhion's feet. Then the light and dark halves dissipated like mist before a wind.

Seeing what had happened to its partner, the remaining shadevar shrieked in fury. The beast it rode turned in time to avoid the magical wall and winged swiftly away from the pinnacle. The spells of light and dark expired. The wall vanished. Morhion swore vehemently. He had destroyed one shadevar, but the last one remained.

"Quickly, conjure another wall!" Serafi hissed.

Morhion shook his head. "I cannot. You know the nature of magic, Serafi. Once used, a spell is gone from my mind. It would take me an hour to learn the spells of light and dark again. And we do not have even a minute."

His rage beyond words, Serafi let out a blood-chilling cry, then vanished in a dark cyclone. A strange peace descended over Morhion. He turned to gaze at the throne.

Slowly, the shadowking rose to its feet. It was horrifying in its darkness, yet majestic as well, a vast creature of sculpted onyx muscle, with horns and talons like black ice. Against its chest, the Shadowstar pulsated frenetically. The outlines of the creature's face flowed, taking shape. It was nearly complete.

"Behold the King of Shadows," Morhion whispered in awe.

A high-pitched scream pierced the air. The mage turned to see the remaining shadowsteed winging rapidly across the vale, coming straight for him.

Twenty-One

K'shar's breath rattled in his chest as he whispered the numbers.

" . . . five hundred four . . . five hundred five . . . five hundred six . . ."

He had to keep counting. Yet he was not certain he could hold on much longer. The pain that racked his ruined body seemed to have merged with the crimson glow that filled the furnacelike cavern, so that he floated in a blood-red sea of agony. He was only dully aware of the jagged stump of bone that stuck out of a rip in his leather breeches, and of the pool of dark blood that spread beneath him. His crushed right arm was numb, which was a blessing, but the ragged cuts on his face and head burned fiercely. However, he could use that pain, could focus on it and let it anchor him so that he did not drift away from the haze of scarlet fire and into endless darkness.

" . . . seven hundred thirty . . . .seven hundred thirty-one . . ."

Embedded in the stone wall next to K'shar was the circular portal. Its metallic surface gleamed dully in the cast-off light of the lava flow. Beside the portal, protruding from the wall, was a lever—a rod carved with unrecognizable symbols. K'shar did not need to read the runes to understand the lever's function. Pulling it would slide back the metal catch that held the portal shut. He could hear the gurgling rush of water on the other side of the door. The sound made him maddeningly thirsty. He licked his parched lips with a dust-dry tongue, tasting the rust of blood.

" . . . nine hundred ninety-six . . . nine hundred ninety-seven . . ."

Agonizingly, he reached his left hand toward the lever and clenched his fingers around the shaft. There was a sizzling sound, followed by the rank stench of burning meat, as the hot metal seared the flesh of his hand. He did not loosen his grip. His lips curled back in a grin that was part agony, part feral mirth.

" . . . nine hundred ninety-eight . . . nine hundred ninety-nine . . ."

K'shar's heart beat crazily in his crushed chest. Something told him he was about to embark on a new chase, one far beyond his wildest imaginings.

" . . . one thousand!"

With all his remaining strength, K'shar pulled the lever. There was a groaning sound, and a grinding of metal on metal. For a second, nothing happened. Then, with a sound like thunder, the portal flew open. A roaring flood of frothy water gushed through the opening, carrying K'shar away with it like a piece of flotsam.

Cold water struck molten lava, and the entire cavern exploded.

* * * * *

Mari raced through the labyrinth, counting under her breath. The caustic air burned in her lungs. Sweat poured down her forehead, stinging her eyes, blinding her. The crimson glow faded as she ran farther and farther from the cavern. She let her fingertips slip over the smooth stone wall as she ran, finding her way by touch.

At first she relied on memory to tell her which twists and turns would take her closer to the surface. Yet as she went, recall began to fail her. Finally she reached a fork in the tunnel and came to a dead halt. Which way led up to the vale? Desperately she fought off panic and concentrated, searching for any sign—a wisp of cool air, a gentle upward slope—that might indicate which passage would take her back to the surface. She detected nothing. Numbers continued to tumble from her cracked lips.

" . . . eight hundred sixteen . . . eight hundred seventeen . . ."

She could hesitate no longer. Guessing blindly, she moved toward the left-hand passage. After a moment she faltered. No—this felt *wrong*. She turned, retraced her steps, and plunged into the right-hand passage. There was no more time to consider her decision. She careened down the tunnel at a dead run.

She was brought up short as the passage ended in a stone wall. Something sinuous brushed against her cheek, and she batted the thing away. With a start, she realized it was a rope. She craned her neck. Above, hovering in the blackness, were three dim circles of gray light. The shaft that led to the surface!

" . . . one thousand."

Time was up. Mari cast a nervous glance at the dim tunnel behind her. Hand over hand, she heaved herself up the rope.

She was halfway up when a sound like rumbling thunder echoed from the labyrinth below. Mari froze. Then, biting her lip, she climbed faster. Her arms ached with effort. A few moments later, she heard the first onrush of sound.

"Damn it, Al'maren!" she snarled to herself. "Climb!"

Clenching her jaw, she kept moving. Her shoulders were on fire now, and the rope bit painfully into her blistered hands. Her palms bled, making the rope slippery. She screamed as she slipped down several feet, barely managing to catch herself. The rushing had grown to a low rumbling. A puff of warm, moist air ruffled her hair.

The openings were close now. The rumbling became a stentorian roar, like the sound of an angry river crashing over jagged rapids. Mari reached up and clutched the edge of one of the openings. The roaring filled her mind, drowning out her terror. Forcing her trembling arms to function, she pulled herself upward. Sharp rock sliced her hands. With a cry of pain and desperation, she heaved herself up and out of the hole, then rolled away from the stone outcrop.

A heartbeat later, three geysers of boiling hot steam and molten rock burst from the fissures like glowing pillars reaching skyward. At the same moment, three vast, throbbing notes of music rang out. Roiling jets of steam poached the skin of Mari's cheek as she scrambled away from the fissures. Painfully, she pulled herself to her knees, staring at the geysers in awe. Like air through the holes of a flute, each of the columns of steam and melted rock piped a single deep tone.

When the three tones blended with the dissonant sounds made by the vale's other steaming fissures, a thrumming music filled the air: wild, chaotic, and incomprehensibly enormous. It was like nothing Mari had ever heard before—a music as old as time, imprisoned for a thousand years, free once more.

The Valesong.

* * * * *

So, Morhion thought darkly, this is how it ends.

He braced his shoulders, watching grimly as the last shadevar flew toward him across the vale. Then three fiery columns of steam and lava burst out of the ground, shooting toward the iron gray sky. This time, the shadowsteed was not swift enough to correct its course. With shrill screams, beast and shadevar flew directly into the surging pillars. Roiling steam ripped the shadowsteed's midnight wings to shreds while molten slag engulfed the shadevar. In a fiery blaze, the two monsters plummeted through the air, crashing to the ground with violent force. When the swirling steam cleared, all that remained of the two creatures was a smoking heap of sludge. The last of the shadevari was dead.

That was when Morhion heard the Valesong.

An inhuman scream sounded. The mage whirled around and stared in horror. Before the basalt throne, the shadowking writhed in agony. The creature flapped dark wings spasmodically, clenching clawed fingers as if struggling with an invisible foe. Against the shadowking's chest, the Shadowstar pulsated wildly in time to the throbbing music of the Valesong. In moments the star-shaped lump of metal glowed white-hot, sizzling as it burned into the shadowking's flesh. Then, all at once, the medallion turned to liquid; glowing droplets of metal fell to pool before the throne.

As the Shadowstar melted, the shadowking spread its impossibly long arms in an anguished gesture. It tilted its head back as if to let out a bellowing howl of outrage, yet all that issued from its gaping maw was silence. The shadowking straightened. For a second, Morhion thought it gazed at him with faded green eyes, eyes filled with a look of unspeakable sorrow. Then, like a felled tree, the onyx creature toppled to the hard stone platform in front of the throne.

The shadowking was dead.

* * * * *

Mari reached the base of the pinnacle just as Ferret and Kellen, pale and wide eyed, crawled from their hiding place. The thief eyed Mari critically. Her clothing had been reduced to filthy rags that clung wetly to her body. Soot and blood smudged her face; her hair was a tangled rat's-nest.

"By Shar above," Ferret swore with a low whistle, "you look like a she-orc after a bad night of drinking, Mari."

"Thanks, Ferret," she replied with a weak smile. "You sure know how to compliment a girl." Abruptly she slumped toward the ground. Ferret and Kellen rushed forward to support her.

"I think something has happened up there," Kellen said quietly, gazing toward the summit.

"Maybe we should go see," Ferret suggested, his beady eyes shifting nervously.

Mari agreed. Together, the three ascended the spiral staircase. They reached the pinnacle's summit to see Morhion kneeling before the basalt throne. Prostrate beside him was a huge, dark creature.

"It's dead," Morhion said without looking up, his voice haggard. "*He's* dead."

Mari choked back tears. They had saved the world from the darkness of a second shadowking. Yet it was no victory to her. Caledan was gone, and she felt utterly hollow. Reluctantly, her eyes moved to the fallen shadowking. The dark body, once gleaming with sinuous life, now seemed merely a shell, the horned countenance a mask.

"I'm sorry, Mari," Ferret said softly, reaching out to squeeze her shoulder.

She gave the thief a grateful look, then limped toward Morhion. Reaching down, she gripped the mage's hand, pulling him to his feet. "Come," she said, leading him away from the throne. "Let's be gone from this place. There is nothing left for us here."

"Wait."

Mari looked up in surprise. It was Kellen. In his small hands he clutched the obsidian pipes, the instrument forged by Caledan's shadow magic.

"I would like to play a song for my father."

A sharp pang pierced Mari's chest. For the second time now, she realized, Kellen had witnessed a parent destroyed by the dark magic of a shadowking. Yet his round face was calm, like a cherub carved of alabaster. Somehow, Mari knew, this child was stronger than any of them.

"Of course," she murmured.

Kellen approached the fallen figure before the throne and lifted the glossy black pipes to his lips. For a moment he hesitated. A hush fell over the crater. Even the Valesong seemed to recede into the distance. It was as if the blasted land itself held its breath, waiting for him to play. Then play he did.

A melody rose from the pipes, gentle, mournful, and achingly beautiful in its simplicity. The voice of the pipes was so sweet and expressive that it seemed almost human, and Mari half-believed that, if she listened carefully, she could hear words in the music:

The Winter King lies sleeping
Beneath the barren briar—
All mantled in snow,
And crowned below,

With berries red as fire.

The Winter Queen stands weeping
Above her pale lord's rest—
Awaiting the Spring,
In garb of green,
To bear her away on his breast.

So skillful was Kellen's playing that it took Mari several moments to realize the song was one she knew. A time-honored ballad, "The Winter King" was one of the first songs learned by an apprentice bard. Mari shivered; the ballad seemed especially poignant in this desolate place.

Ferret let out a gasp. "Did you see that?" Mari and Morhion stared in shock.

The shadowking moved.

No—that wasn't quite it. The limp body of the creature had twitched, but not of its own volition. It was as if something had moved beneath the dark skin. The shadowking moved again, and its torso expanded. For a terrified moment, Mari feared that it was breathing. Then she realized that whatever was struggling was not beneath the corpse of the shadowking. It was *inside* of it.

Kellen lowered his pipes. "Cut it open!" he cried. "Hurry!"

Ferret reacted immediately. The thief leapt forward, brandishing his dagger, and slipped the tip of the blade beneath the scaly skin of the shadowking's belly and tore a jagged opening from navel to throat. A flood of dark, gelatinous ichor poured out. Inside the husk of the shadowking, something struggled. Something alive.

"I don't believe this," Ferret rasped. "Mari, Morhion! Help me!"

The thief plunged his hands into the slime and began

to pull. Mari and the mage rushed forward to aid the thief. It was hard to get a grip on the slippery thing. Finally, as one, the three gave a heave. They nearly tumbled backward as a slime-covered form burst free of the shadowking's body.

For a stunned moment, Mari could only stare. Then she approached the thing, kneeling beside it. Hesitantly at first, then with growing urgency, she used her bare hands to wipe the dark ichor away. She uncovered naked arms, a bare chest, and finally . . . a face. Gasping, she backed away. Two eyes fluttered open—faded, familiar green eyes. For a moment they stared in wild confusion, then they settled on Mari.

"Hello, Al'maren," a hoarse voice whispered.

It was Caledan.

* * * * *

They built a fire in a small hollow at the base of the pinnacle, but Caledan did not think he would ever feel warm again. Mari had cleaned the worst of the slime from his gaunt body, and they had wrapped him in blankets and moved him close to the fire. Still he shivered. But a toothy grin lent life to his haggard visage, and the light in his green eyes, though feverish, was bright and keen.

"Actually, I've been meaning to drop a few pounds for a while now," he said wryly, scratching his bony ribs. "I just didn't realize it would require such drastic measures."

Absently, he ran his hand over his chest, wincing as his fingers brushed the oozing, star-shaped wound above his heart. Although it was the shadowking who had been burned by the molten Shadowstar, Caledan bore the brand.

"I don't understand, Caledan," Mari said softly. "It

seemed that the song Kellen played helped free you from
the shadowking. But I know that song, 'The Winter King.'
Half the apprentice bards in the Heartlands can play
that tune. There's nothing magical about it."

Caledan shook his head. "No, there isn't." His eyes
grew distant. "You see, as I journeyed toward the Shadowstar, and then on to Ebenfar, my memories became
dimmer and dimmer. As the shadowking grew within me,
little by little it obscured who I was, like weeds choking a
garden. I began to forget myself—my friends, my history,
even my . . ." He swallowed hard. " . . . even the people I
loved most."

Mari clapped a hand to her mouth but made no com-
ment.

"That's why I decided to leave something of myself
behind, for you to find," Caledan went on. "Something
that, if I did forget myself entirely, might be able to
remind me of who and what I was. 'The Winter King' was
the first song I ever learned to play on my pipes as a
child. I figured that, if it couldn't help me remember
myself, then nothing would. The problem was, I couldn't
let the part of me that was the shadowking know what I
intended. I had to find a way to leave behind my message
without letting the *other* discover what I was doing. And
I did. I wasn't certain anyone would understand what I
was doing"—he smiled at Kellen—"but someone did after
all."

"Of course!" Mari said. "The signs you left behind!"

Kellen nodded solemnly. "The signs were clues to a
song. I didn't understand, though—not until I saw the
last sign, the dark pipes." Kellen ran a thumb over the
instrument. "The pipes made me think that my father
wanted me to play something, but I didn't know what.
Then I thought about all the other signs, and suddenly it
was so clear. If I took the first letter of each of the signs—

face, eyes, fist, and all the others—they were the notes of a song. I didn't know what would happen when I played it, but I knew I had to try."

Caledan gazed thoughtfully at the boy. "I am glad you did, Kellen. I was lost in a dark place. I thought I would be lost forever. But when I heard the music, it was like a light drawing me back. And I did remember. The first thing I remembered was you."

Kellen ran to his father. Caledan encircled his son tightly in his arms.

"Don't ever leave me again, Father," Kellen said sternly.

"I won't," Caledan said fiercely. "I promise."

Morhion did not wish to interrupt the reunion between father and son. However . . . "It is growing dark," the mage said, "and this vale is filled with dire magic. We should be moving—if you are well enough, Caledan."

The bard nodded and let Mari help him slowly to his feet. "I think I can manage to—"

His words were cut off by a howling gust of wind. A hazy form stepped out of thin air, crimson eyes blazing. Cold dread filled Morhion. In all the strange events, he had forgotten about . . .

"Serafi," he whispered. I will not show fear! he vowed inwardly, though he could not keep his body from trembling as the spectral knight drifted closer.

"Your quest is over, mage," the ancient spirit hissed. "Our pact is fulfilled. Now it is time for you to pay me my due."

Morhion stared hatefully at the malevolent apparition. "So be it," he spat.

"No!" Mari screamed, interposing herself between spirit and mage. "No, Morhion! You can't!"

Serafi's laughter echoed all around. "I am afraid the mage has no choice in the matter. For the second time I have helped him save his precious friend. Now his body is mine!" He raised his gauntleted hands. A sudden burst of frigid air knocked Mari roughly aside. Ferret hurled a dagger at the knight, but the blade passed harmlessly through his smoky form.

"What is going on?" Caledan cried.

"I made a bargain with this spirit for his help in finding the Shadowstar," Morhion said simply. "The price was my mortal body." The mage was beyond terror now, beyond pain. He wished only for the end to be swift. Wistfully he gazed at his friends, lastly at Mari. "I shall miss you all."

"At last!" Serafi cried exultantly. "To know fleshly sensations again . . ."

The spectral knight encircled the mage in vaporous arms. Morhion screamed as cold fire stabbed his chest. He arched his back in agony, his feet leaving the ground as he floated in the ghost's ethereal embrace. "Now you will die, Morhion," Serafi hissed, "and I will live again, as I—"

"Not so fast," Caledan growled, taking a faltering step forward.

"What is this?" Serafi's sepulchral voice dripped venom. "A feeble, half-mad invalid would challenge *me?* Faugh! I have nothing to fear from you, Caldorien. Even I can see that you are without power now. Your shadow magic is gone."

"Really?" Caledan said dangerously. "You're awfully confident of that."

The hot flames of Serafi's eyes flickered. "A pact is a pact," the dark spirit shrieked. "The mage is mine!"

"You're wrong," Caledan countered. He seemed ill no longer. An aura of dark majesty surrounded him. This man had been, however briefly, the King of Shadows. "Morhion belongs to all of us, and bargain or no bargain, I'm not going to let you take him."

Before the spectral knight could react, Caledan whistled three sharp notes of music. A rift appeared in the air above him, like a dark wound in the fabric of the world.

"You wish to experience a new plane of existence, Serafi?" Caledan thundered. "Then how about the deepest pits of the Abyss?"

As the others watched in awe, Caledan thrust his arms above his head. Tatters of shadow streamed out of the rift to coil around the spectral knight. Serafi howled in fury. Above, engulfed by strands of shadow, Serafi began to spin, turning faster and faster, until his form was a dark blur.

"No!" the spectral knight's voice screeched pitifully. "This cannot be!" Like foul water spinning down a drain, the cyclone emptied into the rift. Serafi's voice became a terrified wail. "But he made a pact—" His words were cut short as the rift closed with a clap of thunder.

Caledan collapsed to the ground. Morhion dashed to him and picked Caledan up, shocked at how light his friend was, as if he were merely the husk of a man.

Caledan coughed weakly, leaning against the mage. "Well, the spirit was right about one thing," he croaked. "I think that was the last of my shadow magic. It's gone now. I know it." Mari and Ferret approached quietly. "Something tells me I owe you a great deal, friend," Caledan continued to Morhion. "Perhaps more than I can know. But I hope now you can consider that debt repaid."

"I have never sought repayment, my friend," Morhion said intently. "But I do thank you."

Ferret looked around. "Hey, where did that kid go?"

"I'm here!" Kellen cried, bounding off the last few steps of the staircase that wound up the outside of the pinnacle. "I had to get something we left up by the throne."

"What is it?" Mari asked, kneeling beside the boy.

"This." Kellen held out his hand. In it was a star-shaped

piece of metal attached to a silvery chain. The Shadowstar. It had cooled and solidified once more.

Mari took in a sharp breath. "I thought it was destroyed!"

"Don't worry, Mari," Kellen said solemnly. "I'll keep it safe."

Carefully, the boy slipped the medallion around his neck. The Shadowstar gleamed dully against his tunic, looking like an ordinary piece of jewelry. Mari cast a frightened glance at Morhion. Almost imperceptibly, the mage shook his head. If there was anywhere on the face of Toril that the Shadowstar was truly safe, it was with this strange and powerful child. Smiling, Kellen reached up and gripped Caledan's hand.

"Can we go home now?" he asked.

Epilogue

 One of the advantages of being a child, Kellen had learned, was that adults tended to forget that children were in the same room with them. Thus, simply by being quiet, Kellen managed to learn all sorts of interesting things. True, it was a little like eavesdropping, but it was the adults' fault for not being more observant, or at least so it seemed to him.

Outside the window, snow was drifting like white goose-down between Iriaebor's countless towers. Kellen sat in a corner of the common room of the Sign of the Dreaming Dragon, stringing together red berries and pine cones to make a garland. Everyone at the inn was getting ready for a celebration, for tomorrow was Midwinter Day. And this year, as Estah had said, there was more cause than usual for celebration.

As the blue winter dusk gathered outside, bright laughter filled the common room. At a long trestle table, the Fellowship of the Dreaming Dragon—with a few additional members—had been reunited.

"And you did *what* with my pickpockets?" Ferret rasped incredulously.

"Don't get excited, my dear weasel-faced boy," Cormik rumbled indignantly. "It was a business decision, that's all." As usual, the corpulent proprietor of the Prince and Pauper was opulently attired. Tonight he wore a doublet of thick fir-green wool slashed to reveal silk of holly berry crimson.

"Your legion of pickpockets was competing with your corps of beggars," Jewel expounded. The ageless thief had traded her traveling leathers for a graceful velvet gown the same dusk-purple hue as her eyes. "All too often your beggars were wasting time groveling before people who had already had their purses lifted."

"It was terribly inefficient," Cormik chided, adjusting his jeweled eye patch. "Under the new plan, the beggars approach a target first. If the mark doesn't cough up some gold out of pity, the pickpockets move in to take it from him. It's really a much more elegant solution."

"And we doubled the profits from both beggars and pickpockets," Jewel added. The matriarch of the Talondim clan reached out and patted her grandson's hand affectionately. "I'm so glad you've decided to move your base of operations to Iriaebor, love. Cormik and I really have so much more to teach you."

"That's right, Ferret." Cormik pressed his cheek to Jewel's. "And now that I'm part of the family, you can be certain I'll be checking up on you with great regularity."

Ferret rolled his beady eyes. "Lucky me," he said sourly.

Everyone ignored him.

With a puff of wintry air, Jolle came in from outside bearing an armful of firewood. The stout halfling stamped the snow from his boots and proceeded to build the fire into a cheerful blaze. Pog and Nog ran shrieking through the common room. The tiny halfling children were engaged in some game that only they could comprehend. Estah bustled in from the kitchen bearing a huge tray of steaming honey rolls. The red-cheeked halfling plunked the tray onto the table and stood, hands on hips.

"All right, Tyveris," she said sternly, "I defy you to finish off a third platter."

The bespectacled monk looked up from his pewter plate and grinned. Tyveris had managed to steal away from his duties in the High Tower for the evening. "Well now, that's a challenge I really can't refuse," the big Chultan said with a laugh. He picked up a sticky honey roll in each hand and promptly began to devour the entire platter as Estah watched with a mixture of chagrin and amazement. The battle between Estah's cooking ability and Tyveris's appetite had been going on for a decade now, with little indication of a truce in sight.

Booming laughter rang out. The others turned in surprise. It was Caledan.

As always these days, he had sat quietly at the end of the table nearest the fire, neatly clad in his slate blue tunic with a fine wool blanket around his shoulders. Now he was laughing. The others stared in amazement. Since they had returned from their journey over a month ago, Caledan had smiled often enough, but he had not laughed once. Now he was laughing so hard his shoulders shook.

Abruptly, his laughter turned into coughing that racked his body. As one, the others leapt from their chairs. Mari and Ferret were first to Caledan's side. They eased him back in his chair, and Estah hurriedly brought a steaming cup of herb tea. Caledan managed to gulp some down, and his coughing ceased. He ran the back of his hand across his mouth, and it came away with a smear of blood. The others looked on in concern.

"I've spoiled the fun," he said huskily. "I'm sorry."

"Don't be," Mari said fiercely.

He gave her a grateful look, then testily waved her and the others away. "I'm all right. Really. Now, don't we have a celebration to get ready for?" After that, the merriment continued, though more subdued than before.

At last it grew late. Estah and Jolle went upstairs to put Pog and Nog to bed. Tyveris bid his farewell, followed by Ferret, Jewel, and Cormik. All of them promised to return tomorrow for the Midwinter feast, then departed into the snowy night. Mari, Morhion, and Caledan remained at the table, bathed in the glow of the fire.

"So what will you two do, now that you are no longer Harpers?" Morhion asked after a while.

Caledan shrugged. "I suppose, when I'm well enough, I'll think of something. After all, I had seven years to practice not being a Harper. It won't be that big a switch . . . for me." His eyes flickered toward Mari.

Mari took a deep breath. "Ever since I was a child, I wanted to be a Harper like my guardian, Master Andros. When I finally donned the moon-and-harp badge, it was like a dream come true." She shook her head sadly. "But that's what it was. A dream. I thought I loved the Harpers. I didn't. It was an ideal I loved. Still, after all we've been through, I don't hate the Harpers. How can I? They are simply men, mortal and fallible. Just like the rest of us." She gave a wry smile. "Besides, they've kindly decided to leave us alone."

"So what will you do?" Morhion repeated intently.

She tossed her auburn hair, winking at the mage. "Oh, like Caledan, I'll think of something. The ideal remains. And the Harpers hardly have a monopoly on fighting evil in the world."

After that, they sat together in silence. Finally Mari

stood. "I'm going to turn in." She moved to the staircase, then paused to cast a glance over her shoulder. With a start, Morhion realized that her gaze fell, not on Caledan, but on himself. The shadow of a smile curled about her lips. Then Mari disappeared upstairs.

"You love her, don't you, mage?"

Morhion stared at Caledan in shock.

"Oh, don't act so surprised," Caledan growled. "I'm an invalid, not an idiot. I'm right, aren't I?"

At last, Morhion's cool expression melted. He nodded. "Yes, you're right." He shook his head. "But what does it matter? It is a mage's lot to—"

"—to dwell in solitude," Caledan finished in annoyance. "Yes, yes. I've heard you spout that foolishness a hundred times." He sighed in exasperation. "You know, for all your knowledge, you mages can be pretty boneheaded sometimes." A gentle note crept into his gruff voice. "She cares for you Morhion. Even if you can't see it, I can."

Morhion opened his mouth to say something, but no words came out.

"And she's afraid," Caledan went on sadly. "She's put a brave face on it, but it's true. Mari has just given up everything that was ever important to her. She's afraid—and she's lonely." He reached out to grip Morhion's hand. "Don't you think you should go talk to her, my friend?"

At last Morhion nodded. "Thank you," he said quietly. "For everything." With that, the mage stood and disappeared up the stairs.

For a time, Caledan sat by himself in the light of the dying fire, a bemused expression on face. Suddenly a shudder passed through his body, and he doubled over in his chair. He clutched his chest, stifling a moan of pain. Despite all Estah's efforts, the wound on Caledan's chest had not healed. Nor would it ever.

Kellen rose from his corner and moved into the firelight. Caledan looked up in surprise. "Kellen," he gasped
hoarsely, trying valiantly to mask his pain. "I didn't know
you were still there."

"We should go to bed," Kellen said simply.

Caledan nodded. Weakly, he tried to rise from his chair
but slumped back down. Kellen gripped Caledan's arm
and draped it around his shoulder.

"You can lean on me, Father."

"Thank you, Kellen," Caledan whispered gratefully.
"You're a good son."

Later, Kellen sat on the bed in his attic chamber,
bathed in the light of a single candle. Before him was a
small iron box. Morhion said that iron blocked magic,
which made it useful for storing enchanted objects. Carefully, Kellen opened the box. Inside were two things. The
first was the set of obsidian pipes. The second was the
Shadowstar.

Lightly, he ran a finger over the star-shaped medallion.
The Shadowstar itself was not evil. It had been forged by
the god Gond for Azuth, the High One, as a weapon
against evil. Still, when he touched the medallion, Kellen
could feel a distant, menacing presence. The shadevari.

If Kellen listened, he could hear the ancient beings,
shrilly demanding that he release them from their
bondage. However, he did not have to listen if he did not
want to. All he had to do was concentrate, and the shrieking voices of the shadevari fell silent in his mind, though
they did make the symbol of magic on his left palm itch
fiercely.

Kellen knew this was what made him different from
all the others who had come before him—all the others
with shadow magic. They hadn't been able to silence the
voices of the shadevari when they touched the Shadowstar. That was why both Verraketh and Caledan had

become shadowkings. Now Kellen was the last person in the world with shadow magic, and he could shut out the shadevari whenever he wanted. There would never be another shadowking. Still, Kellen sensed a great potential within the Shadowstar. Something told him its work was not done. Not yet.

Kellen shut the box and placed it in the wooden trunk where he kept his treasures. From the trunk he drew out the bone flute his father had carved for him. He raised the instrument to his lips and played a quiet song. On the wall, the shadows cast by the flickering candle swirled and danced. Kellen concentrated. Though he could easily summon shadows of the past, no matter how hard he tried, he could never seem to conjure shadows of the future. At last, Kellen gave up and lowered the flute. It was time for sleep. He gave the shadows on the wall one last curious glance.

Then he blew out the candle.

DragonLance® Saga

THE HISTORIC SAGA OF THE DWARVEN CLANS

Dwarven Nations Trilogy

Dan Parkinson

The Covenant of the Forge   **Volume One**

As the drums of Balladine thunder forth, calling humans to trade
with the dwarves of Thorin, Grayfen, a human struck by the magic of
the Graystone, infiltrates the dwarven stronghold, determined to
annihilate the dwarves and steal their treasure.   ISBN 1-56076-558-5

Hammer and Axe   **Volume Two**

The dwarven clans unite against the threat of encroaching humans
and create the fortress of Thorbardin. But old rivalries are not easily
forgotten, and the resulting political intrigue brings about
catastrophic change.   ISBN 1-56076-627-1

The Swordsheath Scroll   **Volume Three**

Despite the stubborn courage of the dwarves, the Wilderness War
ends as a no-win. The Swordsheath Scroll is signed, and the dwarves
join the elves of Qualinesti to build a symbol of peace among the
races: Pax Tharkas.   ISBN 1-56076-686-7

Sug. Retail Each $4.95; CAN $5.95